Praise for the Aimée Leduc Series

"Forever young, forever stylish, forever in love with Paris—forever Aimée."
—*New York Times Book Review*

"Today's Paris, both international and quintessentially French, an intriguing blend of centuries of decay and mod futurism, is a fine backdrop for a modern noir, and Leduc finds herself navigating a tightly spun web worthy of a classic spy thriller, complete with a Métro bombing and shadowy assignations with Kurds and Sunnis. Leduc's City of Light is a stylish, dangerous place throbbing by night to an ominous techno world beat, and Aimée Leduc is a marvelous invention, a third-generation Sam Spade in couture."
—*Washington Post Book World*

"If its expert plotting and intense characterizations aren't enough, the book is absolutely drenched with the sights, sounds and smells of Paris and will surely be treasured by every Francophile lucky enough to read it."
—*Denver Post*

"No contemporary writer of noir mysteries evokes the spirit of Paris more than Cara Black in her atmospheric series starring P.I. Aimée Leduc . . . The fearless, risk-taking Aimée is constantly running, hiding, fighting and risking her life—all while dressed in vintage Chanel and Dior and Louboutin heels."
—*USA Today*

"Kinsey Millhone turned loose in *Before Sunset* . . . In Leduc's ninth outing, Paris, as always, sparkles in all its gargoyled, dusty, cobblestoned glory."
—*Entertainment Weekly*

"Wry, complex, sophisticated, intensely Parisian . . . One of the very best heroines in crime fiction today."
—*Lee Child*

"A reliably pleasurable serial guide and a parade of fashionable footwear, thanks to the well-shod Leduc . . . They're corkers."
—*The Seattle Times*

"Smashing and suspenseful."
—The BBC's *Between the Lines*

"Don't be daunted by the depth you find here. These books will go every bit as quickly as your vacation in Paris, if they do not in fact become your vacation in Paris."
—Rick Kleffel, KQED San Francisco

MURDER

in the MARAIS

Cara Black

Published by
Soho Press
853 Broadway
New York, NY 10003

Library of Congress Cataloging-in-Publication Data
Black, Cara
Murder in the Marais / Cara Black.

ISBN 978-1-61695-730-8
eISBN 978-1-56947-727-4
I. Title.
PS3552.L297M8   1999
813'.54—dc21   98-52070

Printed in the United States

10   9   8   7   6   5   4   3   2

Dedicated to the "real" Sarah and all the ghosts, past and present

Fate knows no distance.
—a French saying

THE MARAIS

PARIS

NOVEMBER 1993

WEDNESDAY

AIMÉE LEDUC FELT HIS presence before she saw him. As if ghosts floated in his wake in the once elegant hall. She paused, pulling her black leather jacket closer against the Parisian winter morning slicing through her building, and reached for her keys. The man emerged from the shadows by her frosted paned office door. A baby's cry wafted up from the floor below, then the concierge's door slammed.

"Mademoiselle, I need your help," he said. Leathery, freckled skin stretched over his skull and his ears pointed out at right angles. He wore a crumpled navy blue suit and leaned crookedly on a malacca cane.

"No missing persons, Monsieur," she said. As winter settled, the days gray and the memories vivid, old survivors revived hopes of lost ones. She slid her tongue across her teeth to check for anything stuck, smoothed her short brown hair and smiled. She stuffed the chocolate croissant back in the bag. "I don't find lost relatives. My field is corporate security." Thirty-four years old, Aimée, at five feet eight inches, loomed above him. "*Je suis désolée*, Monsieur, but computer forensics are my speciality."

"That's what I want." He straightened his posture slowly, his large eyes fearful. "My name is Soli Hecht. I must talk with you."

Behind his fear she saw sadness tinged by keen perception. She tried to be polite. Walk-in clients were rare. Most came through corporate connections or by word of mouth. "It's not that I don't want your business, but we're carrying a full caseload. I can refer you to someone very good."

"I knew your father, an honorable man. He told me to come to you if I needed help."

Startled, she dropped her keys and looked away. "But my father was killed five years ago."

"As always, he is in my prayers." Hecht bowed his head. When he looked up, his eyes bored into hers. "Your father and I met when he was in Le Commissariat."

She knew she had to hear him out. Still she hesitated. The cold seeped from the floorboards but it wasn't the only thing making her shiver.

"Please come inside."

She unlocked the door that read LEDUC DETECTIVE that led to the office she'd taken over after her father's death, flipped on the lights, and draped her jacket over her armchair. Nineteenth-century sepia prints of Egyptian excavations hung on the walls above digitally enhanced Parisian sewer maps.

Hecht moved his cadaverous frame across the parquet floor. Something about him struck her as familiar. As he lifted his arm onto her desk, she saw faint blue numbers tattooed on his forearm peeking out from his jacket sleeve. Did he want her to find Nazi loot in numbered Swiss bank accounts? She scooped ground coffee into the filter, poured water, and switched on the espresso machine, which grumbled to life.

"Specifically, Monsieur Hecht, what is the job?"

"Computer penetration is your field." His eyes scanned the equipment lining the walls. He thrust a folder at her. "Decipher this computer code. The Temple Emanuel is hiring you."

"Regarding?"

"We need proof that a woman's relatives avoided deportation to Buchenwald. But I don't want to raise her hopes." He looked away, as if there was more he could say, but didn't.

"I've stopped doing that kind of work, Monsieur Hecht. That was more my father's field. To be honest, if I kept his promise you'd get less than the best."

"I knew your father, I trusted him." Hecht gripped the edge of her desk.

"How did you know him?"

"A man of honor, he told me I could rely on you." Soli Hecht hung his head. "We had many dealings before the explosion. I need your expertise."

She drummed her chipped red nails on her desk and pushed the painful memories aside. Steaming muddy liquid dripped into the waiting demitasse cup. "Monsieur, *un petit café?*"

"*Non, merci.*" He shook his head.

Aimée unwrapped a sugar cube and plopped it in her cup. "I do computer security," she repeated. "Not missing persons."

"He said you would help me . . . that I could always come to you."

Short of going back on her father's word, one path remained. "*D'accord,*" she relented with inner misgivings. "I'll show you my standard contract form."

"My word must be enough." He extended his hand. "As far as you are concerned, you don't know me. Agreed?"

She shook his gnarled hand.

"This will take several days? I was told it could be slow work."

"Maybe a few hours. I type one hundred and twenty conventional words a minute."

She smiled and sat down, shoved last night's faxes to the side of her desk, and leaned towards him.

"You were in school in America when I knew your father."

Full of hope, she'd searched for her American roots and the mother who'd disappeared when she was eight. She hadn't found either. "Briefly. I was an exchange student in New York."

"Your father articulated his casework philosophy to me and I've always remembered it."

"Things weren't usually what they seemed or he'd be out of business?"

Hecht nodded. "You're independent, no ties or affiliations to anyone." His crooked fist drummed the table. "I like that about you."

He knew a lot about her. She also had the distinct impression he was leaving something out. "Our fees are seven hundred and fifty francs a day."

Hecht nodded dismissively. Now she remembered. She'd seen his photo years ago when his evidence helped bring Klaus Barbie to trial.

"Look inside the folder," Hecht said.

Aimée opened his file, noticing the digits and slash marks, a distinctive trademark of Israeli military encryption. Her expertise was in hacking into systems, huge corporate ones. But this code spoke of the Cold War—a slippery tunneling job. She hesitated.

"Two thousand francs are in the folder. Deliver your results to 64 rue des Rosiers to Lili Stein. She's home after her shop closes. I've told her to expect a visitor."

Aimée felt she had to be honest; breaking an encrypted code had never taken her that long. "You've given me too much."

He shook his head. "Take it. She has a hard time getting around. Remember, give this only to Lili Stein."

She shrugged. "No problem."

"You must put this in Lili Stein's hands." Hecht's tone had changed, from fervent to pleading. "Swear to me on your father's grave. On his honor." His eyes locked on to hers.

What kind of Holocaust secret was this? Slowly she nodded in agreement.

"We will have no more contact, Mademoiselle."

Soli Hecht's joints cracked as he rose. His face wrinkled in pain.

"You could have faxed me this query, Monsieur Hecht. It would have saved you this trip."

"But we've neither talked nor met, Mademoiselle Leduc," he said.

Aimée bit back her reply and opened the door for him. Warped floorboards, a tarnished mirror, and scuffed plaster adorned the unheated landing. She buzzed for the turn-of-the-century wire elevator grating noisily up the shaft. Slowly and painfully he made his way to the hall.

Back in her office, she stuffed the francs into her pocket. The overdue France Télécom bill and horse meat for Miles Davis—pronounced Meels Daveez, her bichon frise—would wait until she'd done the promised work.

Eurocom, the cable giant, had royally screwed up her finances by breaking Leduc's security service contract and hiring a rival Seattle firm, the only other firm that did the same work as she and her partner. She hoped there'd be enough money left to spring her suits from the dry cleaner's.

Her standard software keys enabled her to crack coded encryptions. They opened information stored in a database, in this case, she figured, a military one.

After punching in her standard key, "Access denied" flashed on the screen. She tried another software key, Réseau Militaire, an obscure military network. Still the screen flashed "Access denied." Intrigued, she tried various other keys but got nowhere.

Morning turned into afternoon, shadows lengthened, and dusk settled.

After several hours she realized she would earn her francs on this one. So far, nothing worked.

LATER THAT EVENING, on one of her last decoding attempts, she used an old postwar retrieval key. She was surprised when the system responded, "For access enter via auditory/visual format." A rare but not unheard-of access path.

Nothing came up with audio. She opened the visual file using NATO documents decoding software. Suddenly her screen filled with black and white. After several seconds, she could clearly make out a photograph. No text appeared, only the photo. She enhanced the pixel quality, enlarging it as much as she dared without distorting the image.

The torn black-and-white snapshot with its smudged white margins showed a café scene next to a park full of children. People sat at the sidewalk café and stood in small groups. The ones standing were SS. Their backs were turned, but she recognized the lightning bolts on the sides of their collars.

No one looked at the camera. Most of the civilians wore dark shapeless clothes. A candid shot of occupied Paris. Almost half of the snapshot was torn away.

Shaken, she stared at the photo. She'd eaten at that café plenty of times, knew many of its habitués. But now she would always think of the Nazis who'd been there before her.

This marked the first time she'd cracked a code revealing a photo without text. How would this documentation be proof for the old woman? But that, she reminded herself, wasn't her job.

After saving the image, Aimée printed a copy. She couldn't help wondering what this woman's reaction would be.

With the photo tucked in her Hermès bag, a flea-market find, she wound a leopard-print scarf around her neck, belted her leather jacket, and locked the office door.

Below her office, she hailed a taxi that skidded to a stop on wet rue du Louvre. Late-evening crowds filled the awninged sidewalk cafés. The Seine glittered on her right as the floodlit gray stone of the Pont Neuf flashed by.

The buildings changed as the taxi entered the Marais, the Jewish district, full of sixteenth-century *hôtels particuliers*, once abandoned and now often restored. Figures scuttled over the glistening cobblestones. In foggy, narrow rue de Béarn the taxi bumped over the curb and let her off. Fetid air hovered from the *bouches d'égouts*, gutters leading to the sewers.

Her destination, 64 rue des Rosiers, stood above a dusty window lettered DÉLICES DE STEIN in faded gold, advertising kosher goods in Hebrew and French. Opposite stood a falafel stand with trays of chopped red cabbage, onions, and pickled carrots peeking out from under a striped canopy.

Dark green paint flaked off the massive arched entry doors in front of her. She made her way past a bicycle leaning against the stone wall below a peeling circus poster. The cobbled courtyard smelled of yesterday's garbage. To her left, a vacant concierge's loge guarded the entrance.

On the second-floor landing, the dark wood door of Lili Stein's apartment stood ajar. From inside, a radio program blared. She knocked loudly several times. No answer. She pushed the creaking front door open.

"*Allô?*"

Slowly she entered the dim hallway of a musty apartment, reluctant to invade someone's privacy. She hesitated. Still no answer.

Inside, her eyes adjusted to the darkness. From the hall, she peered into the dim living room, then walked inside. A pine sideboard held a cloth runner embroidered with the Star of David and bearing brass candlesticks. Beside that, a vintage radio stood next to a recliner, the upholstery worn and spattered with grease spots. Approaching the radio, she saw a framed sepia photo on the wall. In it a young girl, wearing an old-fashioned school uniform, stood arm in arm with a stout aproned woman before a shop window. Both wore stars embroidered with JUIF on their chests. Aimée paused, saddened. She recognized that window as the one below on rue des Rosiers belonging to Délices de Stein. Under the photo a single white rose bloomed in a vase.

Lili Stein must be deaf to play the radio so loud, she thought. Maybe the old woman had a serious hearing loss.

She approached the radio, an old crystal set with knobby dials and yellowed channel band. She turned the volume lower. Used tissues littered the floor. "Madame Stein, I'm here with your packet!"

No response.

Her neck muscles tightened. Water trickled from somewhere out in the hallway. She didn't like this. Wasn't the old lady expecting her?

She paused beneath the living-room door frame. Across from her in the bathroom, a leaky faucet dripped onto a brown stain in the basin.

Her hand brushed the dark paneled wall searching for a switch. But her fingers only came back greasy.

Her anxiety mounted. She passed the dingy bathroom and edged down the narrow hallway. At the end, what looked to be a bedroom door stood partly open. She felt for her keys in her leather bag, positioning the pointed edges between her fingers as a weapon, her first lesson from the martial-arts dojo.

Carefully, she wedged the door open wider. In the dim light an old woman was sprawled on the bed, her stockings rolled down.

"Madame, Madame?"

She switched on the light. The woman's ashen face stared vacantly at the cobwebbed ceiling. Aimée walked towards the bed, then froze. Someone had carved a swastika into the woman's forehead. She gasped, gripping the bed frame as her legs buckled. Her heart pounded. She took a breath, then forced herself to touch the cheek. Smooth and cold like marble . . .

What if the killer was still there?

She reached for her Phillips screwdriver, part of the mini-tool set she carried in her bag, scanning the room for the attacker. But the only other inhabitant was a bloated angelfish, its silvery bubbles rising in the tank on the old rolltop desk. Wooden slats were nailed over the room's lone window, blocking all but a ribbon of light from the light well.

She stepped gingerly around the bed. After checking the armoire and peering into dust balls under the sagging mattress, she felt convinced no attacker lurked in the bedroom. A fly buzzed, circling near the unblinking eyes whose gaze was locked on the ceiling. Disgusted, she shooed it away.

Alert for an intruder, she padded down the hallway, examining each closet and scouting every room. Empty.

She hadn't come face to face with a homicide since working with her father. Her impulse was to run out of the apartment, call the *flics*, and return Hecht's money. But she forced herself to go back.

In the bedroom she surveyed the dead woman more carefully. Deep and bloodless, the swastika stretched from her eyebrows to the wispy gray hairs at her hairline, exposing bone and pulpy tissue. A gold chain with Hebrew letters hung twisted in the bloody ligature mark around her neck.

She swore, shooing the persistent fly, who'd alighted on the woman's wool skirt that crumpled up at her knees. Swollen ankles puffed out over scuffed shoes. Aimée noticed the scratches and bruising on the pasty legs; the hands, in half fists, lay at her side as if she'd died struggling.

"In Lili Stein's hands" was what she'd promised Soli Hecht. That no longer made sense as the woman was dead. She wasn't superstitious but . . . she bent down, peering at the woman's hand. Bits of wood splinters were embedded in her palms. Aimée looked around her. No marks were scratched in the wood slats nailed over the window. Crutches lay uselessly on the floor. Her fingernails were broken and jagged. Like a cornered animal, Aimée thought, she'd tried to claw her way out.

Aimée carefully put her fingers on the blue-veined wrist. She pulled out the envelope with the photo image and touched it to Lili's cold hand, not yet stiff with rigor mortis.

In that moment she felt the murderer hovering in this dank room. Foreboding washed over her. She became aware of the nasal-voiced radio announcer. In a prerecorded message yesterday to the labor unions at Lille, Cazaux, the French trade minister and expected appointee for prime minister, had promised strict foreign immigration quotas. "French industry, French workers, French products!" Cazaux's familiar voice ranted as crowds roared.

Just what France needed, she thought, more fascism.

"Maman?" A man's deep voice came from the hallway.

Startled, she stood up too quickly and knocked into the bedroom's rolltop desk. The angelfish tank swayed, and she reached out to steady it. That's when she saw the torn photo under the tank, barely visible through the black gravel. She pulled it out, quickly aligning the encrypted photo next to this torn piece. They matched. Shaken, she realized she held the missing corner of the photo that this woman might have been murdered for.

"Maman, *ça va?*"

She slid the photos into the envelope and stuffed it down the calf of her leather boot.

"Monsieur, don't come in here," she said loudly, summoning authority in her voice. "Call the police."

"Eh? Who . . ." A middle-aged man, rail thin and tall, walked in. He stooped as if apologizing for taking up space. His forelocks were worn long in the Hasidic style under a black felt hat with an upturned brim.

She blocked his view. "Is Lili Stein your mother?"

"What's happened?" He stiffened. "Maman is ill?" He peered over Aimée's shoulder before she could stop him. "No, no," he said shaking his head.

She edged toward this man, trying to help him.

"Who are you?" Fear registered in his eyes.

"I'm working with . . ." She caught herself before she mentioned Hecht. "Temple Emanuel. I'm a private detective, we had an appointment." She guided him towards an alcove hung with rolled scriptures. "Sit down."

He shook her off. "How did you get in here?" His eyes grew wide in terror.

"Monsieur Stein?" She kneeled at his eye level, willing him to meet her gaze.

He nodded.

"I'm sorry. The door was ajar. I found her a few minutes ago."

He collapsed, sobbing. She pulled out her cell phone, punched in 15 for SAMU, the emergency service, and gave the address. Then she called 17, Police Centrale.

"*Yisgadal v'yiskadash shmei raboh.*" He began the Hebrew prayer for the dead. Then he broke off. She wanted to put her arm around his thin shoulders, make the sign of the cross. But instead she just whispered, "May she rest in peace."

By the time the SAMU van screeched to a halt in the courtyard, waves of the Brigade Criminelle then the Brigade Territoriale had already tramped through. The Police from the 4th arrondissement came next. A rotund figure puffed up the stairs, a droopy mustache above the half smile on his face. Aimée blinked in surprise. "Inspecteur Morbier!"

She hadn't seen Morbier, an old friend of her father's and Aimée's own godfather, for several years. Not since the day of the explosion. Everything came flooding back to her: the reek of cordite and TNT, the hiss and pop of cold rain falling on twisted hot metal, her palm burning on the surveillance van's door handle. She had watched as the force blew her father into a smoking hulk.

"Aimée . . . !" Then Morbier quickly corrected himself in the presence of the Brigade members. "Mademoiselle Leduc."

He'd changed little. His blue suspenders strained over his wide belly. He flicked a kitchen match, lit up a Gauloise, and inhaled deeply. She could almost taste the tobacco in the stuffy hallway.

"Smoking at a murder scene, Morbier?"

"I'm supposed to ask the questions." He flicked ash into his cupped palm.

Crime-scene technicians, their lab coats drooping under short yellow rain jackets, glided efficiently amid muffled conversations up and down the stairs.

"Don't tell me you're involved in this dog and pony show," he said.

"I'm not involved." She wasn't really lying. She looked away, unable to meet his gaze. When she was little he'd always caught her out faster than her father.

The threadbare Turkish carpet in the hall was already tracked with mud. Stein rocked back and forth on a chair, dazedly shaking his head.

Aimée and Morbier sidestepped the crime photographer loaded with camera equipment, heading for the kitchen down the hall.

Stein sputtered to life. "I'm Abraham Stein. This woman was here when I found Maman."

Morbier's eyes narrowed. "Explain how you happened to find the body."

She shook her head, indicating she wouldn't speak in front of Stein and tugged Morbier's sleeve, nodding her head towards the kitchen. He rolled his eyes, then lumbered after her.

"Temple Emanuel hired me to trail her." She kept her voice low, remembering that the best defense is a good offense. "Explain to me why Brigade Criminelle arrived and secured the scene before"—

loud banging erupted in the hallway as the stretcher hit the door frame and she stared at him—"you did."

"Inspecteur Morbier!" A hoarse-voiced detective beckoned to him. "Forensics needs you. Now."

Morbier growled and left.

She turned away to hide her relief.

He stopped a few steps away and jerked his thumb at the nearby pockmark-faced sergeant. "Investigating officer, check the contents of her bag."

Her shoulders sagged. "Why?"

He blustered, "A possible suspect at a homicide should cooperate."

She attempted to check her anger, keep her tone even. "I have nothing to hide."

She dumped her cell phone, expired Metro pass, extra modem cable, two tubes of ultrablack mascara, business cards, pack of Nicorette stop-smoking gum, mini-tool set, and a well-thumbed manual on software encryption smudged with red nail polish.

At Lili Stein's bedroom door Morbier turned to her, his expression masked. "I want you at the Commissariat. First thing in the morning." He nodded to the sergeant. "Escort her home."

AS THE PILOT ANNOUNCED descent into Charles de Gaulle Airport, Hartmuth Griffe, the German trade advisor, felt an acid taste, drier than the cabin atmosphere, fill his mouth.

Fifty years and now he was back. His heart raced. Despite the surgery, he feared recognition even after all these years. And the past. *What if somehow she'd survived?*

Suddenly, below the mist, tiny pinpricks of light twinkled in the dusk. The landing gear ground heavily below his feet and his stomach lurched. He fought nausea as the wheels hit the runway squealing and the plane taxied along the blue-green lighted lines. He'd promised himself he'd never come back. The plane braked with a jolt.

Ilse Häckl, his bureau administrator, greeted him at the gate, with a wide dimpled smile.

Hartmuth caught himself and compressed his lips in a quick grin. What was she doing here?

Plump, rosy cheeked, her snow white hair in a bun, Ilse was often mistaken by newcomers to his office for someone's grandmother. However, she supervised one arm of the trade ministry and newcomers either caught on quickly or left.

"Ilse, aren't you supposed to be on holiday in . . ." He paused, racking his brains. Where had she been going?

"The Tyrol." She shrugged and smoothed down her shapeless dress. "*Ja.* My orders, I mean my job, Herr Griffe, is to assist you in any way possible." She stood at attention as much as an older woman in flesh-colored orthopedic hose could.

"*Danke schön,* Ilse. I appreciate it," he said, disturbed but determined to take it in stride.

At the curb, she whisked Hartmuth into a black Mercedes. As they glided into Paris on Autoroute 1, flat streams of light hinted at the monotonous strips of housing projects along the highway. On the right after the interchange, the cathedral of Sacré Coeur emerged like an elliptical pearl bathed in lunar light.

The skyline of Paris shone, but not as he remembered it. It was bigger, brighter, a jagged vista ready to swallow him. Already he was desperate to escape.

"These came this afternoon," Ilse said, as she sat beside him in the back seat. She cleared her throat and thrust a pile of stapled faxes at him. "And this just now, a memo from Bonn."

Surprised at this direct approach from the ministry, he leaned forward. Why all of a sudden, he wondered.

"You've read this, Ilse?" Hartmuth's eyes narrowed as he scanned the Bonn printout.

"*Mein Herr . . .*" she began.

"*Ja, ja,*" Hartmuth said, looking straight at her. "But you are here to make sure I lobby for this trade treaty." He punched the paper. "Is that correct?"

Ilse shifted slightly but kept her head high. She pinned a stray white hair back into her thick bun. "*Unter den Linden, mein Herr,*" she murmured.

Hartmuth shuddered. *Mein Gott, she was one of them.*

Now he understood why, without warning, he'd been sent to Paris. The Werewolves, descendants of the old SS, still operated in Blitzkrieg style.

The Mercedes pulled into the cobblestoned courtyard of the seventeenth-century Hôtel Pavillion de la Reine, tucked unobtrusively in a corner of the Marais. This part of the *quartier*, residence of nobility until the court moved to Versailles, once filled with rundown mansions, decrepit *hôtels particuliers*, had become a Jewish ghetto until Malraux saved most of the area from the wrecking ball. Gentrification had made it the trendiest address in Paris.

Hartmuth could imagine a liveried footman in powdered wig running out to greet him. But the door sprang open courtesy of a bland-faced man wearing a headset with a microphone cupped under his chin.

"*Willkommen et bienvenu*, Monsieur," he said.

Upstairs, Ilse disappeared into the room next door to Hartmuth's. In his suite, he stared at his luggage without unpacking and his fingers trembled as they raked through his still thick white hair. He barely felt the old scars but knew they still webbed his scalp.

Sixty-eight years old, lean, tan, with a craggy face etched in a permanent squint, Griffe was too vain to wear glasses. Alone among the antique armoires and gilt-framed paintings, he felt empty. He opened the glass balcony doors, stepping out into the frosty chill air. The vacant playground and fountains of the fenced Place des Vosges spread below him.

Why hadn't he ignored the minister? But he knew the reason why. As the silent architect of previous trade agreements and treaties, only his lobbying glued the EU delegates together. But did the trade summit have to be here?

Under the pigeon-spattered statue of Louis XIII straddling his horse, he'd said goodbye so many, many years ago to the only woman he'd loved. A Frenchwoman. A Jew.

Sarah.

The cooing of pigeons and soggy chill of an early November evening floated past his open balcony doors. His hands shook as he grasped the door handle. What if someone recognized him and screamed his past out loud?

Unter den Linden; that was an order. Also the Werewolves' code-word meaning: one day we will meet under the flowering linden trees in Berlin under a new Reich. The Third Reich reborn.

Unable to work, he gazed at the restored rose brick facades of the square opposite the window. I'm just an old man with memories, he thought. Everyone else had been ground into dust long ago.

Fifty years ago he'd been young, and the City of Light had spread before him, ripe for the plucking. Very ripe, for Hartmuth Griffe had been an officer with the SiPo-SD Sicherheitspolizei und Sicherheitsdienst Security Police and Gestapo, responsible for sweeping the Jews from the Marais.

THURSDAY

Thursday Morning

THE SEINE FLOWED SILVER, chill mist hovered, and along the mossy-stoned quai Aimée walked, debating whether to call Hecht. No contact, he'd said. But as far as she was concerned, the rules had changed when she'd found Lili Stein dead.

She crossed the Pont Neuf with the still-lighted *bâteaux mouches* gliding below as dawn crept over the Seine. Thick fog silhouetted Café Magritte under her office on rue du Louvre.

Inside, at the zinc counter, she dunked a buttery croissant in a steamy bowl of café au lait. The espresso machine rumbled like a jet at takeoff.

She'd accepted a simple job but the stakes had skyrocketed with this grisly murder. Morbier had treated her as a suspect and had her escorted home, whether to establish authority with his minions or—she didn't like to finish the thought. Nothing about this felt good. She shivered, remembering the look on Lili Stein's face.

Warm coffee vapors laced the windows overlooking the Louvre's western wing. She especially didn't want to lie to Morbier about some odd Nazi hunter who would deny knowing her.

Revived, she slipped twenty francs across the counter to Zazie, the owner's freckle-faced ten-year-old, who worked the cash register before school.

"Mind if I get ready for work?" she said, pulling out her battered makeup kit.

Four-foot-tall Zazie stared awestruck as Aimée applied red lipstick in the mirrorlike espresso machine, ran mascara through her lashes, and outlined her large eyes with kohl pencil. She smoothed her short brown spiky hair, pinched her pale cheeks for color, and winked at Zazie.

"Buy yourself a *goûter* after school." She wrapped Zazie's fist around her change.

"*Merci*, Aimée." Zazie grinned.

"Tell your papa l'Américaine wants to settle her tab later, *d'accord?*"

Zazie's brown eyes grew serious. "Why does Papa call you l'Américaine? You never wear cowboy boots."

Aimée struggled not to smile. "I keep them in my closet. Real snakeskin. My *maman* sent them from *le* Texas." She had the cowboy boots but she'd bought them herself at the Houston airport.

Upstairs, lights glowed behind her frosted-glass office door.

"Soli Hecht left you a present," said her partner, René Friant, a handsome dwarf with green eyes and goatee. He wore a three-piece navy blue suit and tasseled loafers. René pumped the hydraulic lift handle of his custom orthopedic chair with his foot.

Curious, she picked up the thick manila envelope with her name scribbled on it.

Fifty thousand francs were inside along with a note.

Find her killer—tell no one. I don't trust the flics. I trust you.

Wads of franc notes tumbled out as she grabbed the desk edge to steady herself.

"He must like you!" René's eyes grew wide. "We'll convince the tax board to . . ."

She shook her head. "I can't . . ."

René pumped furiously until the seat aligned with his desk.

"Look at this." He thrust one of several threatening letters from the bank manager at her. "Our tax extension is up in the air, the bank is calling in our note. Now, the Eurocom accountant refuses to pay us the eight months of back payments we're owed, he's quibbling about a clause in the contract; it could take months." He struggled to adjust a knob on his seat. "Time you got out of the computer clouds, Aimée, and got back in the field."

"I don't do murder." She winced.

"You make it sound like there's a choice."

"INSPECTEUR MORBIER is expecting me," Aimée said to Madame Noiret, gritting her teeth at the Commissariat de Police reception desk. Not only did her jaws ache from the biting cold outside, she was dying for a smoke.

"*Bonjour*, Aimée, *ça va?*" Madame Noiret, the gray-haired clerk peered through reading glasses and smiled. "I'll let him know you're here."

"*Ça va bien, merci*, Madame."

She hated coming back to the Commissariat in Place Baudoyer; her father's memory stabbed her from every corner. There was the cold marble floor of his office where she'd done homework as a little girl when he worked late, later helping him clean out his desk when he joined Grandfather at Leduc Detective, then collecting his posthumous medal from the Commissaire.

Aimée's American mother had disappeared from her life one evening when she was eight years old. On weekends, Aimée's father took her to the Luxembourg Gardens. On a bench under the row of plane trees by the puppet theater, she once asked him about her mother. His normally sympathetic eyes hardened. "We don't talk about her anymore." And they never had.

Three weeks without a cigarette and Aimée's tailored jeans pinched, so she paced instead of sitting. She'd always thought the crimes investigated by the Commissariat of Police in the Marais rarely matched the division's elegant accommodations. High-tech weapon sensors hid nestled in brass wall sconces of this Second Empire style nineteenth century mansion. Rose lead-paned windows funneled pink patterns across the marble walls. But the dead cigarettes in overflowing ashtrays, greasy

crumbs, and stale sweaty fear made it smell like every other
police station she'd been in.

This palatial building neighbored Napoleon's former barracks
and the 4th arrondissement's Trésor Public, the tax office on rue
de la Verrerie. But Parisians called it *flics et taxes, la double
morte*—cops and taxes, the double death.

She drifted over the scuffed parquet floor to read the bulletin
board in the waiting area. A torn notice, dated eight months earlier, announced that Pétanque leagues were forming and serious
bowlers were encouraged to sign up early. Next to that, an Interpol poster of wanted criminals still included Carlos the Jackal's
photo. Below that, a sign advertised a sublet in Montsouris, a
"*studio économique*" for five thousand francs a month, cheap for
the 14th arrondissement. She figured that meant a sixth-floor
walk-up closet with a pull-chain squat toilet down the hall.

Aimée stood in front of the board, reknotting her silk scarf,
knowing she'd got it right the first time. She hated lying to *flics*,
especially Morbier.

Maybe she should convince Morbier she was thinking of con-
verting to Judaism instead of telling him the truth about an old
Nazi hunter who had made her fifty thousand francs richer, hiring
her to deliver half a photo to a dead woman. Then hiring her to
find her killer.

Madame Noiret pushed sliding glasses up her nose and pointed
inside.

"Go ahead, Aimée, Inspecteur Morbier will see you."

She walked into the seventeen-foot-high-ceilinged room of
the investigative unit. Few desks were occupied. Morbier's was
littered with a stack of well-thumbed files. A demitasse of
espresso sat next to his flashing computer screen. His pudgy
fifty-nine-year-old body leaned back in a dangerously tilted
chair. He cradled the phone against his shoulder while one
hand scratched his salt-and-pepper head and the other held a
cigarette conspiratorially between his thumb and forefinger. As

he hung up, she watched his nicotine-stained fingers with their short splayed nails, rifling in the cellophane-crumpled pack of Gauloises for another cigarette. High above the desks, a TV tuned to France 2 displayed continuous car wrecks, tanker accidents on the high seas, and train fatalities.

He lit the cigarette, cupping it as if there were a gale wind blowing through the Commissariat's investigative unit. He'd known her father since they'd been on the force together, had attended Aimée's baptism—but after the accident he'd kept his distance.

He gazed at her meaningfully as he gestured toward a chipped metal chair. "You know I had to put on a show, especially for the Brigade."

She figured that was probably the closest to an apology she'd get for his behavior at Lili Stein's apartment.

"I'm happy to furnish a statement, Morbier." She tried to keep the frost out of her voice. "The Temple Emanuel has retained my services."

"So the Temple hired you before she was killed?" Morbier nodded. "Just in case she got butchered?"

She shook her head, then sat on the edge of the metal chair.

"Humor me and explain."

Morbier could pass for an academic until he opened his mouth. Pure gutter French was what her father used to call it, but then most *flics* didn't have graduate degrees from the Sorbonne.

"It's not delicate to incriminate the dead, Morbier." She crossed her legs, hoping her tight jeans wouldn't cut off her circulation.

Now he looked interested. "You found her, Leduc. You are my *première suspecte*. Talk to me."

She hesitated.

"Trust me. I never prosecute dead people." He winked. "Nothing goes further than this desk."

And cows can fly. Mentally, she asked Lili Stein's forgiveness. "Please don't tell her son."

"I'll keep that under consideration."

"Do better than that, Morbier," she said. "The Temple doesn't want the family hurt. There were rumors about shoplifting."

Morbier snorted. "What's this?"

"You know how old people conveniently forget items in their pockets," she said. "The rabbi asked me to talk with her, convince her to bring the items back. On the quiet."

"What kinds of things?"

"Scarves from Monoprix, flashlights from Samaritaine. Nothing valuable." She tried not to squirm in the hard-backed chair.

Morbier consulted a file on his desk. "We found brass candlesticks, religious type."

Aimée shook her head. "She hid things. Like a child, then she forgot where." She stood up, stuck her hand in her pocket.

On her way to the Commissariat she'd come up with a logical reason for being in the area. The radio had reported large rightwing demonstrations all over the Marais protesting the European Summit.

"I'd followed her from Les Halles but I lost her at that demonstration. Neo-Nazis were all over. I figured she returned to her apartment so this evening I went there and then . . ."

At least the part she told him about how she found the body was true.

"Let me be sure I understand." Morbier inhaled deeply from a newly lit cigarette then blew smoke rings over Aimée's head. "You followed her in case she shoplifted, lost her in Les Halles at a fascist demonstration, then went to her apartment and found her carved Nazi-style?" His eyes narrowed. "Why were your fingerprints on the radio dials?"

She did her best to ignore his look.

"*Mais bien sûr!* Because I had to lower the volume. The killer turned the radio up to hide Lili's screams, then dropped used tissues on the floor after wiping off his or her fingerprints." Eagerly she pointed to the crime-scene photos covering his desk. "But that's an interesting point, Morbier!"

"What's that?"

"The perpetrator might be used to someone cleaning up after him- or herself."

"Or might be a slob."

She studied the swastika carved into Lili Stein's forehead in the photograph. It was then she noticed how this particular swastika slanted differently from the graffiti in the Métro. She grabbed a paper clip from his desk, rubbed it on her silk shirt, and then stuck it in her mouth. Chewing and moving it with her tongue helped her think.

In the photograph reddish discoloration under Lili Stein's ears continued along her neck. The thin line of congealed blood showed the ligature that had strangled her. Nothing explained her half-clenched fists except fear. Or anger.

"I'll corroborate your alibi after I check with your dwarf." Morbier plopped himself back into his chair, rubbing his jowl with one hand. "We make a deal, you and me . . ."

"Leave René out of it."

"Why should I?"

"You want to use me. No one in the Marais will talk to your *flics*."

She knew that ever since uniformed French police had rounded up Jews for the Nazis during the Occupation, no Jew trusted them. Morbier must have figured that if the Temple employed her they trusted her, even though she wasn't Jewish.

"Leduc, trust me."

She paused. Maybe she could trust him, maybe not. But didn't they say if you knew your enemy you were at least one step ahead?

"I'll agree to share information. Deal?"

He nodded. *"D'accord."*

"Give me the forensics?"

He snorted. "You did notice the ligature mark under her ears?"

"Of course. I am my father's daughter." She wanted to add, "And more."

Morbier winced at the mention of her father.

"That wasn't all I noticed, Morbier," she said grimly. "What about the lack of blood?"

"You wouldn't be suggesting that the homicide took place elsewhere and the victim was dragged?" he said.

"Since the swastika was carved after strangulation, not to mention her stockings were rolled down, her fingernails broken and her palm full of splinters, it would follow."

"That thought had occurred to me." He flicked his cigarette into the espresso cup. It sizzled and went *thupt*. Typical Gallic response, she thought. She noticed his mismatched socks: one blue, the other gray.

"The technicians have been combing the courtyard," he said. "If there's something there, they will find it."

"Time of death?" She riffled her hair, creating more spiky tufts.

He ignored her scarred hand as he usually did. "Say between three and seven last night. The autopsy may pinpoint the time closer."

She stood.

"Beyond sharing information, I'd appreciate your help in my investigation."

Now Morbier sounded like her father. He had actually asked for her help. Nicely. She almost sat back down.

"In other words if I don't, I'd be hindering it?"

"I didn't say that." He shook his head.

She started towards the door.

"Yet." He smiled.

"Remember why I got out of this field?"

"That happened five years ago," he said after a pause.

"I've quit this kind of work, I do corporate investigation," she said. "Why can't you ever look at my hand? If you don't answer me I won't consider working with you." She gripped the edge of his desk, her knuckles white.

His voice sounded tired. "Because if I look at that burn mark, everything comes back. I see your bloody . . ." He covered his eyes, shaking his head.

"You see Papa burning on the cobblestones, thrown by the blast against the pillar in Place Vendôme. Our surveillance van, a smoking rubble from the bomb. And me screaming, running in circles, waving my hand, still gripping the molten door handle."

She stopped. Several plainclothes types hurriedly put their heads back behind their computers. She recognized some of their faces.

"I'm sorry, Morbier." She nudged the base of his chair with her foot. "This doesn't usually happen. Nightmares generally take care of it."

"There's one remedy for shell shock," he said after a while. "Climb into the trenches again."

But he didn't know Soli Hecht had already thrown her back in.

AIMÉE WALKED along the Seine, speculating about the photo fragments. The sunlight glittered feebly off the water and a fisherman's nearby bait bucket stank ripely of sardines.

She trudged over the grooves worn in the stone staircase to her dark, cold apartment, unable to get Lili Stein's corpse out of her mind.

She'd inherited the apartment on the Ile St. Louis from her grandfather. This seven-block island in the middle of the Seine rarely, if ever, had seen real estate change hands during the last century. Drafty, damp, and unheated, her seventeenth century *hôtel particulier* had been the mansion of the Duc de Guise. He'd been assassinated by Henri III at the royal chateau in Blois, but she'd forgotten why.

The ancient pearwood trees in the courtyard and the view from her window overlooking the Seine kept her there. Every winter, the bone-chilling cold and archaic plumbing almost drove her out. The year before, she'd pitched an army surplus tent around her bed that held the heat in nicely. She couldn't afford repairs or the monstrous inheritance taxes due if she sold her apartment.

Miles Davis licked her in greeting. In her tall-windowed kitchen, she turned on the faucet jutting out of the old blue-tiled back-splash. She washed her hands, letting the warm water run over them a long time.

Mechanically she opened her small 1950s refrigerator. A moldy round of Brie, a six-pack of yogurt, and a magnum of decent cham-pagne that she would pop the cork on some day took up one shelf. Beneath a bunch of wilted spinach was a white-papered package of raw horse meat that she spooned into Miles's chipped bowl. He gobbled it up, wagging his tail as he ate. She chiseled the mold off the Brie and found a baguette, hard as a crowbar, in her pantry. She left it there and found some crackers. But when she sat down, she couldn't eat.

She put on two pairs of gloves, leather over angora. Down-stairs in her apartment foyer, she pulled her *mobylette* from under the stairs, checked the oil, and hit the kick start. She headed over the Seine towards Gare de Lyon and her favorite *piscine* for swimming. Reuilly wasn't crowded at this time, its humid aqua blue phosphorescence splashed jellylike against the shiny white tiles.

"Bad girl." Dax, the lifeguard, waved his finger. "Didn't see you yesterday."

"I'll make up for it. Fifteen extra laps." She dove into the deep lap lane, her mind and body ready to become one with the heavy warm water. She loved the tingly sensations in her arms and legs until her body temperature stabilized with the water. She estab-lished her rhythm: stroke kick breathe kick, stroke kick breath kick, completing lap after lap.

Too bad she couldn't persuade René to join her. Heat helped

ease the hip displacement common to dwarves. But, of course, he was self-concious about his appearance.

The steamy shower stalls stood empty except for the mildewed tile and soapy aroma. She padded into the changing room, wrapping her old beach towel with ST. CROIX in faded letters around her chest. From her locker she pulled out her cell phone and punched in René's number. Then she stopped. He wouldn't be back yet from the martial-arts dojo where he practiced. She punched in the number again. This time she left a message. Her cell phone trilled and she answered eagerly.

"Leduc, I checked that demonstration you mentioned passing in Les Halles," Morbier said. "The group's called Les Blancs Nationaux, infamous for harassment in the Marais."

She cringed.

"What if a member of Les Blancs Nationaux followed her home?" he said.

Guilt caused her to hesitate . . . what if there was some link?

"You still there?" he said.

"What do you want me to do about it?" she snapped.

"Jump-start your brain and help me. I need more than info sharing."

There was no way to put him off. Besides, it would be a logical place for her to start.

Abstractedly, she dressed and applied makeup. After she shuffled everything into her gym bag, she looked in the mirror. Her feet were rooted to the damp floor in fear. She realized her black wool trousers were inside out and the label hung outside her silk shirt. Mascara had run on her pale cheeks and given her panda eyes. Her thin lips were smudged with red.

She looked like a scared clown. She didn't want to investigate neo-Nazi punks. Or this old woman's murder. She wanted to keep the hovering ghosts at bay.

Thursday Morning

HARTMUTH STARED AT THE fluorescent dial of his Tag Heuer watch—5:45 A.M. Place des Vosges, swathed in mist, lay below him. A lone starling twittered from his balcony ledge, lost when its flock headed south, Hartmuth imagined. He sipped his café au lait in the gray light. The aroma of buttery croissants filled his room.

He felt overwhelmed by regrets—his guilt in loving Sarah and most of all for not saving her all those years ago. A knock on the adjoining door of his suite startled him. He pulled his flannel robe around himself, redirecting his thoughts.

"*Guten Tag*, Ilse." Hartmuth smiled as she entered.

Ilse beamed, eyeing the work pile on the desk. With her snowy white hair and scrubbed cheeks, a gaggle of grandchildren should be trailing behind her begging for freshly baked *Mandelgebäck*. Instead, she stood alone, her stout figure encased in a boxlike brown suit with matching support hose, pressing her palms together.

Almost as if in prayer, he thought.

"A milestone for our cause!" she said, her voice low with emotion. "I am proud, *mein Herr*, to be allowed to assist you."

Hartmuth averted his eyes. She bustled over to close the balcony doors.

"Has the diplomatic courier pouch arrived yet, Ilse?"

"*Ja, mein Herr,* and you have an early meeting." She held out a sheaf of faxes. "These came earlier."

"Thank you, Ilse, but"—he raised his arm to ward off the faxes—"coffee first."

Ilse did a double take. "What's that on your hand?"

Startled, Hartmuth looked at the rusty crescents of dried blood in his palm. The fluffy white duvet cover on his bed was streaked with brown stains, too. He knew he clenched his fists to combat his stutter. Had he done this in his sleep?

Ilse's eyes narrowed. She hesitated, as if making a decision, then thrust the blue leatherette pouch at him. "Diplomatic courier pouch, sir."

"*Ja*, call me before the meeting, Ilse."

"I'll organize the trade comparisons, sir," she said, and closed the door of the adjoining room behind her.

Hartmuth punched 6:03 A.M. into the keypad attached to the pouch handle and then his four-digit code. He waited for a series of beeps, then entered his alphanumeric access code. He paused, recalling a time when a courier's honor had been enough.

A hasp clicked open, revealing new addenda restricting immigration. He shook his head, remembering. These were like the old Vichy laws, only then it had been quotas for the Jews.

The treaty mandated that any immigrant without proper documentation would be incarcerated, without benefit of a trial. He knew France's crippling 12.8 percent unemployment rate, highest since the war, was the reason behind this. Even Germany's unemployment statistics had grown alarmingly since the Reunification.

The phone trilled insistently next to him, jolting him back to the present.

"*Grüssen Sie*, Hartmuth," came the unmistakable grating voice from Bonn. "The prime minister wishes to thank you for excellent work so far."

So far?

Mentally snapping to attention, Hartmuth replied, "Thank you sir, I feel prepared."

He wasn't prepared for what came next, however. "He is also appointing you senior trade advisor. Hearty congratulations!"

Stunned, Hartmuth remained silent.

"After you sign the treaty, Hartmuth," the voice continued, "the French trade minister will expect you to stay and lead the tariff delegation."

More surprise. Fear jolted up his spine.

"But, sir, this is beyond my scope. My ministry only analyzes reports from participating countries." He scrambled to make sense of this. "Wouldn't you call this posting to the European Union more of a figurehead position?"

The voice ignored his question. "Sunday at the Place de la Concorde, all the European Union delegates will attend the trade summit opening. In the tariff negotiations you will propel the new addenda towards a consensus. By that, we mean a unanimous approval. A masterful double stroke, wouldn't you agree?"

Hartmuth began, "I don't understand. Surely for an internal advisory post, this seems . . ."

The voice interrupted.

"You will sign the treaty, Hartmuth. We will be watching. *Unter den Linden.*"

The voice cut off. Hartmuth's hand shook as he replaced the receiver.

Unter den Linden. Circa 1943, when Nazi generals realized Hitler was losing the war, the SS had organized into a political group, code word "Werewolf," to continue the thousand-year Reich. When they'd helped him escape death in a Siberian POW camp in 1946, these same generals had bestowed a new identity on him—that of Hartmuth Griffe, a blameless Wehrmacht foot soldier fallen at Stalingrad with no Gestapo or SS connections. This identity gave Hartmuth a clean bill of social health acceptable to the occupying Allied forces, a common though secret practice used to launder Nazi pasts. These "clean" pasts had to be real, so they were plucked from the dead. With typical Werewolf efficiency, names were chosen closest to the person's own so they would be comfortable using them and less prone to mistakes. How could the dead contest? But if, by chance, someone survived or a family member questioned, there were more mountains of dead to choose from. Besides, who would check?

The Werewolves demanded repayment, which translated to a lifetime commitment. Ilse was here to guarantee it.

He felt trapped, suffocated. He quickly pulled on his double-breasted suit from the day before, smoothing out the wrinkles, and strode into the adjoining suite. Ilse looked up in surprise from her laptop.

"I'll return for the meeting," he said, escaping before she could reply.

He had to get out. Clear out the memories. Breaking into a cold sweat, he almost flew down the hallway.

He turned the corner, abruptly bouncing into a stocky black-suited figure ahead of him.

"Ça va, Monsieur Griffe? So wonderful you are here," said Henri Quimper, rosy-cheeked and smiling.

Too late to escape. Henri Quimper, Hartmuth's Belgian trade counterpart, embraced and kissed him on both cheeks. He nudged Hartmuth conspiratorially. "The French think they can put one over on us, eh?"

Hartmuth, his brow beading with sweat, nodded uneasily. He had no idea what Quimper meant.

Heralded by prodigious clouds of cigar smoke, a group of delegates walked towards them down the hall.

Cazaux, the French trade minister and probable appointee for the prime minister, strode among them. He beamed, seeing Quimper and Hartmuth together.

"Ah, Monsieur Griffe, bienvenu!" he said, greeting Hartmuth warmly and gripping his shoulder. His cheeks were mapped by spidery purple veins. "Spare me a few words? All these meetings . . ." Cazaux shrugged, smiling.

Hartmuth had forgotten how Frenchmen punctuated their sentences by throwing their arms in the air. The muscles in Cazaux's ropy neck twitched when he spoke.

Hartmuth nodded. He knew the election was to take place the next week, and Cazaux's party was heavily invested in the trade issue. Hartmuth's job would be to bolster Cazaux by signing the trade agreement. The Werewolves had ordered it. *Unter den Linden*.

Cazaux and Hartmuth moved to an alcove overlooking the limestone courtyard.

"I'm concerned," Cazaux said. "This new addendum, these exclusionary quotas—frankly, I'm worried about what might happen."

"Minister Cazaux, I'm not sure of your meaning," Hartmuth replied cautiously.

"You know and I know parts of this treaty carry things a bit far," Cazaux said. "I'll speak for myself. The quotas border on fascism."

Mentally, Hartmuth agreed. After being in diplomatic circles for so many years, however, he knew enough to keep his real feeling to himself. "After a thorough review I'll have a better understanding," he said.

"I feel our thinking is probably very close on this," Cazaux said, lowering his voice. "A dilemma for me because my government prefers to maintain the status quo, reduce unemployment, and pacify *les conservatives*. This treaty is the only way we can pass economic benefits on throughout Europe, standardize trade, and get uniform guidelines."

"I understand," Hartmuth said, not eager for Cazaux's added pressure. No more needed to be said.

The two men rejoined Quimper and the other delegates in the hall. More kissing and jovial greetings were exchanged. Hartmuth excused himself as soon as it was diplomatically possible and escaped down the staircase. He paused on the marble landing, a floor below, and leaned against an antique tapestry, a forested scene with a naked wood nymph stuffing grapes into her mouth, juice dribbling down her chin.

As he stood there, alone between floors, Sarah's face appeared to him in a vision, her incredibly blue eyes laughing. What he wouldn't give to change the past!

But he was just a lonely old man full of regrets he'd tried to leave behind with the war. I'm pathetic, he thought, and waited for the ache in his heart to subside to a dull throb.

Thursday Afternoon

A PUNGENT SMELL OF cabbage borscht clung to the hallway of 64 rue des Rosiers. Abraham Stein answered Aimée's knock, his faded maroon yarmulke nestled among his gray streaked black curls, a purple scarf riding his thin shoulders. She wanted to turn away, ashamed to intrude upon his grief.

"What do you want?" he said.

Aimée twisted her hair, still damp from swimming, behind her ears.

"Monsieur Stein, I need to talk with you about your mother," she said.

"This isn't the time." He turned to close the door.

"I'm sorry. Please forgive me but murder is never convenient," she said, wedging behind him, afraid he'd shut the door in her face.

"We're sitting shiva."

Her blank look and foot inside the door forced him to explain.

"A ritual mourning. Shiva helps acknowledge our suffering while we pray for the dead."

"Please excuse me, this will only take a few minutes of your time," she said. "Then I promise I'll go."

He put his scarf over his head and led her into the dark-paneled living room. An open prayer book rested on the polished pine sideboard. The dining-room mirror was swathed in black cloth. Lit tapers sputtered in pools of wax, giving off only a faint light. Women clad in black, moaning, rocked back and forth on stick-like chairs and orange crates.

She kept her head down. She didn't want to breathe the old, sad smell of these people.

A young rabbi, his ill-fitting jacket hanging off him, greeted her in a jumble of Hebrew and French as they passed him. She wanted to flee this apartment, so dark and heavy with grief.

She overheard French rap from a radio in a back room, where sulky teenagers congregated by an open door.

The crime-scene tape was gone but the insistent noise of the leaky faucet in the dingy bathroom and aura of death remained. She'd always see the scuffed black shoe with the worn heel and the vacant white face carved by that swastika. An odd, tilted swastika with rounded edges.

The crime-scene technicians had left neat stacks of Lili Stein's personal items on the rolltop desk. The bloated angelfish and tank were gone. A knitting basket full of thick needles and multicolored yarn spilled out across the hand-crocheted bedspread. Issues of the *Hebrew Times* were piled in the corner and beside the bed.

"Yours?" She picked up a folded section. The paper crinkled and a color supplement fell out.

"Maman ignored French newspapers," he said. "Refused to own a television. Her only extravagance was a subscription to the Hebrew newspaper from Tel Aviv."

The boards on the window facing the cobbled courtyard were gone. Ribbons of yellow crime-scene tape crisscrossed the view of the drab light well below.

"Why did your mother board up the window?"

He shrugged. "She always said the noise bothered her and she wanted privacy."

Aimée pulled a wicker chair, the only chair in the room, towards the window. The uneven chair legs wobbled, one didn't touch the floor. She indicated he should sit on the bed.

"Monsieur Stein, let's . . ."

He interrupted. "What were you doing in this room?"

She wanted to tell him the truth, tell him how cornered and confused she felt. After the explosion, when her father's charred remains had been carted away, she had lain in the hospital. No one had talked to her, explained their investigation. Some young *flic* had questioned her during burn treatment as if she'd been the perpetrator.

Mentally, she made a sign of the cross, again begging for the dead woman's forgiveness.

"Frankly, this is classified but, Monsieur, I think you deserve to know," she said.

"Eh?" But he sat down on the bed.

"Your mother was the focus of a police operation mounted to obtain evidence against right-wing groups like Les Blancs Nationaux."

Abraham Stein's eyes widened.

How could she lie to this poor man?

But she didn't know any other way.

Not only Leduc Detective's depleted bank account and overdue taxes forced her to take this case. Part of her had to prove she could still be a detective: *flics* or not, justice would be done her way, administered in a way victims' families rarely saw. The other part was her father's honor.

Abraham cleared his throat, "She was cooperating with the *flics*? Doesn't make sense. Maman avoided anything to do with the war, politics, or police."

"Rare though female detectives are in Paris, Monsieur, I'm one of them. I am going to find out who killed your mother."

He shook his head. She pulled out her PI license with the less than flattering photo on it. He examined it quickly.

Aimée ran a hand over the worn rolltop desk, trying to get the feel of Lili Stein. Yellowed account books were shelved inside.

"Why would a private investigator care?" he asked.

"I lost my father to terrorists, Monsieur. We worked with the Brigade Criminelle, as part of surveillance, until the plastic explosive taped under our van incinerated my father." She leaned forward. "What eats at me still is how his murderers disappeared. The case closed. No one acknowledges the victims' families . . . I know this and I want to help you."

He looked away. From down the hall came the muted moaning

of the old women. Medieval and dark, this apartment echoed with grief. Ghosts emanated from the walls. Centuries of birth, love, betrayal, and death had soaked into them.

"Tell me about your mother."

His face softened. Perhaps the sincerity in her tone or the isolation Abraham Stein felt caused him to open up.

"Maman was always busy knitting or crocheting. Never still." He spread his arms around the room, every surface covered by lace doilies. "If she wasn't in the shop below, she'd be by the radio knitting."

Dampness seeped into this unheated room. "Can you tell me why someone would kill her this way?"

Deep worry lines etched his brow. "I haven't thought about this in years but once Maman told me 'Never forgive or forget.'"

Aimée nodded. "Can you explain?"

He unwound the scarf from his shoulders. "I was a child but I remember one day she picked me up after school. For some reason we took the wrong bus, ending up near Odéon on the busy rue Raspail. Maman looked sadder than I'd ever seen her. I asked her why. She pointed to the rundown, boarded-up Hôtel Lutétia opposite. 'This is where I waited every day after school to find my family,' Maman said. She pulled the crocheting from her little flowered basket in her shopping bag, like she always did. The rhythmic hook, pause, loop of the white thread wound by her silver crochet needle always hypnotized me."

He paused, "Now Hôtel Lutétia is a four-star hotel, but then it was the terminus for trucks bringing camp survivors. Maman said she held up signs and photos, running from stretcher to stretcher, asking if someone had seen her family. Person to person, by word of mouth, maybe a chance encounter or remembrance . . . maybe someone would recall. One man remembered seeing her sister, my aunt, stumble off the train at Auschwitz. That was all."

Abraham's eyes fluttered but he continued. "A year after Liberation, she found my *grand-père*, almost unrecognizable. I remember him as a quiet man who jumped at little noises. She told me she'd never forget those who took her family. '*Chéri*,' she told me, 'I can't let them be forgotten. You must remember.' "

Aimée figured little had changed in this dim room with its musty old-lady smell since then. She pulled her gloves back on to ward off the chill. "Why didn't the Gestapo take your mother, Monsieur Stein?"

"But it was the French police, madamoiselle, who rounded them up under Gestapo orders. Even they made mistakes with their famous lists. Several survivors I know were in the park or at a piano lesson when their families were taken. Maman said she came home from school but the satchels, filled with clothing and necessities in the hallway, were gone. Hers, too. That's how she knew."

"Knew what?"

"That her parents had saved her."

Aimée remembered her own mother's note taped to their front door: *"Gone for a few days—Stay with Sophie next door until daddy comes home."* She'd never returned. But how awful to come home from school and find your whole family gone!

"Your mother stayed here, a young girl by herself?"

He nodded. "For a while with the concierge's help. She never talked about the rest of the war."

Aimée hesitated, then pulled out the photo image she'd deciphered for Soli Hecht. "Do you recognize this?"

He stared intently. After a moment, he shoved a pile of invoices aside to reveal a group of faded old photos on the wood-paneled wall. There was a blank spot.

He shook his head. "There was a photo here. Similar, but no Nazis. Maman hated Nazis. Never touched anything German."

Abraham jiggled the bottom desk drawer open. Inside were several empty envelopes addressed to the Centre de Documentation

Juive Contemporaine, the Contemporary Jewish Center, at 17 rue Geoffrey l'Asnier, 75004 Paris.

"She donated to their Holocaust fund." He stood up, rubbing his eyes tiredly. "I can't think of anything else." He shook his head. "I don't believe the past has anything to do with this."

More than ever, Aimée wanted to tell him about Soli Hecht. However, the last thing she wanted was to put Abraham in any danger.

He threw up his hands. "I can't believe she would have gotten involved in some operation. But she did mention recently she had been seeing ghosts."

"The antiterrorist squad . . ."

He interrupted her. "I don't want trouble, I live here," he said. "What about the present . . . the massacres in Serbia? I'm sick of the past, it's over. Nothing will bring her back."

She felt his denial was to avoid pain. Something she had tried to do with her own father's death.

Outside in the light well, a black crow, shiny as licorice, cawed incessantly. She stroked the crocheted bedspread, brushing against the knitting basket, and stopped. A scrap of paper in bold, angular handwriting was stuck in the variegated wool.

"What's this?"

He shrugged.

She carefully spread the wrinkled paper. On it, colors were listed in a row with check marks next to them:

navy blue   *ivory*
dark green

Scribbled on the side were the names. *Soli H, Sarah,*

She stopped. Soli Hecht? That name triggered questions about the encrypted photo. More important, she wondered what the photo would have told Lili Stein.

Arrows from the names went off the torn page. She hesitated whether to tell Abraham Stein about Hecht. "Recognize these names?"

Abraham looked puzzled. "I don't know, maybe members of the synagogue."

Before he could say more, there was a faint knock on the open door. She looked up to see a white-haired woman apologetically beckoning to him.

"I'm sorry"—she motioned helplessly with gnarled hands— "but Sinta wants you. More visitors have come."

Abraham nodded. "Thank you, Rachel." He turned to Aimée. "This is Rachel Blum, Maman's friend. Why don't you speak with her while I go to my wife." He left to meet the visitors.

Rachel's hair was stretched tightly back in a bun. Her black dress had a faint odor of lavender mixed with mothballs. She sank down onto the bed, her slightly stooped frame still bent. Sliding off her shoe and rubbing her foot, she sighed. "Bunions! Doctor wants to fix them, but no thank you, no knife for me, I told him. They've carried me this far, they'll carry me the rest of the way."

Aimée nodded sympathetically.

"Lili had no time for fools—I'm like that myself. I lived in Narbonne until my sister passed away last year. Then I decided to come back to the Marais."

"How long had you known her?" Aimée ventured.

Rachel squinted in thought. "Too long."

"Rachel, do you recognize this snapshot?" Aimée asked, passing it to her.

"My glasses, where are they? Can't see without them." Rachel scrabbled down around her neck. "Must be at home."

Aimée reached for a pair of readers from the top of Lili's desk.

Rachel grunted, "That's better." She squinted through Lili's reading glasses. "Hmm, what's this?"

"Anything look familiar, Rachel?"

A wistful look came over her. "The Square Georges-Cain. A lifetime ago." She sighed, then indicated some figures near a tree. "Our school uniform. See the smocks," and she pointed to a girl turned away from the camera.

Rachel seemed grateful to be resting her feet and exercising her mouth. She was vigorously rubbing her other foot now.

"Did you and Lili go to school together during the war?"

Something shuttered behind Rachel's eyes and she turned away. Aimée knew that look, a deliberately vacant stare that came into old people's eyes when the war was mentioned. Rachel shrugged and didn't answer.

Aimée sat down on the bed next to her and smiled. "Were you in class together?"

"Lili was younger than me. I didn't have much to do with her."

"Didn't you know her parents?"

"I'm only half Jewish," Rachel said. "Am I supposed to know everybody? A lot of people disappeared."

Why had Rachel become defensive?

A tingle went up her spine, the same tingling she'd felt when she'd made that promise to Hecht. She edged closer to the old woman and lowered her voice confidentially.

"Rachel, she looked up to you, didn't she?"

Rachel looked surprised but not displeased. "I'm not sure . . ."

She kept going. "Have I embarrassed you, Rachel? You know how schoolgirls idolize older girls!"

Rachel shook her head slightly and paused. "I vaguely remember her father. He came back after the war."

Aimée noticed that Rachel's gaze was focused on the window crisscrossed with crime-scene tape. So there was something, Aimée thought, her heart starting to pound.

"Why did Lili board up the window, Rachel?"

A stony look came over Rachel's face. "The winter of 1943 was cold. No one had coal for heat."

"Lili boarded up the window for warmth?" Aimée said. "But she wasn't here during the whole war, was she?"

"Water froze in the pipes," Rachel said woodenly.

Aimée prayed for patience. "Wasn't it hard for Lili here after her parents were taken?"

"We chipped ice off the fountains. Boiled it for cooking and washing," Rachel continued.

"What about Lili?"

"She stayed with the concierge. Downstairs when . . ." Rachel stopped and covered her mouth.

Aimée leaned forward and gripped Rachel's arm.

"Go ahead, Rachel, what were you about to say?"

Aimée was surprised to see fear in Rachel's eyes.

"Why are you afraid?"

Rachel nodded and spoke slowly. "You think I'm just a silly old woman."

"No, Rachel. Not at all." Aimée reached for her hand and held it.

Finally, Rachel spoke. "They found the body."

"A body? Who?" Aimée asked. Startled, she leaned forward. Why hadn't Abraham Stein mentioned this to her?

"Down in the light well." Rachel twisted her neck as far as her bent back would allow.

"Whose body?"

"This window looked right out on it."

"Yes, Rachel, but who was it?"

"Things happened in 1943," she said.

Aimée gritted her teeth and nodded. "I know it must be difficult to talk about the Occupation. Especially to my generation, but I want to understand. Let me try."

Rachel turned to her, her eyes boring into Aimée's. "You'll never understand. You can't."

Aimée put her arm around the thin stooped woman. "Talk to me, Rachel. What did Lili see?"

"We had to survive. We did what we had to do." Rachel's stale breath hit Aimée's face. "She told me once that she saw the murder."

"A murder that happened in the light well?" Aimée said, keeping her excitement in check. "So that's why she boarded up the window?"

Rachel nodded.

Aimée willed her face muscles to be still and kept her arm around Rachel's shoulder.

"That's all she said, wouldn't talk about it after that," Rachel said finally. "There's not many people around who'd remember, there were so many deportations."

"Was it the Nazis?" Aimée said.

"All I know is Lili's concierge was murdered." Rachel shook her head. "It's not something people talk about." Her eyes were far away.

"What do you mean, Rachel?"

"Only Félix Javel, the cobbler, he'd remember the bloody footsteps . . ." She trailed off, lost in thought. "Past is past. I don't want to talk anymore."

Sinta, Abraham's wife, clomped into the room. "Listen, Mademoiselle Detective—" She planted her feet apart as if supporting her wide hips and repinned her thick black hair with tortoiseshell combs. Loud beeping interrupted from the folds of her faded apron. "*Alors!*" she muttered, pulling a Nintendo Game Boy out of her pocket. She clicked several buttons then slid it back inside her apron.

"Neo-Nazi *salopes!*" Her voice rang curiously melodic, with a strong Israeli accent. "Day and night, they harass us in the shop," she continued matter-of-factly. "Lili always yelled at them to go away. Told me she wasn't afraid of them, but I guess she should have been."

"A gang? What did they look like?" Aimée asked. The damp cold permeated her wool jacket. Why couldn't they turn the heat on?

"Never paid much attention," Sinta shrugged. "I baked in the back kitchen and she handled the customers."

"Your husband mentioned that she'd been seeing ghosts," Aimée said.

"Yes, old people do that." Sinta rolled her eyes at Rachel, who nodded knowingly.

"I don't speak ill of the dead, she was my mother-in-law. We lived under the same roof for thirteen years," Sinta said. "But she could be difficult. Lately she'd taken to seeing shadows everywhere—in her closet, out the window, on the street. Ghosts."

"Shadows?"

Sinta had turned away, as if dismissing her. Aimée stood up and grasped Sinta's elbow, forcing the woman to turn and face her directly.

"What do you mean by that?" Aimée asked.

Reluctantly, Sinta spoke. "Talking about the past, seeing ghosts around the corner." She shook her head and sighed. "Imagining some collaborator had come back to haunt her." Sinta cocked her head and rested her hands on her hips. "She grew so agitated the other day that I finally said, 'Show me this ghost,' so we walked to rue des Francs Bourgeois and up rue de Sévigné to that park with Roman ruins. We sat there for a long time, quietly. Then she seemed calm and said, 'It comes full circle in the end, always does,' and that was that. No more mention of ghosts."

"Collaborators?" Aimée said, surprised.

Sinta repinned a lock of hair that wouldn't behave. "Yes, all that old talk."

"Why wouldn't you believe her?" Aimée said.

"Up and down rue des Rosiers, Les Blancs Nationaux spray graffiti and smash windows. Seems obvious."

This was the second time she had heard Les Blancs Nationaux mentioned.

Sinta paused and looked around the room. Rachel's eyes had closed, low snores rattling from her open mouth.

"Lately, Lili had become very paranoid." Sinta lowered her voice. "Between you and me, she didn't have many friends. Poor Rachel put up with her, the others wouldn't. Go investigate that trash, that's where you should be looking." Sinta sighed. "I don't have time for the past anymore."

Sinta opened Lili's cracked wooden wardrobe and a strong

whiff of cedar came out. Sinta shoved some black skirts together and moved aside a pair of freshly heeled shoes, a repair tag hanging off them. "Too bad. She had just picked these up from the cobbler's." Sinta shook her head. "All this goes to the synagogue sale benefiting Jews in Serbia."

"What's the hurry, Sinta?"

"Time to clean things out," Sinta said with determination. "No more living in the past."

As Sinta reached in the back, Aimée noticed a coat half-covered in yellowed paper with an old cleaning tag labeled MADAME L. STEIN pinned to it. The cut and drape spoke couture, but the combed wool with nubby black tufts resembled a postwar concoction of available materials.

"That's beautiful," she said.

Sinta grabbed it from the wardrobe and threw it in the pile.

Aimée stared into Sinta's eyes as she lifted the coat up. "Maybe you should keep this."

"Why?"

Aimée looked at it wistfully. Her mother had worn a coat like this. "Don't you feel this coat was from a happier time in her life?"

Rachel snorted awake. Her eyes brightened, seeing what Aimée held. "Ah, the new look from Dior . . . 1948! Lili sewed a coat for me like this one. Mine had bows down the back seam."

"*Schmates!* Rags! Everything goes to the synagogue; Serbian refugees will use the cloth. Make it functional and useful, not just a moth-eaten memory."

Aimée felt something intensely personal from Lili Stein emanated from that coat. "Instead, let me keep the coat and I will donate money to the synagogue fund. In honor of my mother. I didn't know her either."

Sinta stood back. "I'm supposed to feel sorry for you?" Her black eyes glittered. "Grieving for a mother you didn't know?" She planted herself close to Aimée. "My sympathy market is closed. I had a mother born in Treblinka. As far as I'm concerned, mentally she never left. Couldn't leave the past. Kept scratching for lice and begging for food even on the kibbutz in 1973 . . ." She stopped as Abraham came in.

He glared at Sinta.

"That's enough." He picked up the coat and handed it to Aimée. "Maman hadn't worn it in years. Take it."

"Thank you, Monsieur Stein," she said. She picked some piled Hebrew newspapers from the corner and wrapped the coat in them.

Down the hallway, she heard Sinta's raised voice, which she knew was meant to be heard. "She doesn't look like a detective . . . why did you take that shiksa's side, Abraham?"

Sinta's words in her ears, Aimée retraced her steps down the stairs. Out in the courtyard, garbage bins blocked the light well. She pushed them to the side, trying to ignore the rotten vegetable smell. Inside the circular space, a patch of weak light shone. Lili's boarded-up window had looked right down to where she stood.

Mentally, she filed away Rachel's comment about the bloody footsteps to check out later. Right now, it was time to pay Les Blancs Nationaux a visit.

Thursday Evening

"TOTAL SHUTDOWN," MINISTER CAZAUX said under his breath. "The left Confédération Française du Travail, the trade unions, promise stoppages across the board if the trade treaty passes." He shrugged. "On the other hand, the rightists lead the popular vote."

Hartmuth had learned techniques for controlling his stutter; clenching his fists was one of them. He was using it now.

"A work shutdown is a socialist tradition here," Hartmuth said, keeping his hands in his pockets. He knew who wielded real power. Parliament belonged to the right, not the CFDT. "It's purely a statement, and then it's over."

"This is true," Cazaux nodded. "But there will be lots of unpleasantness first."

They stood under the chandeliers in the partially refurbished eighteenth-century Salle des Fêtes in the Elysée Palace. In the reception line, Hartmuth had noticed uneasily how Cazaux assessed him with laserlike intensity. He could all but hear the gears shift in Cazaux's brain amid the clink of cutlery and low buzz of conversation. Like an astute diplomat. Like Hartmuth himself.

Tall windows overlooked the Elysée's neglected back garden. Ahead in the Salon des Ambassadeurs, which was closed for renovations, the ornate ceiling sagged alarmingly. He had been surprised to see the palace, a national symbol, in such disrepair. In Germany, it wouldn't be allowed. But he'd never understood the French and doubted he'd understand them any better now.

Across from him he noted Ilse, in beige polyester, chatting amiably with Quimper's wife, in tailored Versace.

The red and white wine flowed freely. He picked at his food and tasted almost nothing.

He pretended this ornate banquet room was in Hamburg, not Paris. He pretended he was safe. But being in the Marais made it harder to shut the memories out. Sunday, too, he would pretend at the opening of the trade summit, the symbolic gesture ordered by Bonn to weave harmony. *Unter den Linden.*

Cheese and fruit were served on an ice sculpture in the shape of La Marianne, the French Republic symbol, while the orchestra played "La Marseillaise." Cazaux slid in next to him, his cheeks flushed. Television makeup couldn't quite hide his uneven complexion. He offered a flute of champagne to Hartmuth.

"I must do lip service to pacify the conservatives, it's the only way," Cazaux said.

Hartmuth held back. "Essentially, these provisions validate concentration camps for immigrants. We need to rework and rethink . . ."

"More riots will erupt if this treaty doesn't pass. But that's only the beginning . . ." A loud buzzing of voices caught Cazaux's attention and he stopped. He turned to the crowd and smiled. "Let us toast a harmonious working relationship."

Hartmuth raised his glass, which sparkled in the light from the drooping chandelier. The photographer caught them lifting their tulip-shaped champagne glasses to each other in a toast.

Hartmuth was about to lunge at the photographer when the flash went off again. Quimper's tipsy wife appeared, giggling, and wrapped her arms around them both. After that, everything was a blur of congratulations and backslapping.

As a trade advisor, he shaped policy, wielded power, but remained in the shadows, out of the public eye. He had never allowed his face to appear in newspapers. Never.

Would anyone be alive today who remembered him? Hadn't the Auschwitz-bound convoys taken care of them? Of course, the surgery on his burned face after Stalingrad changed his appearance. Nevertheless he was worried the rest of the evening.

Later that night he got up and went to his window. He couldn't sleep. Everything about Sarah that had been dead and buried for so many years bobbed to the surface.

As he stared out to the Place des Vosges, hazy globes of light shone through the tree branches, illuminating the metal grill fence and spurting water fountains. Every impulse told him to give in to what he really wanted to do. Their meeting place was so close. When he closed his eyes he saw it again. Hidden under some branches like it had been in 1942, when she'd shown it to him. When Sarah had been there, slipping inside, beckoning him with her almond-shaped eyes.

Only time for a brief goodbye before his troop was shipped to Stalingrad in 1943. Stuck in a POW camp in Siberia for two years, he'd gone snow-blind and whimpered from frostbite. Until the Werewolves helped him escape, giving him a new identity and part of a new face.

They'd used him to sabotage and infiltrate the allies. With their help, he'd prospered in the new Germany. He had slowly been eased into more powerful and influential positions in the Bonn government. Bonn was peppered with others like him. Hartmuth had never cared much either way. He was alive, but he'd lost what he really wanted. Sarah.

If the French detectives he'd hired through diplomatic channels hadn't been able to find her in the 1950s, how could she be here now? Probably shot dead in a field as a collaborator, they'd said, or had her head shaved and been sent to a work camp in Poland to die.

Inside his briefcase he released a hidden spring. Gingerly, he took out a thick envelope. Dog-eared and yellowed with age, this was all that was left of Sarah, except for the ache that hadn't gone away. He spilled the contents onto the hotel desk and began to methodically sort through his memories.

After seven months of dogged work, the Parisian detective agency had found only these few musty-smelling documents. But he always carried the torn photo, a faded sepia print of just half her face, ripped from her family dossier, when his superior's head was turned. The detectives' report had stated that prisoners didn't last long in Polish work camps. What wouldn't he do for even the chance to visit her grave? Hartmuth sighed. His little Jewess had made him a man and she'd only been fourteen.

He couldn't stand it any longer. He had to go and see. Why not? Maybe it would put some of the devils and ghosts to rest. As he left the lobby he politely informed the night porter that he'd keep his key. After all, he was just taking a walk around the square. He patted his stomach and the night porter smiled and nodded knowingly.

She wouldn't be there, of course, he kept telling himself; this all happened fifty years ago. He wondered at time's passing, as his footsteps echoed down the narrow rue des Francs Bourgeois.

The only other people out were a laughing, entangled couple who stopped to embrace every few meters until they reached their door and disappeared inside. He followed rue des Francs Bourgeois until he found the building he recognized as the old *Kommandantur* where he'd worked.

Now it was the Marais post office. He turned right into the dark cobbled alleyway he remembered all too well.

Much of the Marais was honeycombed with medieval passage-ways and cramped courtyards like this, damp and smelling of the sewer. He stopped and listened, but there was no one behind him. The occasional dull glow behind a drawn curtain was the only light beside the street lamp.

Hartmuth looked up but there were no watchful eyes as in the past, just the carved marble salamander above the courtyard entrance. His stomach constricted in an even tighter knot.

He remembered the salamander very well and the family that had lived behind it. The French police he supervised had hurried them along, yellow stars sewn on their coats, while they protested that there was some mistake. The roundup had happened in the daytime, while she'd been at school. But the neighbors had seen everything as they hid behind the closed windows. He'd known they would be watching. The van had been parked right where he was standing under the arcade off the rue du Parc Royal with the marble salamander sculpted into it, bearing François the First's royal arms.

The buildings now held boutiques and trendy shoe shops instead of kosher delicatessens and garment sweatshops. Where the street joined the crooked medieval alley to the rue de Payenne, Hartmuth took as deep a breath as he could. He walked slowly and softly and he was eighteen again. He begged God that she would be there, even though he knew she couldn't be. She wasn't.

The Square Georges-Cain was still there, the archaeological graveyard of Paris. Roman columns stood randomly, sculpted stone rosettes lay on the ground, and marble figures leaned against the walls. But he wasn't eighteen and he wasn't going to meet his lover, Sarah, hiding in the catacombs. He sat down and cried.

FRIDAY

AIMÉE HUNG HER PANTSUIT in the armoire of her frosty bedroom, still smarting from Sinta's remark. She kicked her uncooperative radiator until it sputtered to life, not waiting for the dribble of heat.

Her grandfather had scavenged old bricks during the Occupation, tossing them in the fire to retain heat. He'd lined his bed with the warmed bricks, wrapped blankets over them, and slept toasty all night. Too bad the fireplace had been blocked shut since the sixties. She paged René, who phoned her back a moment later.

"How do I find out if a group like Les Blancs Nationaux—"

René interrupted her. "Their Web site is infamous, but it's not for the faint of heart."

"Care to elaborate?" She heard a low moan and muted, rhythmic thuds in the background. "Am I interrupting something, René?"

"I wish you were," he chuckled. "I'm at the laundromat in Vincennes next to a spin cycle. Proof that I can't afford the dry cleaners like you."

Too bad she couldn't even afford to pick up her one decent suit. "Tell me about Les Blancs Nationaux."

"Why the sudden interest?"

"The victim's daughter-in-law blames them for the murder," she said. "Morbier said they were demonstrating nearby."

"You mean that old lady carved with the fifty-thousand-franc swastika?"

"You're a regular Sherlock Holmes."

"Rumor is they videotape their meetings," he said.

"You mean show them on the Internet?"

"Just for true initiates," he said. "Part of a gruesome ritual for full Aryan brotherhood at their meetings."

Were Les Blancs Nationaux hard-core enough to tape murder? There was only one way to find out.

She accessed the Paris directory via Minitel on her home phone. Les Blancs Nationaux came up listed with a Porte Bagnolet address. She pulled the tall paneled doors of her armoire open wider and gazed inside. She still had all her costumes from when she'd worked with her father. Somewhere inside was the right outfit in which to pay them a visit.

Her cousin Sebastian's biker jacket, which she'd conveniently neglected to return, hung beside a purple-veiled harem costume. Next to the green Paris street-cleaner jumpsuit, behind a starched crisp white sous-chef apron, she found her ripped pair of black jeans from Thank God I'm a VIP boutique on rue Greneta.

She opened her stage makeup kit, a battered box that still occupied a full drawer in her bathroom though she hadn't used it for years. She went to work on her face. That done, she pulled out her wig box, dusty from neglect under her bed, then chose a black one from her collection. She snipped and teased it to the style she wanted.

A beep and hum came over the fax machine from her office. She leaned in anticipation, hoping for an update regarding an overdue account that would enable them to cover last month's office expenses. She grabbed the sheet, then stopped in mid-arc. The top header was the address of a self-serve fax/copy depot near Bastille. The paper held one sentence.

Leave the ghosts alone or you will join them.

She dropped the fax and grabbed the table edge for support, as the image of the Nazi carving in Lili Stein's forehead flashed before her. Someone considered her worth threatening and she hadn't even begun to investigate.

* * *

"SELF-SERVE MEANS exactly that," the harassed manager of the Bastille fax/copy place told her.

"Wait a minute," Aimée said threateningly, "here's the time and date. Who sent this fax?"

"Stick the francs in the machine and it faxes." He shrugged.

"Somebody's trying to kill me, Fifi." She edged closer. Perspiration beaded his upper lip. "Who was in here today?"

"Little or no contact is made with clerks." He retreated to safety behind the counter.

Her ripped leather biker jacket was fastened with chains; the torn black jeans were welded to her legs. Clunky black biker boots and a tank top with holes that showed tattoos completed her ensemble. SS lightning bolts and iron crosses peeked from her chest amid safety pins, skulls, and swastikas. Her large eyes were outlined blackly with kohl, matching her purple-black lipstick. And her black wig was spiked into a scruffy mohawk.

She questioned the other clerk anyway. He winked, saying it had been too busy. But if she met him later, she could call him Fifi as much as she wanted.

From Bastille she took the Métro to Porte Bagnolet. En route she mentally narrowed possible fax senders from the general public to a few old Jews plus Morbier who knew she was investigating Lili's murder.

Would someone who sat shiva at the Steins' have threatened her? Had Sinta, sparked by anger, faxed her a warning to leave the past alone? No, no matter what Sinta's feelings were about her detecting skills, she wouldn't do that. It didn't make sense, and whatever else Sinta was, Aimée instinctively sensed her practicality.

She found Avenue Jean-Jaurès, a broad tree-lined boulevard. Every village, town, and city in France had an Avenue Jean-Jaurès named after the famed Socialist leader and Paris was no exception.

Next to the front door of a flat brown building indistinguishable from the others, a piece of paper with "L B N" typed on it was fitted into the address slot. Simple and anonymous.

A metallic buzzer above it said *rez-de-chaussée.* She wouldn't have to climb up stairs in these skintight jeans. Imitation parquet flooring led down a fluorescent hallway that echoed with her footsteps. Posted on a wooden door was a typewritten notice: "Free Videos: Learn the Real History!"

The smell of fresh paint and disinfectant hit her as she knocked loudly. The door was opened by a thin woman in a black jumpsuit who scowled at her. One of the woman's gray eyes wandered. The other looked Aimée up and down.

"You're late!" she said.

Disconcerted, Aimée sucked in her breath and half smiled. The phrase about joining Les Blancs Nationaux evaporated on her lips.

"Don't just stand there," the woman snapped. *"Entrez."*

She followed the woman into the office, minimally furnished with steel desks and chairs.

"Traffic. You were expecting . . ." Aimée said.

"Your arrival twenty minutes ago," the woman barked. She sat down and appeared calmer. Her wandering eye wobbled less as her fingers thumped expectantly on the metal reception desk. "Where are they?"

Aimée slid her purple-black fingernails into her tight jeans pockets. She shrugged, then scratched her head.

"Don't even start," the woman said. She looked angry enough to spit.

Aimée jumped. "Look, I . . ."

"Last time was enough!" the woman interrupted.

There definitely was a bee in this skinny, funny-eyed woman's bonnet.

Aimée heard noises from the hallway.

An expression of alarm crossed the woman's face. She was scared, Aimée knew that much. The woman bolted from her chair.

"You explain it to him!" she said, striding to the door.

Cold fear of the unknown coursed through Aimée's veins. Now she wished she'd brought René as backup.

The door shot open. A tall man with dark stubble shading his skull wheeled in a dolly piled high with boxes. His pinstriped suit showed behind the top of the cardboard boxes.

"Just got back," he said. He called to the woman, "There's more in the car."

She moved quickly. "You deal with her," she said, then she was gone.

The man heaved the boxes with a grunt, set them down, then noticed Aimée. His tan, hard-lined face contrasted with his bright, sharp turquoise eyes. He picked a plastic-cased video from the box, tossed it at her, and began stacking a pile of videos in the corner.

Aimée read the blurb inside the clear plastic: IT'S ALL HERE, SEE THE TRUTH, VISIT WHAT THEY CALL A "DEATH CAMP" AND SEE THE HOAX THAT HAS BEEN PERPETUATED FOR FIFTY YEARS.

"Impressive!" she said.

He turned around and took her in with one look.

She blanched. SS lightning bolts were tattooed bracelet-like around his wrist.

"We discuss ideal art forms, comparing today's degenerate art and exposing myths in twentieth-century philosophy like the fallacy of death camps." He pointed to a poster in front of her.

She pretended to study the slogan on the poster: GUIDELINES TO RECOGNIZE ZIONIST TENTACLES IN LITERATURE!

He stretched his arm out and jabbed at it, pantomiming shooting up with a needle. "Our bodies are Aryan temples and we don't do dope." His icy turquoise eyes never left her face.

He didn't miss a beat, she thought. And he was scarier than the wandering-eyed receptionist. "No problem, I'm clean, really clean," she said too earnestly.

"Who are you?"

She shrugged. "That's something I wonder about, too."

"Where are they?" he said.

"Not ready." She panicked. What were they expecting? What if the real messenger arrived while she was talking?

The phone rang on the desk behind him and he picked it up. He turned away from her, scribbling on a note pad.

If that was someone calling about her supposed item she was in big trouble. She began studying the pamphlets in the racks along the wall, edging towards the door, as he spoke into the phone. She was almost at the door when he slammed the phone down.

"Not so fast," he said. "Take these with you," he said, handing her a bunch of videos. He seemed more relaxed. "It's been rearranged. Bring them to our Saturday meeting. At Montgallet, upstairs from the ClicClac video."

"*D'accord,*" she agreed. She pulled out her card. "This is my real job."

He appeared almost amiable now. Her card read LUNA OF SOUNDGARDEN, EVENTS PRODUCER/PERFORMANCE SOUND, LES HALLES. It was one she had picked from her alias file.

Theatrically he dusted his hands off, then reached for his. As they exchanged cards she noticed his hands were ice cold. His card read THIERRY RAMBUTEAU, DOCUPRODUCTIONS with a short list of phone/fax/email addresses and numbers.

Loud shouts erupted from the hallway. At the sounds of breaking glass and scuffling she gripped the brass knuckles deep in her leather jacket pocket. Thierry's face remained masklike as raucous laughter echoed in the outer hallway. He herded her towards the door.

"Stay and talk after our meeting, Luna," he said, his tone

changed. Warmth shone from his blue eyes. "Our cause will change your life. It changed mine."

Fat chance, she wanted to say. Outside the door, shards of glass sprinkled the parquet hallway flooring. There was no trace of anyone, but the bathroom door opposite stood slightly ajar.

She emerged into the sunlight on Avenue Jean-Jaurès, curious to know what had happened but glad to leave. What was going on?

She waited ten minutes then retraced her steps into the building. Silence. A citrus scent lingered in the hallway. The glass had been swept up and the door to Les Blancs Nationaux had been padlocked.

Had Thierry Rambuteau discovered Aimée wasn't who the skinny woman with the wandering eye took her to be? What if he'd played along? She could find out if Morbier helped her.

She'd left Lili Stein's cedar-smelling coat in a locker at the station, intending to drop in at the cleaner's. Now she put it on, tired of the reactions of others in the Métro.

She thought about Lili Stein and her own mother. The mother whose face remained blurry, hovering dimly on the outskirts of memory. She put her arms around the coat that covered her tattoos and black leather. "Maman," she whispered quietly, hugging the coat to her body.

Friday Noon

"SARAH!" A HIGH-PITCHED GIGGLING voice came from behind her.

The old woman stopped, half smiling, and turned around. Too late she realized a group of young girls were talking to each other, not to her. No one had called her that for fifty years. Why had she turned after all this time?

She reached the corner and stood in front of reflecting shop windows. And for the first time in a long time, she took a good look at the way she appeared to the world. Staring back at her was a sixty-five-year-old woman, a thin, lined face with strong cheekbones, and full shopping bags between her feet. She didn't see any sign of the Sarah she used to be.

She stopped for a café au lait on Boulevard Voltaire across from Tati, the cut-rate store. Above the espresso machine hung a gilt mirror framed by smudged business cards and old lotto stubs.

Marie, the pudgy, aproned proprietress, sucked in her breath and asked her, "You made it to Monoprix's big sale, eh?"

Sarah nodded. *"Oui."* She pulled strands of hair over her ears, careful not to disturb her wig.

Marie shook her head approvingly as she wiped the counter. "I want to go before it's too late; it's only once a year. Much left?"

Sarah managed a tired smile as she adjusted the scarf over her forehead. "I couldn't make it up to the fourth floor, too jammed, but housewares still had quite a bit, people hadn't started fighting yet."

"Ah," Marie sighed, "that's a good sign." She moved to wash some glasses near the end of the counter.

Sarah pulled a newspaper from the rack. Her bursitis ached and she knew that it would be too hard to get up again if she sat down. She'd enjoy her coffee standing, not to mention the francs she'd save by not sitting at a table.

She glanced at *Aujourd'hui*, scanning the photos of models and celebrities caught in various scandals. Rarely, if ever, did she read the pulpy, skimpy articles below them.

Suddenly, her cup fell from her fingers and café au lait splashed all over the zinc counter. Staring at her was a face she knew.

How could it be? She pulled her reading glasses from her purse and stared at the photo. The nose was different but the eyes were the same. Then, taking a pen from her purse, she colored the white hair black. She couldn't believe it. Wasn't he long dead? Unconsciously, she began to shake and gasped shallowly for air.

"*Ça va?* You don't look well," Marie said as she appeared with a cloth to wipe the counter. "Feeling sick, eh?"

She just nodded, afraid to tell the truth. The awful truth.

"Come sit down," Marie said as she guided her to a booth.

The normal movements of walking and sitting didn't calm her. She laid her head down on the sticky table littered with cups and saucers, took deep breaths, and closed her eyes. She'd been so sure he was dead. When she'd stopped shaking and her breathing was normal, she stood up and retrieved the paper.

It read like any other glossy name-dropping article. Below the photo the caption identified the man as Hartmuth Griffe. She used the pen again and drew epaulets and a swastika on the black jacket he was wearing and she knew. It was Helmut.

"GET A TAXI!" RENÉ yelled. "Our tax extension appointment got moved up."

"Wait a minute." Aimée clutched the cell phone in front of the locker in the Métro station. "Our appointment is—"

"I'm at La Double Morte," he interrupted. "Tomorrow, the tax board goes on a monthlong recess. If we don't meet now, our case goes in default and we'll be liable for an eighty-thousand-franc fine. We're scheduled for arbitration in five minutes!"

That ate up Soli Hecht's retainer and more. They wouldn't have enough left in the business account for the rent check. She grabbed a taxi.

As she ran up the marble staircase of La Double Morte, the clink of the metal chains from her leather jacket brought a low wolf whistle from the janitor. He eyed her suggestively and wiggled his tongue as he wet-mopped the steps. She just missed tripping on the slippery marble and clomped heavily up the staircase. The leering janitor approached as if to talk with her.

Aimée growled, "Watch out, I bite!"

"Good!" he said. "I like that."

She hissed, "Get a rabies shot."

Trapped in her skinhead attire, she wrapped Lili Stein's coat tightly around her. A murdered woman's couture coat, from the fifties and smelling of mothballs, was not the outfit for a meeting with number crunchers.

Her dressed-to-kill look should have been more along the lines of a gray pinstripe suit. She smoothed down her hair, rubbed off the black lipstick, and trudged carefully up the rest of the stairs. When in doubt, brazen it out!

Quite a few heads arose from their desks as she darted to the room marked ARBITRATION.

René Friant's perspiring face held a mixture of relief and horror as she entered. His short legs dangled from the seat. Every centimeter of him recoiled as she sat down beside him.

Eight pairs of eyes, all male, stared at her from across the long wooden table. A glass of water sat at each place. Computer toner cartridges were piled on the table near her, next to an ancient copy machine. Most of the men wore gray suits. One wore a yarmulke.

"Excuse me," she said demurely and cast her eyes down. "I just received word that this meeting was moved up."

Silence.

The one in the yarmulke glared at her, adjusting the short cuffs of his tight-fitting jacket. "I see no records of past income in the file received from Leduc Detective," he said, without taking his eyes off her. "No statement of deductions either."

He rolled his sleeve up and she saw faded tattooed numbers on his forearm. He'd been in a concentration camp like Soli Hecht. She slipped her hands, covered with SS lightning-bolt tattoos, into her lap.

The man to her left joined in. "I concur, Superintendent Foborski. I also found no record of these."

Here was the superintendent—a concentration-camp survivor—and she was dressed as a neo-Nazi skinhead.

René stole a glance at her and rolled his eyes. Under the table she could see his pudgy hands clasped in prayer.

"Sir, these records—" Aimée began.

But the man next to her reached for his glass, promptly spilling water and knocking toner all over her coat. Accidentally or on purpose, it didn't matter. The powdery toner turned into a clumpy charcoal mess all over her.

Even sopping wet and cold, she wouldn't take the coat off. The fake tattoos were probably bleeding all over her chest.

"Pardon, I'm very sorry," he said. "Please, let me help."

Lili Stein's coat was ruined. She tried to wipe the mess up.

"I insist," he said, pulling at her sleeves. "This could be toxic."

"Leave me alone, Monsieur!" she warned.

"Are you hiding a weapon, Mademoiselle Leduc?" Superintendent Foborski's eyes glittered. "If you don't remove that garment, I'll call security to assist you."

Her shoulders sagged. Gently, she pulled her arms out of the soggy coat, dripping and smelling of wet wool. Swastikas and lightning bolts lay exposed through the holes of her tank top.

Eight pairs of eyes fastened on her tattoos.

"This has nothing to do with that—"

"This board will look at no request without the proper forms," interrupted Foborski, "it's impossible to conduct any further business. Consider your tax in default. Penalties will be levied retroactively in addition to a five-thousand-franc fine." He waved his hands dismissively.

"No!" Aimée stood up and looked him straight in the eye. "What I was attempting to say," she began levelly, "is that all those forms have been sent to you."

She rifled through René's file and immediately pulled out a blue sheet. "You are," she stopped and spoke slowly, "Superintendent Foborski, I take it?"

He nodded imperceptibly, glaring.

She continued, "Your office accepted and time-dated this receipt." Aimée strutted over to Foborski and laid the sheet in front of him. "Keep it, I've got several."

"Why don't I have a copy in my file?" He looked at it suspiciously. "I'll need to have this authenticated."

She'd dealt with bourgeois bureaucracy before, so she was prepared. "Here's a copy of the sign-in log stating the time I submitted them, with the tax revenuer's stamp, if that's any help to you."

He stared at the paper and shook his head. "Take this for verification," he said to his colleague.

Aimée went back, sat down, and gave them what she hoped was a professional smile. "As you know from the form, I'm a private investigator. I don't usually look like this, but in my current case"—she turned to Foborski and looked again in his eyes—"the part demands it."

Aimée passed her investigator's license, with the orange code symbol on it, around the table. She focused on the next most hostile pair of eyes and said matter-of-factly, "Can you bring me up to speed on what points my partner and you have negotiated so far?"

AFTER AN hour of negotiations, she and René walked down the marble staircase, partially triumphant.

"Only a seven-day extension." She looked at René ruefully. "We need three months."

"Even with Hecht's retainer, we're short. Of course, if our overdue accounts paid their balance we'd make it." He half smiled. "But we'd have better odds buying lottery tickets."

Near the exit to Place Baudoyer, they sat down on the wooden bench. René pulled out his ever-present laptop. Aimée hesitated—should she confide in René?

Years after the bombing, she still woke up screaming from the same nightmare. She'd be crawling on cobblestones slippery with blood amid broken glass in the Place Vendôme. Her father would angrily demand that she hurry and piece his charred limbs together so he wouldn't be late for his award dinner. "Vite, Aimée, quickly!" he'd say out of his melted, burned mouth. "I have no intention of missing this!" She'd wake up terrified and run through her dark, cold apartment.

Only once, after too much Pernod, had she told René about her nightmares and the bombing. Right now, she had to talk with someone she trusted.

"I need a sounding board," she said. "Got an ear?"

He nodded and left his laptop unopened. "I thought you'd never ask."

She told René most of what had happened since Soli Hecht had hobbled into their office. She'd already told him about finding Lili Stein.

"I wonder if Foborski attends Temple Emanuel Synagogue, the ones who supposedly hired me," Aimée continued. "Or if Abraham Stein does."

"So?" René said. "I can't see Stein asking a fellow synagogue member to deny you a tax extension."

"No, of course not." Aimée shook her head. "It's just strange that Foborski didn't have those forms."

"Let me help you."

She shook her head. "I'm reserving you for computer work." His hacking skills were the best she'd ever seen besides her own. Even better than her own. She saw the rejection in René's downcast eyes.

"Because I'm small?"

"Stop that. I dealt with your size long ago. You're my best friend."

"And tact is not your strong suit, Aimée," René said. "Even though you're my best friend, too. Do you think if I were tall I'd be able to help you?"

"*Alors!* This has nothing to do with your size, René. Lili Stein's homicide isn't our usual corporate crime."

"Don't count me out, Aimée."

"I swore on my father's grave." She put her head down. "Now I've blabbed to you."

"You swore to deliver something to Lili Stein. You did. Remember, I'm a black belt." He nudged her proudly. "And a good backup."

She sighed. "You keep reminding me."

"What about Soli Hecht?"

"He said no contact."

"Come to the dojo with me. You need all the self-defense kicks you can master."

"*Merci.*" She squeezed his hand. "I'm going to see Morbier. He should have the forensics report by now."

"What is that stuff on your fingernails?"

"Like it? It's called Urban Decay," she said. "I'm going to Les Blancs Nationaux meeting tomorrow."

"Why?"

"If they murdered Lili Stein . . ."

He interrupted. "You need backup with those types, Aimée."

She hesitated. That might not be a bad idea. But if it was a setup . . . She decided against exposing him to danger.

"If I need you I'll call you." She kissed him on both cheeks. "Pressure Eurocom's accountant, make him sweat. See you later at the office."

LE COMMISSARIAT de Police seemed quiet for an early Friday afternoon. Few desks were occupied and the television blared an old American rerun of *Hunter*. As Aimée approached, Morbier's head appeared from under his desk.

"Lost the grip that holds up my suspenders," he said with a sheepish grin.

"Try this." Aimée plucked a safety pin from her jeans and passed it to him. "I've got plenty."

Morbier hitched up his trousers and pinned them.

"Just for that, I won't comment on your appearance." He smiled and sat down heavily at his desk.

Her father would have said something like that.

"Look, Morbier," she began. "I need a favor."

"You're a big girl now, I know," he said stiffly. "Our investigation will remain professional." He winked.

She controlled her impulse to stuff the cigarette dangling from his mouth down his throat. One minute he played hard-line and by the book. The next, he became a paternalistic old coot who couldn't express his feelings. She wished he'd decide on the role, then play it.

"I'd appreciate Les Blancs Nationaux's phone records, calls made and calls received," she said. "I want to know who Rambuteau talked with when I was in the office."

"Back up here. Who's Rambuteau?"

"A born-again Nazi who could be setting me up."

"Why?"

She hesitated. "I'll know when I infiltrate Les Blancs Nationaux's meeting."

His eyebrows lifted. "How did you manage an invitation? They don't let just anyone in—the scum level is high."

She told him.

"Maybe you shouldn't go."

"It's a bit late now."

He whistled. "Could be a trap."

"Exactly. Can you get me the phone numbers?"

Morbier's mouth hardened. "Before I do anything, hit me with the real reason you're mixed up in this Stein pot-au-feu."

"Maybe if you believed in community policing and made friends with the rabbi at Temple Emanuel"—her shoulders tightened— "he wouldn't have called me about Lili's shoplifting." She paused, realizing she had to be more careful . . . what if Morbier contacted the rabbi? She shifted the conversation's focus. "I'd like to see the forensics report."

"Me, too." Morbier scowled. "Somehow it's lost in the shuffle between the Brigade de Recherche et d'Intervention, the Brigade Criminelle, and the Commissariat," he said. "You know, the usual rivalry in our three-pronged justice system. Either of the other two would sooner let someone escape than let us at the Commissariat grab them."

To avoid him venting his frustration on her, she tried being sympathetic. She sighed, "Why don't the branches work together?"

"Our squad car radios can't even communicate with each

other. Napoleon's theory of divisiveness still prevents us from ever getting together to overthrow the government."

She grinned. "An interesting idea that makes for lousy police work."

"Supposedly, the feds at BRI have a covert operation." He rolled his eyes.

She could tell he was warming up, testing whether to toss a few morsels her way.

"Far as I'm concerned they're all clowns. But you never heard that from me."

"In other words, be careful not to step on anyone's territorial toes?" she said.

"That's one way to put it," he said. He opened his desk drawer and pulled out the crime scene photographs and a clear plastic baggie which he dangled in front of her eyes. Jumbled inside were dirt, scraps, and leaves.

"*Voilà.*"

She reached up but he slipped the baggie behind his back.

"My commissaire has become extremely interested in this case." He shook his thick finger at her. "Share and share alike, Leduc?"

He'd make her pay for every particle of information. She bit back her nasty reply. "*D'accord.*"

He pulled out two pairs of tweezers, gauze masks, and sterile plastic bags. Aimée put on a mask. He wiped his arm across the top of his computer terminal, laid down newspaper, and dribbled the baggie contents.

"Where did your men find these?"

"You tell me." His eyes narrowed.

She remembered the splinters in Lili Stein's palm and the bloodless swastika. "You mean she was murdered in the light well?"

He nodded. "There's evidence of a struggle—forearm bruising, linear marks on fingertips from the ligature, concrete bits under her fingernails, metal scratches from the screws in her crutches. Points to the perp dragging her upstairs."

One hell of a struggle, Aimée thought. She leaned over and smelled the damp earth from a cluster of dirt-encrusted leaves. She gripped the tweezers and picked up a mud-spattered paper strip covered with numbers. Carefully, she lifted a length of variegated-colored wool, then a centime-sized cloudy, plastic cylinder. She peered intensely at each. She left the knobby pink button in the baggie. Aimée turned the baggie over, pointing out the double interlocked C's on the button.

"Odd," she said. "Lili Stein didn't look the Chanel type."

"Aha!" He let out a big sigh. "The killer wore Chanel and lost a button in the struggle pulling her upstairs." Morbier poked the chunky button. "A designer murder!" He smiled.

She ignored him. "Assuming that's Lili Stein's wool, where are her knitting needles? Or the bag she carried her knitting in?"

And what about Soli Hecht's name in Lili's knitting, the photo, or the threatening fax? She didn't mention any of this to Morbier, especially since Morbier had mentioned the federal BRI, the government's strong-arm enforcement. She'd figured Hecht didn't want *flics* involved due to his innate suspicion of them. But maybe it was something else . . . maybe he suspected corruption.

"Checked the dustbins, public and private?" she asked.

"Dustbins, that's quaint," he said. Morbier made a long face and consulted his notes. "Garbage pickup was that morning and the hotel bin had just been emptied."

She cocked her head sideways. "Which hotel?"

"Hôtel Pavilion de la Reine nearby." She'd heard of this exclusive hotel, multi-starred in the Michelin guide.

"What about this?" She pointed to the scrap of paper in the baggie. "How near to Lili's body was it?"

"The crime-scene unit noted this was found in the courtyard entrance," he said.

"See the numbers. That looks like a receipt. Let me make a copy," she said. "And I'd like to borrow the photographs."

He nodded.

She took a sterile strip of Saran Wrap, laid it on the copier plate, picked up the paper scrap with tweezers, and set it down. Then she laid another sterile Saran strip over it, put down the lid, and pressed "Copy."

The ripped edge had a number, like the bottom of a receipt. She decided to check the shops near the alley.

"Thanks, Morbier." She eyed a Columbo-style trench coat with a patched lining on a hook. "Yours?"

Morbier shook his head. "I'm on call. Inform me if you find out anything."

"Think someone would mind if I borrowed the trench coat for a while?" she said.

He grinned. "Be my guest, your tattoos are guaranteed to offend every group."

"I do try," she said, donning the coat.

OUTSIDE OF La Double Morte, Aimée walked smack into a large knot of people clogging one side of the rue de François Miron. Orthodox Hasidic Jews in black stood grouped among bystanders in suits and jeans.

"*Nom de Dieu*, Soli Hecht!" she heard an old woman wail.

Aimée flinched at hearing Soli's name.

Red lights flashed from an ambulance straddling the sidewalk ahead. She pulled the trench coat tighter and started running. She made it to the corner before the ambulance pulled away. White-coated attendants slid a stretcher into the back door. She caught a glimpse of a blanketed mound before the doors clanged shut. The siren echoed off the cobblestones as it sped down rue Geoffroy l'Asnier toward the Seine.

Worried, she shook her head as she stood in front of the bronze six-pointed star on the gate of the Centre de Documentation Juive Contemporaine.

Two men conversed beside her in Yiddish. Both wore the black upturned hats; one was bearded, the other's skimpy suit pants didn't quite reach his white ankle socks.

"What's happened?" she asked.

"Soli Hecht got clipped by the Bastille bus," said the bearded one, switching into French. A Hebrew magazine stuck out of his pocket.

"An accident? Is he all right?" she said.

The bearded man turned to look at her and shrugged. "Hard to say, but they didn't pull the sheet over his head. No *panier à salade*," he said, referring to the blue van that picked up corpses. "An accident? If you believe it was an accident . . ." He didn't finish.

Startled, she backed into the stone wall. "But he's an old man . . ." she trailed off as the men walked away.

The bearded man looked back over his shoulder at her. "Do recriminations ever stop?"

Now, with the crowd mostly dispersed, she saw the blood-stained cobblestones by her feet. A shiver ran down her spine. Lili Stein had been murdered less than three blocks away.

The institutional-looking Centre de Documentation Juive Contemporaine stood close to the Seine. A bronze memorial to the Martyr Juif Inconnu filled the entrance. Aimée strode briskly past it to the gravel quai.

She remembered the envelopes in Lili Stein's desk drawer addressed to the center, the list in her knitting with "Soli H" on it. Most of all, she thought about Hecht's words. She had put the photo in Lili Stein's hand. But it had been too late. What did Hecht know that put him in danger?

Uneasiness gnawed at her. First Lili, now Soli.

Pigeons swarmed near her feet hoping for bread crumbs as she pulled out her cell phone. Her footsteps popped gravel and the pewter-colored Seine flowed lazily beside her. She shooed the pigeons away as Morbier answered.

"I just saw Soli Hecht put into an ambulance," she said. "Rumor is he got pushed in front of the bus."

Aimée wanted to hear the official spin from Morbier. See if the police were treating it as an accident or attempted homicide.

"*Alors!*" came Morbier's reply. "Someone trips in front of a bus and you call me at le Commissariat! Anybody see him pushed? Eh? A perpetrator and a motive would help, too. *Voilà*, then you have something."

"Just sharing information." She clicked off.

She didn't like this at all. She hadn't from the beginning. Things didn't smell right, as her father would say. She entered the Center's paved square to inquire if Soli had been there or if someone noticed something. On the memorial, death camp names were chiseled. She gazed, saddened by the long list: Auschwitz, Belzec, Birkenau, Chelmno, Ravensbruck, Sobibor—so many places she'd never heard of. "Never forget" was handwritten in bold letters on a placard propped below.

"Never forget," Lili Stein had told her young son, Abraham. What had Lili meant? Aimée wondered—had it killed her?

The interior of the five-story building blended fifties architecture with anonymous high-tech features. State-of-the-art alarm sensors and high-density vision cameras perched in marble niches above her. On the wall in the sparse reception area hung a directory of the Center's services in several languages.

A small young woman with a thick black braid down the back of her denim smock bustled out to greet her. Her name tag read "Solange Goutal, Administration Assistant."

"Yes, may I help you?" Behind rimless glasses her bright eyes were puffy.

Aimée displayed her ID. "Did you know Soli Hecht was involved in an accident in front of this building?"

"Why, yes," Solange said. Anguish was printed on her face. "I spoke with him as he left."

Aimée hoped her surprise didn't show. "When was this?"

"Are you from the police? Show me your ID again," said Solange. Aimée kept her smile businesslike. This woman could have been the last person to speak with Hecht before his accident. "I'm a private detective, investigating the murder of the Jewish woman near here."

"Of course I want to be helpful, but how is it related?" Solange said. She pulled a lace *mouchoir* from her pocket and blew her nose loudly.

"My job," Aimée said, frustrated that Solange Goutal was the curious type, "consists of eliminating coincidences to find solid clues and build a case."

Solange's eyes crinkled. "I see." But Aimée could tell she didn't. "Vandals set fire to our Star of David last week. Les Blancs Nationaux didn't claim responsibility, but it wouldn't surprise me if they had."

"Hard to say." Aimée gritted her teeth but kept smiling. She wanted this woman to answer her questions, not pose other questions. "Why don't you tell me about Hecht."

"Well, he needed assistance down the stairs because of his arthritis." She indicated the curved marble stairway. "I helped him with his coat. I always helped Soli if I could. His work is so important." She smiled sadly.

"Did you see the accident?"

She sniffled, holding back tears. "My back was turned, deactivating the security system," she said. "I heard brakes squeal, then a thud. I ran outside but . . ." She closed her eyes.

"You deactivated the security system after Soli Hecht left?" Aimée said. That didn't make sense. "Why?"

"If Soli is involved with a project, he works here any time. We close at noon Fridays for Shabbat. However, today, for the deportation memorial services I came in to finish up some work. Sometime after three Soli buzzed the office so I deactivated the alarm, then let him in. I reactivated the alarm but he only stayed a short time. To let him out I had to deactivate again. In doing so, I forgot to disarm his office alarm code."

"But I just walked in," Aimée interrupted.

"My mistake." Solange shook her head. "I was supposed to activate the process again. But it's so hard to remember."

"He has special access?" Aimée asked.

"Of course!" Solange sounded surprised. "Soli got the grant from the 4th arrondissement for this building space. His foundation maintains an office upstairs. Since the Jews lived and died in the Marais, he always said, their history should be shown here. But this week was the first time I'd seen him in several months."

Startled, Aimée realized that this information fit if his recent contact with Lili involved his work at the center. Keeping her excitement in check, she asked, "What was he working on?"

"That's confidential information," Solange said. She glanced at her watch. "I need to close the center."

"Is there anyone in his office whom I can talk to?" Aimée asked.

"Only Soli could tell you that. There's no one else in today."

Why wouldn't Solange talk? Supposedly there'd been an attempt on Soli's life, so why worry about confidentiality?

"Solange, I need to know about this work he's involved in."

"I told you it's confidential," she snapped.

Hecht had slipped her fifty thousand francs to find Lili Stein's killer and now he'd been hurt. There must be a connection to Hecht's foundation, but she wouldn't find out if this braided lackey kept blocking her way.

"Your director better be more helpful." She leaned close to Solange.

"She's involved in the memorial at the deportation monument today, but she'll be in Sunday." Solange backed up against the highly polished wood reception desk.

"What if Soli doesn't make it until tomorrow and you've obstructed my investigation—would you like that on your conscience?"

Solange's chin quivered. "I don't make the rules, I'm sorry."

"Answer me this." Aimée crossed her arms. "Did Soli act differently today than before?"

Solange paused, knotting her fingers. "His rheumatoid arthritis had become worse. He was in constant pain," she said, then sighed, "That's why it seemed unusual."

"Unusual?" Aimée said, alerted by the change in Solange's tone.

"That he was at a bus stop," Solange said matter-of-factly. "He told me he was going to take a taxi home."

Aimée willed her face muscles to stay put, hiding her excitement. Her suspicious feeling about Solange evaporated. "Did you report the accident to the police?"

"They didn't even respond when I called. Told me to dial SAMU, the emergency. Soli's a special man. This doesn't seem fair."

Outside, Aimée stared at the now dull brownish spot on the cobblestoned street. It didn't make sense for Hecht, in constant pain, to wait at a bus stop when a taxi stand was a few meters away. Especially since he'd said he would take a taxi. Somehow she'd unearth this mess, cobblestone by cobblestone if need be.

"YOU SAY SOLI HECHT is in a coma?" Aimée asked Morbier as she stood across from his desk. "Is he going to wake up?"

"Severe trauma, internal injuries." Morbier shrugged. "Then again, I'm not a doctor."

"If he wakes, can you arrange it so I talk with him?" she said.

France 2 droned above them on the TV in the Commissariat's investigative unit. On the screen, angry demonstrators at the Elysée palace gates paraded near a newscaster who vainly attempted to interview them.

"A big if. He's in his eighties, amazing that his heart is pumping at all. Round-the-clock surveillance, too," Morbier added.

Her heart raced. Something was very off here.

"Wait a minute, weren't you calling this an accident? Not even investigating when I called you . . ."

Morbier cut her off. "Not me. Word came down the pipe."

"Meaning what?" she asked.

"From above. Not my dominion anymore. My men and I have been ordered clear of this investigation for safety and precaution. You, too." He stared at Aimée.

"Hold on." She hated being told thirdhand. "Does this include Lili Stein's case?"

"BRI has been assigned to the 3rd and 4th arrondissement," he said.

If Solange Goutal's emergency call had been ignored but Soli Hecht was abruptly put under hospital surveillance, a lot more was happening than met the eye. Her eye, anyway. "You're no longer handling this case?"

He shook a nicotine-stained finger at her. "Stick to your computer, Leduc; that's all you need to know."

"What about getting me the phone numbers dialed from Les Blancs Nationaux's office?"

He shook his head. "I can't help you."

Typical Gallic evasion, she thought; the French had perfected the art of sitting on the fence. He cupped his palm and took a deep drag of the Gauloise stub held between his thumb and middle finger. His bushy eyebrows lifted high on his forehead.

"Talk to me, Morbier," she said. It came out more intimately than she meant it to.

"First time in twenty-six years I've had a case taken away." He regarded his desk with a sour expression and ignored the tone in her voice. "For what it's worth, I don't like it either."

She felt her temper erupting, but she thanked him and walked out.

Late-afternoon traffic had choked to a standstill on rue du Louvre as she walked to her office. Morbier's comment spun in her head and she longed for a cigarette.

Instead, she bought a baguette at the *boulangerie* next to her building. In the small *supermarché* wedged on the other side, she picked up chèvre cheese, tapénade relish, and a bottle of Orangina. She waved to Zazie, who was doing her homework by the window in Café Magritte.

As she mounted the worn stairs to her office she decided she had to keep investigating, no matter what Morbier said. They might be able to push him around but no one could tell her what to do.

Inside the office Miles Davis greeted her, excitedly sniffing her bag of food. He'd spent the night with René. She fed him some scraps from the butcher's. The only trace of René was a message taped to his computer screen with one word: "later."

Miles Davis fell asleep perched near the heater and René's chair. Aimée poured the Orangina into a crystal Baccarat wineglass left over from her grandfather. She folded the cheese and tapenade into the crusty baguette and ate.

After she finished her meal, she carefully taped the photo image and torn snapshot piece from Lili Stein's room together. She scanned the complete image into her computer and digitally enhanced the photo and printed a copy.

Aimée placed this image among the spread-out photos from the police folder and her own archive files. Then in chronological order, she tacked them up along her wall and looked for connections to the swastika.

She peered at them though a magnifying glass. The black-and-white photos cast everything in a timeless past. Each snapshot held a different scene, but they were all views of the Marais. She recognized the café, Ma Bourgogne, she often went to. A group of booted Nazis sat drinking at the corner table. Next to it, women with rolled pompadour hair wearing ankle socks and t-strap shoes stood in line holding ration books.

Another photo showed the local *Kommandantur* on the rue des Francs Bourgeois, with armed Nazis guarding the heavy wood entrance doors. She almost dropped her goblet of Orangina.

On flags flying above the *Kommandantur*, the swastikas were tilted $\mathcal{G}$, with rounded edges, exactly like the one carved in Lili Stein's forehead.

Miles Davis growled, then someone knocked loudly on the office door. Had René forgotten his keys? She slipped her unlicensed Glock 9-mm from the desk drawer into her back jeans pocket.

"Who's there?" she said.

A muffled voice came from behind the door. "Herve Vitold with BRI."

"Show me your identification."

A laminated photo identity card with Brigade de Recherche et d'Intervention flashed in front of the peephole.

"*Un moment.*" She shuffled the photos together and slid them back into a large envelope in her drawer.

"Excuse the caution." She opened the door slowly. "I've had some threats."

Aimée had never seen a Saville Row suit before but figured the Nordic-looking man standing at her door wore one. Probably a Turnbull and Asser handmade shirt, too.

"Of course," he said. His white blond hair glinted in the hall light but his features remained hidden. "Mademoiselle Leduc?"

Aimée nodded, keeping her hand cocked on the gun's safety.

"I have no appointment, but I'd like half an hour of your time. With commensurate compensation, of course," he said.

Aimée opened the door wider and let him in. She tried to appear as professional as possible in her too tight jeans and a torn Asterix vs. Romans T-shirt. A whiff of something expensive laced with lime hit her.

"Please come in and have a seat, I'll be with you right away," she said.

"Herve Vitold." He held out his hand as she showed him into her office. "Security administrator." He had gold-green eyes and an expensive tan for November.

"Please sit down," she said, surprised he didn't wear a uniform.

He leaned forward, took out a leather checkbook, and flashed a kilowatt smile at her. "Your rates, please. I want to take care of the business first."

Aimée briefly wondered why a *Gentlemen's Quarterly* type from the federals at BRI would walk into her office and want to pay money to talk to her.

"Five hundred francs for a half hour," she said promptly.

Let him put his money where his mouth was. See if this handsome man in an expensive suit was real or joking.

Immediately he pulled out a Montblanc pen, filled in the amount, and slid it across the desk, briefly touching her fingertips. She could have sworn his fleshy, manicured fingers lingered a second too long. Shell-shocked at receiving such a check though she was, she didn't react. Her mind was mostly on his very curly blond eyelashes and the green in his eyes. Consciously, she ignored a danger signal in her brain flashing "Too good to be true."

"How may I help you?" she smiled.

"First, may I say I appreciate your taking the time. A business like yours . . ." Here he vaguely gestured around the office, not exactly a beehive of activity. "And with a busy schedule, I'm sure." He flashed his brilliant smile. "But I'll get right down to it, shall I?"

"It's your franc."

"My branch works with precautionary services, sort of a field unit, out of La Défense," he said.

Get with it, girl, and ask a question, she told herself. "Sorry to interrupt, but I'm not familiar with government security. Don't you wear uniforms?"

Again that smile. "No uniforms. We exist and we don't exist, if you get my meaning."

Talking in tongues was what it sounded like to her. "Not really. Maybe you should get to the point."

A glimmer of amusement crossed his face.

The shadows lengthened across her office walls and she stood up to switch on the office lights.

"*Mais bien sûr*," he said. "Special branch out of Bourget, responsible for terrorist management, has taken over the Stein case. All inquiries, surveillance, and follow-up are to be handled by us."

That fit Morbier's dictum. "Why?"

"Given the present political climate and sensitivity of the issue, Special Branch feels it must be handled with care." Vitold sat back, crossing his trousered legs precisely at a ninety-degree angle. "This is a historic moment. Finally, for the first time since the last war, the European Union delegates will sit together and sign a treaty that binds Europe. Nothing must endanger this or the covert operation we've mounted to nab terrorists intent on destroying this process."

Too good to be true, all right. "Are you telling me to, let us say, butt out?" she said.

"Mademoiselle Leduc, I'm asking you." His eyes flickered again with amusement, then hardened. "I know how important the tax extension is to your firm right now and I wouldn't want anything to interfere with the process."

"Is this some kind of veiled threat?"

He stood up with a perfect crease down his pant leg and a still wrinkle-free shirt. "Now, now," he clucked patronizingly.

She stood up, too. "You walk in here, write a check, and expect me to back off a paid case by threatening to interfere with my taxes? Who do you think you are?"

"Vitold, as I've said, but I neglected to mention that your investigator's license is about to expire, since you've not renewed it."

"My investigator's license is code orange. Permanent and non-renewable," she said.

"Not anymore."

"Threaten somebody else." She glared at him, ripping his check into franc-sized bites.

He grabbed her wrists, imprisoning them in a viselike grip. Little white pieces of his check fluttered onto the parquet floor. She realized his large manicured fingers could snap her bones in half like matchsticks.

"Must be careful of your little hands." He stroked the scar on her palm.

She jerked her head towards the video camera mounted into the deco molding. "Go ahead, the security camera is capturing our moment as we speak."

An odd smile washed over his face and he let go.

Then he was outside her office, striding toward the glass-paned hallway door.

"Consider carefully. I would if I were you," he said.

She whipped out the Glock. But he was gone. Only a whiff of lime lingered in the air.

She was shaking so much she couldn't keep her hands steady. She forced herself to take deep breaths and slip the safety back on. How deep had she waded in—and what kind of trouble was this anyway?

The indentations where Herve Vitold's fingers had pinched her wrists were still visibly white. She rewound the videotape and printed a photo of him. She remembered that Texas saying "Not fit for dog meat," and wrote that in red across Vitold's image.

After she grew calm enough to work, she sat back at her computer. She knew access codes changed daily in the security branch at La Défense. Within ten minutes, she had bypassed the "secure" government system, accessed their database, and found Bourget Special Branch.

The Bourget chain of command, responsible for antiterrorism functions, only crossed municipal police lines in the event of attack bombings, hostage situations, and the like. Not cold bodies of old women with swastikas carved into their foreheads.

Then she checked BRI's files, but no Herve Vitold came up. She spent two hours logging into all government branches with corresponding security.

If Vitold was who he purported to be, then Aimée was Madame Charles de Gaulle, God rest her soul. She found no one named Herve Vitold existing in any data bank.

Friday Evening

THE GRAVELLY VOICE DIDN'T sound happy.

"Consider this an order, Hartmuth. The chancellor is very set on this item of the trade agenda."

Hartmuth kept his voice level. "*Jawohl.* I've said I'll review the adjunct waiver proposal before I decide."

He clicked off. Briefly he wondered about Bonn's reaction if he didn't sign the agreement.

Hartmuth wearily set his briefcase down on the Aubusson carpet, collapsing into the récamier's brocade. All the rooms were furnished in authentic antiques, yet they were so comfortable, he thought. This silver-and-silk-threaded pillow was familiar, like the kind his mother embroidered on winter evenings long ago.

But that world had been shattered out of existence. Setting his stockinged feet upon the pillow, he lay back exhausted and closed his eyes.

Yet he couldn't sleep. He relived the journey, the one in which he returned to his father's home on the outskirts of Hamburg. Of ninety-one thousand taken at the defeat of Stalingrad he'd been one of the five thousand Germans limping back after the Siberian work camps.

At the end of the muddy road, rutted with bomb craters, he'd recognized the blistered paint and blown-out windows. Entering the doorless shell, now empty and deserted, he'd seen that even the fireplace bricks had been taken. He shuffled to the back, looking for his fiancée, Grete. His family had arranged their betrothal while they were in the Gymnasium, before the war.

A steady chopping and then a sound of splintering wood came from a dilapidated outbuilding in the crisp, bitter air. Red-faced, her breath frosty on a chill March afternoon, Grete was chopping down the back garden shed for firewood, using a rusty ax. She clapped a cracked and bleeding hand over her mouth, stifling her cries, and hugged him.

"You're alive!" she'd finally managed to say, her voice breaking with emotion. "Katia, Papi is here. Your Papi!" Grete said, shivering in the icy wind.

A child, wrapped in sewn-together burlap sacks, sat in a nearby wheelbarrow. Oddly, he felt no affection for this hollow-cheeked, runny-nosed creature with yellow ooze dripping out of her eyes. The baby had been playing with a warped photo album and his father's violin bow, all that remained of his family. Grete assured him proudly that Katia was his, born of their coupling on his last furlough in 1942. Yes, he remembered that. He'd been so anxious, after his fiancée's doughlike legs and desperate embrace, to return to Paris and Sarah.

He knew Katia was his and he resented her. He wished he didn't. Guilt flooded through him for not wanting his own child.

Because of Katia he knew he'd have to stay and take care of them, marry Grete, and keep his promise. She deserved it, for bearing his child, protecting the house. She told him herself what had happened to his parents.

"Helmut, the snow hadn't melted by April and Mutti and Papi couldn't stand to see Katia shiver so badly. They decided to investigate a rumor about black-market blankets in Hamburg. Only one tram was left running, painted white and red to resemble medical transport," she said. "I'm sorry." Grete put her head down. "I'm sure they didn't feel a thing, Helmut. We saw yellow-white light." She pointed beyond the muddy, rutted road. "After the explosion, smoke billowed into the sky and a rain of little red slivers fell on the snowy field."

He wondered if she was telling the truth or was the truth too painful to tell? It sounded like the explosions in the Siberian oil field where he'd been a POW. Working at the camp in the frozen tundra, men had been burnt by eruptions of fire on ice into charred cinders before his eyes. He wore gloves to cover the skin grafts crisscrossing the old burns on his hands.

He sat up in a cold sweat. Loyal and steadfast Grete, she hadn't deserved his gift of an empty heart. But he couldn't very well go back to France then—he, an ex-Nazi just out of a POW camp, to search for a Jewish girl, a collaborator.

Postwar Germany had no services, no food. Grete cooked the roots and tubers he found by clawing under the snow. Scavenging in the forest, he dreamed of Sarah, seeing her face in the catacombs as they shared tins of black-market pâté.

But all around him, people boiled and ate their shoe leather if they had any. He sold his mother's pearls for a sack of half-rotten potatoes that kept their hunger at bay. Gangs of children ran after the few running trains, fighting over burned pieces of coal that fell onto the tracks, hoping to find some only half-burned. They weren't allowed back into the basements under the rubble until they brought something to eat or burn.

Hollow and numb most of the time, he survived by his wits and by scavenging. At night, spooned between Grete and Katia for warmth, he'd see Sarah's curved white thighs, feel her velvety skin, and imagine her blue eyes.

Grete knew right away he didn't love her, that he loved someone else. But they married with no regrets. No one had time for regrets in postwar Germany, and he and Grete worked well together. They were a team of two dragging Katia along. Her eyes never seemed to heal. One eye stayed closed and continually dripped. There was no penicillin to be had and no money for the black market.

Grete appeared one day with tubes and packets stuffed in the pockets of her too-small winter coat. She pulled out a fat tube of metallic-smelling ointment.

"Helmut, hold her, please. This will help her eyes," Grete said. Firmly she rubbed it around and inside Katia's lids as much as she could, while he held his squirming child. Then Grete pulled some huge yellow-and-black pellets out of a paper packet. "Good girl, Katia, now just swallow these. Here's some cold tea to help them go down," Grete said soothingly.

Katia made a face and spit them out. Grete stuffed them back in her mouth.

"Grete, Grete, what are you doing?" He thought Grete had gone crazy and was giving Katia dead bees to eat because she was so hungry.

Her eyes flashed angrily, "It's medicine! She has to take them or she'll be blind, *Gott im Himmel*, help me!"

And he did. He never forgot what those huge penicillin tablets looked like and how Grete's face had looked as they got them down Katia. Only the GIs had them. Katia's eyes got better and he never asked Grete how she had got the penicillin.

SATURDAY

AIMÉE, IN BROWN wool jacket and pants, strode through the narrow passage behind the rue des Rosiers. She rested her gloved hand in her lined pocket, keeping it warm. Fog crept through the Marais, almost to Place des Vosges. Centuries-old stone, worn smooth by countless footsteps, lined the alley. Above her, red geraniums spilled from window boxes.

A broken street lamp buzzed and blinked randomly. Nearby, on rue Pavée, stood a fancy *charcuterie* selling imported meats, Javel's cobbler shop, and a small dry cleaner's. She held the partial receipt copy she'd made at Homicide and hoped she'd find the other half.

First she checked the *charcuterie*. The owner busily informed her that all his customer receipts were yellow copies, unlike the scrap of paper in her hand. Try next door, he suggested.

Aimée opened the spotlessly clean door of Madame Tallard's dry cleaning establishment. Warm air redolent of laundry starch drifted from behind the chipped formica counter.

"*Bonjour,*" said a white-haired woman from behind a steamy laundry press.

"*Bonjour, Madame.*" Aimée held up her copy of the paper. "Would you recognize this?"

The woman emerged from behind the press, feeling her way along the counter. She grinned sightlessly. "Put it in my hand. There's a lot I can tell from touch."

The woman was blind. Aimée couldn't believe her bad luck. "I wondered if this was a cleaning receipt from your shop," she said.

One of Madame Tallard's eyes was milky white, veiled by a cataract, the other crossed. "I'm minding the shop for my daughter.

The baby's sick." She reached for something on the counter. "Here, check yourself." She thrust a receipt book in Aimée's direction.

"Thank you." Aimée flipped through a standard receipt book with smudged carbon copies.

No numbers matched, but the forms did.

"Hmm, don't see it," she said. "But the receipt looks like one of yours."

"I help my daughter if the items don't have spots or touch-up areas." Madame Tallard cleared her throat. "My good eye gets tired easily. We do a very careful job and pay attention to detail. Nothing's too important, I always tell my daughter, for a customer with couture wear."

Aimée tried being hopeful. Madame Tallard might recall something. "A Chanel! Maybe you remember it?"

"My daughter mentioned one . . . hot pink?"

"Why, yes," Aimée said. "With big knobby buttons."

"Like these?" She pulled a box of buttons from a drawer under the counter. Her fingers moved over them until she handed Aimée a pearl button with raised interlocking C's. "I keep buttons in case a customer needs one."

"Exactly. Only pink," Aimée said, recognizing the type of Chanel button from Morbier's evidence bag.

"The suit was picked up Wednesday night." Madame Tallard slapped her palm on the counter. "But it's not yours . . ."

"I apologize." Aimée automatically took out her ID. "I'm a private investigator with Leduc Detective. Who picked up the hot pink Chanel suit?"

Madame Tallard bristled. "My clientele is private. This is intrusion!"

"Murder is more intrusive, Madame Tallard," said Aimée. "Especially when it's around the corner. Your corner."

"You mean the woman with the swastika?" Old Madame Tallard's hands trembled.

"I'd like your cooperation, Madame."

Madame Tallard shook her head. "My daughter told me about it."

"And what did she say?"

"That being old in the Marais is getting dangerous these days." She felt her way and perched on a three-legged stool. Aimée leaned over the counter.

"I'm working on behalf of the victim," she said.

"Did any of those *imbéciles* see you enter?"

Aimée paused. "Who exactly do you mean?"

"*Imbéciles* who paint swastikas on my windows!"

Madame Tallard was afraid, she realized.

"The street was deserted when I came in." Aimée peered out the window. Nobody. "Still deserted."

Madame sighed. "The suit belongs to Albertine Clouzot. She lives on Impasse de la Poissonnerie."

Aimée nodded. Impasse de la Poissonnerie, a passage with a neo-classical fountain of the kind noted by Voltaire, led to private cobbled courtyards. Very exclusive.

"Madame Clouzot always sends her dry cleaning here," Madame Tallard said. "Tells me we're the only ones who clean the pockets. That's true. What would it have to do with her?"

Aimée felt excited. Maybe Madame Clouzot had been an eye-witness. "What time did she pick up the suit on Wednesday?"

"Not Madame. Her housekeeper," Madame Tallard said primly. "I have nothing to hide."

"The housekeeper?"

"She came just before I closed. Said that Madame Clouzot needed her suit for a late supper party. And that's all I know."

"When you closed up the shop did you hear a radio playing loudly?"

Madame Tallard rubbed her lined forehead. "I didn't linger, I went home."

She asked more questions but Madame Tallard assured her that she hadn't heard anything unusual. Aimée's heart raced excitedly.

Now she could question the owner of the Chanel suit and her housekeeper.

But how would a neo-Nazi from Les Blancs Nationaux following Lili Stein fit with the Chanel suit picked up by the housekeeper? She filed that in her memory and continued down the narrow street.

Her goal, the cobbler shop Chaussures Javel, stood several doors down from the dry cleaner's. She'd been wanting to talk with Javel ever since Rachel Blum mentioned the long-ago concierge's murder the night they met at Lili Stein's.

Bells jingled on the door as she entered. The purr of a cat, industrial strength, came from the window ledge under dingy lace curtains.

"*Bonjour*. Monsieur Javel?"

"*Oui*." He pronounced it "*Wae*" as Parisians did. A shriveled brown walnut of a man with thick white hair, he was working on a pair of black lizard pumps. His once blue apron, smudged by shoe polish, was tied behind his back.

After being surprised by Madame Tallard, Aimée decided to be up-front with Javel. That didn't mean she couldn't get her boots reheeled at the same time.

"Can you fix this heel?" she asked.

Javel's face matched the leather he worked on. "*Un moment*, sit down." He indicated a gouged wooden stool with his hand.

The water-stained walls were lined with a yellowish dado border. The dark veneer wooden floor sagged as she stepped on some loose slats near a modest showcase of arch supports and heels. In the corner, a heater emitted dribbles of heat with kerosene fumes. A sense of neglect pervaded his shop.

As Javel stood, reaching for a tool above him, she saw his legs. They were so extremely bowed, they resembled parentheses. He hobbled as he took a step and it was almost painful to watch.

He motioned to her to take off her boot. "I'll try." He began to root through his work tray. "Safer to reheel them before they wear down this far," he said.

"Did you know Lili Stein?" she said, watching for his reaction.

He didn't look up and kept on working. "One who had the shop on rue des Rosiers?"

Aimée nodded.

"People told me about it." His eyes remained neutral as he attached a new heel to her boot. "Brutal. What's the world coming to?"

Too neutral, she thought. "Didn't you know her a long time ago?" she said.

"Are you a *flic*?" He still didn't look up.

"I'm a private detective," she said. "Rachel Blum told me you would know about the concierge bludgeoned in Lili's building."

He handed the boot back to her. She reached in her bag as he pointed to the sign that said 15 FRANCS NEW HEEL.

He looked stonily at her. "What's it to you?"

"Lili Stein boarded up her window so she wouldn't have to be reminded of the scene," she said. "Did you know her then?"

He snorted. "Expect me to remember what some Yid schoolgirl did fifty years ago?"

She knew he was hiding something. Only someone who'd known Lili as a schoolgirl would reply like that.

"What do you remember?" she said calmly.

"Cooking up some crazy theory, aren't you?" He shook his head. "About Arlette and that swastika carving. Then listen up, Arlette wasn't Jewish or with the Nazis. Go bother those skinheads who kick in my window for fun!"

"Tell me about Arlette," she said. "Was she the concierge?"

He slammed down his hammer, spattering nails and metal grommets that pinged off the walls. "She was my fiancée, Arlette Mazenc. Why the sudden interest? The *flics* beat me up. Never investigated . . . why now? Just because some old Jew is killed by punks, someone pays attention, eh?"

She felt sorry for this angry little man.

"Monsieur Javel, I feel a connection. Something threading these murders. If I could be more concrete, I would," she said.

"When you do find something, look me up. Not before."

"Guess who?" said Aimée, her hands clapped over the eyes of an older woman who stood in front of rows of aluminum spindles, sorting buttons. The scent of rosemary and roasted garlic wafted through the factory air.

Small and wiry, Leah stood in wool socks and clogs, wearing a sweater buttoned over her work smock. She grabbed Aimée's hands with her rough ones. "Don't be such a stranger, Aimée," she said, twisting herself around and grinning. "You think you can surprise me?"

"I try, Leah." Aimée laughed and gave her a hug. "Something smells wonderful."

Leah, an old friend of her father's, lived with her family above their button factory, Mon Bouton. She cooked the midday meal for her workers in a kitchen by the melting presses and button die forms.

"You don't have to be domestic to cook, Aimée," Leah said, referring to their ongoing argument about Aimée's lack of culinary skills. "I only see you when you're hungry. Cooking is a creative expression, let me teach you."

"Right now, teach me about Chanel buttons. I want to learn from an expert," she said.

"A case?" Leah's eyes lit up. She read a new spy thriller every week and loved to hear about Aimée's work.

"Leah, you know I can't talk about ongoing cases." Aimée pulled out a rough sketch of the Chanel button she'd made after seeing it. "Just give me an idea about this button."

"Color and material?" Leah said, wiping her hands on the worn smock.

"Hot pink, and the interlocking C's were kind of brassy, shiny metal."

Leah, shortsighted, pushed her glasses onto her forehead and peered intently. "I'd say the button came from a suit in the spring collection. A mohair suit. We made a prototype but the head honcho shipped it out to Malaysia for production. Couture used to mean couture made in France—thread, ribbon, zippers, lining, and buttons. Not anymore."

"Care to generalize about the owner of the suit?"

"Twenties or thirties. Rich and bored. With good legs."

"Why good legs?"

"All the mohair suits were minis."

Saturday Noon

"MADAME IS WORKING IN her office. May I say who's calling?" The smiling housekeeper dusted the white flour off her hands. Tall and thin, her liquid eyes contrasted with her starched maid's uniform.

"Aimée Leduc. I'm a private investigator. This should take only a few moments." Aimée fished a card out of her bag.

Curiosity flickered in the housekeeper's gaze. "*Un moment,*" she said. Her scuffed mules clicked down the marble hallway.

Aimée had changed into a pleated dark blue wool skirt and blazer, her generic security-type uniform. Sometimes she stuck badges on the lapel from her extensive collection. For this interview she'd slicked her hair under a blue wedge-type hat, similar to that of a female gendarme, and wore a touch of mascara with no lipstick.

This drafty marble-floored hallway of Albertine Clouzot's apartment on the exclusive Impasse de la Poissonerie could have fit two trucks comfortably. Littered among a child's bicycle and roller blades were Roman bronze statues and busts resting on pillars.

Almost immediately, the housekeeper emerged and beckoned Aimée down the echoing hallway. Aimée entered a drawing room—for that was the only thing to call it—that could have come from the eighteenth century. And it probably did. Aimée thought it hadn't been heated since then either as she saw her own breath turn to frost in the air. She kept her angora-lined gloves on.

Tapestries with pastoral scenes hung on the twenty-foot-high walls. In the corner, framed by a window with a private court-yard behind it, sat a woman in her late thirties, working on a huge dollhouse, a Southern mansion styled with pillars and "Mint Julep" chiseled above the miniature door. A small portable heater stood by a tray of white wicker doll furniture.

"Thank you for sparing me the time, Madame Clouzot," Aimée said.

"I'm intrigued. Why would a private investigator wish to talk with me?" said Albertine Clouzot. She put a miniature chest down and stood; she wore fishnet stockings, a black leather miniskirt, and maroon lipstick. Her perfectly cut straight blond hair grazed her shoulders. She tottered on faux leopard platform heels. "What's this about? Florence, you may go."

"It might be better if she stayed." Aimée smiled broadly, turning to the housekeeper. She certainly didn't want Florence to leave. "I'd like to talk with both of you."

She reached in her bag and pulled out a note pad that she pretended to consult.

"Madame, do you own a pink Chanel suit?"

"Why, yes."

"Did you receive it from the dry cleaner's with a button missing?"

"That's right. I had to wear something else." Florence stood woodenly as Albertine preened in front of a floor-length gilded mirror. "First time I've ever had trouble at Madame Tallard's."

"I see. You didn't go to the dry cleaner's, am I correct?" Aimée kept a matter-of-fact tone.

"No." Albertine Clouzot's face looked incredulous. "Why would I?"

Albertine belonged to the world that hired other people to do their mundane chores.

"Florence, your housekeeper, did, am I correct?"

Albertine Clouzot nodded absently. She'd lost interest and was pulling open the little doll chest's drawers.

"What time did Florence leave your house on Wednesday evening?"

"Is this an inquisition? I won't tell you any more until you tell me what this is about."

I'm losing her, Aimée thought. "Madame, please bear with me." Aimée smiled broadly again. She stuck the pencil behind her ear and shook her head. "Detecting isn't like the movies. Tedious checking of details makes up most of it. All we know is that a pink Chanel button was found near the body of a murdered woman, not two blocks from your apartment."

"It must have come off . . . my God, you're not trying to suggest that I killed that woman! That woman with the . . ."

Out of the corner of her eye, Aimée saw Florence's arm jerk. Either this housekeeper was the nervous type or Aimée had struck a nerve.

"Madame," she spoke reassuringly, "I'm checking out pieces of evidence and constructing a timetable of the murder."

She looked straight at Florence. "What time did you pick up Madame's suit?"

Florence covered her mouth with her hands. Little feathery spots of white flour were left on her cheeks. "Just before the shop closed," she stammered.

I've hit it, Aimée thought excitedly.

She remembered Sinta commenting on the pair of shoes in Lili Stein's closet, looking at the repair tag and saying Lili had just picked them up. If Lili had picked up her shoes at Javel's, been trailed by an LBN member, and Florence had followed . . . But that didn't explain *why* Florence would trail her.

Aimée stifled her eagerness and kept her tone businesslike. "What time was that?"

If Florence had seen a neo-Nazi trailing an old Jewish woman on crutches she might have been alerted and followed her. Maybe she'd witnessed something.

Florence hesitated and looked down at the floor.

"Speak up, Florence." Albertine clicked her long maroon nails irritably on the dollhouse roof.

Florence shrugged, "Close to 6:15 or 6:30. Madame Tallard was about to lock her door and so I just got in to grab the suit."

But when Aimée found the body rigor mortis hadn't set fully in. She knew that the cold could retard the onset of rigor mortis but the intense muscular activity, due to Lili's struggle, could have released lactic acids hastening the process. Puzzled, she realized that wouldn't fit with Florence's timetable. But she had to check with Morbier for the inquest findings.

Florence turned to her employer. "Madame, I'm so sorry. We must check your suit to be sure but . . ."

"Am I being implicated in a murder?" Indignant, Albertine strode up to Aimée, towering over her in the leopard platform heels.

"Of course not, that just explains one piece of evidence that can be ruled out. The button, unnoticed by Florence in the darkness, fell off," Aimée said, keeping her voice matter-of-fact. "Of course, now I understand. It's perfectly plausible."

"But the police haven't questioned me," Albertine said. "Why you?"

"I can't speak for the police," Aimée said, tucking her almost empty pad back into her bag.

"This is absurd." Albertine turned coldly to her. "If you have any more questions, go through my lawyer."

As Aimée turned to leave, she saw Albertine Clouzot glare at her housekeeper. "I'll speak with you later," Albertine said.

Florence walked behind Aimée, their footsteps echoing off the marble walls. "I've just recently joined Madame Clouzot's employ," she said hesitantly. "Two weeks ago."

Pain or fear, Aimée wasn't sure which, was etched across the older woman's face. Aimée felt sorry for her.

"Florence, my intention is not to get you in trouble," she said. "I'm investigating a murder. I had to be sure who picked up the suit from the dry cleaner's and if indeed a button was missing. Tell me what you remember hearing and seeing after you walked out of the shop."

"Nothing." She shook her head. "I hurried back. Madame was waiting."

But Aimée saw fear in Florence's eyes.

"You might have crossed the killer's path." Aimée's eyes narrowed. "Are you sure about the time?"

Florence nodded, looking away.

"As you walked from the dry cleaner's did you see an old woman on crutches?"

"No."

Was she lying?

"Did you notice any skinheads hanging around?"

"I just walked quickly."

"Or a radio blaring?"

Florence stiffened. "I mind my own business, that's all," she said. She smoothed her floured hands on her apron, sending white powdery mist onto the floor. "I told you I don't mind anything but my own business."

"The Temple Emanuel hired me. Here's my card," Aimée said.

Hesitating, Florence slowly took the card. Her hand shook as she thanked Aimée.

"The Marais is small. Phone me if you recall anything. This reaches me directly, day or night, no answering machine," Aimée said. She felt eyes on her back as she walked down the short passage.

Aimée didn't think Albertine Clouzot or Florence had killed Lili Stein. Neither had a motive that she could discern. But why was Florence afraid?

"GO EAT SOMETHING," LEAH said.

As Aimée nibbled on *cul de lapin au basilic*, she read the head-line NEO-NAZI MOBS OVERRUN DEMONSTRATION AT JEWISH DEPOR-TATION MONUMENT in *Le Figaro*. The terse report mentioned several right-wing groups, Les Blancs Nationaux among them.

Leah's kitchen, toasty and warm from the hot button presses, helped her forget the cold. So did the *vin rouge* she poured from the bottle into a smudged wineglass. The dense, oak-flavored taste trickled down her throat.

She rooted around for Thierry Rambuteau's card in her bag. Since Morbier wouldn't help her, she knew it was up to her to iden-tify who Thierry spoke with on the telephone. Otherwise, when she went to the LBN meeting, she could be walking into a trap.

She hooked up a code enabler to Leah's phone Minitel, then spliced the cable and ran it to the small television off the eating area.

She phoned the main branch of Post and Telecommunica-tions. "Operations, please," she said.

"Yes," a man's voice said.

Aimée clicked on the TV screen and fiddled with adjustments. "My ex-husband is threatening me. He's calling day and night, threatening the children but I can't prove it." Aimée's pitch went higher and higher. "The judge won't do anything unless I can document it. Can you check my number at work? At least your records would verify that he calls there."

"I can verify that incoming calls occur," the man said, not unkindly. "I'm only allowed to check your office number to see calls received."

Perfect, she thought. This would reveal who called Thierry

while she was in the LBN office. And it would be even more perfect if this enabler worked.

"*Merci, Monsieur.*" She switched it on. "That's a huge help!" she said. "My office number is 43.43.25.45."

She watched Leah's TV screen display the LBN office number she'd given him as he typed from his keyboard. This generated several phone numbers on the screen that were phone numbers calling into the office that day. She copied them all.

"What is the number your husband would call from?" he said.

She made up a number and saw those numbers punched in, which resulted in "no correspondence" flashing on the screen.

"Pardon, Madam. I'm afraid it wasn't your husband this time," he said. She thanked him and hung up.

Next Aimée identified herself as a secretary with the LBN, calling to verify charges on their office bill. There were five phone numbers. The first number was a small office-supply store holding an account with Les Blancs Nationaux, the second was a local café that delivered pastries to them. Aimée seriously doubted if the skinny woman ate any.

The third and fourth were from Crédit Agricole regarding account information. Aimée called the fifth number, which proved to be Jetpresse, a twenty-four-hour printing company in Vincennes. She had all but given up, but, to be thorough, she mentioned Thierry's name.

She was startled to hear the clerk begin apologizing. "They're ready, Mademoiselle," she said. "Seems there was a mix-up, we apologize. We don't deliver, that's in our contract. Somehow that wasn't clear to you."

"I'll pick them up," Aimée said quickly. "Er, what was the final count?"

"Let's see. Twenty-five editions, bound deluxe, of *Mein Kampf*," the clerk said.

Aimée almost choked. "I'll be there within the hour."

Saturday Evening

AIMÉE APPROACHED THE NEO-NAZIS congregating by the shuttered ClicClac video shop. She had slicked back her hair and donned her skinhead outfit. Her fingers, more for protection than decoration, were filled to the knuckle with silver rings. She wished her heart wasn't pounding so hard, keeping rhythm with the flashing purple-and-green neon sign over the storefront.

A balding Arab shopkeeper in a flowing gray robe swept the sidewalk near her in front of his produce shop. Strains of whining Arab music blared from inside.

"Your type, *chérie?*" several skinheads jeered. "You like sharing the street, why not share the Arab's tent?"

She growled. The box with twenty-five editions of *Mein Kampf* was heavy. She'd liked to have thrown it in their leering faces. Instead, their taunts forced her to establish some Aryan credentials. Hating to do it, she jostled the storekeeper, then bumped into him.

"Abdul, keep to your side," she said.

He kept his shiny head down and pushed his broom further away, mumbling something in broken French that she pretended not to understand. She kept advancing toward him, angling him into a corner. His head glistened with perspiration as he tried to sweep around her biker boots.

"Can't you speak French, Abdul?" Aimée said. "Go back where you came from!" She kicked the broom from his hands.

He cowered against the shop door, while scattered cheers erupted among the skin-heads. He scurried back to his shop and closed his doors.

As she mounted the side steps of the ClicClac shop she heard, "Who's the kick-ass Eva Braun?"

Many pairs of suspicious eyes checked her out. Her heart beat so fast she was afraid it would jump out of her chest. What if she had to do more than kick a defenseless Arab's broom away? She pushed that out of her mind as she joined a motley heavy-metal-type pair, their arms entwined, filing upstairs.

A panorama of shining Hitleriana greeted her as she entered an upstairs room. Blown-up photos of Adolf Hitler saluting to gathered masses and huge red swastikas covered the black walls along with a photo of barbed wire and wooden stalags with a red circle and line through it. The caption above it read AUSCHWITZ=JEW HOAX.

Where were the photos of the living skeletons in rags next to empty canisters of Zyklon B gas that had greeted the Allies who liberated Auschwitz? She figured details like that would probably be missing from the evening.

There was a photo of a Vietnamese whose brains were being blown out by an American officer and one of a toothless, grinning Palestinian boy, with burned-out Beirut in the background, pointing a machine gun at a corpse riddled with holes. But all in all, the vignettes of hate were predominantly Nazi.

Thierry Rambuteau, in an ankle-length black leather stormtrooper coat, stood at the front of the room. Despite his youthful shaved stubble, faded blue jeans, and hi-tech track shoes, he looked old for this crowd. Around his piercing blue eyes were age lines; he could be fifty, she thought. Something about Thierry was off, he didn't belong. Maybe it was his attempt at a youthful appearance or maybe that he had brains.

She shoved the box of *Mein Kampf*s on the table. Thierry nodded at her, indicating a seat he'd saved for her. She sat down. Many of the faces in the smoky room surprised her. Scattered among the shaved heads were truckers in overalls, a few professor types in corduroys, and what looked like several account executives in suits. But the crowd was mostly skinheads, average age mid-twenties, who milled around the room. Among the thirty or so assembled, most wore black, smoked, or were busy shoving cigarette butts in empty beer bottles.

She felt eyes on her and looked over at the man sitting beside her. He had dark sideburns, slicked-back hair, and wore a mousy brown sweater vest with black jeans cinched over nonexistent hips. His deep black eyes and curled lip were what got to her. Like metal filings to a magnet, she felt repelled and attracted at the same time. His eyes lingered a second too long before he averted his gaze. Behind that look she saw intelligence and felt animal attraction. Bad boys were always her downfall.

A table had been set up with stacks of free videos, a keg of beer and plastic cups, SS armbands, and Third Reich crosses on chains. There wasn't exactly a rush for the videos but the beer and crosses were going fast. She quickly snagged a pointy-edged cross to complete her fashion statement.

"*Kameradschaft!*" Thierry had moved to the dais. "Welcome! Let us begin our meeting, as always, with our moment of reflection."

Heads bowed briefly, then, on a signal Aimée didn't hear, loud shouts of "*Sieg Heil*" rang through the room in unison. Arms shot up in the Nazi salute.

Thierry saluted back. This quasi-religious brotherhood feeling sickened her. Even though she knew the philosophy of the neo-Nazis, it shocked her to watch them in action.

He launched into a diatribe about Jews being scum. She surveyed the crowd's reaction. Hate was reflected in every face. True, Thierry carried fervor and a certain charisma. He explained earnestly that scientists had proven that certain races were genetically inferior. A historic fact, he pointed out simply, shown by culture and society. She felt that Thierry had convinced himself of his own words.

Then the lights dimmed and the video was shown. This was no amateur home video, but a slick production costing real money.

The title, in large letters, read "The Hoax That Is Auschwitz." Scenes of present-day Auschwitz, surrounded by bucolic farmlands tucked into a green pastoral valley, flashed by while a pleasant, businesslike voice narrated, "As a nonpartisan group, we came to view the so-called 'death camp' using state-of-the-art equipment to detect mineral and bone content in soil compositions. After careful measurement in many areas of the camp where there had supposedly been gas chambers, we found no chemical residue or traces of Zyklon B gas. We discovered no evidence of mass graveyards, or anything resembling them, for that matter. The remaining compound buildings, of solid wooden construction, attest to its use as a work camp and to the skill of the German builders, in that they are still standing after more than fifty years." The camera focused then on the railroad tracks that ended at the iron gate of Auschwitz with the slogan wrought in iron still above it: *"Arbeit Macht Frei"*—"Work Makes You Free."

After the video, a skinhead wearing tight lederhosen and a leather vest exposing pierced nipple rings connected by chains shouted, "I'm proud to be a member of the *Kameradschaft*."

A chorus of grunts backed him up. She noticed a banner near him emblazoned with '1889 Hitler's birthdate—When the world began!'

"We are heroic *Volk*," someone shouted from the back. "Like the Führer says in *Mein Kampf*. We have to start at the root of the problem, the mutant bacteria that contaminates everything it touches, to halt its growth. We have to strike now!"

Thierry slammed his fist down as he emphasized the Nazi tenets. "In every way, the Aryan is superior; our confidence should rise and soar."

She figured their video archives, her goal, were stored in the back room. She intended to check the area behind a life-size photo of Hitler saluting, but a finger dug into her arm as she stood up.

"Sit down," said a trucker in grimy overalls.

"Who's she?" grumbled his friend, in a slightly more stained jumpsuit.

Nervously, she sat down. Someone elbowed her in the ribs. She turned sharply to see the one in lederhosen smiling at her. His white blond hair poked straight up, as if standing at attention.

"Boys wear tattoos, little lady," he said to the accompaniment of sniggering around her. "Aryan women don't."

"Some do and some don't." She jerked her head around, indicating other women. Not many had tattoos. Some wore dirndls but all had on clunky Doc Martens. "Depends on individual preference."

"Using big words. Do you know what they mean?" he said.

She didn't answer, just cracked her gum.

"Women look better on their knees," he said. "I know you would."

He leaned on her arm, cupping her shoulder with an iron grip. She couldn't move.

A voice next to him barked, "Service your own harem, Leif."

The dark-sideburned man glided next to her, picked Leif's fingers off her shoulder, and grinned. He wedged himself between them. Mockingly, Leif raised his eyes in surprise.

Aimée wondered if she'd gone from the frying pan into the fire but she smiled back at him. She stood up and raised her hand until Thierry acknowledged her.

Aimée forced herself to grin. "Why don't the Jews get honest? They were only victims of wartime food shortage like everyone else."

Snorts of approval greeted her as she sat down. Besides her, she felt the warm body heat emanating from the one with sideburns.

"I'm Luna," she said.

"Yves," he said, without turning his head.

Thierry continued, "Leif will outline our plans for the next few days. He'll give the details of our evening mission and protocol for tomorrow's demonstration."

Leif strutted towards a blackboard standing under an original

SS recruiting poster. To her horror, he outlined a plan to bash orthodox synagogues that night. She feared one would be Temple Emanuel.

Thierry sat down beside her. "I appreciate your bringing our literature. Ignore Leif's crudeness; he's better at planning and organization details."

He motioned to Yves. "Get the equipment ready."

Yves slid out of his chair and Aimée started to follow him.

Thierry leaned over to her. "Listen to this, it will be helpful for you."

Aimée nodded, trying not to squirm in her seat. Was Yves the video cameraman? If they were taping this meeting, she hadn't spotted the camera yet.

"Vans will transport us to the synagogue," Leif said in a tone devoid of emotion. "To do the job, it has to be in and out, quick and vicious."

Aimée wondered if that was how he treated his women. Instinct told her to find out which synagogue, tell Morbier, and get the hell out of there.

Thierry nodded approvingly at Aimée. "I bet you learn quick. You'll do better sticking with us than sticking something in your arm."

If those were my only choices, she thought, I'd pick junkie any day. Thierry seemed to be trying to help her, in his own Aryan way.

He went on. "A feeling of unity is born on our missions. We join together and accomplish our goals. We achieve satisfaction transforming ideas into concrete operations."

She sensed he was speaking of himself, as if he needed a cause to justify his existence.

"We attack first. No Aryan will be a victim anymore!" Leif yelled from the podium to the crowd, who roared approval.

"Our stomachs wrench," Thierry added. "But we do it out of love."

She sidled next to Leif to find out which synagogue he'd

targeted. Now he wore a Tyrolean-style short jacket, epauletted with metal lightning bolts and iron crosses. Neo-Nazi meets *Sound of Music*, Aimée thought.

"Do we get to hurt anybody?" she pouted, loud enough so he could hear it.

"If you're lucky," he said, eyeing her up and down. "You look healthy enough to be a breeder sow."

The neon green light of the ClicClac sign shone through the window, giving his eyes a reptilian look. He was scary. She felt like a piece of meat about to be skewered.

But she clicked her heels together and stuck her arm out in a *Sieg Heil*. "Is that right?"

"It'll do. Let's go," Leif said.

"All right! Where are we going?"

"That's for me to know and you to find out," he grinned. "Just Jew land. If you're a good girl you can kick somebody. C'mon."

"Cool, I gotta pee." She went toward the back door, passing a huddle of skinheads all in black leather.

Thierry grabbed her tightly by the arms. "That way." He pointed her in the opposite direction.

Great, Aimée thought, how do I get out of this one? Thierry sure is a piece of work and he's got his eye on me. She locked the door to the toilet and checked the battery pack of her tape recorder. Pencil thin and molded to the curve of her back, this state-of-the-art recording machine caught everything, even a yawn at fifty paces. She'd bought it at the spy store before the *flics* outlawed the place and closed it down.

Now if she just didn't sweat too much, since it was a highly moisture-sensitive device . . . She placed it in a plastic baggie she carried, made a hole for the microphone cord, then taped it to her back. She pulled out the cell phone from her jeans pocket and punched in Morbier's direct line. Right now she didn't care if he'd been called off the Stein case, she needed backup. While she did that, she put the toilet lid down, stood on top of it, and peered out the narrow window. Down below she could see two vans under the streetlight next to glimmering rain puddles.

No answer.

There was a pounding on the bathroom door.

"*Salope!* Can't someone crap in peace?" she yelled.

The pounding stopped.

Finally a disembodied voice came on the line. "Yes?"

"Get me Morbier, it's urgent," she whispered.

"He's on call," the voice said. "I'll patch you through."

This was taking too long. "Hurry up," she said.

Click, click, and a hearty voice boomed, "Morbier."

Without benefit of introduction she began. "It's going down right now," she whispered slowly. "Two vans with skinheads are headed to attack synagogues in the Marais."

The pounding started again. Aimée flushed the toilet, clicked off the cell phone, and wedged it in her jeans pocket. She opened the door in time to see Leif, his back to her, helping Yves move something heavy in the dark hallway. Bumping noises echoed from the stairs and Aimée figured they were carrying equipment down. Next to her, a black-painted door stood ajar and she quickly scooted inside. Shelves of videos cataloged by date stood before her in the green-purple light from the blinking video sign. Which one?

Musty smells emanated from the threadbare carpet, which barely covered the worn tiled floor. Dates, Aimée thought, that's it! She scanned the shelves for the last two meetings, found them, and quickly stuck them inside her black leather jacket. Holding her breath, she zipped her jacket up, which sounded like a buzzing chainsaw in her ear. She held her breath but no one came in. Out in the hallway, more shuffling and dull thuds rose from the staircase.

She looked out and scanned the hall. Seeing no one, she tried the back door. Locked. Impossible to jimmy open without more noise than she felt prepared to make. All the windows faced the street, where the vans were parked. She edged down the stairs.

The party-like atmosphere still reigned as members congregated and moved towards the vans, formerly blue dairy trucks. The group numbered about twenty now. As she slowly backed out of the crowd towards the corner, Thierry caught her eye. He motioned to her.

"Carry this." He handed her a heavy gym bag. "Ride up front." He started herding the group into the vans.

In front, taking up most of the passenger seat, was a stocky skin-head with a shiny scalp dressed paramilitary style. He squeezed her knee. "Stick with me," he said.

"A privilege to be here." She removed his paw from her knee then executed a mock bow in the cramped front seat. "Don't they like me?"

"They're always suspicious of newcomers." He jerked his thumb towards the back of the van. "Everybody gets jittery when it comes to business." He grinned, showing decayed jagged stubs of brown teeth. "Ready for some fun? You're gonna like it, I know."

A whiff from his mouth caused her to look away. Uneasily, she speculated about her newcomer initiation. When Thierry told him to move over so Aimée could sit between them, she shook her head.

"Motion sickness, I need air on my face." She rolled the window down as far as it would go, which was barely more than a crack.

At least she was by the door. Thierry turned the heater on high and it hit her full blast. Conversation en route consisted of Thierry berating the paramilitary type for erasing some message from the answering machine. Sullen and surly, he ignored Thierry, his eyes focused on Aimée. She was starting to sweat inside her leather jacket. The two videos stuck to her like glue, spearing her lower ribs.

Thierry left the broad boulevards of Bastille, turning into dark narrow streets, deserted and quiet. She felt beads of sweat on her brow.

"I'm getting sick. Turn the heat down," Aimée said.

Cries of "It's freezing back here, turn the heat up" came from the back of the van.

"We're almost there," Thierry said.

Businesses were shuttered and the streets deserted. Silence except for the murmuring in the back. That's when she started sizzling. Her perspiration had short-circuited the tape recorder and she was about to fry.

She reached forward and switched off the heat, growling, "It's too hot."

Discontented rumblings came loudly from the back. She grabbed a rag from the sticky van floor and wiped off as much sweat as she could reach. Unfortunately, it turned out to be the skinhead's bandana, reeking of patchouli.

"Keep it." He grinned at her. "So you don't forget me."

The patchouli oil rose from her pores, making her nauseous. Something to do with the sixties.

"Shut up," Aimée grunted.

He giggled. "You're one of my kind."

She noticed another tattoo on Thierry's wrist as he gripped the steering wheel.

"What's that say?" she asked.

"*My honor's name is loyalty*," he said proudly. His eyes narrowed as if to challenge her.

"Of course! Couldn't read it from here." She nodded. "The SS Waffen motto."

What were they going to do and where would they do it? Could Morbier get *flics* to the Marais in time? And how long would this stinking patchouli ooze out of her?

Sweat trickled off her while the tattered tank top and videos glued stickily to her chest. She used the greasy bandana again to dab at her perspiration, keeping the videos in place.

"An eye for an eye . . . isn't that what this is about?" She pounded her fist on the cracked dashboard. "*Sieg Heil* and all that stuff is fine, but getting nasty with some of the kike population . . ." She chuckled, giving Thierry time to fill in the blanks.

"Violent assertion is part and parcel of the solution, but only as a means to an end," Thierry said.

The paramilitary skinhead frowned. "Cut the high and mighty talk! We kick Jew butt."

Thierry steered the van through a slim notch in the medieval cloister's wall into the small square of Marché-Sainte-Catherine.

Aimée pressed further, "No, you know, like help with the final solution. Take care of them, one on one?"

She never heard the answer. Motorcycle engines gunned loudly as an amplified voice instructed them to pull over. From out of nowhere the small square filled with blue flashing lights and motorcycle police.

"Alcohol check. Out of the van. *Allez-y!*" said a helmeted patrolman.

"*Merde!*" Thierry said under his breath. "Of all nights."

"Funny coincidence," someone said from the rear. "Since she graced us with her presence."

"Save your bad breath for the *flics*," Aimée said and hoped Morbier's tactic worked.

"Out!" the *flics* shouted. They tore her door open and slid the van door back. She struggled and elbowed the surprised *flic* in the ribs, shouting, "Get your hands off me." She started to kick him in the ankles.

She wanted to be arrested. Desperately. Get out while undercover and with the videos under her jacket. She'd take advantage of the police check, whether a ploy of Morbier's or not.

Suddenly a boot slammed against her hip, knocking her across the *flics* and their raised billy clubs. There were hoarse shouts of "Fascist pigs" and then all hell broke loose. Cries of pain echoed in the small square. She started crawling on the wet cobblestones. She made it to the other side of the van and almost got away.

"Hurry up," Thierry yelled, pushing her in, and flicked on the ignition.

She didn't have time to appreciate the irony of the situation or plan how she could escape. As they pulled away, Leif jumped in the open sliding door and clanged it shut.

Thierry's foot jammed down the accelerator. That caused the van to careen wildly and Aimée to shield her face with her arms. The van lunged towards a gurgling, mossy waterspout over Ste. Catherine's statue. Scraping the side of the van and chipping the statue, Thierry righted the steering wheel and gunned out of the square.

"Who are you?" Leif said from behind her, sticking something sharp in her rib. He slapped her hard with the back of his hand.

Thierry shouted, "Cut it out, Leif . . ."

"In my past life?" she said. Her cheeks stung as she peered down. "Get that knife out of my chest."

"After you convince me you had nothing to do with what just happened," Leif growled.

"What are you talking about? I'm with you," she said.

"Lay off," Thierry said. "You're too paranoid."

"*Alors!*" Leif said. "Look what happened last time." He plunged the knife into the already cracked dashboard, causing the windshield seam to split.

In one movement, she pulled the handle, kicked the door open, and flung herself out. As she landed, she tried to roll away from the wheels of a car following right behind. Her shoulder crunched as it hit the pavement. White-yellow pain seared up her arm. Dislocated shoulder if I'm lucky, she thought. Scrabbling to her feet, she stumbled, then ran. Behind her she heard the squeal of tires, a crash and the tinkle of breaking glass as a car hit Thierry's van. That gave her an extra minute before she heard loud pounding footsteps behind her. The van coughed, sputtered, and started up loudly.

The narrow one-way street echoed with her running steps. Behind her she heard more footsteps and the gunning of the van's motor. Around her were silent, dark stone buildings. Only a few scattered windows showed a faint glow from behind a curtain. Don't other streets connect here, she wondered frantically, vainly searching for another street to turn into. But she was surrounded by the last medieval vestiges left in the Marais. The long circular lanes designed the keep invaders out were keeping her in. She heard labored breaths right behind her. Puffing and sweating, she willed her rising panic down. A lichen-covered wall looking ten feet thick and reaching two stories high blocked her way.

Dead end. A dead-end dungeon.

To her left she saw a narrow stone passageway between the walls. Swerving into it, she ricocheted off some metal garbage cans that banged noisily, and kept on running. She heard the clanging of metal as someone behind her ran into them, too, stumbled, and yelled "*Merde*." This was too narrow for a vehicle. The damp air hit her lungs and her breath chugged painfully. From the dark corners she could hear the squeal of rats. Ahead, down the shadowy passageway, shone the fuzzy yellow globe of a street lamp.

When she reached it, she veered away from the sound of an engine to her left. Behind her she caught a glimpse of a taxi with a blue light signaling that it was free.

She switched back, keeping up her pace, and yelled, "Over here."

The taxi started to speed away.

"Rape! Help, rape!" she screamed.

The taxi slowed down. Aimée realized the chasing figure had probably appeared in the taxi's rearview mirror. Just as she was reaching for the door handle she heard heavy breathing and shouting right behind her. This person could easily pull her out of the taxi. She feinted to the right. Whoever was behind her lunged and just missed grabbing her jacket as she turned. She heard an "Ouff" and a heavy thud as she sprinted away. The taxi gunned its engine and sped off.

Down the slippery, glistening pavement she ran. Keep going, she told herself. Her lungs burned and dull slivers of pain shot up her arm, still hugging the videos to her chest.

Finally she saw the welcome traffic and lights of rue St. Antoine with plenty of taxis. Thank God, she thought, and took as deep a breath as her painful shoulder allowed. As she stepped out, the other blue van from the ClicClac screeched to a stop in front of her.

"Get in," Yves shouted and gestured to her.

Behind her she heard the running footsteps again, echoing off the walls. Coming closer.

"Hurry up!" Yves pulled the handle from the driver's side and the dented blue door swung open.

Before she could pull the door shut, he'd shot down busy rue St. Antoine.

"Where were you?" Aimée asked suspiciously. Why hadn't he been with the rest of the group?

"Behind everyone." He jerked his arm towards the back of the van. "Since I do most of the video I carry the equipment. Thierry trusts me."

Aimée groaned.

"What happened to you?" His dark eyes held concern. He threw his jacket at her. "Take mine. It's warmer."

"No thanks." She couldn't take her smelly, ripped leather jacket off since the recorder was still taped to her back and the videos bulged out of her tank top.

"I need some anesthetic," she said. "Let's get a drink."

Yves jerked the van to a stop in a narrow alley off Bastille, still in the Marais. A waiter shuttered the windows from inside a murky bistro on the corner. She heard strains of a jazz guitar as the door opened and a laughing couple spilled out. If she concentrated, she could probably make her feet walk to the corner and cause a ruckus so the bistro would let them in.

"Listen, this shoulder hurts," she said, feeling giddy.

"I've got just the right thing for that." His black eyes bored into her with a laserlike intensity.

"I seriously need a drink." She started to giggle and didn't know why.

"I've got that too," he smiled.

And a beautiful smile, she noted. Here she was with a neo-Nazi carrying stolen videos—possibly containing an old woman's murder recorded by him. And incredibly attracted to him. He'd seemingly helped her for the second time that night.

"My flat is over here," he said, pointing to a darkened brick turn-of-the-century warehouse. "Can you make it?"

"You leave the equipment in your van on the street?" she said and wondered at her own coherent thinking.

"No one messes with our blue vans," he said. "That's for sure. But"—he pulled out a digicode remote and punched some numbers—"I don't park on the street."

As the metal awning rolled up slowly, Yves eased the van into the warehouse courtyard.

Aimée didn't like the sound of the awning rolling back down and looked for a way out. A narrow side entrance showed a pinhole of light.

"Thinking of leaving?" Yves said, unlocking a door under the vaulted arches of the brick building.

"Not yet," Aimée grinned. "I'm thirsty."

"Let me help you, this is tricky," Yves said, scooping her up. He flicked on a set of lights and carried her down a spiral metal staircase to a brick basement flat.

Warm air hit her, laced with a strong familiar tang. They

descended onto a bleached wood floor lined by deep white sofas, a long metal table, and open kitchen. The vaulted arches in the walls had been bricked in and covered by bright batik fabric.

"Site of the old tanning vats," Yves explained, setting her down on a sofa. "This was an old saddle factory. Police and cavalry saddles," he grinned.

Aimée felt sticky and hot but didn't dare take off her leather jacket. Her arm had started throbbing. Funny how things hurt when you had time to think about them, she thought. Sure that the grease and patchouli oil had been absorbed into her pores, she wanted a wash.

"Rémy, okay?" Yves said as he handed her a bowl-like brandy snifter.

Aimée hadn't had Rémy Martin VSOP in years. She almost purred as it slid down her throat. This neo-Nazi definitely had more class than his comrades.

"I need to clean up," she said.

He gestured. "Be my guest."

She gripped the Rémy and hobbled towards the kitchen. Inside his white-tiled bathroom, she put her clothes in a pile on the floor, making sure the videos were secure in the inside pocket of her jacket.

One good thing, her shoulder hurt so much she couldn't feel much else. She turned the hot water on. Praying there was enough for a tubful, she knelt on a thick towel in front of an old gilt mirror. After she downed another shot of brandy, she noticed the thin red line of singed skin along her spine.

Her shoulder drooped, but this had happened before and she knew what to do. And with enough brandy she could do it. Gritting her teeth, she rotated her shoulder socket counter-clockwise up to a three o'clock position. Taking another gulp of the brandy, she reached with her left hand to grip her right shoulder. She took a deep breath, pulled her arm straight out, swiveled it slightly, and popped the socket back into twelve o'clock. The pain shot from her fingertips to her neck. She heard a gasp behind her. Yves was in the mirror wincing, still in his jeans and sweater.

He knelt down beside her and took her gently in his arms. "Are you all right?"

She nodded and gave him a lopsided smile.

"You're not going to pass out, are you?" He kept her cradled in his arms.

"Not yet."

He poured another snifter and she sipped slowly. "I'm fine."

Softly, he stroked her wet hair. "What kind of outlaw are you?"

"Mad, bad, and dangerous to know. But I should be asking you that."

"If you do, I'll give the same answer." He laughed and then Aimée knew she was headed for trouble.

They ended up in the tub with the bottle of Rémy, surrounded by steam, most of it of their own making.

AIMÉE SLID back into her greasy jeans and left Yves asleep. But not before stealing his brown sweater and checking out his apartment. Off the open kitchen space she found a small office with a state-of-the-art computer, printer, and color scanner. Yves obviously had a decent day job. She searched high and low but couldn't find any other videos.

She grabbed a taxi, switched to another one at St. Paul, and rode home. Just to be sure, she doubled back along the quai twice. Dawn was an hour away. Miles Davis greeted her in the dark flat, sniffed her noisily, then burrowed into her patchouli-scented jacket. Silhouetted against the quai's street lamp, the black shadow of the Seine snaked outside her window.

Aimée felt more guilty than she ever had in her life. Somehow she should have gotten away from him. But she'd drunk too much and enjoyed how Yves had made her feel. The brandy hadn't dulled her brain, she'd known what she was doing. And she'd wanted to do it. What if he'd been a part of the old woman's murder? Sick, she made herself sick. How could she have slept with him?

She opened a bottle of Volvic spring water and popped a handful of vitamin B and C. She slid Les Blancs Nationaux's video labeled "Meeting November 1993" into her VCR. Miles Davis nestled into her lap and she hugged him, trying to prepare for the awful truth.

SUNDAY

Sunday Morning

"CONGRATULATIONS, *MEIN HERR*," ILSE squeezed his arm tightly and whispered. "We will make the past live again!"

Hartmuth was afraid his smile looked like a grimace of pain, and he glanced away. He concentrated his gaze on the balding mayor of Paris, standing among the European diplomats at the ceremony. Only once did his eyes drift to the gray wainscotting of the room.

He remembered these walls well. In this very room he had routinely filed Jewish Population Removal Orders in quadruplicate. His *Kommandant* viewed "removal" as a simple business function of the Occupation. Jews were "removal material" subject to tiresome but routine formalities, formalities Hartmuth was required to perform every time he swept the Marais in a Jewish roundup. He'd found Sarah's family too late. They'd already been deported on the convoy to Auschwitz.

Ilse beamed from under the brim of her rose-colored hat. Across from them, Cazaux laughed familiarly with the mayor. After the opening ceremony, Hartmuth escorted Ilse in her brown orthopedics across the rotunda of black-and-white tiles.

He entered the waiting limo that would take them to Saint Sulpice Church. There under the smoky, incense-filled nave, below the leering phantoms imprisoned in Delacroix's mural, he exhaled quickly. He realized that he'd been holding his breath. Soon, he told himself, soon this whole thing would be over. A few more days and he would be safely back in Hamburg.

As the bells pealed and the party descended the marble stairs of Saint Sulpice, the hairs lifted on his neck.

He had the oddest sensation of being watched. Of course, the

Werewolves were watching, but this felt different. And he didn't know if he minded at all.

At the reception following, Cazaux smiled and pulled him aside. "We must talk of the trade commission's future. You know, I think you would be best qualified to lead negotiations."

Hartmuth did not want to have this conversation. Nor did he believe in the unfair treaty that he was being pressured to sign. He'd stall Cazaux and buy time. Maybe he could lobby other delegates to effect compromise on the harshest policies. He didn't hold out much hope but he would try.

"I'm flattered," he said. "Others are more qualified than I."

"Politicians can't afford to be modest." Cazaux winked and patted him on the back. "Of course, the commission gets in place after the treaty is signed. First things first."

Quimper, the rosy-cheeked Belgian delegate, joined them. "This pâté is superb!" he said, gently dabbing at his mustache with a napkin.

Cazaux grinned. "May I offer you the privacy of my office to conduct your perusal of the treaty clauses?"

Hartmuth had already seen the addendum. He figured Cazaux wanted to get Belgium's and Germany's approval first, then convince other delegates to agree.

"My understanding, Minister Cazaux," Hartmuth said, "is that the European Union delegates, as a body, are presented with the treaty tomorrow and we discuss any details or changes before we ratify."

A shadow passed briefly over Cazaux's face but it was gone in an instant.

"But of course you are right, Monsieur Griffe." He nodded his head sadly. He put his arms around their shoulders and steered them away from the babbling crowd.

"You know and I know, this isn't the best answer," Cazaux said. "However, France's economy and our relationship with you, our close European neighbors, will suffer if this isn't signed." He sighed. "Mass unemployment—well, that's just the tip of it."

Quimper nodded in agreement. Cazaux dropped his arms and studied the floor.

Hartmuth stared at Cazaux. "This treaty sidesteps due legal proceedings for immigrants. The mandate allows them to be held in detention centers indefinitely, without trial by judge or jury. No high court will sanction this."

"High court? No, dear Monsieur Griffe, it will never come to that. Once the treaty is passed and signed, discouraging new immigrants, we begin proceedings to strike those clauses." Cazaux smiled expansively. "The clauses will be deleted, like they never were there! Immigration will have slowed to a trickle. Eh, voilà, our consciences will rest quietly after that."

"Plenty of time for us to deal with that tomorrow," Hartmuth said.

"Of course, gentlemen." Cazaux smiled, putting his arms again around both of them. "As the host, where are my manners? And where is that pâté?"

Hartmuth felt Cazaux's clawlike grip on his shoulder. More than ever, he wished he was far away.

SARAH PULLED THE HAT lower over her eyes. She felt disoriented, grappling with the old Paris she knew and the changes in the fifty years since she'd left.

"*Bonjour*, Monsieur, the evening *Le Figaro*, please."

She paid and passed under the damp colonnades of Place des Vosges. The Marais felt oddly the same yet different, memories accosting her at every corner.

The wind whipped crackly brown leaves around her legs and she pulled her raincoat tightly around her thin body. The smell of roasting chestnuts wafted across the square. At the bottom of the back page, she saw the article she'd been looking for.

Marais Murder

Lili Stein, sixty-seven years old, of 64 rue des Rosiers, was found dead on late Wednesday evening. According to autopsy findings she was a victim of homicide. Police inquiries are centered in the Marais and surrounding 4th arrondissement. The Temple Emanuel has posted a reward for information leading to the conviction of person/s involved.

Here was Lili's murder, confirmed in black and white! She must have missed the first mention during the week. Above her, the strains of a violin, playing "Coeur Vagabond," drifted from an open window.

Her mother had hummed that old song on laundry days before

the French garde mobiles, supervised by the Gestapo, rounded up her family in The Vélodrome d'Hiver raid and deported them to Auschwitz in July 1942. She trembled and it wasn't from the chill November wind. Were they after her, too? Or was Helmut?

Sunday Noon

AIMÉE FOUND ABRAHAM STEIN in the storefront synagogue on rue des Écouffes, a sliverlike street crossing rue des Rosiers. Formerly a stationery store, the synagogue stood next to a vegetable shop that displayed bins of dark purple aubergines, shiny green peppers, and scabbed potatoes on the curb.

Abraham looked thinner, if that was possible. Dark circles ringed his eyes and his dark blue striped shirt gave him the appearance of a concentration-camp inmate from old newsreels. Lili Stein's memorial service had brought the small community together inside this tiny dark synagogue.

Everything bespoke tradition to Aimée—the low tones, the smell of fat before it got skimmed off chicken soup somewhere in a nearby kitchen, the gleam from brass candlesticks, and the feel of the rough wooden bench. Present time faded.

She became a little girl again, with ankle socks that always slid down and itchy wool sweaters that scratched her neck. Fidgety as usual. Trying to be as French as everyone else, the continual struggle of her childhood. Her mother holding her hands, making the sign of the cross, telling her to stop speaking English mixed with French. "*Mais*, Maman, I can't help it!" she had begged. "Stop that Frenglish, Amy, you're old enough to know," her mother had said. But that was as foreign to her as feeling French. "Sooner you learn, the better it is," she remembered her mother saying. "You can take care of yourself!"

"*Baruch hata adonai.*"

She slowly came back to the present, while a pair of wizened hands gripped hers and helped her make hand motions. But it wasn't her mother. It was a white-haired woman, eyes clouded by cataracts, whom she'd never seen before.

"*Très bien, mon enfant!*" the old woman with misfitting dentures beamed, hugging her.

Aimée sank back in disappointment. Her childhood was gone and her mother wasn't coming back. She took a deep breath and gently, she extricated herself, clasping the woman's gnarled hands in thanks.

Outside, she nodded at Sinta and approached Abraham Stein on the curb. He appeared melancholy as usual.

Rachel Blum, stooped and clad in an old sagging floral-print dress, disappeared behind a wooden door opposite the storefront synagogue.

"Excuse me," Aimée said to Abraham. She knocked on the wooden door several times. Finally a wooden slat slid open a crack.

"Hello, Rachel, it's Aimée Leduc. May I come in a few moments?" she said.

Rachel didn't smile as she peered out. "Why?"

"I forgot to ask you something."

Rachel slowly pulled open the heavy, creaking door.

"How are you, Rachel?" Aimée said, walking inside the moldy smelling entrance.

Rachel sighed. "Fallen arches, that's what the doctor calls it now. Can't take too much standing, my feet can't anyway, not like I used to."

She motioned to Aimée. They sat together on a wooden bench in the dark paved entrance.

"Walking on stone too much—that does it." She'd taken off her shoe and was rubbing the sole of her foot. "Those stairs going to Lili's used to be wooden. This stone gets my bunions hurting."

"Is that where the bloody footsteps were?" Startled, Aimée remembered Rachel's description. Morbier's men had found evidence of Lili Stein's blood there also.

"You don't give up, do you?"

"No one deserves to die like that," Aimée said, her face flushed. "Yet every time I ask questions about Lili's past, people don't want to talk. Why don't I chase the neo-Nazis, they say, do something concrete?"

Rachel kept rubbing her foot and didn't look at Aimée.

"I don't care where you fit into Lili Stein's past," Aimée said. "You won't talk to me because you think I'll judge you. No one my age would understand what you went through during the Occupation, right?"

Aimée attempted to keep her voice neutral, but she wasn't succeeding. "Who gives you the right to decide? And even if I can't understand, do you want the horror of what happened to be hidden forever?"

Rachel still avoided Aimée's gaze.

"Look at my face, Rachel," Aimée said.

Rachel shook her head.

"Lili's murder wasn't a skinhead special. That swastika was SS Waffen style," she said. "The SS . . . don't you see that? Or maybe you don't want to."

Rachel shrugged. "You're the one with the big theories."

Aimée sat back, feeling defeated as the hard bench cut into the burned spot on her spine. She shook her head and spoke as if to herself. "Who's next?"

Rachel sighed. "Arlette's murder happened after a big roundup of Jews in the Marais," she said.

Aimée froze.

Rachel's hands sliced the air, punctuating her words. "Jews kept indoors after that. We only bought things at certain hours of the day, we were even afraid to do that. That's when the Gestapo started more night raids. Almost every night. I'll never forget. Middle of the night, the squeal of brakes in the street and footsteps came pounding up the stairs. Would they stop at your apartment? Yell 'Open up' and bash in your door with their jackboots? Or would they keep going and pick on someone else that night? My neighbor down the hall beat them to it. When they were breaking down her door, she grabbed her two sleeping babies and jumped out the window, right onto rue des Rosiers." Rachel pointed to the street. "In front of this building. I like to think those babies slept on through to heaven."

Aimée sensed something odd in the way Rachel spoke, but she couldn't put her finger on it. Rachel took a deep breath and continued. "At Lili's apartment they couldn't get the blood off those wood steps. No one would go upstairs, they ended up just paving them over with stucco." She leaned close to Aimée's ear.

Aimée shifted on the dark, narrow bench.

Rachel whispered, "Some say they were Lili's bloody footprints because they were small. But Lili was gone. She didn't come back until Liberation and so much was going on, no one thought to question her. I asked her once about the concierge's murder she witnessed but she wouldn't elaborate. She never wanted to talk about the Occupation, said the war was over. She liked telling her son how she dealt with collaborators, though." She added, "Lili could be mean sometimes."

"Who found Arlette, the concierge?" Aimée asked.

"Javel. Seems he came courting later in the evening, saw a lot of blood. He found her in the light well, her brains all over."

"What do you mean, 'a lot of blood'?" Aimée said.

"I wasn't there but that's what I heard." Rachel Blum wedged her shoe back on and slowly rose to her feet. "I tell you, people did wonder about Arlette's murder since she wasn't Jewish. Rumor had it she was a BOF, but then everyone in Paris who could did that."

"BOF?"

"*Beurre, oeufs, fromage*—butter, eggs, and cheese," Rachel said. "That was the currency of the black market. You'd be surprised to know how many supposed Resistance members made fortunes that way. Everyone was jealous of those BOFs. I remember Arlette as silly and greedy. Always talking about her fiancé. With Lili gone, I suppose no one will ever know."

Aimée wondered why, if Lili had seen a murder, she hadn't told anyone.

Rachel turned and stared hard at Aimée. "No good comes of bringing all this up again," she said. "Leave the dead alone."

"This isn't the first time I've heard that. Are you going to put more obstacles in my way, Rachel? Threaten me again?"

Rachel shook her head stubbornly.

"You sent me the fax!" Aimée said.

"I'll say it once more." Rachel's eyes hardened. "Forget the past, it's over."

"No, Rachel." Aimée stood up. The story made sense now. "You must relive it every day. Were you an informer? Fifty years isn't punishment enough, is it?"

Rachel's bravado disintegrated and she covered her face with her hands. "It wasn't supposed to happen that way," she wailed. "They got the wrong apartment. I didn't mean to!"

"How can you tell me to forget the past?" Aimée said. "You are haunted by it."

"Three days later they took all of us."

Aimée shook her head. Rachel remained hunched over, her eyes glazed and far off.

Aimée let herself out, emerging into busy rue des Rosiers. Lili's staircase contained answers. How to obtain them was the problem. A big problem.

She approached Abraham, ignoring Sinta's look. He cleared his throat.

"We need to talk," she said.

"*D'accord.*" He turned to Sinta, but she'd already gone.

They walked slowly down the rue des Rosiers, past the Stein shop and towards the rue Vieille du Temple. At the Place des Singes, opposite the graffitied covered market at les Blancs Manteaux, they sat down at an outdoor café.

"I apologize, Mademoiselle Leduc. You mean well, I know. The rabbi at Temple Emanuel told me I should be more helpful, not so intolerant." Abraham Stein looked down at his hands.

She kept silent until the waiter served him a mineral water and her a double café crème.

"Things are difficult for you now, Monsieur Stein," she said. "I understand."

On the sidewalk, a father grabbed his toddler daughter, who'd tripped on the curb, catching her before she tumbled into an oncoming car. He smothered her tears in a hug, then plopped her on his shoulders.

Aimée recalled her twelfth birthday when she refused to let her father continue chaperoning her to ballet lessons. Oddly, he hadn't been upset. He'd just shaken his head in exasperation, saying, "You may be half French but you're all Parisian, every stubborn bit of you." Then he hugged her long and hard, something he'd done rarely after her mother had left.

"What have you found out?" he said.

She shook off the memories. "Last night I enlisted with Les Blancs Nationaux and almost bashed your synagogue."

Abraham choked on his mineral water. "What?"

She told him about the neo-Nazi meeting at the ClicClac and their target. She neglected the part about her shoulder and Yves.

His eyes opened wide in alarm.

"Please detail for me what your mother did last Wednesday afternoon."

He stopped and thought. "Wednesdays she usually took the afternoon off, ran errands, bought special food for Shabbat."

"Did she cook?"

He shook his head. "Normally we have Wednesday supper at my nephew Ital's apartment. But that evening Maman never showed up. So I came looking for her."

"Ital lives nearby?"

"Around the corner on rue Pavée."

She stirred her coffee excitedly. "Near the cobbler Javel's shop?"

"Next door."

Somehow this all fit, she thought, remembering the newly heeled shoes in the closet Sinta had commented on. "Had she picked up a pair of shoes from Javel's that day?"

He paused. "Ital's daughter's bat mitzvah is next week. Maman mentioned something about shoes. I'm not sure."

"What else did she do?"

"She'd sort the garbage Wednesdays for me to put in the light well, then come over."

Aimée almost dropped her spoon. Morbier's men had found evidence of a struggle near the garbage.

"Your mother had already been down in the light well."

Stein shook his head. "Maman never went in there. Refused."

Something clicked in her brain—the closeness of Javel's shop, the light well where his fiancée had been found, and now where Lili Stein's blood traces were fifty years later. Everything was pointing to Javel.

She braced herself to explore an ugly avenue. "Monsieur Stein . . ."

"Abraham." He smiled for the first time.

"*D'accord.* Call me Aimée." This made it harder. Too bad, she liked this man, felt his pain almost as her own. "Please don't be offended. I'm sorry to ask this. Many women who fraternized with the Nazis got branded with swastikas on their foreheads after Liberation. Would there be a connection?"

Abraham sighed. "I've heard that, too. But Maman was definitely not a collaborator. On the contrary, she pointed them out, as she self-righteously told me one time."

His eyes squinted in pain and he buried his face in his hands. She waited until he stopped shaking and gave him a napkin.

Giggling students scurried across the cobbled street, past the almost empty sidewalk café. She reached in her backpack and pulled out the first thing her hand touched. It was the wrinkled copy of *The Hebrew Times* she'd wrapped Lili Stein's coat in.

She gasped. *Cochon assassin*—Swine assassin—in bold angular handwriting was scrawled across a small photo and accompanying article. She smoothed the newspaper. Politicians and ministers were outlined by fat red lines in that writing. Aimée couldn't make out the faces but she could read the names.

She thrust the paper at him. "Your mother wrote that, didn't she?"

"Ah yes, Maman ranted about this one night. A Nazi liar strutting in black boots, she knew all about him. She carried on so but when I asked her particulars, she shut up. Wouldn't discuss it. Maman wasn't the easiest person to deal with." Abraham grimaced. "But family is family, you know how that is."

Aimée nodded as if she did, but she didn't.

He continued. "Last week, Sinta noticed Maman went out a lot." Abraham paused to drink some mineral water. "Sinta remembers her saying that she wasn't going to be put off by ghosts anymore." He stopped, hesitating.

"Go ahead, Abraham." She wondered what he was afraid to tell her.

"I doubted you before, Aimée." He looked down. "Blame it on my old-fashioned thinking about women. But now, wrong or right, I worry for you."

She was touched by his concern and didn't know what to say.

Abraham spoke in a measured tone. "The last words I can remember Maman saying were 'I'll come to Ital's later,' as if she was expecting something."

Aimée felt conflicted, wanting to tell Abraham that his mother had been expecting her. But if she did, that could put Abraham in danger and put her no closer to Lili's murderer.

Abraham continued. "Then Maman said, 'You will take the boards down from my window tonight.' "

She sat up. "What did she mean by that, Abraham?"

"I don't know," he said.

"Obviously it struck you as unusual," she said. "What do you think she meant?"

"With Maman you never knew . . . but maybe she felt guilty."

"Guilty? For what?"

"That's just a feeling I got," he said. "No concrete basis."

He looked upset. "I have to get back." He slapped some francs on the table and hurried away.

She rose, carefully putting the folded newspaper in her backpack, more confused than before. What did the boarded-up window have to do with the photo she'd deciphered?

AIMÉE STOPPED at the corner kiosk near her office on rue du Louvre. Maurice, the owner, nodded at her. He had a clipped mustache and bright sparrowlike eyes.

"Usual?" he said.

She smiled and placed some francs on a fat pile of newspapers.

Maurice whisked a copy of *Le Figaro* with his wooden arm into hers. An Algerian war veteran, he ran several kiosks but wasn't above dog-sitting Miles Davis occasionally.

She clutched her paper and climbed the old, worn stairs to her floor. All the way up she wondered why Lili would feel guilt over Arlette's murder she supposedly hadn't even seen. And if she'd recognized an old Nazi, why hadn't she talked about it?

Back in her office, she logged onto both her and René's computer terminals. She knew where she had to look. Files not destroyed by the Germans had been centralized. On René's terminal she accessed the Yad Vashem Memorial in Jerusalem and downloaded the *R.F. SS Sicherheits-Dienst Memorandum file 1941–45*. Thick black Gestapo lightning bolts were emblazoned across her computer screen as the documents came up.

On her terminal she bypassed a tracer link and downloaded GROUPER, the back door into Interpol. She accessed GROUPER and queried under Griffe, Hartmuth, the name under the newspaper

photo Lili had written over. A pleasantly robotic, digitally mas-
tered voice said, "Estimated retrieval time is four minutes twenty
seconds."

René's screen displayed a long report in German titled
Nachtrichten-Nebermittlung, dated August 21, 1942. Even with
her rudimentary grasp of German she could figure out the general
idea. Addressed to Adolf Eichmann in Berlin, the subject of the
report was *"Abtransport von Juden aus Frankreich nach Auschwitz"*
or "Transportation for French Jews to Auschwitz." According to
Aimée's rough translation, there had been no provisions made for
Jewish transport to Auschwitz in October and the Gestapo chief
was asking Eichmann what he was going to do about it.

Well, here was a zealous Nazi, she thought; in August he was
already worried about getting enough people to the gas chambers
in October. An Adolf brown-noser, he probably stayed up nights
worrying about the possibility of empty ovens. The report had
been signed R. A. Rausch, *Obersturmführer*. Two other signatures,
those of K. Oblath and H. Volpe, were listed as underling Si-Po
Sicherheitspolizei und Sicherheitsdienst responsible for Jewish
roundups.

Back on her terminal, she checked for a reply to her GROUPER
query. A loud whir, then a reggae version of the *2001: A Space
Odyssey* theme came on. GROUPER access came via an eclectic
server today, she thought. Old Soviet war records flashed on the
screen. She ran the names of the three Gestapo she had found:
Rausch, Oblath, and Volpe. Each name came up as deceased.
That was odd.

Searching deeper, she found each one separately listed as dead
in the Battle of Stalingrad in 1943. Why would Rausch, the head
of the Gestapo, be sent to the front in 1943, Aimée wondered.

She checked other memorandums from the file. Rausch was still
signing memos deporting Jews from Paris in 1944 but he'd been
listed as dead in 1943? Aimée sat back and let out a low whistle.

Interpol identity files cross-referenced to the postwar US Documents Center in Berlin, circa 1948, appeared on her screen. In them, a Hartmuth Griffe had been listed dead, as a combatant in the Battle of Stalingrad. That was all.

These records had obviously been tampered with. Here was proof. But not enough proof to identify who, if any, of these Nazis was still alive.

Sinta had told her that Lili felt ghosts were haunting her. But it had been Rachel's threatening fax that warned her to leave the ghosts alone.

"RESERVE A SEAT FOR me on the late flight to Hamburg, please." Hartmuth's fingers thumped on the elegant walnut secretary that served as the hotel's reception desk.

That afternoon he'd realized he'd had enough. He'd placate Cazaux by signing the treaty, and make the Werewolves happy. The European Union agreement sanctioned concentration camps but maybe Cazaux meant it when he'd promised to delete the racist provisions afterwards.

Hartmuth had thought he could stop it. He realized now how futile that was—the Werewolves couldn't be stopped. Now he just wanted to toe the accepted party line and get back to Germany. The Werewolves would win, no matter what; their claws stretched everywhere.

"Of course, Monsieur, I'll inform you when the reservations are completed," the clerk said.

And I can escape the ghost of Sarah hovering in my mind, Hartmuth thought, courteously thanking him. How foolish he'd been to think she might have survived! But deep inside, a tiny hope had fluttered. There would be no records of her either, he'd taken care of that himself in 1943. Hartmuth gazed sadly over Place des Vosges below him.

"Excuse me, Herr Griffe," the clerk bowed abjectly. "I almost forgot, this came for you." He handed Hartmuth a large white envelope.

Hartmuth thanked him again absentmindedly and went to the elevator. As he entered and nodded to the other occupants, he idly noticed his name on the envelope. It was scrawled in the familiar cursive script of his time, not how people wrote these days, squat and uniform. The system had changed after the war, like so much else. As the elevator stopped and let a couple off, he looked forward to this evening when his plane took off. Finally he would be safe. He'd make it out of Paris.

Hartmuth noticed a bulge in the envelope. And then he panicked. Had he trustingly picked up a letter bomb? This was Paris, after all. Terrorist attacks happened all the time! His hands started shaking so much he dropped the envelope. But the only thing that happened was that a piece of ivory bone wrapped in faded yellow cloth rolled soundlessly onto the carpeted elevator floor.

He kneeled and gently unfolded the tattered yellow star, the childishly embroidered J with broken black threads that every Jew had been required to wear. Could this be Sarah's? He'd seen it for so many years in his dreams, reminding him of her. He cupped the bone in his hands. Nothing else was in the envelope. Could she be alive after all these years? Had she survived?

The bone had been their signal. She would leave a bone lying on a ledge outside the catacombs. It had meant "Meet me tonight." Who else would send a message like this? Tears brimmed in his eyes.

He would go and meet her where they had always met. When night fell and the lights hid behind the marble salamander on the arch.

Hartmuth took the elevator back down and he went to the reception desk.

He smiled. "Excuse me again, there's been another last-minute change. Cancel that flight for me tonight. Who delivered that last message for me?"

"I'm sorry, Herr Griffe, I just came on duty at two and the message was already here."

"Of course, thank you," Hartmuth said. He felt the pounding of his heart must be audible to the clerk. In several hours it would be dark. They had always met just after sunset, the safest time since Jews were forbidden on the streets after 8:00 P.M.

He walked out of the lobby, through the courtyard bursting with red geraniums, to the sun-dappled Place des Vosges. He entered the gate, closed it behind him, and let his feet and mind wander. Duty. Hartmuth knew all about that since most of his life was based on it—his political life, marriage, and being an upright German.

The plane trees still held some foliage, but yellow leaves fell and danced in the bubbling fountains. Toddlers bundled in warm jackets chased pigeons and tumbled onto the grass with cries of glee. Like his daughter, Katia, had done once. Before she'd blindly stepped in front of a GI troop truck on the outskirts of Hamburg and died in Grete's arms. She was only six years old.

But he couldn't forget the first time he'd seen Sarah. She could have stepped right off the shelf of porcelain figurines that lined his grandmother's Bremerhaven cottage.

As a young boy, he'd spent every summer at the cottage playing with his cousins near the sea. Sometimes for hours at a time, he would stare at his grandmother's collection and make up stories about each figurine. Grandmother never allowed him to touch, that was forbidden, but he had been content to look.

His favorite, though it had been a hard decision, was the shepherdess, with her coal black wavy hair, azure eyes with dark blue pinpoints, and white porcelain skin. She held a staff and beckoned to her fluffy sheep, whose hooves were forever poised in flight.

Of course, it was all gone. His grandmother's cottage, as well as miles of other suburban cottages, had been firebombed during early raids on the Bremerhaven harbor.

But Hartmuth had seen his shepherdess alive and in the flesh that day in 1942. He'd been checking the Marais again near the building with the salamander. In the courtyard with sleepy midday shuttered windows, a figure leaned over, petting an orange marmalade–colored cat.

A girl with wavy black hair had looked up, smiling, as he'd approached. She had incredible sky blue eyes and alabaster skin. Her expression had changed when she saw the black uniform with the lightning bolts of the Waffen SS on his sleeve and his heavy jackboots. He'd ignored her look of terror as she haltingly rose. Hartmuth always remembered her as the only French girl who had ever greeted him with a smile. Love at first sight can happen when you're eighteen, he thought. It had lasted all his life.

She'd recoiled in fear, but he'd put a finger to his lips and knelt down to pet the cat. Its fur was uneven and it had scaly patches of mange, which probably explained why no one had eaten it. He opened his heart to her and smiled. Then she nodded, kneeling down beside the cat and next to him.

Her schoolbooks peeked out of the worn satchel on the cobblestones. Something about her was so defenseless that he decided to ignore the yellow star embroidered on her school smock. They took turns petting the cat, who was purring furiously now and hoping for something to eat. She had the biggest blue eyes he'd ever seen. Hartmuth couldn't stop staring into them. When she looked up at him he pulled a bit of chalk out his pocket. He drew a whiskered cat and they both smiled. His French was so minimal and his urge to communicate so desperate that he did the only thing he could think of.

"Woof, woof," he barked.

Her incredulous look gave way to stifled giggles and then outright laughter as he stood up and started scratching like a monkey and jumping around. Hartmuth didn't care how he embarrassed himself, he just wanted to make her laugh. She was so beautiful. He remembered something his uncle, a bachelor who had many mistresses, had said: once you've got them laughing, they're yours.

It was important to him that she want him, too, that he wasn't just her captor. He gently put his hand on her shoulder, feeling bones and her thinness, and gestured with his other hand. Trembling, she reached into her satchel and handed him her school card with the *Ausweis* permit attached to the back. He recognized the address. His men had raided it during the Vel d'Hiver roundup in July. He gestured forward with his arm and led her through the courtyard, up the staircase with a winding metal rail.

"*Ja. C'est bien, kein Problem.*" He smiled and patted her arm to reassure her.

Just as they approached the apartment, a door across the hall opened and an old man hobbled out using a cane. His rheumy eyes took a long look as he stopped and clicked his tongue in disapproval. Sarah had looked up in fear, but Hartmuth purposely ignored the old man, who shuffled down the hall. In front of her door, Hartmuth pantomimed eating, trying to make her understand that he would bring food.

Hartmuth used the little French he knew and motioned with his hands for her to wait. He showed her his watch and what time he would be back. She seemed to understand and nodded vigorously. He took her chin in his hand, it was warm and smooth, and he smiled. He still couldn't stop staring at her. Then he left.

The apartment was empty when he came back. She'd run away from him.

So he waited and watched in the Marais. He would find her. On the third day he saw her, emerging from the boarded-up courtyard of a derelict mansion, an *hôtel particulier*, off the rue Payenne. Dusk had fallen when she finally returned. He stood waiting. Waiting to follow her. She wouldn't get away this time. He watched her pick her way through debris, then disappear behind a pile of rubbish.

Clutching his parcel of food, he slicked his dark hair under his cap, brushed the dust off his epaulets, and buffed his black leather jackboots quickly with his handkerchief. He approached the bushes, his boots crunching branches and bits of broken furniture as he walked.

He came face to face with an old rusted wire bed frame. He kicked it aside, the wire rattling drunkenly askew, and he saw the opening. He found the footholds and climbed down, realizing he'd entered a candle-lit cavern sprinkled with bones, part of the old Roman catacombs that honeycombed Paris. She was curled up in a fetal position in a dim corner, wedging herself into the damp earth. Her hands quivered as she tried to ward him off.

"*Non, s'il vous plaît. Non!*" she pleaded.

"*Mangez, mangez.*" He smiled, putting his fingers to his lips to indicate food.

In a corner of the catacomb, a patched blanket lay spread over a lumpy mattress while a battered wooden tea chest doubled as a table. He beckoned to her and pointed to his package of food. From under his arm he pulled out some dog-eared books.

"*Ja. Amis. Etudiez f-français?*"

He removed his Gestapo dagger from its hilt, setting it flat on the tea chest. Eagerly, he motioned with his arms and she slowly crawled forward, her eyes never leaving the dagger shining in the candlelight.

Her eyes widened as he opened the parcel and spread out tins of foie gras, chewy Montelimar nougat, calissons d'Aix from Provence, and crusty brown bread.

In the primitive French he'd rehearsed he said, "Let's be friends, share."

As if to offer hospitality in return she spread her arms, thrust bottled water into his lap, and kept her eyes down.

At first, she was reluctant to eat but after he opened the bottle of red wine, she almost inhaled the contents of the chewy nougat tin. Hartmuth started talking in German while she ate. Constantly consulting a French-German dictionary, standard Third Reich army issuance, and an old phrase book he'd found in a book stall on the quai des Célestins, he tried to relax her. He punctuated each word with looks in the dictionary to make sure.

She would raise her eyes when he stuttered. It had begun when he was ten and his brother died. Now his mouth wasn't cooperating again. Watching him intently, she saw his frustration. Then she took his hand and put it on her lips to feel how she formed the words with her mouth.

"*Je m'appelle* Sarah. SA' RAH."

"*Ich b-b . . . bin* He . . . Helmut. HELM' MOOT," he stammered as he held her small white hands on his mouth, kissing them.

She pulled her hands away immediately and said seriously, "*Enchantée*, HELM'MOOT."

"*Enchanté*, S-SARAH." He bowed as low as he could with his knees crunched beneath him.

A faint odor of decay clung to the cavern walls pocked with bits of bone. Damp chill crept from the darkness beyond the candlelight.

"I w-won't hurt you, S-SARAH," he whispered. "N-never."

His night shift at the *Kommandantur* began at midnight, and he left her just in time to walk the few blocks there. Eighteen families on her street had been turned in by a collaborator, she'd said. He had promised to search for her parents but that would be an exercise in futility.

Everyone had boarded convoy number 10 bound for Auschwitz.

The only thing he could do was save her. If he was careful. Fear, gratitude, and a promise of safety might be all she had now. But he would wait.

Every night before his shift he visited the catacombs. His loneliness would evaporate as he climbed down and met Sarah's face. Hopeful and grateful.

In 1942 all the detainees from Drancy prison had been required to send home a cheerful missive before being herded into the trains. The next week he'd found the card from her parents and brought it to her. Ecstatically happy, she'd hugged him and cried. Quickly she'd sent her one extra blanket to the prison.

Hartmuth knew he could never tell her the truth. Sarah would not understand why he lied. It was all he could do to bring the food with his meager army pay swallowed in bribes. The evening his *Kommandant* visited the opera, Hartmuth had slipped into the office at the *Kommandantur* where Missing-Active Search files were kept. He'd crossed out her name, the only thing he knew to do to save her.

MONDAY

MARTINE SITBON, AIMÉE'S FRIEND since algebra class in the *lycée*, sounded tired. Her graveyard shift at the newspaper *Le Figaro* had fifteen minutes left.

"*Ça va*, Martine? Got a minute or two?" Aimée said.

"Well, Aimée, long time no hear," came the husky voice. "Is this a friend-in-need-is-a-friend-indeed call?"

"You could say that and I'll owe you dinner big-time," Aimée chuckled.

Martine yawned deeply. "Hit me now before I fade; you're keeping me from the warm body in my bed, about whom I'll tell you more at dinner. We'll go to La Grande Vefour—the pâté and the tête de veau are superb."

Aimée flinched. A meal without wine began at six hundred francs. But Martine, a gourmet, always dictated the restaurant.

"Agreed, you'll definitely earn your dinner on this stuff. First, you still have that friend in social security?"

"*Bien sûr!* I love and nurture my connections, Aimée. I'm a journalist."

"Great. Need everything you can get on some members of Les Blancs Nationaux. I want to know where their money comes from." She gave Martine Thierry's and Yves's names.

Martine paused. "What's this about, Aimée?"

"A case."

"Aimée, Aryan supremacist types don't play by the rules. This EU trade summit is causing lots of rats to surface. Just a word of caution."

"*Merci.* One more thing. Check on a non-Jew murder in 1943

on the rue des Rosiers, reported or not. And while you're at it, collaborators in the Marais."

"As in Nazi collaborators?" Martine said. "Touchy stuff! No one likes to talk about them. But I'll sniff around if you promise to be careful."

"Careful as lice staring at delousing powder," Aimée said.

"Keep that smart mouth in line. I know that during the Occupation all newspapers were taken over, turned into essentially rote German propaganda. Some arrondissements printed their own one-pager cheat sheets with local info such as births, deaths, electricity rates. But I'll check on that and get back to you. One more thing."

"I'm listening, Martine."

"Make three reservations, in case my boyfriend wants to come."

Aimée groaned. This really would cost.

"MONSIEUR JAVEL, you remember me, right?" Aimée smiled brightly at the cobbler. "How about something to drink? Let's discuss our mutual interest." She held up an apple green bottle of Pernod.

"Eh, what could that be?" Félix Javel growled, swaying on his bowed legs.

"Arlette's murder," she said. "Maybe if we share information, things will be mutually beneficial."

Before he could hesitate, she nudged herself between him and the door leading out the back of his shop. She was determined to find out what he really saw in 1943. Despite the Gallic genius for evasion, she counted on the Pernod to loosen his tongue.

He shrugged. "As you like. I don't have much to say." He scrubbed the back of his neck with a grayish flannel washcloth as he led her down the narrow hallway lit by a yellowed bulb. Sliding off his shoes, he indicated that she should do the same before entering a parlor sitting room.

This room, suffocatingly warm due to a modern oil heater,

smelled of used kitty litter. A Victorian rocker plumped with threadbare chintz cushions sat in front of a sixties greenish chrome television set. A bent rabbit-ear antenna sat on top of it. Cascading strands of blue crystal beads formed an opaque curtain that hung from the door frame to the floor, separating the small cooking area. Javel returned from the kitchen balancing a tray with two glasses and a pitcher of water. Aimée willed herself not to get up and help him while he laboriously set the rattling tray on a scrubbed oak table. She pulled a small tin of pâté out with the bottle and his eyes lit up.

"I have just the thing to go with that," he said.

He clinked past the beads again, carrying a chipped Sèvres bowl full of stale, damp soda crackers. Aimée watched him set out embroidered lace-fringe linen napkins and picked one up.

"These are almost too beautiful to use," she said, noting the ornately intertwined A and F.

"Arlette did these. The whole set is still stored in our wedding chest. I don't have guests much, figured might as well use them."

"You knew Lili Stein," she said. "Why keep it a secret from me?"

Slowly he mixed the water with Pernod until it became properly milky. He rubbed some pâté on a cracker. "Why are you snooping around?" he said.

"Doing my job." She moved her chair closer to his. "Lili's murder is connected to Arlette's."

He chuckled and poured himself more Pernod. "The prewar Pernod absinthe got made with wormwood and ate one's brain away."

"Who killed Arlette?" she said.

He drank it down and poured himself another glass.

"Aren't you the detective?" he said.

"But you have your own theory," she said. "Something you saw that the *flics* didn't?" she said.

Surprise flitted briefly across his face.

"What did you see?" she said, excited by the look in his eyes.

A long, loud burp erupted from deep in his stomach.

"Buggers," he said. "Beat me."

"Why? Why did they beat you, Javel?"

His eyes narrowed. "You're a Jew, aren't you?"

She shook her head. "What if I was?"

"I don't like your type," he said. "Whatever it is."

"Then don't vote for me at the Miss World pageant," she said.

He smeared pâté on more stale crackers and shoveled them on the plate.

There had to be some way to reach this concrete-headed little man. "Aren't you afraid, Javel? I mean, you mentioned hate attacks and random neo-Nazi violence in the Marais. But you don't seem very nervous to me."

He sputtered, "Why should I be?" He poured himself another glass.

"Exactly. Especially if you knew that Lili's murder had something to do with the past."

"Leave me alone," he said. "Go away." He turned, his mouth twitching.

"Tell me what you saw."

He shook his fist in the air but still wouldn't look at her.

Now she wanted to shake it out of him.

"Look, I know you don't like me but holding it in won't bring Arlette back! You want justice, so do I. And we both know we have to find it ourselves. Right? Did the *flics* do anything but beat you?"

She couldn't see his face. Finally he spoke, his back still turned toward her. "Everything started with that damned tinned salmon," he said.

"What do you mean?" she asked, surprised.

"Stuffed in her wardrobe. Everywhere," he said.

"Black market?"

He turned and reached for his glass. She slowly poured him another. Rachel Blum's words spun in her head.

"Arlette sold black-market food. She was a BOF, right?" she said.

Shaken, he looked up. "I haven't heard that term in years." He sighed. "She graduated to petrol, watches, even silk stockings. I told Arlette these things were too dangerous."

"Did Lili help her?" she said.

Saliva bubbled at the corner of his mouth.

"Where was Lili? Did you see her?"

"I tried to apologize," he shrugged. "But there were so many bloody footsteps. All over."

"Why were you sorry? Did you and Arlette argue?"

He nodded.

"The footsteps went upstairs?" Aimée asked. "You thought they were Lili's?"

He raised his eyebrows.

"Javel, Lili saw what happened. Why didn't you ask her?"

He shook his head. "She was gone. There were so many footsteps by the sink."

"Lili wasn't there? Maybe hiding somewhere?"

His eyes had narrowed to slits. She was afraid he was about to pass out. She took a gulp of Pernod to combat the pervasive ammonia smell from the kitty litter.

"Javel," she said loudly and tiredly. "Tell me why."

"I told the inspector." He spoke more lucidly, unaware of the tears trickling down his cheeks in thin silvery lines. "They beat me bloody at Double Morte. Called me a cripple. Said I couldn't get it up and laughed at me. First inspector got too greedy for a black-market collabo."

"What was his name?" Aimée asked.

"Lartigue. Run over by a Nazi troop truck accidentally, they say."

"Lili knew who killed Arlette, didn't she?" she said.

He shoved the empty glass towards her and she poured him more Pernod with a generous dash of water.

"Rachel said Lili knew," Aimée said. "Come on, Javel, who else would know?"

He shrugged, then leaned forward. "That Yid collabo who slept with a *Boche*." He whispered, squinting his eyes, "With her bastard baby." His shoulder sagged. "Had the same eyes."

"Same eyes?" Who was he talking about?

"Such bright blue eyes for a Jew!" he said.

"When was the last time you saw her?" Aimée asked excitedly.

His head landed heavily on the table. Passed out. Only when he was snoring did Aimée tuck the crocheted blanket around him. She put milk in a bowl for the missing cat, rinsed out the glasses in his dingy sink, and shut the door quietly behind her.

LE RENARD, "THE FOX," was a relic of Les Halles in the fifties. Somehow it had missed the wrecking ball that had swung on rue des Prêcheurs when they razed the old central market of Les Halles. There, Violette and Georges served their famous *soupe à l'oignon gratinée* at 5:00 A.M. for the few fish sellers who still plied their trade nearby.

Aimée had arranged to meet Morbier here. After Javel's information, she counted on getting Morbier's approval to set her plan in motion.

She entered the haze of cigarette smoke and loud laughter. Georges winked as she smoothed down her black dress, inched her toes comfortably in the black heels, and adjusted her one good strand of pearls. She slid around the corner of the zinc bar to kiss him on both cheeks.

"Eh, where have you been? The snooping business keep you too busy to shoot the bull with old *flics*?" Georges teased with a straight face.

"I had to raise my standards sometime, Georges, my reputation was getting tarnished," she threw back affectionately.

Morbier perched at the counter, poking in his pants pockets for something. He found an empty pack of Gauloises, crumpled the cellophane, then searched his overcoat.

"Any chance of Violette's cassoulet for me and this one?" She nudged Morbier as she said it.

Georges smiled and said, "I'll check."

Aimée motioned to Morbier. "I'm inviting you."

He feigned indifference. "What's the occasion?"

"It goes on the business account," she said. "Under purchasing information."

He chuckled as he lit up a nonfiltered Gauloise blue. "You can try."

They edged toward a booth with cracked brown leather seats. Dingy and comfortable, a cop hangout with good food. Several others from the Commissariat nodded and raised their glasses of *vin rouge* in mock salute as they walked by. She recognized several from her father's time. A table of men in pinstriped suits were busily arguing and slurping Georges's signature dish. Bankers, stockbrokers from the Bourse, even a famous designer would roll up here. Many a time, Aimée had seen the prime minister's chauffeured Renault out front while he came in for a bowl. It was that good.

"No dice on the forensics. Lili Stein's file has disappeared upstairs." He tore off a piece of crusty baguette.

"I need to know when she was killed."

"Formulating some theory that I should know about?"

"Just a theory," Aimée said.

"Like what?" He lifted the edge of the white tablecloth and wiped his mustache.

She frowned and tossed him a linen napkin.

"Nothing points directly to the LBN. The swastikas I saw at the meeting were different from what was on . . ." Aimée stopped. She remembered the bloodless lines carved in Lili Stein's forehead and heard the bland voice from the Auschwitz=Hoax video. Burning anger rose in her throat.

"Is something wrong?" he said.

She stopped herself. Anger would get her nowhere.

"No. The closest hate crime in the videos I borrowed was burning the Star of David in front of the Jewish Center."

Solange Goutal, the receptionist at the Jewish Center, had guessed right.

"Borrowed?" he said.

After watching the videos, she'd been relieved to see Les Blancs Nationaux hadn't recorded killing Lili. But that didn't mean they hadn't done it. Just that she hadn't found a tape, if any existed. Not only had she slept with Yves, deep down she wanted to do so again.

"Like a lending library," she said. Her back still ached as if large logs had rolled over it.

Morbier snorted.

"All I know for sure is that they're sick misfits," she said.

"Misfits. That's quaint." Morbier nodded. "They figured you were some kind of plant. And they're not sure from who."

"Mystery is my middle name, Morbier," she said. "Nail anybody in the alcohol check?"

"Got one of the cockroaches for parole violation. That's it," he said.

"At least they didn't bash a synagogue."

"You sure bring 'em out of the woodwork, Leduc."

Just then, Georges appeared with two steaming, fragrant bowls of *soupe à l'oignon gratinée*. Big chunky pieces of half-melted cheese sitting on a piece of baguette floated lazily in the middle. For eons, these huge blue bowls had fed butchers, fishmongers, sellers of vegetables, cheese, and fruits in early dawn.

"Sorry, we're out of cassoulet," Georges apologized. That was the running joke. Le Renard never had cassoulet, only the best onion soup in Paris.

For a time, the only sound between them was the serious dunking of chunks of bread.

"I want the records of a murder in 1943," she said.

Georges, a blue-and-white-checked towel draped over his arm, stood by the counter. She nodded at him and mouthed "Espresso." He winked back in reply.

Morbier shrugged. "Would this murder be related?"

"Inspector called Lartigue investigated in 1943." Aimée plopped a brown sugar cube in her espresso. "Victim named Arlette Mazenc."

"Before my time. What's it got to do with anything?" he said.

She had to be careful what she told him since her suspicions derived from information illegally obtained off the computer. Too illegal to tell Morbier.

"I've got another theory," she said.

"In 1943 a lot of people disappeared and there weren't exactly detailed investigations being conducted," Morbier said.

"She didn't disappear, Morbier. Murdered. Indulge me here, check the records," she said.

His voice changed. "Why?"

She motioned to Georges for the check. "Because you asked for my help, remember? It's awfully odd that another woman was bludgeoned to death in Lili's building. Somehow it's connected."

He snorted. "Connected? Not even coincidental, Leduc. If there's a link, it's all in your mind."

"This woman, Arlette, was murdered under Lili's window . . ."

Morbier interrupted. "And fifty years later Lili got snuffed by some Nazi type. Where's the connection?"

"The forensics would tell us."

Georges brought them each a thimble-sized glass of amber liquid with Aimée's change. "My brother's Calvados. Home brewed," he said proudly.

Aimée downed it, feeling the coarse tang of the apple brandy burn her throat.

"No wonder we never see your brother, Georges." Aimée grinned. The tart sting became a slow, toasty aftertaste.

Morbier continued. "Forget it. I'm off the case."

"But you have authority to get old files. Morbier, I can't prove anything yet; I need to explore my way."

"You still haven't told me the possible connection," he said, looking up. He dropped ashes onto the white butcher-paper tablecloth scattered with bread crumbs.

"I think Lili saw who murdered Arlette," she said.

"So what? It doesn't explain the swastika."

"It doesn't explain anything, Morbier, but I've got to start somewhere. Get me the file, let me prove that Lili's murder . . ."

He stopped her. "I'm off the case, remember? Leduc, stick with computers. You're way off the track here."

She put her elbows on the table and tented her fingers as she began. "Morbier, you never heard this from me and if you talk, I'll deny everything."

He leaned forward.

"But I've got an idea. It's rough, but it could tell us something," she said. "I need Luminol to test a theory about bloodstain traces left in Lili's light well. Some trace could point to the killer."

In the end he agreed.

LATER ON, as they were bidding adieu to Georges, she noticed how quiet Morbier had become.

"Maybe I should retire," he said as he put his hands in his pockets.

Outside on narrow rue des Prêcheurs, she searched her shoulder bag for her Metro pass. "What's that, Morbier?" she asked distractedly. "You've just had too much to drink tonight." Then she looked at his forlorn expression.

"Never been pulled off a case before," he said.

"Who exactly pulled you off?" she said.

He shrugged. "My superintendent informed me on his way out."

"His way out? Relieved of his post?" She looked directly at Morbier.

"Promoted. Now I report directly to the antiterrorist unit chief. At the Commissariat, instead of onward and upward, we say wayward and francword. You get the meaning, eh?"

"Are you talking bribery?" She cocked her head sideways in disbelief. "The chief superintendent of greater Paris?"

Morbier shrugged. "Well, to be fair, he was up for promotion in a few months anyway. Just happened sooner than expected."

"So what are you saying, Morbier?"

"Could be a coincidence or"—he peered at the luminous fingernail of a moon hanging in the cold sky—"vagaries of nature due to the cyclical spheres of the moon. I don't know."

"Why would someone from the antiterrorism bureau override you?" she asked.

"Certain things happen and you accept them or leave. That's all. Let's walk."

She hooked her arm in his and they walked. They walked in silence for a long time. Like she used to with her father. Paris was the city for walking when words failed.

They walked down past the Hôtel de Ville with the tricolor flags flying from balconies, across the Pont d'Arcole to the flood-lit Notre Dame, now camouflaged by sheeted scaffolding, where a crew was giving her a face-lift, down the Ile de la Cité to the Pont Neuf and past the shadowy Louvre and her darkened office, across the shimmery Seine on Pont Royal to the Left Bank.

Down the elegant rue du Bac they strolled along lively, crowded Boulevard Saint Germain, where even on this cool November night the sidewalk tables were full of smoking, drinking patrons gesturing, laughing, and people-watching. Models, students, tourists, and the cell-phone set.

On Ile St. Louis, around the corner from her apartment, they stopped for a sorbet at Berthillon, famous for the best *glace* in Paris. Aimée chose mango lime and Morbier, vanilla bean. Finally they stopped in front of her dark building.

She kissed him on both cheeks. He clutched her arms, not letting her go. Uneasily, she tried to back away.

"Invite me up?" he whispered in her ear.

"We have a beautiful friendship, Morbier, let's keep it that way. Don't forget about our plan," she said. She entered the door before he could make another advance that he would feel embarrassed about in the morning.

Miles Davis greeted her enthusiastically at her door. She laughed and scooped him up in her arms.

She picked up her phone on the first ring.

"Luna?" breathed Yves.

Aimée's throat caught before she could answer.

"You left without saying goodbye."

Aimée paused, what do I do?

As if he could read her thoughts, he said, "Get back over here. The entry code is 2223. I'm waiting." He hung up.

He sounded so sure of himself that it made her angry. Well, she wouldn't go. How could a coherent, rational woman voluntarily want to sleep with a member of an Aryan supremacist group?

Quickly, Aimée unzipped her dress, tossed her pearls in the drawer, and pulled on her ripped jeans and black leather jacket. "You're going to stay with Uncle Maurice," she told Miles Davis. She grabbed his carrier, throwing in extra dog biscuits. "Help him mind the kiosk. You like his poodle, Bizou, don't you?" He jumped in his bag, eagerly wagging his tail. "I thought so." She ran back down her stairway and hailed a taxi.

HARTMUTH SAT WAITING ON the bench in the Square Georges-Cain and watched the shadows lengthen. He'd bought Provençal sweets, the same fruit *calissons* he used to bring Sarah. But what he really wanted to give her was himself.

What would she look like? He'd been eighteen and she fourteen the last time he'd seen her. Now they were in their sixties and briefly he wondered if he'd still be attracted to her. But all these years he'd dreamed of her, Sarah. Only her. The one woman who had entered the core of his being.

He had to take this second chance, no matter what. He refused to die full of regret. He'd draft a letter of resignation to the trade ministry citing ill health. Somehow he'd escape the Werewolves. He'd camp on her doorstep until she accepted him.

There was a slight rustle and thump in the bushes near him. He went over to investigate and found only pebbles. When he returned to the bench a figure sat huddled in a large cape. He nodded and sat back down. Then Hartmuth turned back to look.

Those eyes. Cerulean blue pools so deep he started to lose himself again and the years fell away. There was no doubt.

For a moment he was as shy and awkward as when they'd first touched. A stuttering, gangling eighteen-year-old.

Wrinkles webbed in a fine pattern from the corners of her eyes. Dark hollows lay under them and her pale skin glowed translucently in the dim streetlight. Exactly how he remembered: pearl-like and shining. A hooded cape covered all but her eyes and prominent cheekbones. And she was still beautiful.

His plastic surgery hadn't fooled her, he knew. She would

notice the deep lines etched in his face and the crepey folds in his neck. And his hair, once black, had turned completely white.

She searched his face, then spoke quietly. "You look different, Helmut."

No one had called him Helmut in fifty years.

"Your face changed but your eyes are the same. I could tell it was you."

"Sarah," he breathed, hypnotized again by her eyes. "I've l-looked for you."

"You lied, Helmut, you deported my parents." She lapsed into the jumble of French and German they'd spoken. "They were dead and you knew all the time."

He'd expected anything but this. In his dreams she was as eager as he. He realized she was waiting for him to say something.

"W-we d-deported everyone then. I found out later that they were gone but I s-saved you. I kept looking for you after the war, but it was always a d-dead end, because I'd erased your r-records myself." He reached for her hands.

She pulled away and shook her head. "Is that all you can say?"

"You're the only one," he said softly, reaching again for her hands. "*Ja*, I'll never let you g-go again, n-never." His voice shook.

"You ruined my life," she said hoarsely. "I stayed here. Saw 'Nazi whore' written in everyone's eyes. Fifteen years old and I gave birth on a wooden floor while the concierge used metal ice tongs as forceps to pull our bastard out. At Liberation, they threw us in the street. The mob tried to lynch me while I clutched the baby and they screamed, '*Boche* bastard.' Even Lili."

She paused and took a deep breath. "Of all the collabos, I was the one they hated the most, even though I'd shared your food with them."

Her eyes glittered in the dim glow of a far-off streetlight. "I stood on a statue's pedestal for eighteen hours. They tarred my forehead with a swastika. Jeering, they asked me how I could sleep with a Nazi while my family burned in the Auschwitz ovens."

He shook his head in disbelief. "We had a baby? What happened?" he rasped in pain.

"The baby died when my breast milk dried up. You know, Helmut, I've had so many reasons to hate you it's hard to pick the crucial one. After Liberation, I hid in a freezing farm cellar and fought with the hogs for their food because collaborators with shaved heads had to hide. After a year, the swastika on my forehead finally began to heal. But for years, constant infections occurred. I had to leave Europe, go away. There was nothing here for me. Nothing. No one. The only ship leaving Marseilles was bound for Algeria, so I—once a strict kosher Jew—ended up cooking for *pieds-noirs*, what they call French colonials, in Oran. Fair and decent people. I became part of their large household. They left after the sixties coup d'état. Later, I married an Algerian with French blood who worked at Michelin. He understood me and we lived well, better than I ever imagined. But for me life held a hole never to be filled."

She slowly pulled the hood off until it draped in folds on her shoulders. Short, white bristly hair surrounded her head like a halo, highlighting the jagged, pinkish swastika scar on her forehead. It glowed in the dim light.

Hartmuth gasped.

Her voice wobbled when she spoke again. "I never really liked men to touch me, after you and after the baby. At first, it was hard even with my husband. He was a good, patient man and put up with me until I was ready. My insides had been butchered with those tongs, I couldn't have children."

Hartmuth listened in anguish. He took her hand and caressed it but she was oblivious, determined to finish.

"Algeria changed, I'd grown no roots there. But now I had papers, a little money. After my poor husband died this year, I felt so lonely that I returned to France. In Paris, at least I felt that any ghosts would be ghosts I knew. I wanted to live in the Marais again, the only home I knew. I could walk by my parents' apartment every day, even if another generation born after the war lived there. But it's so expensive here. With my references I found a job. I found out what happened to my family. I found out what you did to the tenants in our building."

Hartmuth stammered, "A-l-ll I c-could do was save your life and love you, I couldn't save the others, we had to f-follow orders, it was war. I was eighteen and you were the most beautiful being that I had ever t-touched. I wrote poetry after I'd see you. Dreams swam in my head. I wanted to take you to live in Hamburg."

"You've living in the past," she said.

He took her face in his hands. "I love you, Sarah."

She turned her head away for the first time. How could he make her feel like that again? That longing! She almost reached out to him but her parents' faces floated in front of her. She shook her head. "Your mind is in a past we never had."

"You don't have to speak, I know your heart. You feel guilty that you still love the enemy," he said. "What we have doesn't recognize borders or religion."

"Rooting in the dirt?" she said. "Eating like pigs while others starved? Hiding in the catacombs, always hiding, afraid to be seen . . . what was that?"

He hung his head. "I never wanted you to have pain, n-never. Even when there was no hope that you were still alive, you haunted me."

Her voice quavered. "I want to kill you, I planned to do it but"—she put her head down, defeated—"I can't."

"Sarah, can you f-ff-orgive me?" Hartmuth sobbed, his head in his hands. When he finally looked up, she was gone. He had never felt more alone.

SARAH BOLTED HER GARRET door and curled up on the bed. Several hours were left until her shift began the next morning. She clutched the spot where her yellow star had been and tried not to remember. Tried to forget but she couldn't.

It was 1942, the stickiest and most humid day recorded in a September for thirty years. Not a breath of air stirred. School, already started and with compositions due, had settled into a tedious routine. As routine as the Nazi Occupation allowed. Only she and Lili Stein wore yellow stars embroidered on their school smocks.

"Want to see something?" Lili, plain and pigeon-toed, asked her after school.

Surprised that a sixteen-year-old would deign to notice her, she'd nodded eagerly and followed. At fourteen, she felt proud that an older girl wanted her company. Cool air wafted from darkened courtyards as they passed quiet rue Payenne. Lace curtains hung lifelessly from windows normally shuttered against the heat.

At the Square Georges-Cain they sat on benches in the shade of plane trees, by the Roman pillars. No one was out, it was too hot. There was no petrol for cars and horse carts clomped over cobblestones in the distance. Fetid, dense air clung over the Seine in a wide band.

They took off their white pinafores and dipped them in the urnlike fountain. Giggling, they swabbed their sweaty necks and faces with cool, clear cistern water. Lili sat back, her small eyes full of concern.

"Something fell out of your satchel before mathematics," Lili said. "But I picked it up so no one would see it."

She pulled a almond-shaped *calisson*, a speciality of Aix-en-Provence, from her pocket.

Sarah stirred guiltily.

"Where'd this come from?" Lili asked.

"Look, Lili," Sarah said.

"Stop." Lili interrupted her. "Don't tell me because then I'd have to turn you in. I might have to do that anyway, Sarah Strauss!"

Sarah pulled a box out of her satchel and thrust it into Lili's palm.

Lili squealed in delight, "I can't believe it." She opened the box and popped a sweet in her mouth, moaning. "Luscious!" Savoring the taste, she grabbed some more. "The pink ones taste the best."

Sarah let Lili finish the sweets in the Provençal metal box painted with fruit and vines. Their legs dangled in the cool, bubbling water. Dragonflies buzzed in the green hedge. Everything felt smooth, peaceful—as if the war wasn't happening.

Lili's eyes narrowed. "What else do you have?"

"I can get more if you keep this between us," Sarah said. "Are you ready to leave Paris if Madame Pagnol finds a way to help us escape to the unoccupied zone?"

"Of course, I'm waiting for her to give the word, she said it might happen next week," Lili confided. "Madame told me trains are still running down south but you have to hike over the mountains to get to the free zone. Village scouts will take you but they want a lot of this." Lili rubbed her fingertips together and gave her a knowing look.

"Money?" Sarah asked naively.

"Of course, or jewelry, maybe even food," Lili said.

Sarah tugged her satchel nervously. She had never traveled outside of the Marais, let alone Paris. "Will we go together?"

"Two yellow stars at once? Hard to say." Lili eyed her. "Bring more of these. I need to keep the welcome warm with my concierge."

"But that might draw attention." Uneasy, Sarah shook her head. "I don't want that."

"You'll get Gestapo attention, Sarah Strauss, if I can't shut her up!"

The next day at school, their teacher, Madame Pagnol, informed them that an escape opportunity might occur at a moment's notice. So for several weeks after school, they met at the Square Georges-Cain to discuss plans.

Lili's identity card, with the J for Jewish, had been issued on her sixteenth birthday, as was the custom in France. Sarah knew if Lili claimed ration coupons, the Nazis would demand her identity card and then ship her directly to Drancy prison. She also realized Lili subsisted on whatever food she shared with her.

Every night Helmut reassured Sarah that he had checked the holding camps for her parents. He promised to find them and do his best to get them food. But he was so generous, she felt guilty. Guilty in taking the food even though she fed Lili and others in her old building.

Most of the time she succeeded in ignoring her warring emotions—her guilt versus her growing feelings for him. She didn't like to admit to herself how handsome he looked, his dark eyes glowing in the candle-lit cavern, like those of film stars she'd seen in her older sister's cinema magazines before the war. She told herself he'd understand when she escaped. As a Jew, it was her duty to escape.

Most of Helmut's food was quite exotic, especially for Jews who were raised kosher. She didn't care much for the foie gras in the Fauchon tins.

"My concierge says Fauchon is the fanciest food store in Paris," Lili said one day, munching eagerly. "The rabbi will excuse us for eating food not kosher, won't he?"

She heard doubt in Lili's voice for the first time. "There's not much choice. Anyway, it's goose liver, not pork."

Lili had looked away but not before Sarah saw relief on her face.

That night another roundup occurred in the Marais. Bottle green open-backed buses rumbled through the dark streets, full of Jews clutching crying babies and suitcases. She and Lili grew nervous. Every day it became more dangerous to walk on the street with a yellow star.

An unusual orange dusk had painted the sky, she remembered, in late October. One afternoon after Sarah had said goodbye to Lili she returned to the catacomb. She had always liked coming back to its dark, cool safety. She had even discovered another exit to the Square Georges-Cain and some large marble busts poking through the dirt. One looked like the picture of Caesar Augustus Madame Pagnol had pointed out in their history book. Like the bust they'd seen on a class field trip to the park when Madame took their photo.

Behind a wooden post, she heard crackling and looked up. Lili stood, wedged in a niche littered with femur bones. "Who are you informing on?" she said matter-of-factly, her mouth half-full of nougat.

Sarah stood bolt upright in surprise, bumping her head on the earthen ceiling. "How did you get in here?"

Lili ignored her question. "You must be an informer to get this food. Come on, I won't say anything." She paused. "You better be careful, you don't look so thin anymore."

"How did you get in here?"

"I've followed you for days, silly. You're not very observant," Lili said, crawling through the dirt. "Nice and cool in here."

"You followed me—why?" Then Sarah added it up. "Lili, don't be greedy. I share with others. You get enough."

"My concierge is greedy. Another family moved into my apartment," Lili said, picking at stones embedded in the dirt wall. "If I don't give her more I can't stay with her."

Sarah registered the dark shadows under Lili's eyes, her gaunt cheeks, and the patched soles of her shoes. "I'll try to get more. The trains will be running again soon. We'll escape!"

Lili stared at her. "Who do you inform on?"

"No one! A soldier trades with me," Sarah said defensively.

"What kind of soldier? What do you do for him?"

"What do you care, Lili? Thanks to me you're eating." She tried not to feel ashamed. "Leave it at that."

Some clods of dirt fell. Panic-stricken, she saw Helmut descend, blocking the weak light. Lili began screaming and backed into the wall. A black-uniformed Helmut smiled quizzically, staring from one to the other. Then he gently put his hand over Lili's mouth, sat her down, and beckoned to Sarah with his finger.

"It's all right, Lili, he won't hurt you," she mumbled.

Lili's terror-stricken expression alternated between accusing glances and a dawning recognition of why this Nazi was visiting Sarah. Helmut pulled some fancy tinned salmon out of his pocket and put it in Lili's hands.

"*Ja, ja*, take it, *s'il vous plaît*," and he put his finger over his mouth. "Shhh . . . *ça va?*"

His eyes narrowed. Lili's blotchy red face registered both hunger and fear. She opened her fists and gingerly took the tins of salmon without touching his fingers.

He shrugged. "Sarah," he said, putting his arm around her waist. "*Ja*, your guest has few manners."

Her cheeks were on fire. Lili looked jealously at the two of them. She realized Lili viewed them as lovers.

"Tell him thank you and leave quietly," Sarah said, averting her eyes from Lili's face.

"*Merci*," came out of Lili's mouth in a high-pitched squeak. She quickly scrambled up the ladder rungs.

Helmut asked, "Who is she?"

Sarah rolled her eyes. "Just my schoolmate, silly and stupid, she wears a yellow star. Don't worry." She pushed Lili's expression out of her mind.

Helmut looked at his watch. "I just came to say I've something to pick up then I'll be back." He'd traded his shift because he hated leaving her alone at night.

He pulled out a string of oily bratwurst from his SS kit bag and winked. "Some butcher in Hanover's contribution to the war effort."

Later he returned with duck terrine marbled in aspic and herbs. They ate while candle wax dripped lazily across the tea box. She tutored him in French after they ate, as she usually did. Her large wool sweater fell off her shoulders as she corrected his verb conjugations with a thick pencil.

"*Très bien*, Helmut, good work." She smiled. "Bravo."

He set the notebook down and pulled her toward him. Unbuttoning his uniform with one hand, he spread the jacket down as a pillow over the dense earth. She grew alarmed and gripped her fingers in the dirt. She'd had no brothers, never even seen her own father without his shirt. Taut muscles spread above Helmut's lean chest, his skin glistened.

Torn between gratitude and fear, she was paralyzed. Wasn't he looking for her parents? Giving her food? The Nazis who'd supervised the police roundups in her neighborhood hadn't been like him. Helmut was always so funny and generous with food. Under the flickering candlelight he laid her down and her black hair tangled in the storm trooper insignia glinting off his jacket. She went rigid.

She shook her head. "*Non*, Helmut."

Tracing her features with his finger, he cupped her face in his other hand. As he opened his mouth to speak, she winced. She wanted him to stop.

"Don't worry, Sarah, I won't h-hurt you." He drew close, rubbing her pearl white cheek with his.

She inhaled his smoky scent as he burrowed his face in her neck. He gently brushed the side of her neck with his lips, his kisses went down the front of her throat.

Tears welled in her eyes. Why was he doing this? His lips trailed down her navel and waves of heat passed through her. He kissed under her nipple and up the side of her breast, all the time caressing her face. For a long time he stroked the hollows of her cheeks and kissed behind her ears and her eyes, just holding her. She moaned. Now she didn't want him to stop. Finally their shadows entwined and rocked back and forth on the cavern walls of the old Roman catacomb.

On her way to school the next morning, she thought everyone would notice the straining seams of her school uniform. Too much rich food. But they only noticed the star. She entered the "synagogue," the last Métro car and the only one Jews were allowed to ride in, feeling so tired. She'd only fallen asleep at dawn when Helmut left. In her classroom there was a new teacher and an empty desk. Madame Pagnol was gone. So was Lili.

TUESDAY

AIMÉE WOKE UP AND pulled on a crumpled T-shirt full of Yves's musky smell. He'd gone. Part of her felt angry with herself for jumping in his bed last night. And part of her purred contentedly. A year had passed since Bertrand, her hacker boyfriend, had waffled on his commitment and moved to Silicon Valley.

She and Yves had spent a lot of time in the tub again. Things had only gotten better. *La relation fluide* seemed a good term to describe their involvement. She decided to mop up the tiled bathroom.

Aimée paused to savor the previous night's pleasure. Yellow sunlight streamed from the street-level windows above the bed. Mentally and physically they'd moved in rhythm, which so seldom happened to her. Something felt right about him. Except for his Nazi affiliations.

There was no way to get around that.

Her bare leg scraped something and she reached to move it. Her state-of-the-art tape recorder, out of its plastic bag, came back in her hand.

How long had this been here? She'd been concentrating on the videos and had forgotten this the other night. She must have been drunker than she'd thought. Had Yves noticed? She clicked the play button and the tape started. The tape had definitely been rewound to the beginning.

Her heart sank. Yves must know she wasn't who she pretended to be. Had he planned on confronting her but got carried away? Had he told the others? If he'd known, why hadn't he told her? What an idiot I am, she thought.

Disgusted with herself, she bolted from the bed and pulled on her black jeans and jacket. Whatever game he'd been playing, she quit. Perhaps he'd been about to expose her tape recorder and illustrate his loyalty. Lili's mutilated forehead swam before her eyes. All the way to her office, she wondered how she could have been so wrong.

RENÉ FOLDED THE CORNER of the page and slammed the paperback down as Aimée entered the office.

"I've got a bank promissory note from Eurocom. Twenty thousand francs," he said.

Aimée hugged him. *"Superbe!"* She picked up the book, *The Second Sex* by Simone de Beauvoir, flipping the pages. "You read too much, René."

"Nom de Dieu!" René covered his eyes with his short arms. "This is a classic, Aimée. You might pick up some pointers."

"Pointers?" She snorted. "I thought I got lucky last night. Turns out I couldn't have been more wrong."

She chewed her Nicorette gum furiously. "Why don't you badger our overdue Lyon account? Explain it to that nice director, face to face. It would be hard to throw you out of the office," she said.

"Are you trying to get rid of me?" René said.

She threw his Citroën keys at him. "Go on. You love to drive. Just don't kill yourself. And while you're there, get an advance out of him."

He grinned. On his way out, he looked back over his shoulder. "Where's your protection?"

She patted the pistol bulging in her silk pants pocket. "Here."

BY 3:00 P.M., Aimée had obtained permission from Abraham Stein and the other tenants, a clearance from the MCCHB (Marais Citizens' Council of Historic Buildings), a writ of permission from the 4th Arrondissement Supplemental Housing Federation, and the required demolition permit to expose the wooden staircase. Having a search warrant from Morbier certainly had expedited the process. He was grumbling because he couldn't smoke. Luminol was highly flammable.

"Where the hell is that crowbar, Leduc?" he said.

But she couldn't hear. Inside the tent in the darkened courtyard of the Steins' apartment on rue des Rosiers, Aimée and Serge, the middle-aged, bearded criminologist, were busy. Wearing fluorescent Day-Glo jumpsuits to avoid the chemical's being absorbed into their skin, they sprayed Luminol on the old oak boards exposed in the courtyard by the sink. Luminol showed blood and its traces on any porous surface. Despite whatever had been painted or scrubbed over it, traces of blood would remain.

"An unsolved homicide fifty years ago and you think you'll find the murderer's footprints?" Serge's voice was muffled through his mask. "Seven years is the outside edge, maximum has been shown at eleven years. Why do you think it'll show traces?"

"If it's worked on a seven-year-old stain, why couldn't it work on a fifty-year-old one as well?" she said. "No one has ever proved it wouldn't."

Her arguments for using Luminol had been predicated on that assumption. But now she wondered if it would work. And what if it didn't?

She went outside the tent to look for Morbier and came face to face with a camera crew. Immediately, the bright lights glared on her.

Reporters shouted, "Are you with the Brigade Criminelle? What do you hope to uncover?"

Her jumpsuit was already causing her to sweat as if she was in a sauna. The lights made it worse.

"Official crime recovery scene. Press is not allowed," she said. She whistled to a blue-uniformed *flic*, who approached the camera crew.

She hadn't counted on this Luminol test to go public. Wouldn't the killer become suspicious if there was a connection between the two murders?

Her silence would be the killer's objective. She filed that disturbing thought away. If this caused the rat to surface, all the better, she told herself.

Back inside the tent, she put on another pair of booties to avoid contamination, and began taping everything with a low-light-sensor camera. Serge sprayed Luminol on the cobblestones in the courtyard and on the old concrete around the sink to see if anything would show. He continued spraying as he backed away from the old boards in the light well and slowly retreated up the stairs. He saturated the original wood steps, all the way along the wooden planks that stretched to the Steins' door.

He yelled down at Aimée, "Get Morbier. If it's gonna work, and I said IF, there should be a light show in three minutes."

Aimée knew the wood should show blood traces in cracks or fissures and hoped that the concrete and stones over it had protected and preserved any remaining evidence. Well, they would find out. After five years, the blood couldn't be typed, but that didn't matter to her. That wasn't what she was looking for.

Morbier entered the tent, letting in a wide slice of light.

"Hurry up," Serge shouted, pausing at the Steins' door. He couldn't move until the Luminol took.

If it did.

"Secure the panel from the outside," Morbier shouted as he fumbled blindly with his Day-Glo booties.

Inside the tent it was pitch dark.

"Jesus, Leduc, this had better work. My ass is in a harness here. We've blocked off half the street, relocated these tenants courtesy of the Parisian taxpayers, who are as tight as ticks, there's some idiot from the 4th arrondissement who thinks we're making a science-fiction movie and tells the press. On top of all that, Agronski, some sharp-eyed inspector from Brigade Criminelle, came because he told me he 'just loves Luminol.' "

"Keep going, Morbier, I'm getting everything you say on tape even if I can't see you," Aimée told him.

He was fuming now. "Leduc, I told you . . . Aaah!"

Aimée shone the portable LumaLite as she and Serge chorused, "Fireworks!"

The Luminol glowed, displaying a fluorescent scene of fifty-year-old carnage.

"Oh my God," she said into the camera, which was catching every streak and splatter of blood. Javel had been right. Blood was everywhere. Arcs sprayed up the light well and a jagged stream snaked to the drain and disappeared. Luminol lasted less than a minute but she captured it all on video.

"It's unbelievable!" Serge inched his way down the stairs beside the trail of bloody footprints. "Blood preserved under concrete and stone for fifty years. I'll get into police bulletins all over the world!" he said.

"Let's spray the staircase again," she said grimly.

She prepared her ruler and laid it quickly next to a pair of footprints that fluorescently appeared. The prints led up the stairs and measured nine centimeters. Something else of a muted color was mixed in with the blood.

"Tissue or organ probably; this area has been remarkably protected," Serge said.

She looked up at Lili's dirty windowpane above them. Aimée figured it had been quick, brutal, and more messy than even the Luminol showed. Her fast take, from the angle of the arc of the blood spray, indicated an attack from above the victim. Footprints walked out of the light well. They resembled a solid shoe, like boots with splayed heels, worn on one edge as if the wearer was slightly pigeon-toed. The ball of the foot was more pronounced and they stopped at the troughlike concrete sink. Smudged bloodstains were on the chipped concrete. It was creepy to think that she'd walked over this. No one had lived in the concierge's rooms for years; now she realized why they'd been abandoned.

Morbier stood next to Aimée.

"Two tracks." She pointed the camera at a path of footprints. "A small person and a slightly larger one." She peered down at the sink, examining it with her magnifying glass. "The smaller ones must be Lili's but whose are the other ones?"

They stopped.

Another set of footprints led out from the light well to the sink and stopped.

Smeared blood and a fine spray of droplets in the sink had been absorbed by the porous stones and concrete. She peered at the cracked porcelain knobs on the faucet.

"Little bit here, when he turned the water on. He even had time to wash his shoes before going into the street," she said. "Or were they boots?"

She felt like she was right next to the murderer. Agonizingly close, but so far away. Fifty years too far. What could she prove?

HOURS LATER, when the criminologist had finished his job and Inspector Agronski was so suitably impressed that he invited Morbier to supper, Aimée still couldn't leave.

She kept retracing the area where the footsteps had appeared next to the smaller ones, trying to figure out what the murderer had been thinking. Then she carefully mounted the stairs.

She tried imagining herself as the scared sixteen-year-old Lili Stein. A young Jewish girl, her family gone, living alone and dependent on the concierge. A concierge who, according to Javel, had been dangerously involved in the black market.

"All recorded now, Leduc," Serge was saying. "I'm packed up, the plasterers are ready to come in, time to go." He tapped his heel impatiently. "This is union time we're talking about here, Leduc."

Aimée was still not satisfied. "I need one more look. I'll meet you on rue des Rosiers."

The plasterers, in white-caked coveralls, waited, grumbling, in the courtyard. The Steins' building was getting a reconstructive face-lift long overdue and major renovation, courtesy of the city of Paris and the 4th arrondissement. Records showed that the most recent construction had been done in 1795. She figured it would be that long again before another renovation.

She had the nagging feeling she was missing something, something that was crying out to her but she couldn't get it. The high-pitched "beep beep beep" of the plasterers' van was deafening as it backed into the courtyard and almost drove over her toe.

"Hey, watch out!" Frustrated, she kicked at the bumper, pounding the metal.

That's when she realized the one place she hadn't looked. The one place a killer would pause, maybe grip the sink, to wash his hands. Wash the blood off his hands.

She ran back into the courtyard and crawled under the sink. Sharp cobblestones dug into her sore shoulder, mildew assailed her nostrils. Shining her flashlight in every crevice and knobby ridge, she strained to reach as far as she could, lying on her back. Then she saw it.

"Get your Luminol out again, Serge. Tent and cover the sink. See the very faint ridges of a fingerprint in the crack?" she said. "This fingerprint will shine up nicely when you've done your stuff. I've got him!"

RENÉ BUMPED THE CITROËN over the narrow gutter lining rue des Rosiers.

"I thought you were in Lyon," she said, surprised.

"Get in, Aimée," he said.

René's Citroën was customized for his short legs and arms, allowing him to clutch, shift, and zoom like any other speed demon in Paris. And did he ever. The car was adjustable, so Aimée could manipulate the levers to fold her five-foot, eight-inch frame into the marshmallowy interior.

"I got him, René, I knew the answer was here," she said. "Now I just have to figure out who he is or was." Her eyes shone brightly and her cheeks were flushed. "I took a Polaroid of the fingerprint. At the office I'll magnify and scan it into the computer."

"How does this involve Lili Stein?" René asked as they roared around the curb into another medieval one-way street.

"I'm working on that," she said. "I'll find it."

"You and Morbier are stars on the evening news. Not worried about undercover anymore, Leduc?" he said.

"The press weren't there at my invitation, René, I tried to stay away from the cameras."

"Cut the defensiveness, Aimée. I saw your feet in those fluorescent little booties on France 2," he said. "That Luminol might illuminate things you hadn't bargained on. Stay at my place."

She rubbed her hands at the memory of Herve Vitold's scissor-like grip.

"When was the last time you cleaned it up? I'm not a snob, René, but certain standards of hygiene need to be maintained."

"Haven't you considered someone doesn't want this Pandora's box opened?"

Vitold had made that loud and clear.

"That's why it has to be opened," she said.

Several horns blared as his Citroën swerved into the oncoming lane of traffic. Grudgingly, she took the spare key to his flat.

René let her off on the corner of rue de Rivoli. "Miles Davis is upstairs." She bounded up the stairs of her office building, anxious to log into FRAPOL 1, the police system, and search for a match with the Luminol fingerprint.

The muffled bark of Miles Davis didn't sound right as she ran up the last flight of stairs. And the frosted-glass door of her office stood slightly ajar, so she couldn't put her uneasy feeling down to intuition. René would never leave the door like that. Someone had been inside and today wasn't the cleaner's day. Instead of entering, she kept on climbing to the next flight. Editions Photogravure Lapousse had its door open and she could hear the click of computer keys.

"*Bonjour, ça va?* Permit me," she said to the older woman with headphones typing data entry who nodded distractedly and then ignored her.

Aimée walked past her and opened the double windowed doors to the street. She climbed over the black wrought-iron balcony guard, gripping the thick rail, and was greeted by a dusky sunset over the Louvre and the Seine beyond. It was almost enough to sweep away the anticipation of finding out who was in her office.

The moon dangled over the distant Tour Eiffel and the traffic hummed below her. Carefully, she wedged her toe into a crack in the limestone facade and rested her boot heel on the metal sign support. Four stories above the rue du Louvre, she slowly climbed down the first E of the LEDUC DETECTIVE sign to peer into her office window for an intruder.

From the slightly open window, a smell of fresh paint hit her.

Very fresh. She knew René wouldn't schedule the office to be painted and forget to tell her. She slipped her Glock 9-mm from the strap around her leg.

As she molded her body to the semicircular curve of the window, she hesitated. She had the firearms permit but not the license to carry her Glock. Drawing an unlicensed gun on anybody spelled trouble. French firearm laws, still enforced by the Napoleonic code, didn't allow her the right to bear arms. Even in self-defense or equal-force situations. If the *flics* were inside, she'd really be in trouble. Her PI license would be revoked immediately, if Herve Vitold of the Brigade d'Intervention hadn't already done that.

She didn't feel like bursting into her office when the door had been left ajar, without any kind of backup. She pulled her cell phone out and punched in her office number. The phone rang right below her toehold, inside the window.

As the answering machine came on, she waited, then shouted, "You're in my crosshairs, *salope*. I'm at the window directly opposite."

Heavy footsteps beat below her, then the office door slammed shut. This is going to be easy, Aimée thought, I'll just wait and see who comes out of the building.

Five long minutes later, no one had emerged from the entrance. Of course, she'd realized she'd told them they were being watched from across the street. Only an idiot would exit from the front. Now she'd have to go in, not knowing if they'd really left or not. She steadied her gun. The *flics* wouldn't act like that. At least, she didn't think they would.

As she slid down and perched on the rusted tin drain she heard an ominous creak below her and grabbed the big D. Just in time, too. The drain came loose and went crashing down four stories to the street. Luckily, no one was on the pavement below. By the time she'd jimmied the window lock and fallen into her office, it was empty.

Papers and files were strewn everywhere. Her desk drawers had been dumped upside down, every nook and cranny searched. A professional job by the look of it, she thought. She kept her gun drawn as she slowly opened the closet. Miles Davis tumbled out, ecstatic to see her. Cautiously, she searched her office to make sure no one was there.

She inched into the hallway. A chill breeze blew from the open window facing a shadowy passage between prewar boxlike apartments. She heard the creaking of the rusty fire escape swinging below her. Her intruder had probably made it to the Métro station by now. Dusting herself off, she took a swig of mineral water and called Martine.

"Someone's ransacked my office!" she said. "Can you fax those sheets again?"

"Aimée, be careful, I'm serious," Martine said, all in one breath. "Give me the exclusive on this one, please? With this story I'd get into editorials and off my back with Gilles."

"You sleep with Gilles to keep your job?" Aimée couldn't keep the surprise out of her voice. "Of course, this story is yours." She paused. "But no print yet, nothing. I've got to document everything airtight. Do we have an understanding?"

"*D'accord,*" Martine spoke slowly. "It's not that bad with Gilles, we have an arrangement. I know I'm good at what I do but I've never been like you, Aimée. You don't need a man."

"I wouldn't call screwing the neo-Nazi hunk I met at an LBN meeting a smart relationship choice. That's a whole other story."

"Probably spices up his performance," Martine giggled. "I'm still checking one name."

A ring and click signaled a fax coming in. "Is this from you, Martine?"

"Yes. Don't forget—this is my story," Martine said.

The smell of paint was stronger now and came from near the fax machine. Aimée walked around her office partition to confront a terrifying image. A black swastika was painted on the wall, angled and off center like the one incised in Lili's forehead. Next to it were three words in dripping red paint:

YOUR TURN NEXT!

WEDNESDAY

AIMÉE PERCHED ON THE thick black velvet sofa in her red suit, the one she could afford to pick up from the dry cleaner's. She had begrudgingly slipped a few hundred franc notes to the hotel clerk. Plush hotels rated high bribes; it was the cost of doing business.

"Mademoiselle Leduc?" came a deep voice in heavily accented French. "You wish to have a word with me?"

Hartmuth Griffe gave a modified bow, and looked expectantly into her face. He fit perfectly in the Pavillion de la Reine lounge among the discreet clink of crystal and silver. Suave, tan, and very handsome. Curt Jurgens and Klaus Kinski, move over, she thought.

"Herr Griffe, please sit down. I know you have a long day ahead of you. Would you care for coffee?" Aimée spread her arms, indicating the plush sofa.

"Actually, I'm running late," he said, glancing at her café au lait on the table and his watch at the same time.

"Just a quick one. I know you're extremely busy." Aimée caught the waiter's eye and pointed at her cup. She gestured towards a deep burgundy leather armchair. "Please."

"Only for a few moments then," he said. "Of what do you wish to speak?"

She wanted to stall him until he got his coffee.

Loudly she demanded, "Quickly! For the monsieur, *s'il vous plaît!*"

Immediately, a café au lait in a Limoges cup and a bountiful fruit tray appeared.

"Compliments of the hotel," the manager said, almost scraping his chin on the table with a low bow.

"*Merci*," Hartmuth said, reaching for his cup.

She tried not to look at his hands. Tried not to stare at the pigskin leather gloves he wore. Most of all, she tried to hide her disappointment at not being able to lift his fingerprints. She decided to get to the point.

"Did you know Lili Stein?"

"Excuse me, who?" Hartmuth Griffe stared at her.

She noticed the creamy foam in his cup trembled slightly.

"Lili Stein, a Jewish woman maybe a few years younger than you." She paused.

"No." He shook his head. "I'm in Paris for the trade summit. I know no one here."

She sipped, watching his eyes as they met hers. His stare had grown glassy and removed.

"She was murdered near this hotel," Aimée said, slowly setting her cup down on the table. "Strangled. A swastika was carved in her forehead."

"I'm afraid I don't know that n-name," he said. He blinked several times.

She heard the stutter and saw his mouth quiver at the effort to stop it.

"Her family said she'd been very scared before it happened. I think she knew secrets." Aimée watched him. "But you've been to Paris before, maybe you met her then, *non*?"

It was a long shot but worth a try.

"You've mistaken me for someone else. This is my first time in Paris." He stood up quickly.

Aimée stood up also. "Here is my card. Odd bits and pieces lodged in one's memory tend to emerge after conversations like this. Call me any time. One last question. Why are you listed as dead in the Battle of Stalingrad, Herr Griffe?"

He looked truly surprised.

"Ask the war office. All I remember is seeing bodies stacked like cordwood in the snow. Mounds of them. Frozen together. Kilometers of them, as far as the Russian horizon."

Then Hartmuth stiffened like a rod, as if he remembered where he was.

"But go ahead, Mademoiselle Leduc, and pinch me, I'm real. If you'll excuse me." He clicked his heels and was gone.

She slumped on the velvet sofa. Did he wear those gloves to avoid leaving fingerprints? All she knew was that something was bottled up inside him. Tight and close to explosion.

Aimée finished the fruit platter; it would be a shame to waste raspberries in November. But she'd learned at least one thing. He was either an incredible liar or a mistake had been made. She opted for the former. After all, he was a diplomat and a politician.

HORDES OF protesters chanting, "Not again, not again!" blocked her way to the Métro. Buses lined narrow rue des Francs Bourgeois, the air thick with diesel fumes and high tempers. Aimée wished she could get past the seventeenth-century walls, high and solid, hemming her and passersby in to the sidewalk.

Police encased in black Kevlar riot gear squatted between the Zionist youth and skinheads screaming, "France for the French." A light drizzle beaded in crystalline drops on the clear bulletproof shields of the police, who crouched like praying mantises.

Ahead, a polished black Mercedes limousine, stuck in the Hôtel Pavillion de la Reine courtyard, caught Aimée's eye. The driver gestured towards the narrow street, arguing with a riot-squad member. The smoked window rolled down and Aimée saw a veined hand stretch out.

"Phillipe, please, I want to walk," came the unmistakable voice. She remembered the last time she had heard it—on the radio after she discovered Lili Stein's body.

The highly waxed door opened and Minister Cazaux, the probable next prime minister of France, emerged into the stalled traffic. The plainclothes guards rushing to surround his tall, bony figure caught the crowd's attention.

"*S'il vous plaît, Monsieur le Ministre*, these conditions—" a body-guard began.

"Since when can't a government servant walk among the people?" Cazaux grinned. "With the treaty about to be signed, I need every chance to hear their concerns." He winked at the small crowd around the car, his charm melting many of them into smiles as he moved among them shaking hands, totally at ease with the situation.

He smiled directly at Aimée, who'd become awkwardly wedged among the hotel staff. He appeared younger than he did in the media but she was surprised at his heavy makeup. "Bonjour, Mademoiselle. I hope you will support our party's platform!"

Cazaux grasped her hands in his warm ones, as she winced at the sudden pressure.

"*Je m'excuse.*" He pulled back, glancing at her hand.

His charm was laserlike. Once appointed he would be prime minister for five years.

"*Monsieur le Ministre,*" she said, stifling a smile, "you promote social reform, but your party sanctions this racist treaty. Can you explain this contradiction?"

Cazaux nodded and paused. "Mademoiselle, you've made a good point." He turned to the crowd, assorted skinheads, shoppers, and young Zionists. "If there was another way to reduce our crippling 12.8 percent unemployment, I'd be the first one to do it. Right now, France has to get back on its feet, reenter the global market, and nothing is more important than that."

Many in the crowd nodded, but the young Zionists chanted, "No more camps!"

The minister approached them. "Simple answers to immigration don't exist; I wish they did."

He embraced a squealing infant shoved at him by a perspiring mother. With all the time in the world, he rocked the young baby like a practiced grandfather. Then he kissed the cooing baby on both cheeks, gently handing it back to the beaming mother. "Discussion is the foundation of our republic." He smiled at the Zionists. "Bring your concerns to my office."

Cazaux was good, she had to admit. He worked the crowd well. Several photographers caught him in earnest discussion with a Zionist youth. By the time the traffic jam broke up, even the Zionists were almost subdued.

His guards signaled to him, then Cazaux waved, climbed in the limo, and shot down the street. The whole incident had taken less than fifteen minutes, she realized. His adept handling of potential violence triggered her unease. He'd manipulated the volatile situation almost as if he'd planned it. When did I get so cynical, she wondered.

Ahead of her stood an old man in a lopsided blue beret. "Just like the old days. Maybe they'll do it right this time," he muttered. His face was contorted by hate.

"There's blacks and Arabs everywhere," he continued. "My war pension is half what the blacks get. Noisy all night and they can't even speak French."

She turned away and stared straight into the eyes of Leif, the lederhosened skinhead from LBN. He stood by the entrance of a dingy *hôtel particulier*, watching her. Even in a red suit with makeup and heels instead of leather, black lipstick, and chains, she wasn't going to wait and see if he recognized her.

When she looked again, he was gone. Stale sweat and the smell of damp wool surrounded her. She froze when she saw his bristly mohawk appear over the old man's shoulder.

"*Salopes!*" the old man swore into the jostling crowd, Aimée wasn't sure at whom.

She was scared. In this narrow, jammed street, she had nowhere to go. She crouched behind the old man, pulled her red jacket off, and stuck a brown ski cap from her bag over her hair. She shivered in a cream silk top in the now steady drizzle, put on heavy black-framed glasses, and melted into the crowd as best she could.

"They laid my son off, but he doesn't get the fat welfare check those blacks get for nothing," the old man shouted.

Aimée felt groping fingers under her blouse, but she couldn't see who they belonged to. Leaning down, she opened her mouth and bit as hard as she could. Someone yelped loudly in pain and the crowd scattered in fear. Aimée darted and elbowed her way through the grumbling crowd. She didn't stop until she had reached the Métro, where she shoved her pass in the turnstile and ran to the nearest platform. Gusts of hot air shot from the tiled vents as each train pulled in and out. She stood in front of them until her blouse had dried, she'd stopped shaking, and had come up with a plan.

AIMÉE WORKED IN HER apartment on her computer, accessing Thierry Rambuteau's credit-card activity, parking tickets, and even his passport. He drove a classic '59 Porsche, lived with his parents, and had dined the night before at Le Crépuscule on the Left Bank using his American Express card.

On the previous Wednesday morning, the day Lili was murdered, the card showed a gas purchase off the A2 highway near Antwerp, Belgium. That gave him plenty of time to drive into Paris by early evening. She scrolled through the rest and was about to give up, but just to be thorough she checked his passport activity. There it was. Entry into Istanbul, Turkey, a week ago Saturday and no record of return. But most countries didn't stamp your passport on departure. No wonder he had a tan, she thought, when she'd first seen him at LBN office. And a possible alibi.

She took a swig of bottled water and called Martine at *Le Figaro*.

Martine put her on hold briefly, then spoke into the phone. "Here's what I found. Like clockwork, there's a deposit every month into Thierry and Claude Rambuteau's joint account from DFU. That's the Deutsche Freiheit Union, the fascists who burn Turkish families out of their homes. Why are you investigating this guy? I'm just curious."

"He's a suspect in a Jewish woman's murder," Aimée replied.

"Let me guess," Martine yawned. "He's really a Jew."

Aimée choked and almost dropped her bottle of water. "That's an ironic angle I hadn't thought of."

Martine was awake now. "Really? I was just kidding; it would give him some excuse to be screwed up."

"Screwed up enough to strangle a woman and and carve a swastika into her head?" Aimée said.

"Oh God, Gilles told me about that, it's in his follow-up story for the Sunday evening edition. You think he did it?"

"Martine, this is between us. Not Gilles," Aimée said firmly. She tapped the name Claude Rambuteau into her computer as she talked. "Why would Thierry's father . . . ?"

"Wait a minute, Aimée. Who is his father?"

"According to Thierry's Amex application, his father is Claude Rambuteau," she said, pulling up the information from her screen and downloading it.

"Were you wondering why he would have a joint account with his son Thierry and receive DFU money?" Martine asked.

"Something along those lines," Aimée said. "I better go ask him."

RAIN SPLATTERED over the cobblestones as Aimée ran to number twelve. She rang the buzzer next to the faded name Rambuteau, adjusting her long wool skirt and tucking her spiky hair under a matching wool beret.

The outline of a smallish figure materialized, silhouetted in the frosted-glass door. A portly man, short with gray hair and dark glasses and dressed in a fashionable tracksuit, opened the door halfway.

"Yes?" He remained partly in the door's shadow.

"I'm Aimée Leduc, with Leduc Investigation," she said, handing him her card. "I'd like to speak with Thierry Rambuteau."

"Not here, he doesn't live here, you see," the man said. Already she'd caught him in a lie.

"Perhaps I could come in for a minute," she said evenly. Her beret was soaked.

"Is there a problem?" he said.

"Not really. I'm working on a case and—"

Here he interrupted her. "What is this about?"

"Lili Stein, an elderly Jewish woman, was murdered near here.

A local synagogue enlisted my services." She glanced inside the hallway. A black leather storm-trooper coat hung from the hall coatrack. "That's your son's coat, isn't it? Let me talk with him."

He shook his head. "He's not here now. I told you."

"I'd like to clear up a few points, Monsieur Rambuteau. You can help me." She edged closer to him. "I'm getting awfully wet and I promise I'll go away after we talk."

He shrugged. "A few minutes."

Shuffling ahead, he led her into an antiseptically clean windowed breakfast room. A long melamine-topped table held a place setting for one. Next to a sunflower-patterned plate, its matching cup and saucer, and an empty wineglass were vials of multicolored pills. Yellow roses wafted their scent from a bubbled glass vase by the window.

The man motioned for her to sit down on a couch by the window. He leaned forward and took off his dark glasses. From the kitchen she could hear the monotonous tick of a clock. Piles of papers and a cardboard box of yellowed press clippings littered the floor.

Aimée opened her damp backpack and took out a sopping note pad.

Embarrassed, she said, "My ink will run on this wet paper. Can I trouble you for some dry paper?"

Monsieur Rambuteau hesitated, then pointed. "On top of one of those piles should be a writing tablet. I was making a list."

"Merci." She reached for the nearest stack. On top was the empty tablet. She took it and a folder to write on.

He was nervously twisting the knuckle on his ring finger. "Are you investigating Les Blancs Nationaux group?" A note of anguish stuck in his voice.

Aimée replied calmly, "I'm exploring all possibilities."

He let out a big sigh and rested his palms on the spotless white table, facing Aimée. "My wife just passed away." He pointed to a silver-framed photo sitting atop a glass-front china cabinet. "I'm due at Père Lachaise; her funeral is today."

"I'm very sorry, Monsieur Rambuteau," she said.

In the photo, a woman with thin penciled eyebrows wearing shiny leather pants and a rhinestone-flecked sweater peered out from under a helmetlike bob of hair. Her eyes had a surprised look that Aimée attributed to a face-lift.

"Her things," he said, indicating the piles of paper.

"I know this isn't a good time, so I'll be brief," she said. "Did your son know Lili Stein?"

"My son gets carried away sometimes. Is that what this is about?" he said.

"I'll put it another way, Monsieur Rambuteau. Your home isn't far from the victim's deli on rue des Rosiers. Did Thierry know Lili Stein?"

"I don't know if he knew her or not. But I doubt it."

"Why do you say that?" Aimée said.

"He didn't make a habit of . . . er . . . let's say, having social contact with Jews," Monsieur Rambuteau said.

"Would he carry his feelings to an extreme?"

Startled, Monsieur Rambuteau looked away. "No. Never. I told you he can get carried away but that's all. My fault really; you see, I've encouraged him. Well, at the beginning I was happy to see him get involved in politics. A good cause."

Obviously, Aimée thought, Thierry's apple didn't fall far from the tree. She willed herself to speak in an even tone. "A good cause, in your opinion, includes Aryan supremacist groups?"

"I didn't say that." He cleared his throat. "At the beginning, Thierry and I talked about their ideology. There are some points in their program, whether one agrees or not, that make sense. I'm certainly not condoning violence but as far as I know, Thierry hasn't been involved with them recently. Filmmaking is his field."

"Would you say, Monsieur Rambuteau, that your son's upbringing was in a politically conservative vein?" she said.

He raised his eyebrows, then shrugged, "Let's say we served *sucre à la droite*, not *sucre à la gauche*."

He referred to white and brown sugar, the metaphor for right-wing conservatives and leftist socialists. She knew that in many households political leanings were identified by the kind of sugar sitting in sugar bowls.

"Did your wife hold these views?" she said.

"I'm not ashamed to say we held Maréchal Pétain and his Vichy government in the highest regard. You didn't live through a war. You can never understand how Le Maréchal aimed to untarnish the reputation of France," he said.

Aimée leaned forward. "Is that why Thierry receives funds from a German right-wing extremist group and you support Les Blancs Nationaux?"

His eyes narrowed. "You can't prove that."

"Proving that Les Blancs Nationaux are bankrolled by the DFU Aryan supremacists isn't too hard. And that's sure to bother people who still remember Germans as Nazis and *'boches.'* "

Monsieur Rambuteau's cheeks had become red and his breathing labored. He reached for the bottle of yellow pills on the table in front of him. He shook out three, poured a glass of water, and gulped both. His shallow breath came in short spurts.

Finally, he took a deep breath and folded his hands. "I'm a sick man," he said. "You'd better go." He rose with obvious effort, and walked her to the door. "My son couldn't hurt anyone," he said. In his small, tired eyes, Aimée saw pain.

"You haven't convinced me, Monsieur." She adjusted her beret and looked at him resolutely. "I'll be back."

He closed the door and Aimée walked out into the drizzling rain to the bus stop.

She would prove that Les Blancs Nationaux existed on neo-Nazi money with René's help on the computer. Twenty minutes later she stepped off the bus on Ile St. Louis near her flat and entered her neighborhood corner café. Chez Mathieu was inviting and much warmer than her apartment.

"*Bonjour*, Aimée." A short, stout man in a white apron playing a pinball machine in the corner greeted her. Bells clanged as the pinball hit the targets.

"*Ça va*, Ludovice? A café *crème*, please."

He nodded. The café was empty. "I've got bone shanks for your boy." He meant Miles Davis.

"*Merci*." Aimée smiled and chose a table by the fogged-up windows overlooking the Seine. She spread her papers to dry and took out her laptop, but the marble tabletop was sticky and she needed to put something over it. She pulled out some paper and realized she held Monsieur Rambuteau's tablet. And a folder, too, that she'd picked up by mistake. She opened it.

Lists of Nathalie Rambuteau's personal belongings filled two sheets. Well-thumbed film scripts and old theater programs lined the folder next to a sheaf of photocopies, one labeled "Last Will and Testament." Curious, Aimée opened it. On the top was a codicil, dated three months previously: "Suffering from a terminal illness, I, Nathalie Rambuteau, cannot in good conscience keep secret my son's origins. I cannot break the promise I made to my son's biological mother. Upon my death, I request that my son, Thierry Rambuteau, be informed of his real parentage."

Stapled to the back of it was a note in spidery writing: *S.S. letter with Notaire Maurice Barrault.* Shaken, she sat back. Who was Thierry's real mother?

"*Ça va?*" Ludovice asked as he set her *café* on the table.

"God, I don't know. Got a cigarette?"

"I thought you quit." He rubbed his wet hands across his apron and reached in his pocket.

"I did." She accepted a nonfiltered Gauloise and he lit it for her. As she inhaled deeply, the acrid smoke hit the back of her throat, then she felt the familiar jolt as it filled her lungs. She exhaled the smoke, savoring it.

Aimée gestured to the chair. He untied his apron, sat down, and lit a cigarette.

"Let me ask you something—" she began.

"Over a drink. I'll buy." He reached for a bottle of Pernod and two shot glasses and poured. "What's the question?"

The empty café was quiet except for the drizzling rain beating on the roof.

"Do you believe in ghosts?" Aimée asked. "Because I think I'm beginning to."

AIMÉE LEFT the café when the rain stopped and wearily entered her apartment. Before she could kick off her damp clothes her phone began ringing.

She answered. The nurse she'd slipped several hundred francs to inform her of any changes in Soli Hecht's condition spoke quickly.

"Soli Hecht came out of his coma fifteen minutes ago," she said.

"I'll be right over."

Quickly, she put on black stirrup pants and red high-tops, draped her Chanel scarf around her neck under her jean jacket, and ran down two marble flights of stairs. Her mobylette wobbled and bounced over the uneven cobbles on the quai. Rain-freshened air mingled with a faint sewer odor as she crossed the Seine. The perfume of Paris, her father had called it. She kept to small streets in the Marais. Outside l'Hôpital Ste. Catherine, she rammed her moped in a row with all the others and locked it.

Dead cigarette smell and muffled bells on a loudspeaker greeted her as she emerged on the hospital's fifth floor. Overflowing ashtrays littered the waiting area near a row of withering potted plants.

She strode over the scuffed linoleum toward room 525. Loud buzzers sounded as a team of nurses and doctors flew by her.

"*Attention!* Out of the way," yelled a medic, who wheeled a shock unit past them.

She followed him, feeling a terrible sense of foreboding. A doctor kneeled over an unconscious blue-uniformed policeman, sprawled on the linoleum.

Uneasy, she asked, "What's happened?"

"I'm not sure," the doctor said, feeling for a pulse.

She ran into room 525. Hecht lay naked except for a loose sheet across his waist, wires and tubes hooked into his pasty white body. His skin glistened with perspiration. His forearm showed an injection mark with a bubble of blood.

She rushed to the hallway. "Doctor, this patient needs attention!"

Surprised, he nodded to the nurse and they went in.

Aimée reached for the radio clipped to the policeman's pocket and flicked the transmit button. "Request assist; fifth-floor attack on Soli Hecht—officer down. Do you copy?"

All she heard was static. As she reached for the policeman's pocket, her hand raked a cold metal pistol. She wondered why a Paris *flic* would carry a Beretta .765. *Flics* she knew didn't carry this kind of hardware. They carried Manurhins. She slid it into her pocket.

More static, then a voice said, "Copy. Backup is on the way. Who is this?"

But Aimée stood at the foot of the bed where doctors and nurses worked on Soli Hecht.

"Adrenalin, on count of three," said a doctor near Soli's chest, which was heaving spasmodically.

She looked at the bubble on his arm, swollen and purple now, heard the labored breathing. Soli's hollow cheekbones contracted as he desperately sucked air. Recognition flashed in his eyes.

The doctor looked up. "Better get the rabbi. Somebody go look. Any family here?"

Aimée ignored her pounding heart and stepped forward. "I'm his niece. My uncle is on twenty-four-hour protection but someone got to him. Injected him with drugs."

The doctor looked up and gave her a quizzical look. "You mean this on his arm . . . ?" He grabbed Soli's chart, hooked to the bed.

Scanning it, he shook his head. "He's not responding. Check the IV solution."

"Can't you do something?" Aimée moved toward the head of the bed, feeling guilty for lying. Soli's eyes fixed on her and she returned his gaze.

"Vital responses are minimal," the doctor said.

Aimée bent over, gently touching Soli's arm, which was clammy and moist to the touch. Her conscience bothered her but she didn't know how else to find out. She whispered in his ear, "Soli, what does that photo mean?"

His arms broke loose from the tubes and flailed wildly. He reached out to her.

"You know, Soli, don't you?" She searched his eyes. "Why Lili was killed."

His sharp nails dug like needles into her skin. Aimée winced, drawing back, but he pulled her close. He rasped in her ear, "Don't . . . let . . . him . . ."

"Who?" Aimée said as his arid breath hit her cheek.

Someone touched her shoulder. "The rabbi is here. Let your uncle pray with him."

Soli's eyes rolled up in his head.

"Tell me, Soli, tell me . . ." But the nurses started pulling her away.

His head shook and he pulled Aimée tighter, his nails raking into her skin.

"Say it! Say his name," Aimée begged.

Soli's other arm flailed, scrabbling at the sheets. "Lo . . ."

"L'eau, Soli? Water?" she said.

"Ka . . . za . . ."

"What do you mean?"

He blinked several times, then his eyes went vacant. The heart monitor registered flat lines. Blood trickled from Soli's nose. Gently, the doctor pried Soli's fingers loose from Aimée's neck.

"Yit-gadal v'-yitka-dash sh'mei." The rabbi entered, intoning the Hebrew prayer for the dead.

The nurse led Aimée to the hall, where she leaned against the scuffed walls, shaking. She'd seen her father die in front of her eyes. Now Soli Hecht.

Her neck felt scraped raw. Raw like her heart. Another dead end. He'd only been asking for water.

The rabbi tucked his prayer book under his arm and joined her in the hallway. He gave her a long look. "You're not Soli's niece. His whole family was gassed at Treblinka."

Aimée's shoulders tightened. She looked down the hallway, wondering why the police backup hadn't arrived. "Rabbi, Soli Hecht has been murdered."

"You better have a lot more than chutzpah to lie at a dying man's bedside and then say he's been murdered. Explain."

Either the police response time had dwindled or that hadn't been a real police radio she'd talked into. Her uneasiness grew.

"I'm willing to explain, but not here," she said. "Let's walk down the hall slowly, go past the lobby toward the elevator."

They walked by the mobile shock unit, now abandoned in the hallway.

"Temple Emanuel has hired me to investigate."

His eyes opened wide. "You mean this has to do with Lili Stein's murder?"

She nodded. "Didn't you see the policeman who'd guarded the room lying unconscious on the floor? And the injection spot on Soli's arm, a bad job that swelled like a golf ball?"

The rabbi nodded slowly.

"Someone pushed Soli in front of a bus," she said. "That didn't work so when he came out of the coma, they finished him off with a lethal injection. Unfortunately, they got here before I did. I don't know how, but it involves Lili Stein. Was he able to talk at all?"

The rabbi shook his head. "He drifted in and out, never regaining consciousness.

Loud voices came from the corridor. Several plainclothes policemen strode down the hall. Why hadn't a uniformed unit arrived?

Her suspicions increased. Aimée turned away from them, bowed her head, and hooked her arm in the rabbi's. She whispered in his ear, "Let's walk slowly towards the stair exit. I don't want them to see me. Please help me!"

The rabbi sighed. "It's hard to believe anyone would make this up."

He nudged her forward. They walked arm in arm towards the stairs while she buried her face in his scratchy gray beard. As she heard the static and crackle of police radios from down the hall, she burrowed her head further in his shoulder.

Around the corner, the rabbi hissed in her ear, "I'm only helping you because Soli was a good man." He sidled close to the stairs, blocking the view, while Aimée crept through and down the stairway. She moved as quietly and quickly as the old stairs would allow.

"Excuse me, rabbi. Where is the woman you were in conversation with?" a clear voice asked the rabbi.

"Gone to wash her face in the ladies' room," she heard him reply.

Down the stairs, Aimée quickly followed a glassed-in walking bridge to the older part of the hospital. Outside, she unlocked her moped and scanned the area.

A few unmarked police cars were parked at the hospital entrance, but she didn't see anyone. The pungent smell of bleach drifted from the old hospital laundry. She hit the kick start, then pedaled down tree-lined rue Elzevir, quiet at this time of evening.

Le Commissariat de Police didn't carry Berettas. Professional hit men did, she knew that much. Behind her, a motorcycle engine whined loudly. Few cars used narrow rue Elzevir. The engine slowed down, then roared to life. She looked back to see a black leather-clad figure on a sleek Moto Guzzi motorcycle. She veered towards the sidewalk as it came closer. Suddenly, a car darted out from an alley across from her. All she saw was the darkened car window before the front wheel of her bike hit a loose cobblestone and threw her up in the air. Airborne for three seconds, she saw everything happen in slow motion as she registered the motorcycle speeding away.

She ducked her head and rolled into a somersault. Her shoulders smacked against a parked car's windshield. She inhaled the stench of burning rubber before her head cracked the side-view mirror like a hammer. Pain shot across her skull. She rolled off the hood.

Stunned, she sprawled on the sidewalk, partly wedged between a muddy tire and the stone gutter. The car stopped, then backed up, its engine whining loudly. Dizzy, she crawled over grease slicks and rolled under the parked car. She barely fit. She slid her Glock 9-mm from her jean jacket, uncocking the safety. The car door opened, then footsteps sounded on the pavement near her head.

Afraid to breathe, she saw black boot heels. She'd be lucky if she could shoot him in the foot. Loud police sirens hee-hawed down the street. A cigarette, orange-tipped, was flicked onto the pavement near her and fizzled in a puddle. The door clicked open, then the car sped away.

She flipped the gun's safety back on, then slowly rolled out from under the car, her head aching. Her knees shook so badly she staggered in the gutter and fell. She just lay there, hoping her heart would stop pounding. Grease and oil stains coated her black pants and her hands were streaked with a brown smudge that smelled suspiciously of dog shit. She picked up the soggy cigarette stub. Only a well-paid hit man could afford to smoke fancy imported orange-tipped Rothmans.

AIMÉE KNOCKED at the frosted-glass door. She kept her eyes on the blurry outline visible in the hallway.

"I need to speak with you, Monsieur Rambuteau," she shouted. "I'm not leaving until I do."

Finally the door opened and she stared into portly Monsieur Rambuteau's face.

"*Nom de Dieu!* What's happened . . . ?"

"Do you want to discuss your wife's will in the street?"

Pain and fear shot across his face. He opened the door wider, then shuffled towards the breakfast room.

Her head throbbed with dull regularity. "Do you have any aspirin?"

He pointed to a bottle on the table. Aimée shook out two, gulped them down with water, and helped herself to ice from the freezer.

"Merci," she said. She stuck the ice in a clear plastic bag, twisted it, and applied it to the lump on her head, wincing.

"Who are Thierry Rambuteau's real parents?"

He sat down heavily. "Did my son do this to you?"

"That wasn't my question but he's certainly on my list."

"Leave the past alone," he said.

"That phrase is getting monotonous," she said. "I don't like people trying to kill me because I'm curious."

She pulled out the folder and slapped it on the white melamine-topped table. "If you won't tell me, this lawyer, Monsieur Barrault, will."

"You stole that!" Monsieur Rambuteau accused.

"You offered to let me use this, if you want to get technical." She slowly set her Glock on a sunflowered plate, her eyes never leaving his face. Half of her skull had frozen from the ice and the other half ached dully. "I'm not threatening you, Monsieur Rambuteau, but I thought you'd like to see what the big boys use when they need information. But I went to polite detective school. We ask first," she said.

His hand shook as he reached for a bottle of yellow pills. "I'm preventing the reading of my wife's will with a court order. So whatever you do won't matter."

"I'll contest that as public domain information," she said. "Within three days, Monsieur, it can be published as a legal document. What exactly are you hiding?"

"Nathalie was naive, too trusting." He shook his head. "Look,

I'll hire you. Pay you to stop further damage. The war's been over fifty years, people have made new lives. Some secrets are better left that way. My son's certainly is."

"Two Jews have been murdered so far, and I'm next," she said. What would it take to reach him? "You better start talking because everything points to Thierry Rambuteau. Who is he?"

He glanced around furtively, as if someone would overhear.

"I had no idea Nathalie changed her will," he said. "We never agreed over him. Maybe she'd been drinking. Why should the mistakes we make when young stay with us all our life?"

She wasn't sure what he meant but he appeared fatigued and wiped his brow.

"Cut to the chase, Monsieur." Her head pounded and her patience was exhausted. "Who is he?"

"During the war, Nathalie was an actress, I did lighting and camera work for Coliseum. We worked with Allegret, the director, in the same acting troupe with Simone Signoret." A melancholy smile crossed his face. "Nathalie never tired of telling everyone that. Anyway, Coliseum was accused of being a collaborationist film company and later grew to become Paricor. But then we just made movies and Goebbels made the propaganda. And like everyone in France, we had to get Gestapo permission for anything we did. At that time, cutting your toenails required approval from the Gestapo *Kommandantur*, so I've never understood the uproar about collaborators. We all were, if you look at it like that."

Maybe that was true, but it reminded her of the joke about the Resistance. Fewer than five in a hundred of the French had ever joined, but if you talked to anyone today over sixty, they'd all been card-carrying members.

He paused, sadness washing over his face. "Anyway, at Liberation we had a stillborn child. My wife couldn't get over it, but then, you see, so many babies came out stillborn during the war. Maybe it was the lack of food. But Nathalie felt so guilty.

Everyone went crazy happy at Liberation. Our saviors, the Allies, were rolling in and here she was about to commit suicide."

His breath came in labored spurts now and his face was flushed. "On the street we'd see parades of women with their heads shaved. They'd slept with Nazis."

"Monsieur, some water?" she interrupted. She passed the bottle of yellow pills across the table towards him.

"*Merci,*" he said, gulping the water with more pills.

"What does this have to do with Thierry?" she said.

"There was a knock on our door one night. Little Sarah, a girl really, held a baby in her arms. I knew her father, Ruben."

"Sarah?" she said. Where had she seen that name? Then her brain clicked—*she'd seen it on Lili's yarn list next to Hecht's!* "What was her last name?"

Claude Rambuteau shook his head. "I don't remember. Her father worked on the camera crew before the war, a Jew, but . . ." His eyes glazed, then he continued. "Anyway, it was such a shock, I hadn't seen her for several years. Sarah's head had been shaved and an ugly tar swastika branded on her forehead. She cried and moaned at our door. 'My baby is hungry, my milk has dried up, and he's going to die.' The baby cried piteously. I noticed on her torn dress a dark outline of material where a star had been sewn. 'Where is your family?' I asked. She just shook her head. Then she said, 'No one will give me milk for my Nazi bastard.'

"I told her that I couldn't help her. People might suspect me of collaborating. Especially since I'd worked at Coliseum all during the war. She looked at my wife and said that the baby would die if he went with her and she didn't know anyone else to ask. She said she knew we'd had a baby, couldn't my wife nurse hers, too? I told her our baby had died."

Rambuteau closed his eyes. "She begged me, got on her hands and knees in the doorway. She said she knew he'd be safe with us because we had connections. Bands of Resistance vigilantes roamed Paris, out for revenge. I tell you, it was more dangerous to be on the streets after the Germans left than before, if they thought you'd collaborated."

He took a few deep breaths, then kept talking determinedly. "All of a sudden, my wife took the crying baby in her arms. She opened her blouse and instinctively the infant sucked greedily. Nathalie still had milk and her face filled with happiness. I knew then we'd keep the baby. So you see, Nathalie is his real mother. She gave him milk and life, I've always told her that. I never saw Sarah again. She brought us the baby because we were rightists and no one would ever suspect."

Incredulous, Aimée asked, "How could you accept the baby with the way you feel about Jews?"

"I've always regarded him as Aryan, because half of him is."

"Half-Aryan?" Aimée sat up.

"The product of a union between a Jew and a German soldier. Evidently, my wife had made some foolish promise to reveal the past to Thierry. Sometimes her drinking got her into trouble." Wearily, he raised his hand and brushed his thinning gray hair behind his ears. The man had no tears left. Aimée recalled the cobbler Javel mentioning a blue-eyed Jewess with a baby.

"Did this Sarah have bright blue eyes?" she said.

Monsieur Rambuteau looked surprised, then wrinkled his brow. "Yes, like Thierry." He shrugged. "He's as much my son as if he came from my loins. And he's all I have left."

"Tell him the truth. Be honest," she said.

Monsieur Rambuteau looked horror-stricken. "I don't know if I could. You see, he would have such a reaction."

"You mean a violent reaction?" She thought he seemed afraid of his own son.

He shook his head sadly. "His real parentage is against everything I've raised him to believe. And now it's come back to haunt my life. I never meant to be so anti-Semitic when he was growing up. I just felt the races should live separately. And I spoiled him, I could never say no to him. He's very strong-minded, I just don't know what to do."

Aimée was struck by this irony in Monsieur Rambuteau. But his obvious love for his son, even though he was half-Jewish, touched her.

After a minute of quiet, his labored breathing had eased and he smiled faintly. "I'm sorry. I'm a sick old man. And I'm desperate. The truth would destroy him." He sighed. "My son is not the easiest person to deal with. If he asks you lots of questions, tell him that all records of births were destroyed by the Nazis when they abandoned Drancy prison. That's the truth."

"You love him," she said. "But I can't help you."

"The records were destroyed, there's nothing left," he said.

Aimée pulled out a Polaroid of the black swastika painted on her office wall. "This is your son's handiwork."

He shook his head. "Wrong, Detective."

"How do you know, Monsieur Rambuteau?" She searched his face.

"Because that's how Nazis painted them in my day."

Taken aback, she paused and studied it again.

"He could have copied the style," she said.

But even though Aimée pressed him, he just shook his head. "As far as I'm concerned, young lady, we never had this conversation. I'll deny it. Take my advice, no one wants the past dug up."

THIERRY RAMBUTEAU, LEADER OF Les Blancs Nation-aux, paced impatiently in front of a sagging stone mausoleum. Where was his father? They'd arranged to meet before his mother's funeral.

This was ridiculous. He wasn't waiting any longer. Striding between the narrow lanes of crooked headstones in Père Lachaise cemetery, he realized he was lost. Every turn he took seemed to take him further away from where he wanted to go. A trio of seniors involved in a heated discussion stood on the gravel path, their breath puffy clouds in the crisp air.

"*Alors,* is this the western section?" Thierry asked of the one with a shovel. "I'm looking for Row E."

The old man looked up and nodded knowingly. "A new burial, eh? You're in the east corridor, young man, made a wrong turn a few turns back."

The old man pulled his heavy work gloves off, reached into his vest pocket, and pulled out a fluorescent orange map. On it were the faces of celebrities buried in Père Lachaise. Like a Hollywood map to stars' homes Thierry had seen sold in Beverly Hills. Only these stars were in homes of the dead. Just then, a group of tourists wandered past them, rattling away in Dutch and consulting their own maps.

"What is this, a tourist stop?" Thierry asked in disgust.

The old man had lit a Gauloise. "The dead don't mind it." He shrugged and pointed at his map. "Anyway, go left at Oscar Wilde—it's very obvious with the angel; he's a big draw, you know—and then straight until the marble crypt. If you hit Balzac you've gone too far. Then go just to the right past Colette and you should be there."

The old man put the map in Thierry's hands. "Someone in your family?" he asked.

"My mother," Thierry said. He'd been amazed that her love affair with the bottle hadn't killed her. Cancer had done that.

"Ah, well, my condolences. You must have an old family vault; no new space here anymore. But you'll enjoy visiting her. Never a dull moment here, especially over by that rock star Jim Morrison's grave, lots of all-night parties there."

Thierry started on his way and paused at the angel, as the old man had pointed out to him on the map. The name Oscar Wilde and the dates 1854–1900 were carved into the marble with the inscription *"For his mourners will be outcast men and outcasts always mourn."*

A single red rose lay at the angel's foot. Bleakly, Thierry concurred. He knew how it felt to be an outcast.

WHEN THIERRY reached the burial site chosen for his mother, he waited for a long time. His father finally shuffled towards him. Monsieur Rambuteau was red in the face and out of breath.

"Even with a map, this place was hard to find," he puffed. "But at least your mother is in good company." He pointed to the tombstone of Simone Signoret a few plots over.

"Why don't they charge admission like the Eiffel Tower?" Thierry said angrily.

Fifteen people attended the ceremony. Nathalie Rambuteau, an agnostic, had requested a simple graveside service with her family and some friends. Several old hands from her theatrical and film days appeared.

As Thierry and his father walked away from the grave, Monsieur Barrault, the attorney, reminded them that he would be in his office later to read Madame Rambuteau's will.

As they passed the sagging gravestone of Sarah Bernhardt,

blackened and weedy with neglect, Thierry shook his head. "How could they let Jews in here?"

His father's grip on his arm had tightened until it hurt and he leaned heavily on Thierry for support. Surprised, Thierry looked at his father's face and saw his pained expression.

"Papa." Thierry hadn't called him that for a long time. "You look ill. Why don't you go home and rest?"

Monsieur Rambuteau didn't answer.

In Thierry's Porsche on the way back to the apartment Monsieur Rambuteau was quiet. Then he spoke in an odd voice. "Close our joint account, Thierry. I've been meaning to tell you for some time," he said. "It's much safer if you route the funds another way."

"Why, Papa?" Thierry said.

"One can never be too cautious," Monsieur Rambuteau said. His voice changed. "Do you remember how we used to feed the pigeons crumbs in Place des Vosges?"

Thierry was shaken by the softness in his father's voice. "But that happened long ago, Papa. I was a little boy."

"You loved to do that. Every night after supper you begged me to take you," he said. "You told me you were the happiest boy in the world when you sprinkled bread crumbs near the statue of Louis XIII on his horse."

Thierry grinned. "I haven't thought about that in years. What made you bring . . ."

Monsieur Rambuteau had covered his face in his hands. His shoulders shook.

"Papa, what is it?" Thierry reached over, patting his father's arm. "We'll have good times again." He meant like the frequent times his mother had dried out at the Swiss clinic.

Claude Rambuteau nodded, rubbing his eyes. "Thierry, look for a blue envelope near your *maman*'s picture."

Thierry glanced at him quizzically, as his father slumped in the bucket seat.

"In the breakfast room, don't forget!" Monsieur Rambuteau was gasping now.

"My son," he gurgled as Thierry pulled over.

Thierry frantically searched his father's pockets. "Of course, don't worry . . . Papa!" he cried in alarm.

Claude Rambuteau's face was turning from beat red to purple. His knees spasmodically jerked against the leather dashboard.

"Where are your pills? Your pills?" Thierry screamed.

But Claude couldn't hear him as Thierry raced through the half-empty streets to the emergency entrance of the hospital.

AIMÉE CHANGED INTO CRISP wool trousers and a tailored cashmere cardigan. She looped the silk Hermés foulard, another treasure found at the flea market, around her neck. She popped more aspirin as she downed a generous shot of Ricard. Her head felt sore but the ice had prevented any major swelling. The dull throb had subsided and if it recurred she would drink more vermouth. Around the corner from her apartment she climbed onto the open-backed bus bound for the Palais Royal.

The law offices of *notaire* Maurice Barrault were located at street level of what had once been an *hôtel particulier* on rue du Temple. Renovated probably in the seventies, the high-ceilinged salon had been chopped into office suites. Much of the charm had been lost but not the cold drafts, Aimée noted with discomfort.

"Monsieur Barrault is in conference," the clipped secretarial voice behind designer wire-frame glasses informed her.

"Oh, what can I do?" Aimée sighed. "My aunt's will is supposed to be read today. Of all days!"

"I'm sorry. Would you like to reschedule?" The secretary pushed some files to the side of her desk and pulled out an appointment book.

Aimée parted her sleek black shoulder-length wig with her fingers. "But I have a reservation on the TGV to Bordeaux in two hours."

She eyed the framed baby photos lining the secretary's desk. French people loved children, giving excessive warmth and attention to any child.

"My one-year-old came down with croup! The doctor is worried about complications with pneumonia."

The secretary's concerned gaze radiated from behind the wire frames. "I understand. Your name, please." she said.

"Céline Rambuteau," she said. "Nathalie Rambuteau was my aunt."

"I'll see what I can do." The secretary patted the chair next to her desk and there was warmth in her voice. *"Calmez-vous."*

The secretary disappeared behind a wooden partition. Aimée heard a door open, then click shut. She stood up quickly and scanned the file of some fifteen legal briefs piled next to the baby photos. Nothing. Then she rifled through a stack next to them labeled "To be transcribed," fuming to herself. The will was probably right on the lawyer's desk and she'd never be able to get a look at it.

In the secretary's open drawer, she saw hanging files. Under the "To file for probate section," a folder hadn't been shoved in completely. She peeked, then started in excitement. In the middle was a file labeled NATHALIE RAMBUTEAU.

Beside her, the telephone rang loudly on the desk. She jumped. The red light blinked on and off. She wouldn't have time to pull Nathalie Rambuteau's file out. Her hands shook. She knew the secretary would be on her way to answer.

Suddenly the light stopped blinking and went off. Aimée took a deep breath. Deftly, she slid the file out, flipped the cover, and scanned the sheets. She turned the pages hurriedly, looking for anything about Thierry. Deeds of property and legalese. Nothing about Thierry. Behind the wooden partition, she heard a door close and the click of heels. What story had Rambuteau been feeding her? Had he lied about this whole thing to throw her off the track?

Stapled to the back of the will was an envelope with THIERRY RAMBUTEAU in black spidery writing. Aimée coughed, covering the noise as she tore it off and slipped it in her pocket. As the secretary rounded the partition, Aimée dropped the will back in the hanging folder.

"I'm afraid there's been a complication, Madame Rambuteau." The secretary looked worried. "Your aunt's will goes into probate."

"But why?" Aimée said.

"Monsieur Barrault wanted to tell you; unfortunately, he is in conference. He'll call you later this afternoon."

"Probate?" Aimée raised her eyebrows.

"I apologize if this seems unexpected . . ." the secretary began.

"Unprofessional is what it seems to me." Aimée stood up, adjusted her silk scarf, then made for the lawyer's door. "I need an explanation."

The secretary barred the way but her eyes were evasive. "Monsieur Barrault is meeting with a vice president of the Bank of France. As soon as he's finished he'll call and explain."

Aimée was about to make a scene and barge through the tall oak doors but she stopped herself. The reason a will went to probate clicked in her brain.

"My uncle is dead, isn't he?"

The woman's eyes shifted nervously, then she nodded. "I'm sorry. Monsieur Rambuteau suffered a heart attack after the funeral. Now the reading of the will is blocked until your uncle's estate goes through probate."

Aimée sat back down, shaken.

"I'm sorry you heard it from me." The secretary bent down, patting Aimée's arm. Her eyes were kind. "Truly sorry." The woman took Aimée's shocked behavior for grief.

"A heart attack?" Aimée shook her head.

"Right after the funeral, on the way back to his apartment. And you have just seen him at the cemetery! What a shock for you."

"And my poor cousin, Thierry . . . I have to go to him!" More than ever, she had to discover Thierry's identity.

The secretary threw her hands up. "Please don't let Monsieur Barrault know I've told you. My job would be . . ."

"Of course." Aimée nodded and stood up. "I'll find my cousin. We'll keep this between us."

ENTERING HER office, Aimée was immediately alarmed by the look on René's face. He avoided her eyes and concentrated on his computer screen.

"René, what happened?"

He sucked in his breath, bowing his large head and pointing to the fax machine.

Miles Davis scampered noisily into her arms as she bent down to pick him up. He licked and nuzzled her wetly with his nose.

A long fax feed had come in from Martine, curling all the way down to the floor. Martine had scribbled at the top, "I've lost my appetite . . . let's do dinner another time."

Enlarged from microfiche records were one-page cheat sheets titled, in crudely set print, CITOYEN—CITIZEN. Full of vindictive articles and accusations about collaborators, a starved and widowed France vented its spleen. J'ACCUSE headed each of the articles.

There were photos of collaborators hung garroted from streetlights with swastikas painted on their grotesque figures, village squares filled with contorted bodies shot by vigilante firing squads, and groups of women with their heads shaved, being stoned by crowds. The rest was a hideous description. No wonder Martine was sick.

Aimée looked sadly at these photos of women, herded like sheep before a people's street tribunal at Liberation. Just like Claude Rambuteau had said. The line under one photo read:

> Not only did French whores take the Germans' food while their neighbors starved but Jewesses slept with the Nazis as their families burned under Gestapo orders!

In the motley-dressed group of women with shaved heads, one carried a baby. She looked young, her expression stony, her head

held high. Aimée pulled a magnifying glass from her drawer to
see the details more clearly.

The next scene caught by the photographer preserved the
ugly truth forever. A swastika had been tarred into her forehead. The young mother had sagged to the ground in pain, still
holding the baby and keeping it away from the crowd. Could
that be Thierry in the young woman's arms? Was this the Jewess
who'd slept with a Nazi?

In the crowd she noticed a leering adolescent girl. Around the
girl's neck hung a gold chain with odd symbols. Peering closer
through the lens she remembered seeing those same distinctive
symbols before, twisted into the ligature marks. She recognized
that face. A young Lili Stein stood in the crowd.

"I LIKE your theory," René said. His fingers raced over his laptop. "Les Blancs Nationaux works as a front, financing Aryan hit
squads, operating from DFU money via the Rambuteaus' joint
bank account."

"Makes sense," Aimée said. "The German funds provide perfect cover for the final solution Thierry earnestly believes in.
Now we just have to prove it."

René had already started accessing the Rambuteau's bank
account on his computer. "For Thierry to murder Soli Hecht
because he was an interfering Nazi hunter and Lili Stein for an
initiation rite would fit," he said.

Aimée opened the oval window facing rue du Louvre. The
November chill did nothing to disguise the four coats of paint
needed to cover the swastika. Maybe it was her imagination,
but she could still make out the curved edges.

"Look at this," she said, handing the blue envelope to René. "I
stole it off Nathalie Rambuteau's will. Here's confirmation from
his real mother."

"His real mother?" René said. He hit "save" on his laptop.
"Who's that?"

"A woman named Sarah. The irony is, he's part Jew," she said. "Like they say Hitler was."

She would leverage the truth out of Thierry. Not only would she display his incriminating bank account, she would show him the contents of the envelope.

"Then who is his father?" René said after he read the letter. "Or do you have ideas about that?"

"A Si-Po officer who deported Jews from the Marais," she said. "But there's only one way to find out for sure. And Thierry will help me do that."

AIMÉE WRAPPED HER FINGERS around the cold plastic of her 9-mm Glock and knocked on the door with her gloved hand. A white-faced Thierry Rambuteau appeared. He stared at her. A glimmer of recognition passed over his face.

"You! What do you want?" he said.

"We need to talk," she said.

"Who are you, anyway?" He didn't seem to want to know the answer because he started to close the door.

She stuck her boot in the door, still keeping her hand balanced on the gun handle in her pocket. "I have something you should see."

He shook his head.

"And I'm not going away."

He stood aside. "Since you insist."

She strode down the hallway. The breakfast room, formerly so bright and meticulous, appeared dull and gloomy. Papers were scattered over the sofa. Nathalie Rambuteau's framed photo watched her from the mantel.

"Tell me why you tried to kill me," Aimée said evenly, her finger poised on the trigger in her pocket.

"Me? Not me," he said. His wild bloodshot eyes darted around the room. Abruptly he shook his head, then ran his hands across his stubble.

"Who else would?" she said, still not relaxing her grip.

"I thought you were a *flic* but I certainly wouldn't pull a knife. Leif's the vicious one. I tried to stop him, but you got away."

"Leif, the one in lederhosen, chased me?" she said.

"Leif was right about you." He stood up and began mumbling to himself, pacing distractedly back and forth.

"They are all amateurs! I must work harder so they understand." He ignored her and shuffled old newspaper clippings together. His blue eyes shone fiercely. "My obligation, my commitment is to the white race. I work for Les Blancs Nationaux out of love and sacrifice. Who else will keep the world pure if we don't?"

She was appalled. "Was Lili Stein killed to keep the world pure?" she said. "Did you engineer both Lili Stein's and Soli Hecht's murders, then have your minions execute them? Tell me the truth."

"The truth?" He laughed. "My father warned me. You're searching for who cut the old lady, eh? That's LBN turf. But murder is not our style."

"Why should I believe that? You have a motive," Aimée said. "And no real alibi."

"Motive? The *flics* questioned me," he interrupted, irritated. "I was in Istanbul, flew into Antwerp, picked up new videotapes, then drove back. It's stamped on my passport."

She'd seen his credit-card activity on the A2 highway from Belgium the day of Lili's death. "Show me."

"The *flics* kept it. Go ask them. If something juicy comes up, they plan to pin it on me." Thierry's eyes glittered.

"New members of Les Blancs Nationaux kill as part of their initiation rites," she said. "To prove their commitment!"

Thierry shook his head. Wonder shone in his eyes. "Aryan supremacy is real," he said. "No one has to kill for it."

The irritating thing was she believed that he was being honest. It bothered her. Made it difficult to advance her theory of him as the killer.

The harder part followed. He was a human being who had lost both parents. She'd have to push him to the edge, make him reveal the truth, prove or disprove her theory. She began reluctantly, "There's no easy way to do this." She stood in front of Nathalie Rambuteau's photo.

"To tell me I'm adopted?" he said.

She was surprised; how would he know?

"My father told me you would come," he said. "Spin me a pack of lies. Now, get out. Play girl detective somewhere else. I know the truth!"

Of course, Claude Rambuteau would try to discredit her. He'd promised as much.

"My father died in my arms," Thierry said. His voice cracked. "Leave me alone. I didn't kill anyone!"

"You better read this," she said. She tightened her hold on the pistol in her pocket as she withdrew the envelope with spidery writing. "This is for you. Your father planned on blocking the will, but he died and threw everything into probate."

Thierry looked unsure.

"Of course"—she opened it slowly—"I helped matters along at the lawyer's office. I think your real mother is alive, Thierry."

"He said you'd try . . ." Thierry sputtered.

"And you are a Jew."

Thierry stopped dead. "What are you talking about?"

"Technically," Aimée continued, "since you were born of a Jewish mother. Judaism follows matriarchal lines. But you're German too since your father was an occupying soldier. Probably Si-Po, responsible for the Gestapo who pursued enemies of the Reich."

He shook his head. "Why are you doing this?"

"Read it," she said.

Doubt flickered in his eyes.

"Nathalie wanted you to know your real parentage, Thierry," Aimée said. "Her soul couldn't rest after her promise. Secretly, it hurt her to see you hate the Jews. Especially . . ."

Thierry grabbed the letter out of her hands. He went to the

window and read it. For what seemed an eternity, she heard the monotonous tick of the kitchen clock.

"How could this be true?" His eyes flashed at Aimée. He sat down and reread the letter. "All these years? Lies, a pack of lies! Is this why she drank?"

"I can't answer that," she said. She caught his wild gaze and held it. "How does this involve Lili?"

"How would I know?" Thierry's voice dropped. "Nothing makes sense. It's like I've been hit by a wave in the ocean and my feet can't touch the sand. I don't know which way is up for air." Then he asked simply, "Why didn't they ever tell me I wasn't theirs?"

He looked devastated. Even though she felt sorry for him, she still had to know the truth.

"Did you kill Lili? Make an example of her death?" She watched him closely.

He shook his head. "From an airplane? I told you, I flew in from . . ."

"Who did it?" she interrupted.

"Someone's trying to frame me," he said. He began rummaging through papers near the window.

"What are you looking for, Thierry?"

"Something that tells me who I really am." Thierry picked up papers, never taking his eyes off her. "All this reveals is . . ." But he couldn't say it.

"That your mother was Jewish and your father a Nazi?" she finished for him.

"What does this mean?" Thierry said with a strange look. He pulled Nathalie Rambuteau's photo out of the silver frame and lifted up a scrap of paper. "Is this my Jew name?" He thrust it at Aimée.

She took it. *Sarah Tovah Strauss, née 12 avril, 1928*, was printed on a yellowed, otherwise blank scrap of paper.

"Can you believe that?" he said. "Even with all my work in Les Blancs Nationaux I've never really felt like a Nazi," he laughed.

He hurled the frame on the floor. Nathalie Rambuteau stared up, filtered by glittering shards of glass.

"Maybe that's because I'm half-Jew," he said.

SHE HATED going to the Archives of France but if any record of Sarah Tovah Strauss existed, besides in the Centre de Documentation Juive Contemporaine where it was not, that was the only place it would be. The old palace, glacially cold and littered with rodent droppings in its corners, was open late on Wednesdays. Napoleon's records and Nazi documentation along with most of French history filled much of the adjoining mansions, Hôtel de Soubise and Hôtel de Rohan. Her level-two access card allowed her entry twenty-four hours a day.

She followed a clerk with a thinly curled moustache who reeked of garlic-laced rabbit stew. They entered a glassed-in lobby, filled with large wooden reading tables.

"The material is quite heavy. Use a cart." He pointed to a high-tech metal wire construction resembling an Italian sports car.

Off this parquet-floored area, open and light due to myriad skylights, stood racks and racks of leather- and cloth-bound volumes.

She approached the small checkout desk. "*Bonjour,* I'm looking for records from 1939 to 1945 in Archives of the Commissariat general on the Jewish question."

"Something specific?" the librarian asked. "We have thousands of files."

"Strauss, Sarah Tovah," Aimée said.

The librarian clicked on the computer. "Living or deceased?"

"Well," Aimée stumbled. "That's why I'm here."

"I only ask because some patrons already know." The librarian smiled understandingly. "Find the AN—AJ 38 division. The Deceased section is to the left, oddly numbered. Aisle 33, Row

W has volumes with the names starting with S. Unknown or nonreported deceased are to the right." She indicated a much smaller area. "Please call if you need assistance. Good luck."

At the entrance to the racks, a sign proclaimed that the blue labels were German Occupation Documents, orange labels were Allied Forces documentation, and green labels were French National Records. Most of the racks were filled with blue-labeled material. Aimée knew the German reputation for recording details but this was staggering. She picked up a sagging blue volume tied with string and read a five-page itemized list of the contents of a clock factory at 34 rue Cloche-Perce owned by a Yad Stolnitz. A red line had been drawn through his name. She often walked on narrow, medieval rue Cloche-Perce, which angled into busy rue St. Antoine, full of boutiques and sushi bars. Once it had thrived with small Jewish bakeries and falafel stands.

She climbed up the small library stairs and found the Service for Jewish Affairs, the 11—112, of the Sicherheitsdienst-SD, the intelligence agency of the SS. Among the S volumes, "St-" alone took up sixteen volumes. She loaded up her high-tech cart carefully with yellowed documents and wheeled it to a reading table.

Sadly, Aimée sat and turned page after page, filled with Parisian Jews who were no more. Straus, Strausz, Strauz, she read, going down columns of names. Every single derivation of Strauss had been drawn through with a red line. There was a Sara Strausman listed but no Sarah Tovah Strauss. After two hours her eyes ached and she felt guilty. Guilty for being part of a race that had reduced generations to ashes or ooze in mass-grave lime pits.

Convoy lists composed most of the Unknown section. Jews who had arrived at death camps were checked off but no further records existed. No Sarah Tovah Strauss listed here either.

Back in the Deceased section, Aimée discovered that the Germans also cross-referenced deportees with their arrondissements in Paris. They had sectioned the city into areas with *Judenfrei* status.

Probably the idea of that Gestapo brown-noser in the memo to Eichmann who'd worried he couldn't get them to the ovens fast enough. She wondered how human beings could do this to each other.

Well then, she would start with the 4th arrondissement, the Marais, where most of the Jews had lived. Streets, alleys, and boulevards listed names and addresses. Forty minutes later she found a household at 86 rue Payenne cross-referenced from an Strauss, Ruben with this under it:

~~Strauss, Sarah T.~~ *12-4-28 Paris Drancy JudenAKamp Konvoy 10*

A red line ran through the name, like all the others on the page. The Strauss family were routed via the Vel d'Hiver transit camp. Sarah T. Strauss had entered Drancy prison and then was listed on Convoy number 10 to A, meaning Auschwitz. How could this Sarah Strauss be Thierry's mother?

Aimée noticed how bright the red line through Sarah's name was compared to the others. Odd, she thought, every other red line had faded to a rose hue. It almost looked to her as though the A had been squeezed next to the non-Aryan classification column, with its bold black J for Jew. As if the A for Auschwitz had been added later. But that didn't fit with what she'd discovered.

Claude Rambuteau had seen Sarah alive when she handed them the infant Thierry. Aimée remembered Javel's comment. He'd mentioned the bright-blue-eyed Jew who'd given birth to a *Boche* bastard.

As she returned past the desk, wiping her hands of dust, the librarian said that it was their policy for the librarian to reshelve.

"Find what you were looking for?" she inquired.

"Yes, but it raises even more questions," Aimée replied.

"A lot of people who come here say that. Try the National

Library in Washington or the Wiener Library in London. Those are the major sources besides Yad Vashem in Jerusalem."

Aimée thanked her and slowly walked down the sweeping marble stairway. She felt dirty after touching those pages and her fingers reeked with a special musty smell that clung to the catalog of the dead. At home she collapsed and thought over all the events of the day. She took a long shower and stayed under the hot water until it ran out. But she couldn't get rid of the smell or erase the red lines from her mind.

THURSDAY

"I'VE GOTTEN EVERYTHING CHANGED since the break-in," René said. "Here's your new access code and keys to the safe."

"HOPALONG?" She laughed, eagerly punching in her new access code. "Where do you get these, René?"

"My perverted childhood spent with pulp Westerns." He winked. "I'm CASSIDY."

"What a poet!" She frowned. "Finding the Luminol fingerprint is going to be harder than I thought. Fingerprint files have been centralized. It's all through FOMEX out of Neuilly."

"Try to interface with LanguedocZZ via Helsinki," René suggested. "The main menu originated with them."

"Good thinking, Cassidy," she said.

Twenty minutes later, she'd accessed FOMEX, the repository of files from the prefecture of police of every city or town in France that had its own prefecture. By the time she got to the main catalog of fingerprints, the only title that was close was FINGERPRINT, BLOODY, of which there were three subsets: Pending, Active, and Deceased, and thousands of files under each. It could fit all three. She called Morbier.

"Where did the bloody fingerprint go?" she said.

"With the experts," he said.

She heard the scrape of the wooden match on his desk. She knew the videoed fingerprint had been scanned and immediately catalogued on computer files.

"No kidding, Morbier. What's it under?"

"Pending and Interpol. What's it to you?"

She punched in Pending, then Paris, then 4th arrondissement/ 64 rue des Rosiers. Up came a giant index finger on her screen.

"Just like to be included in the twenty-eight percent of the informed population," she said. She'd like to see the expression on his face if he could see the display filling her screen.

"The higher-ups have spoken again. Seems whatever case I touch they like to take over," he said.

"Meaning that they didn't like your face on the evening news?"

"Meaning Luminol use falls under strict rules from the ministry at La Défense," he answered. "Which I didn't follow. So I'm pushed off that case."

"That doesn't make sense," she said.

"Leduc, just a word to the wise. Leave this thing alone."

"So only the big boys get to play and set up their own rules? Is that what you're saying, Morbier?" Aimée asked.

"They already have," he said. "Watch out."

The fingerprint hadn't even been classified or typed yet, but Aimée could tell by the whorls filling her computer screen that it was common to one third of the population. Such a clear readable print; the swirls over the hump of the center finger pad were unique, as everyone's were. But she could start to classify and discard two-thirds of the millions of prints that were stored based on what she saw. She punched into FOMEX on René's terminal and scanned the known fingerprints of Nazis from Nuremberg trial files into the computer. That would give her a base to start from. On the other terminal hooked to his Minitel she downloaded the *R.F. SS Sicherheits-Dienst Memorandum file* emblazoned with thick black Gestapo lightning bolts she'd accessed through the Yad Vashem in Jerusalem.

But that turned into a dead end. She checked other memorandums from the file. Nothing. The Nuremberg trials only yielded prints of those already executed for war crimes and the *R.F. SS* file was limited.

At a loss as to where to go, she delved into Republic of Germany classified documents. After forty more minutes of searching, she accessed the Third Reich database, which flooded the screen with a whole plethora of Nazism. Many of the entries had come from charred remnants scanned and entered into the database from the remains left in the burned Reichstag basement smoldering as Berlin fell. Countrywide lists of Hitler Youth group members and the alliance of German Girls were catalogued alongside SA brown shirt organizations, fingerprint files of Gestapo members, and even the names of German women awarded gold crosses for having the most children.

She entered Gestapo files and searched by surname. Nothing came up that matched the ones she wanted. Then she tried locale, searching the three main headquarters in Munich, Hanover, and Berlin. A "Volpe, Reiner" aged eight years old came up but that was the closest. Then she decided to go year by year. She began in 1933, the first known year on file of an established Gestapo. After an hour and a half she'd found the fingerprints in the Gestapo file of the SS chief and underlings in Paris: Rausch, Oblath, and Volpe. She printed them, amazed at the clear imprints that existed after all this time.

After pulling up the Luminol fingerprints from the FRAPOL 1 file, she peered through her magnifying glass at the two screens full of whorls and swirls. She inputted them together, counted to ten, then pressed the command REQUEST COMPARISON. A soft whir, then a series of small clicks. REQUEST RECEIVED appeared on the screen, then a flashing signal indicating request backlog. All she could do now was wait until the match was or wasn't made.

When the flashing light disappeared from René's terminal and the message came up "No Match of Verified Fingerprints," Aimée wasn't too surprised. She'd eliminated Rausch, Oblath, and Volpe as Arlette's murderer. But they'd been responsible for so many other murders, it didn't mean much. Primitive elimination. She still didn't know Hartmuth Griffe's true identity. Generally, new identities had been found that were close to the person's real

name for easier remembrance and to avoid mistakes. He could be
Rausch or either of the underlings: Oblath or Volpe.

A configuration of jumbled letters appeared on her screen,
followed by clicking noises. Alarmed, she looked up. "René, something weird is happening."

"Mine too," he said. "Something is either scrambling transmis-
sion or we've been hit by a virus."

"I'll check the backup server link. Did you confirm our new
access codes with them?" she said.

"I haven't gotten around to it yet," René moaned. "We're
cooked! Our whole system's down."

Aimée quickly started the automated backup retrieval system,
so files wouldn't be lost or deleted. Automated backup retrieval
cost them a lot, but the system was guaranteed to be fail-safe.

She breathed a sigh of relief after she'd checked the system.
"The fingerprints are saved."

René looked worried as he climbed down from his chair. "I think
you kicked off some warning device in the FOMEX system."

"I think you're right." She glanced at her screen. "That means
I dug deep enough to flip off an alarm."

For the first time she admitted to herself that she might be in
over her head. Way over her head.

"Go home," René said, as he put on his coat. "I'm going to visit
a friend who deals with this kind of thing. Just stay off the system
and wait until you hear from me."

"I'm going to walk home," she said.

"Stay off the phone." He looked grim. "And make sure you're
not followed."

AS SHE walked along the Seine kicking pebbles into the water,
she checked to see that she wasn't being followed. Uneasily, she
forced herself to mentally catalog her recent discoveries.

She'd discovered that a fifty-year-old bloody fingerprint found
at the murder scene of Lili's concierge hadn't matched any Si-Po

officers in occupied Paris. However, she knew that these officers had been listed as dead in the Battle of Stalingrad while they were still signing deportation orders for Jews in Paris. Her office had been broken into, files about Lili and a collabo taken, and a swastika painted on her wall along with a threat. She had heard Soli's last utterance in the hospital of "Ka . . . za" and was almost run over. Not to mention discovering Thierry's real parentage and Javel's statement about the Jew with the bright blue eyes. More of the puzzle pieces had surfaced—fragments and images. They all fit together. Only she didn't know how.

Now she needed to stir things up. Throw her idea in the frying pan and see what happened. Test her suspicions about Hartmuth Griffe. She pulled out her cell phone and called Thierry.

"Meet me in the rear courtyard of the Picasso Museum," she said.

"What for?" His voice sounded flat.

"Has to do with your parentage," she said slowly. "We need to—"

He interrupted excitedly. "Did you find out about my . . ." He paused. "The Jewess?"

"Look for me by the Minotaur statue. Behind the plane trees."

"Why?"

She explained her plan to him, then hung up.

As she crossed the Place des Vosges, she kicked the fallen leaves. She made another phone call to Hartmuth Griffe. This would definitely set wheels in motion. Whether they were the right ones remained to be seen.

THIS FORMER *hôtel particulier*, now the Picasso Museum on rue de Thorigny, still maintained quiet niches of green comfort in the rear courtyard. At this time of year, the small courtyard was deserted of museum-goers. Crisp autumn air skittled leaves over Picasso's bronze figures reclining on the lawn. Several of his voluptuous marble Boisgeloup females bordered the limestone walls.

Thierry stood next to Aimée under a spreading tree, his legs apart, his face expressionless. "Him?"

She nodded. "Keep to the plan."

Hartmuth Griffe huddled on a bench beside the gilded Minotaur, pulling his cashmere coat around him. He stared as they approached.

"Thank you for coming, Monsieur Griffe," Aimée said.

"Your offer intrigued me, Mademoiselle Leduc." He inclined his head in a half bow. "Now what is so interesting for me to come out in this cold?" he said.

Aimée noticed how Hartmuth stared at Thierry's intense blue eyes. She motioned to Thierry. Thierry's arm shot out in a *Sieg Heil* salute from his black leather storm-trooper coat. The worn leather crackled.

Hartmuth's eyes never wavered as he stood up. "So who are you, before I leave?"

Thierry smiled sardonically. "Right now, that's a good question."

Aimée stepped forward. "I have a request to make of you. This may appear audacious, and of course it is, but indulge me, please; it will all make sense later. Please remove your shirt."

"What if I say no?" Hartmuth said, standing and backing up into an ivy-covered trellis. He started towards a rear walkway.

Aimée blocked his exit. "Cooperation is better."

Thierry reached for Hartmuth's arms, holding him from behind. Hartmuth jerked and twisted.

"Struggling isn't wise," Thierry said as he pulled Hartmuth behind leafy bushes directly under the museum windows.

Behind the dense foliage, Aimée stuck her Glock in his temple. "I've asked you nicely. Now do it."

His face a mask, Hartmuth removed his jacket and unbuttoned his shirt, exposing his chest. Tan, muscular, and lean. Aimée draped the coat over Hartmuth's shoulders as she lifted his arm.

"Do you think I'm a drug addict, too? Needing a fix?" Hartmuth's eyes bored into Thierry's. "You two junkies work as a team, right? My wallet is in my pocket. Take the money and get out."

Aimée examined his arm carefully, as Thierry held him from behind. She pushed aside her disgust at discovering the telltale sign.

"What are you d-doing?" Hartmuth said. He jerked his arm back.

"That scar under your left arm comes from removing your SS tattoo, doesn't it?" she said. "Firing a pistol into your armpit so the muzzle flash would burn it—painful but better than the slow death from the Russians if they'd discovered it," she said.

Hartmuth simply stared at them.

"Please put your shirt back on; it's very cold out here," Aimée said. She had him now. Time to gamble that these men matched. But after reading Sarah's letter, she knew they would.

Thierry stared at Hartmuth.

"Who are you and what do you want?" Hartmuth asked. His eyes were cold.

"I don't know what I want," Thierry said.

She stepped forward. "He's your son."

Dumbfounded, Hartmuth's eyes became wide.

"I don't understand," Hartmuth began. "Is this a j-joke?"

"More a bizarre backfire. Tainted in the Aryan sense." Thierry emitted a brittle laugh.

"You expect me t-to . . ." Hartmuth said.

"Monsieur Griffe, if that is your name, I want answers," Aimée said. "Sit down."

Thierry pulled him down on the bench. His eyes never left Hartmuth's face.

Hartmuth shook his head back and forth, staring at Thierry. "What crazy idea are you trying to prove?"

"I had to be sure you were SS," she said.

"My record is clear," Hartmuth said. "This is absurd!"

Aimée thrust the faded blue sheet of paper, covered with spidery writing, at him. "Didn't I promise you interesting reading?" she said. "Read this."

Hartmuth read it slowly. His lower lip twitched once. Motionless, he reread the letter.

"Who gave this to you?" he asked Thierry.

"His stepmother left this to be read with her will."

"But why come to me?" His hands shook as he rebuttoned his cashmere coat.

"You tell us," she said.

Thierry, his arms folded, stared intently at Hartmuth. The only sound came from scraping gravel as Thierry crossed and recrossed his legs. Somewhere in the Marais, low and sonorous in the frosty air, a bell pealed. Hartmuth remained mute, almost paralyzed.

"You had to murder Lili Stein because she recognized you," Aimée said. "From the time you rounded up her family and all the Jews in the Marais!"

Hartmuth stood up. "I'm calling a guard."

Aimée held his arm. "Fifty years later, Lili sees your photo in the paper and knows you."

"You're making this up!" he said.

"Lili couldn't forget your face. You beat down the door and pulled her parents out of bed."

"I-I t-told you it wasn't like that," Hartmuth stumbled.

She noticed how he clenched and unclenched his hands.

"Coincidentally, in the alley behind your hotel, she recognized you." Aimée leaned into his face, pushing him back. "Or maybe she tracked you down. Followed you. 'Nazi butcher,' she screams, or 'Assassin.' Maybe she tries to attack you, gets scared, runs away. But you follow her and you have to keep her quiet like the concierge. Keep your past hidden."

"I-I only saw her once," he said.

Aimée froze. So it was true. The idea she'd thrown into the frying pan was the right one.

"In 1943. I followed her to her apartment," he said. His eyes glazed over.

"Tell me what happened," Aimée said.

"I was afraid if Lili informed," he said, "they would t-trace the food to me. But I found the concierge, beaten to a bloody pulp."

Aimée shivered. "Those were your bloody fingerprints under the sink," she said. She pointed to his hands. "Those gloves hide your prints, preventing anyone from discovering who you are. You're the Gestapo lackey who couldn't get them to the ovens fast enough for Eichmann!"

Hartmuth slowly peeled off his kidskin gloves and thrust his scarred hands in the cold air. Rippled flesh whorled in strange patterns over his shriveled palms. The last two fingers of his left hands were stumps. "These are courtesy of the Siberian oil fields, Mademoiselle."

Unable to disguise her feelings Aimée turned away. Her own seared palm was small compared to his deformity.

"But those were your boot prints!" she persisted. "You washed your boots at the sink, didn't you?"

A brief silence. He looked down. "After the fact, yes. I went back."

"You went back?" she said.

"I knew the concierge would be easy to bribe. But it was too late."

"Who murdered her?" Aimée asked.

"I saw Lili climb out the window, over the rooftop, and escape. That's it, I just protected Sarah."

"Protected Sarah . . . like the way you crossed her name out in the convoy sheets, then added the A to make it appear she had been sent to Auschwitz?" she said.

"Who are you?" Hartmuth demanded.

Thierry sat forward, studying this man, his eyes never leaving Hartmuth's face.

She ignored his question.

"Sarah is in danger." His voice shook. "I don't know how to help her."

"She knew Lili Stein."

A sigh. "Yes."

"Did she kill Lili in revenge because she'd been disfigured at Liberation?"

"N-no," he shouted.

"Isn't she still sympathetic to Germany after being a collaborator, sleeping with you?"

"N-no, it's n-not like that. You have to find her again. Before they do." Hartmuth raised his voice.

Aimée was surprised. "Who?"

"People in the German government . . ." He put his head down.

"Why should I believe you? You were in the Gestapo. I'll never have enough proof to prosecute you for war crimes. The Werewolves erased your past, resurrected a new identity from a dead man. They were masters at that. But deep down I know rats like you live in holes all over Germany."

He rubbed his arm and spoke tonelessly. "I supervised the local French police. They rounded up the Jews from businesses and apartments in every building around here. I worked with the *Direktor* of the *Anti-jüdische Polizei* at the *Kommandantur*. We ticked off sheets when the convoys were loaded. As for shipping them out . . ." He paused, and lowered his voice. "I didn't know what an Auschwitz or Treblinka meant. I found out later. Sarah hid from me but I found her and saved her. All the rest . . . I was one man in a wave that crushed generations. I didn't kill Lili. The only time I ever killed was in hand-to-hand combat at Stalingrad. A little Russian boy aimed a p-pitchfork at me and I sh-shot him. I see that every night when I try to sleep. Other things, too."

"Thierry is your son, isn't he?" Aimée said.

"I don't know. This letter is in Sarah's writing b-but she said," he stopped. "Those eyes, y-yes . . . those are her eyes." He choked. "Sh-she told me we had a b-baby who died as an infant! I j-just find it hard to believe . . ."

"That I'm alive?" Thierry stood in front of him.

Aimée saw something inside of Hartmuth shift.

"*Gott im Himmel*, I never knew, n-never knew," he said. His head started shaking. "Are you my s-son?"

"Lies! Everyone lied to me," said Thierry. His face contorted in hate. "I had a right to know."

Aimée saw the confusion in Hartmuth's eyes. He wondered if this really was his son. His and Sarah's, conceived in the catacombs fifty years ago.

"Sarah told me the b-baby died!" Hartmuth said.

Thierry, a stream of tears running down his own face, tentatively reached over.

"May I touch you, Father?" he asked in a whisper.

"Look at his blue eyes," Aimée said to Hartmuth. "Claude Rambuteau said Thierry had the same eyes as Sarah."

Hartmuth slowly reached out his trembling fingers, and grasped Thierry's. They held hands tightly. Aimée watched as Hartmuth's hand started to explore Thierry's face. His fingers traced Thierry's cheekbones, how his forehead curved, where his ears brushed his black hair.

Fog curled into the courtyard, dimming the spotlights highlighting Picasso's sculptures. The temperature had dropped but the two men were oblivious. As they spoke, clouds of frost in the afternoon air punctuated their words.

Softly Hartmuth spoke. "Your chin is like my grandmother's, jutting out just a little here." He sighed wistfully as he ran his fingers over Thierry's jawline. "Of course your eyes, coloring, and hair are hers," he said.

"Hers?" Thierry asked, letting the question trail in the air.

"She'll come to me, to us . . ." A fierce longing shone in Hartmuth's eyes. "That's why she's doing this, now I understand. Nothing matters anymore but that we're together. Some crazy coincidence and we've all found each other. I always hoped. But never in my fantasies did I dream we—"

"That we'd be reunited, like some happy family?" Thierry laughed sarcastically.

"No. I never knew you existed. But we are meant to be together," Hartmuth said.

"Father, don't forget what you lived by," Thierry said. He flashed his hand in the light so Hartmuth could see the tattoos circling his hand. "The SS motto—'My honor's name is loyalty.' Those ideals have never died."

"Where do you get this old propaganda?" Hartmuth asked, amazed.

Thierry's eyes welled with tears. "My life is a sacrifice for the Aryan way of life."

Hartmuth shook his head. "She's in danger." His voice had become urgent.

"It's good to know some things never change," Thierry said. For the first time he smiled.

"What do you mean? She's your mother," Hartmuth said.

Aimée moved closer to Hartmuth. "What does she look like?"

"Her eyes are incredibly blue," he said. "She wears a black wig. You have to find her."

"She's a Jewish sow, a defiled receptacle for Aryan seed, that's all." Thierry's eyes flashed with hate.

Aimée was alarmed. "Let's go, Thierry."

Hartmuth looked incredulous. "How can you say that? That's old talk, it never mattered."

Thierry bowed abjectly. "Can you accept me as your son, defiled as I am?"

Hartmuth slapped him. "Your brain is defiled!"

Thierry nodded. "True." He knelt down. "I will purify myself, cleanse her presence from me," he begged. "I will find the Jewish sow. Purge our line for the master race."

Aimée pulled him up, grabbing his arm. She had to get him out of the dank, chill courtyard before he did anything else. She shoved him past the Minotaur, almost tripping over the bench.

"You warped, sick . . . !" Hartmuth yelled.

"I will prove myself," Thierry said as Aimée dragged him towards the back door of the museum.

"Wait . . ." Hartmuth cried but they were gone.

THIERRY JERKED Aimée against the wall outside the Picasso Museum.

"Find her!" he said and was gone.

Cold and tired, she trudged over the Seine to her apartment. Miles Davis sprung on her as she entered her unheated flat. She jiggled the light switch until the chandelier shone dimly, then kicked the hall radiator, which sputtered to life and died.

Chilled to the bone, she went to the bathroom and turned on the chrome faucets full blast in her black porcelain tub. Her father's old Turkish robe, frayed and blue, hung over the heated towel rack. When her apartment's heat failed, she'd warm up in her claw-footed tub; there, her thoughts were released and she could order the compartments of her mind. Put ideas together, make sense of what she knew. She sank into the welcome warmth as her mirror fogged with steam and the sweet aroma of lavender Provençal soap filled the room.

She'd proved Thierry was Hartmuth's and Sarah's son. After Hartmuth accepted that, he'd revealed Sarah had survived and was in danger. Not only did Hartmuth want to find her, a crazed Thierry did, too. Thierry's anger frightened her and she still wasn't any closer to knowing who killed Lili. On top of that, René hadn't gotten back to her and she was worried about him.

She heard the click of her answering machine.

"Leduc, answer, I know you're there," came Morbier's voice on her machine.

She got out of the now lukewarm tub, intending not to answer. As she dried her hair, she heard the insistence in his voice. Finally she picked up the phone in her bedroom.

"You don't have to yell, I just got out of the bath," she said.

"Meet me in the Place des Vosges, at Ma Bourgogne, the café with the good apple tarte tatin," he growled.

"Give me one good reason, Morbier," Aimée said in a tired voice.

"Intuition, gut feeling, whatever you want to call it, just that feeling I get that's kept me in this business this long. Get dressed, I'll be waiting." He hung up.

She whistled to Miles Davis who scampered off her bed. "Time for you to stay with Uncle Maurice. I want you safe."

Thursday Afternoon

AIMÉE WALKED THROUGH THE long shadows cast across the courtyard of Hôtel de Sully. Dark green hedgerows manicured thinly into fleur-de-lys shapes broke up the wide gravel expanse. This tall mansion, another restored *hôtel particulier*, gave access to Place des Vosges via a narrow passageway.

She'd left René a message telling him where she was meeting Morbier. René's cautionary tone pulsed in her brain and she felt open to attack. Threatening faxes, graffitied threats, and hostile cars forcing her off her moped hadn't disturbed her as much as the virus attack on their computer system. Computers were their meal ticket. Her Glock, loaded and ready in her jeans pocket, was molded to her hip.

A buttery caramel aroma drifted across the courtyard. Her mind darted to the warm, upside-down apple tart for which Ma Bourgogne was famous. The restaurant lay past this narrow passage, under the shadowy arcade of Place des Vosges. She pulled out her cell phone and punched in René's number again. No answer.

As she turned to open her backpack, a hot burning stung her ear. Powdery plaster spit from the stone arch as a neat row of bullets peppered the wall.

She dove over the damp cobblestones and hugged a thick pillar, quickly grabbing the Glock from her pocket. If she hadn't turned, her brains would be splashed on the cobblestones right now.

She touched her ear, grazed by a bullet. Her shaking fingers came back sticky red and metallic-smelling. It hadn't even hurt. She was scared and didn't know where to go. Bullets that seemed to be coming from above her systematically blasted the pillar's edges. She was an easy target. Already the column had been shaved to a quarter of its size.

She gripped her pistol with two hands to steady her aim, took a deep breath, and fired a round at the roof. Counting her shots before she finished them, she sprang and somersaulted, still firing. Her left arm banged into the arched passage entrance and sharp pain shot through her back. She prayed her shoulder wouldn't go out on her now.

It had to be Morbier! He'd called to meet her at the café around the corner. Consistently he'd warned her off Lili Stein's investigation. He'd set her up. René was the only person, if he'd gotten her message, who'd know she'd be here.

Ahead, the dark passage lay deserted. Keeping under cover behind the crumbling colonnade, she reloaded the Glock. Was he shooting at her himself or had he gotten a B.R.I. marksman? Crouched in the shadow, she took aim at the courtyard in front of her. Her hand shook. She didn't know why he would betray her.

He'd strung her along and she hadn't even suspected him. What a *traître*! She'd trusted him, felt sorry for him. Her godfather, for God's sake!

A puff of air whizzed by her cheek and plaster fell into her eyes. The sand and pebbly grit blinded her. She squirmed over the gravel towards the exit, trying not to go in a straight line. At least towards where she thought it was. Her tearing eyes finally blinked the sandy granules out. She realized she'd crawled to the opposite side of the wormholed doors that led to the Place des Vosges. Further from escape. A short figure pushing a baby stroller appeared near the door, about to enter the passage. Someone innocent was about to be killed; she had to warn them.

"Get out!" Aimée screamed at the figure with the stroller as she scooted backwards, propelling herself against the limestone wall. "Go! Run!"

She twisted back on her stomach and aimed below a dark-paned window. More puffs of ivory dust splattered in a row as her shots hit the colonnade. No thud, grunt, or low-lying shuffle. Nothing. Where were the shots coming from?

And almost too late, she looked up. To her left on another roof, a glinting barrel of a ground-sensor rifle poked over a gargoyle's ugly snout. Pointing at her.

Suddenly, the baby stroller reappeared, sliding into the courtyard. The stroller's wheels popped and hissed, deflating from rifle shots as it sagged into the courtyard hedge. The short figure in the shadow opened a coat revealing a semiautomatic, shooting at the roof.

She gritted her teeth, rolled over, and fired more rounds at the roof. She heard a scraping noise above her as a black-clad body thumped over the gargoyle's pointed ears, then the crunch of breaking bones as the body landed. Some vital organ burst, splattering matter over cobblestones and gravel.

"Aimée, get the hell out of here," René's muffled voice came from inside the coat. "Now!"

She ran over to him, trying to ignore the bloody mess in front of them. She looked long enough to see that it wasn't Morbier. Had her phone been tapped?

"René, my God what's happening?"

His arm was soaked dark red and he gasped, "They're following you." His hand covered his arm but she tried to pull it off to see. "Don't. Pressure to stop the bleeding." He smiled thinly and his green eyes closed. He opened them again with effort. "Don't go back." He moaned, then whispered, "Don't trust anyone, it's too big."

"René, I'll get you to the hospital. Sssh, be quiet until—"

"No, a bullet just grazed my arm." He tried to sit up. "Go quickly before they come. Take my keys, hide." The wailing drone of a siren came from rue St. Antoine. He pulled keys out of his vest pocket. Panic flashed in his eyes.

"Why the paranoia? Morbier will—"

"It's a setup; don't"—René gulped—"go."

She hesitated. "But, René . . ."

"Goddamn it, got to stop them." His eyes closed as he passed out.

Aimée backed slowly out of the courtyard as she heard the ambulance screech to a halt. From behind a moldy pillar she heard attendants running with a stretcher crunching over gravel. How did they know so quickly, she wondered. She peered from behind the fluted pillars and saw a Kevlar-suited swat team striding up to the huddled corpse. They leaned into their collars and she realized they were talking into small radios. She heard the static crackle as one of them stopped in front of her pillar and responded in a low voice.

"Negative. No sign of her."

She recognized the dead shooter sprawled in his own bloody entrails; the swastikas tattooed across his knuckles looked familiar. She flashed on Mr. Lederhosen, Leif, as Thierry had identified him. The one who'd almost knifed her in the van, had chased her through the Marais, and was in the crowd when Cazaux appeared.

Turning towards the back exit, she broke into a run just beyond the last pillar and stopped abruptly, ready to sprint down the arched Place des Vosges through strolling passersby. A police riot van swayed out of narrow rue de Birague and careened to a stop directly in front of her.

The burnt smell of roasted chestnuts wafted down the ancient arcade to where she stood, paralyzed. As the swat team streamed out of the van, she grabbed the elbow of a man next to her. Putting her arms around him, she burrowed into his wrinkled neck. His astounded elderly wife seemed about to bat her with a large handbag when Aimée feigned horror.

"I'm so sorry. Why, you look exactly like Grandpapa!" she exclaimed, keeping her head down.

Most of the swat team entered the Hôtel de Sully courtyard

but a few had fanned out along the Place des Vosges. Aimée kept pace with the old couple as the indignant wife tried to move away from her.

"You greet your grandfather in that manner, young lady?" she inquired sarcastically.

The old man's eyes twinkled as his wife pulled at him. Ahead of Aimée, an accordion wheezed something familiar, echoing off the vaulted brick. At the east corner of Place des Vosges stood an Issey Miyake shop. Aimée swerved through the stainless-steel doors into a stark white interior as the old man winked goodbye.

Bleached white walls, floors, and ceilings provided a minimalist backdrop with nowhere to hide. Black clothing hung from ropes draped from the ceiling like so many dead bodies. Unless you wore black or white you were sure to stick out here, and Aimée's dusty and gravel-pitted blue jeans definitely stuck out. Behind the deserted counter were white smocks worn by the salespeople. She grabbed one and buttoned it over her jeans and denim jacket. She heard the whir of sewing machines from the back and slipped through white metal-mesh curtains before a salesperson came out.

The row of Asian seamstresses busy at their sewing machines didn't even look up as she entered. Many of them kept up low conversations while they guided the material under the punching needles. From the shop exterior she heard voices—loud, officious ones. If she took off the smock, her dirty jeans and scruffy denim jacket would be picked out in a minute. Bins of black and white items of clothing were overflowing and the seamstresses kept adding more finished pieces. Aimée bent over and picked up the bin nearest her. A seamstress looked up questioningly at her.

"Display sent me for floor samples," Aimée smiled. "The requisition order is in my van."

"Inform the floor supervisor," the seamstress said. Her thin black eyebrows arched as she looked Aimée over. "Bring it on your way back."

"*D'accord*," Aimée agreed. She grunted, hefting the heavy bin into her arms. Slogging to the back of the busy work area, she kept her face hidden and set it down with all the others. Piled high, they made an odd-shaped mound.

Aimée slid a few black pieces out before she closed up the bin and stepped behind the pile. She took off her jean jacket, slipped on a tailored, well-cut black wool jacket, then stepped out of her jeans into a form-fitting tight black skirt. She rifled through a hosiery bin and grabbed thin black-ribbed tights. Sample shoes and boots in assorted sizes were strewn helter-skelter on shelves. She tried several pairs of boots on but the only pair that remotely fit her were sexy suede high-heeled pumps. Not exactly what she'd pick for a great escape. She looked like this season's fashion victim but she'd blend in more than she ever had before. The challenge would be, could she run in such a tight skirt and heels?

She bunched her jeans into a ball. The workers' backpacks and handbags hung from hooks behind her. Quickly she emptied the contents of a stylish black leather bag onto the floor and scooped her cell phone, wallet, cards, tube of mascara and Glock, with one remaining bullet cartridge, into the bag. Next to the contents of the bag on the floor she slipped some hundred-franc notes with a scribbled "Sorry, hope this covers it" in red lipstick on one of them. She unlatched the back workers' entrance as she heard a loud voice above the clicking sewing machines.

"Please give your attention to this officer. Have any of you seen . . ."

Not waiting to hear more, she slipped out into the night and the darkened Places des Vosges.

AIMÉE'S HEELS tapped a rhythm on the cobblestones as she searched for René's Citroën. Finally she found it on the rue du

Pas de la Mule, a street that had been named in the seventeenth century after its donkey mounting block." She and René always joked about that, but no smile came to her lips as she saw two policemen examining his vehicle. They weren't just giving it a ticket either.

Going to her office or flat would be stupid, she realized, and hiding at René's would be idiotic. Where could she find a place to hide that contained a computer? She ducked into the patisserie on the corner, bought a bag of warm chocolate croissants, and exited out the rear back to the Place des Vosges. She walked in her Issey Miyake designer suit, munching and looking in boutique windows, slowly working her way under the arcade towards the busy rue St. Antoine. In the children's playground, plainclothes police blocked her way by the side of the square, talking to the mothers, nannies, and assorted caregivers. Where could she go?

A group of tourists clustered in the doorway of the Victor Hugo Museum, which, Aimée noticed, the security forces ignored. All French national museums contained state-of-the-art computers, hooked online with government and educational ministries. This would be perfect—that is, if she could play tourist and sneak in the door.

She slipped among a trio of elderly ladies, greeting them like old acquaintances. She smiled and immediately began chitchat about the weather.

"Of course, being from Rouen," Aimée said, "I savor these ancient parts of the Marais."

"But the Cathedral of Rouen," one of the trio exclaimed, "is such a gem! A perfect example of the best in medieval architecture! How could one compare this Bourbon king's imitation to that!" The old woman spoke passionately. She pointed at the seventeenth-century colonnades above them. Aimée knew little about architecture and nothing of Rouen. She wished she'd kept her mouth shut.

"Are you just joining the architectural tour then, dear?" an almost hunchbacked old woman asked. "You've missed significant parts of the Marais, the *hôtels particuliers* on rue de Sévigné especially."

"I'll catch them next time," Aimée said.

She edged closer to the old lady, who smelled of musty violets. Two policemen walked by and she pressed herself against the rose-colored bricks of the building.

They filed into the foyer and she realized she was the youngest member of this group. The tour leader, a round-faced young man with circular tortoiseshell glasses, spread his arms as if enjoining the spirit of Victor Hugo himself to guide them, and began in a sonorous, droning voice.

"From 1832 to 1848 perhaps the greatest of all men of letters lived on the second floor of this building." He nodded officiously to several older men leaning on walkers. "Those unable to navigate the stairs may follow our journey through the museum on our computer access."

Despite her predicament, she almost laughed out loud as she saw the look of amusement the old men gave their guide. Most eighty-year-olds ignored computers and these didn't seem any different.

The museum, laid out as it had been in his time, showed the daily life of Victor Hugo. Hugo's bedroom, taken up with a canopied bed, overlooked Place des Vosges through leaded bubbled glass. Worn dark wood paneling covered the walls. A showcase held various colored locks of his hair tied with ribbon, labeled and dated. In the study was his *escritoire* and a sheet of half-written yellowed foolscap with a quill pen in a crystal inkwell beside it. Almost as if Hugo had paused to take a pee, which she herself desperately needed to do. Aimée stared longingly at a porcelain eighteenth-century bidet with exquisite floral rosettes. Lining the dining-room walls were portraits of his wife, mistresses, and other prominent writers of his day. The room captured his essence, dark and narcissistic. The only touch that could be called socialist was the heavy peasant glassware on a mahogany sideboard.

The guide continued. "This being the last tour of the day in this historic building, the option of resting is of course available." His arms waved dismissively toward a vestibule.

Aimée sat down, rubbing her heel, and joined several old men. The smell of tobacco floated in the air. She'd already cheated death once today. Tomorrow could be another story. Gratefully, she accepted a cigarette from the old man next to her. She inhaled the smoke greedily, savoring the jolt when it hit her lungs.

After the buzzer clanged, signifying closing time, the men rose and drifted towards the entrance. While no one was looking, she melted into the folds of a faded tapestry near the cloakroom door.

There could be worse places to spend the night than the Victor Hugo Museum, she decided. She backed up against the damp stone wall, and crouched down behind some tapestries while museum workers rang up the day's receipts and tallied ticket sales. All the time she worried about René, hoping he hadn't been badly wounded. And then there was the LBN—since she'd escaped, would they abduct René? And that questionable SWAT team—were they real B.R.I.? But there wasn't much she could do until the museum closed and the workers left for the day.

The staff grumbled about the drafts and chill coming from the stone walls. She smiled to herself. They probably went home to warm, cozy apartments with every modern convenience. But she lived in a place like this, *never mind that she couldn't go back there!* She felt sure her apartment and office were under surveillance.

Morbier, whom she'd known since childhood, had succumbed to pressure in his department, betraying her. Yves, the neo-Nazi hunk, alerted by her listening device, had told Leif that she was undercover. But Leif missed and shot René in the crossfire. And she'd taken care of Leif—so far, the only thing she didn't regret.

She was all alone now. No one to trust.

She pressed closer to the wall as the museum staff took their time about closing up. Finally she heard a voice. "Check the floor and restroom, then I'll activate the alarm." Thank God, Aimée thought, a working restroom. Her legs had been squeezed, holding it in for a long time.

"*Oui, Monsieur le Directeur*," she heard. That's it, they had been waiting for him.

As she peered through moth holes in the tapestry, she saw the tungsten-colored computer, furnished by the French Ministry of Culture, on the director's desk. The French government was obsessed with computer access, letting the taxpayers foot the bill. Right now, that seemed fine with her if only she could get her fingers on that keyboard. The director, his back turned to her, clicked something on the wall and then she heard a staff member shout, "*Ça marche.*"

Probably a Troisus security system, activated by two settings. Pretty standard for government buildings with an indoor switch and one outside. She'd worry about the alarm later or use a skylight since they were rarely wired. She waited a good five minutes, in case anyone forgot something and came back, almost peeing on herself before searching for a restroom.

After she had gratefully relieved herself in Victor Hugo's bidet, which was closer than the toilet, she sat down in the director's chair, clicking on an electric heater to take away the bone-chilling cold.

Familiar with this state-of-the-art system, she tried several versions of the director's initials until she hit the right one that logged her onto his terminal. She slid off her high-heeled pumps and chewed the last chocolate croissant. She tried several generic access codes. On her third try, she accessed the Archives of France.

She rang Martine on her cell phone. "Martine, don't trust the *flics* anymore."

"What do you mean?" Martine sounded more tired than usual.

"They took René out."

"Your partner?" Martine said.

"Listen, I need two things, *d'accord?*"

"Where's my story? You promised me," Martine said.

Aimée pushed the director's chair back and peered out the tall window. Shadows lengthened in Place des Vosges. Figures moved back and forth. They could be passersby or B.R.I., she couldn't tell.

"Send a reporter to check on René in the hospital. I can't go because they're looking for me. Break a story like 'Mysterious Shooting, Neo-Nazi Assassin with Swastika Tattoos.' Blow it up big on the front page. Right now, fax me that last cheat sheet."

"What kind of trouble are you in?" There was concern in Martine's voice. "Who is after you?"

"Take a number, who isn't? Here's the fax where I am." Aimée read it off the machine near the director's computer. "Check on René first, please! Do it right now, okay? And I promise you this whole thing is yours." She didn't add *if I make it.*

On the alert for a night cleaner, she wandered the rooms. Prosperous writers in Hugo's time couldn't be said to have lived in a sumptuous mode. In his bedroom she looked out and saw the dusk settling over the plane trees in the square. If there was a police presence she didn't see it, only parents attempting to round up their children from the playground.

She noticed a placard next to the folds of a brocade canopy that cascaded heavily to the floorboards announcing that the great writer had expired in this bed. Uneasiness washed over her. Did Victor Hugo haunt these rooms? Ghosts, ghosts everywhere.

The fax feed groaned. Startled, she bumped into a wooden armoire, which creaked, sending the mice under it scurrying down the hall. Rodents. She hated rodents. Dust puffed over the wooden floor. From somewhere deep in her shoulder bag, her cell phone tinkled and she choked back a cough.

"Look at this," Martine's voice crackled over the phone. "Can you find her with this photo?"

Aimée ran to the fax machine. She gasped when she saw the face, clear and unmistakable.

"I already have," she said.

"THIS IS AIMÉE LEDUC," she said into her cell phone. "I need to see you."

A long silence.

"You're in danger. Go out the back of your building, there's a courtyard in the rear, right?" Aimée didn't wait for an answer. "Bring a hammer or chisel. Find the door to the alley, there's always one. It's where the horses were stabled; break it open. Do you understand so far?" Aimée waited but all she heard was a sharp intake of breath over the phone.

She continued, "Go to the button factory Mon Bouton, around the corner from Place des Vosges on rue de Turenne. Tonight it's open late. Go inside, but nowhere near a window. Leave now and I should get there just when you do." Still silence at the other end. "Whatever happened between you and Lili Stein is in the past. I'm doing this because she didn't deserve to be murdered. They're after you now. Leave immediately." Aimée hung up.

Aimée's brightly lit goal, the button factory, twinkled from over the rooftops and through the trees. One street over from the Place des Vosges, Mon Bouton inhabited a small courtyard.

Victor Hugo's canopied bed bordered on comfortable and apart from the scurrying noises, she felt safe. But now Aimée had to leave the museum without setting off the alarm. She tied assorted cleaning smocks and rags from a utility closet together with sheets she'd found under the bed of the great writer. She grabbed the guard's chair and slung it over the toilet. Few museums bothered to include skylights more than three stories high in their alarm systems. Here, two metal bars were strung across the thick, webbed glass. She swung the roped rags over the bars and hoisted herself onto the chair. Hunched below the rectangular skylight, she aimed her right foot and kicked one of the bars.

She wished she wore boots instead of several-hundred-franc high heels. After several attempts, the bar loosened enough for her to slowly wedge it out. But it was still too narrow for her to slide through. She kicked again and again. Finally she kicked the second bar loose and pulled herself up slowly. As she released the handle, the skylight popped open. The night air was clear and crisp amid the chimney pots and slanted roofs.

She had to reach the button factory on rue des Tournelles across the roofs of Place des Vosges. With her skirt hiked up over her thighs she climbed the peaked eaves and straddled corbels. The spiky ears and tails of gargoyles perched below her on the right. She made her way across the rooftops sliding over ancient slate tiles, her high heels scrabbling for purchase on the sleek surface. Open windows and skylights exhaled vestiges of classical music, the clatter of cooking pots, the scattered moans of lovemaking. She gripped a moldering brick exhaust cone and felt a wet mushy turd under her palm. Rodents.

Steamy, greasy vapor shot out of the cone as Aimée grabbed at rusty iron rungs leading over a high bricked abutment. Climbing, breathing hard, she pulled herself up each rung slowly. The smell of frying onions from a lighted kitchen below assailed her nostrils as a little boy cried out, "I'm hungry, Maman!"

At another series of roofs she stopped, kneeling high above the Marais, to catch her breath. More rungs led to a sloping roof over the button factory courtyard. Spread-eagled, she worked her way along the chipped shingles, using her toes to find niches when the rungs twisted or came loose. Slipping along, clutching at oily slate shingles broken off in places, she reached a metal overhang above the courtyard. Probably a twenty-foot drop. If she could clamp on to the rusty fire-escape ladder and slide down, it might just be a ten-foot drop.

She aimed for the tin gutter next to it. Lying facedown, she scooted herself forward a few feet at a time until she finally grasped the chute leading to the rain gutter.

She had to say one thing for this designer wear, it held up under tough conditions. If the chute couldn't bear her weight she'd have to reach out, push off the gutter, and grab the fire escape quickly. Which happened as soon as she'd thought it. She grabbed at the tin gutter which squealed as her fingernails raked over it.

She tried desperately to hold on to the narrow ridge of the gutter as her legs swung wildly in the air. Cold air rushed around her as she reached for the fire-escape rail with her other hand. This is it, I'm done for, she thought. A wild circus act before I splatter on the cobblestones in an Issey Miyake suit hiked over my thighs. Her father's grinning face next to a faded sepia likeness of her mother flashed through her mind. Her only chance was a dumpster below her filled with God knew what.

She screamed as the gutter broke and she dove towards the dumpster.

And plunged, somersaulting, into the cold night air.

She landed sitting upright in a dumpster full of buttons that cushioned her fall. Red, green, and yellow ones. Glossy and shining in the moonlight that peeked over the trees. The buttons ground against each other as she reached up to the dumpster rim. Her hand slipped and she was buried under mounds of buttons. Jesus, would she be suffocated by these colored disks after she'd survived a twenty-foot fall from the roof?

She finally managed to pull herself up, crunching scores of buttons. The courtyard seemed amazingly quiet. Pulling her skirt down, she shook herself, and a myriad red, green, and yellow pellets rained on the cobblestones. She'd landed in a batch of defective button rejects. She tramped into the side door of Mon Bouton.

"Ça va, Leah?" Aimée kissed her.

Leah's eyes opened in wonder at her appearance. "Such a nice suit!" She came closer, being myopically shortsighted from sorting buttons for so many years. "Is it . . . ?"

"Murder." Aimée nodded, feeling guilty for abusing Leah's trust.

At that moment the door opened slightly and Aimée turned.

"I'm here." Albertine Clouzot's housekeeper, Florence, hesitated. "I almost didn't come."

Aimée gently took her arm. "You're safe here, Sarah."

The former Sarah Strauss wore a black pageboy wig framing her startling blue eyes. Gaunt and tall, her beauty still glowed. She stuck her trembling hands in the pockets of her raincoat.

She stared at Aimée. "But I noticed the same man who'd been out front when I returned from shopping. He was still there after you called."

"We need to talk. Coffee?"

The only other noise came from the hissing espresso maker on the gas stove top. Leah turned off the workroom lights, leaving only a dim spotlight on the cooktop. She nodded conspiratorially and left the room.

Aimée guided Sarah to a long wooden refectory table, gouged and scarred, alongside galvanized metal tubes and cylinders that sorted buttons. She poured steamy black espresso into two chipped demitasse cups and slid the bowl of brown sugar cubes across the table.

"Someone's out to kill you." Aimée sipped her espresso. "They're after me, too."

Sarah looked up from the demitasse cup, startled.

"What does the swastika carved into Lili Stein's forehead mean?" Aimée said, rubbing her hand on the wooden table.

Sarah shook her head.

Aimée had to get her to talk. "Sarah, this is all about the past. You know it!"

Fear and mostly sadness shone in Sarah's eyes. She whimpered, "A curse, that's what it is. Following me all my life. Why does

God allow this? I read the Torah, trying to understand, but . . ." And she collapsed, crying.

Aimée felt guilty for her outburst. "Look, I'm sorry." She leaned over and put her arm around the woman. "Sarah—do you mind if I call you that?" She lifted Sarah's chin up. "I never would judge your actions fifty years ago. I wasn't alive then. Just tell me what happened." Aimée paused. "Tell me about you and Lili."

"You found her body, didn't you?" Sarah said.

Aimée's stomach tightened.

Sarah looked down, unable to meet Aimée's eyes. "She'd changed."

Aimée's curiosity had been colored by fear. Ever since she saw the photo of Lili in the crowd when Sarah was tarred with the swastika.

Sarah spoke slowly. "That's all so long ago. Some of us spend our lives making up for the past," she sighed.

"Did she . . ." Aimée couldn't finish.

Sarah pulled off her black wig. "Do this?"

The scarred swastika across her forehead showed even in the dim light. Sarah nodded. "If Lili hadn't, someone else in the mob would have."

Aimée was amazed at the weary forgiveness in her voice.

Sarah read her eyes. "But she stopped them from hurting my baby. She persuaded the crowd to leave us alone. Helped me find shelter." Sarah sighed. "After fifty years, I saw her again, it must have been just before . . ."

Aimée bolted to attention. "Before she was murdered?"

"I recently moved back to Paris." Sarah nodded. "As you know, I'd only just begun working at Albertine's. Lili still lived on rue des Rosiers. I followed her. But I couldn't deal with the past."

Aimée asked, "You followed her?"

"She'd been terrified during the Occupation. Filled with jealousy and loathing toward me. Being young, I didn't realize that; I believed Lili abandoned me when she escaped Paris."

She shook her head. "But that day we bumped into each other at the cobbler's. Somehow I got the courage and told her who I was. Jew to Jew, for the first time, we talked. Then she told me about Laurent."

"Laurent?" Aimée said. She felt confused.

"She was afraid of Laurent," Sarah said.

Aimée shook her head. "Who's Laurent?"

"That troublemaker from Madame Pagnol's class so many years ago!" Sarah said. "Rumor had it he informed on parents of children he didn't like. A vicious type. Lili said she'd recognized him and had gone to talk with Soli Hecht."

Aimée stood up and started pacing, her high-heeled pumps crunching loose plastic chips and partial button forms on the floor. "You mean, Lili had recognized Laurent. Now . . . in the present day?"

Sarah rubbed her tired eyes. "Soli Hecht advised her to keep it quiet," she said. "Until he could come up with evidence. Documentation or something to do with her concierge. Help her prove that he wasn't who he said he was. Expose his identity."

"Wait a minute. Who is he?" Aimée said. She thought back to Soli's dying words. Lo . . . *l'eau*. "Who are we talking about?"

Sarah shrugged. "I don't know."

"Let me understand this," Aimée said and stood up. "Lili, using Soli Hecht's help, was about to expose Laurent, a former collaborator, who had hidden his identity. But why wouldn't she tell you who he is?" Aimée began pacing back and forth.

"Lili was getting nervous, then acting almost as if she didn't know me," Sarah said. "That's when she turned abruptly, said she was being followed. Later, after I picked up the dry cleaning, I saw her. She grabbed me, I don't know why, then ran away before I could talk to her."

"That's when the button came off the Chanel suit and got tangled in her bag," Aimée said, pacing faster now. "Did your conversation occur at the cobbler's?"

"No, outside, near the corner of the alley," Sarah said.

"What time?"

"Just before six, I think."

"You're in greater danger than I thought," Aimée said, unable to stop pacing. She had the pieces now to fit in the puzzle.

"Why?" Sarah mumbled. "Is it my son?"

"That's a separate issue. He abhors the fact that you are Jewish because it means he is too."

"Is Helmut after me?"

Of course, now it all made sense. Hartmuth was Helmut Volpe.

"No, he told me you were in trouble. He's trying to save you. And Lili tried to save you too," Aimée said.

"What do you mean?"

"From Laurent. Can't you see?" Aimée said, trying to control her excitement but her words spilled out. "Think about how, as you talked with Lili, she changed. How she pretended not to know you and edge away. He was there, somewhere. She did it so he wouldn't know who you were." Aimée sat down close to Sarah. "I promise, he's not going to get you!"

Friday

Friday Morning

HARTMUTH'S NIGHTMARES WERE FILLED with ice tongs and crying babies. Sleep had eluded him.

There was a slight knock on the door from the adjoining suite. It would be Ilse. He pulled on a robe and shuffled to the door.

"*Mein Herr,*" Ilse said, her eyes bright as they quickly swept his room. "You are back! I checked late last night but your room was empty. We missed you!"

Hartmuth forced a grin. "This rich French food, Ilse, I'm not used to it. If I don't walk, it just curdles in my stomach."

"*Jawohl,* you are so right. Myself," she sidled closer to him, "I miss our German food. Simple yes, but so good and nutritious." Without missing a beat, she continued, "I don't mind telling you, mein Herr, that Monsieur Quimper and Minister Cazaux are of the old school. Because of their sincerity, all the delegates have agreed as of tonight to sign the treaty. But of course, this happens tomorrow at the ceremony. And with your signature to make it unanimous."

"What time is the ceremony, Ilse?" he said in as businesslike a tone as he could summon.

"Nineteen hundred hours, mein Herr," and she smiled. "In time for the CNN worldwide news feed. A nice touch, I thought." She lumbered to the door. "*Unter den Linden.*"

The treaty was as good as signed.

AIMÉE KNOCKED TWICE, THEN again. Slowly, Javel opened the door wearing a tattered undershirt.

"I'm busy," he said, not smiling. "There's nothing more to say."

Aimée put her foot in the door. "Just a few minutes; it won't take long," she said and slid through the doorway.

He grudgingly stood aside in the hallway.

"Does this go into your shop?" Aimée said, pointing at a damp, moldy door.

He nodded, his eyes narrowing.

She quickly climbed the three stairs and pushed the door before he could stop her.

"Eh, what are you doing?" he said.

By the time he had painstakingly climbed the steps she was back out the door again and had shot past him down the narrow hallway.

He caught up with her in the parlor and found his tongue. "You're just a nosy amateur detective running around in circles," he said.

Aimée stared at him. "You heard the whole thing, didn't you?"

"What are you talking about?" he asked angrily, gripping the back of his only chair.

"In this shop and around the rue Pavée. The spot's so close I bet you can spit that far," she said.

He spluttered, his eyes furtive. "None of this makes any sense. You're all the same!" He hastily shut the drawer in his pine kitchen table and moved to his rocking chair.

"Is that why you decided to take the law into your own hands, be a vigilante for a fifty-year-old crime?" she said.

He was obviously hiding something. She sidled next to the table, opening the single drawer by its rusted knob.

"What are you doing? Get away from there!" he yelled.

Aimée felt under Arlette's hand-embroidered napkins and reached towards the back. She pulled out a string bag and yarn from the drawer. "Why did you keep it?"

"Keep what?" he said.

"Lili Stein's bag and her knitting," she said as she lifted it out of the drawer.

"I-I found it," he said.

"On Wednesday you overheard Lili and Sarah talking about the past," she said. "From what you overheard, you thought Lili had killed Arlette, fifty years ago. After Sarah left, you confronted Lili. Lili vehemently denied killing her but she called Arlette a thieving, opportunistic blackmailer who had it coming to her. Didn't she?" She paused, looking at Javel's glittering hate-filled eyes. "Or words to that effect. You reached in your pocket for the only thing available," she said and pulled a thin wire out of her pocket. "You followed her, then strangled her with one like this from your shop. Finally, you carved the swastika to make it look like neo-Nazis."

She dangled the metal shoe wire in the air. "See the clear plastic at the end of this that protects and makes it easy to lace through the holes. That bit came off next to Lili. The other end is in the police evidence bag," she said.

Shaking his head, he screamed, "Stop this fantasy. Stop these lies!"

Aimée continued, "It's this that puts you at the scene of the crime with a motive!" She held up Lili's bag with her knitting.

His face was florid and he was panting.

"But you had killed the wrong person. Arlette's killer was back in Paris," she said.

"No! Idiot!" he said, furiously shaking his head back and forth. "Never left, I tell you."

She watched him carefully. "You were about to kill Hartmuth, only . . ."

"Lies, lies," he screamed.

When he rushed at her with an old pipe he'd lifted from behind the chair, she was prepared. Swiftly she twisted the pipe away and tripped him up. He thudded to the ground and she straddled his legs, immediately pinning him down. She felt sorry for him until he ripped out chunks of her hair while he struggled. "Jew lover! Arlette's murderer is still alive!" he said, gasping.

"Are you going to fight me all the way?" she said. "Okay, little man, I can fight too." Whereupon she punched him solidly in the head. "That's so you won't cause me any more hair loss."

At least he couldn't fight her now. She stood up, attempting to brush her roosterlike hair down. She lifted his bowlegs and began to drag the semiconscious man awkwardly through his hallway. A stinging whack whipped her off balance and she landed under his old television. She envisioned the TV's rabbit-ears antenna about to spear her as they tumbled off, but she couldn't move.

"Javel, Javel!" she mumbled.

Silence. Then the insistent jingle of bells.

AIMÉE WONDERED why they hadn't even bothered to trash the place. Javel's bulging eyes stared at the ceiling. His head was cocked in a way only a dead man's could. He had been strangled by wire from his own shop, just like the kind used on Lili. Someone had tried to make it look like suicide, dangling him from a rafter. The note looked genuine enough, especially if he'd been forced to write it. *I will join you, Arlette.*

Only she had heard him scream. She'd come to and passed out again. Why hadn't she been strangled, too? A distant jangling lodged in her brain. The bells. Then she recognized the noise. Bells from the shop door to the street meant customers who came in and out. A voice asked, "*Il ya a quelqu'un?* Somebody here?"

Then the bells jingled and she heard the door shut as the customer left.

She struggled out from under the TV table and felt guilty. Again. She'd accused Javel and when he started telling her that Arlette's killer was alive she'd slugged him. The killer, entering through the connecting shop door, had probably stood right there and silently thanked her. Until sending her across the room, knocking her and her theory to smithereens. Not only had she barked up the wrong tree but she'd helped the killer.

But why go to the trouble of making it look like suicide? Unless the killer had been about to do Aimée when a customer appeared, but even then? Maybe now the feisty little Javel would join his Arlette after all this time.

Lili's string bag was gone. A puffy white cat slinked around her ankles like a feather boa and meowed.

"Poor thing, who'll take care of you?" Aimée said, rubbing its head. She staggered through the blue beaded curtain to fetch milk for the cat, then she stopped. What had Lili carried in her string bag beside her knitting? Javel would have hidden anything else he'd found.

She started searching, pulling drawers and cupboards apart to find out. Might as well make it look like the crime she figured it was. Poor old Javel, he had little and threw little away. His one armoire held unworn starched white shirts and two musty suits. A pair of lambskin handcrafted shoes, the kind few people could afford to wear anymore, sat unworn on the lowest shelf. His hall cupboard held an unused bed linen set, yellowed by age and probably embroidered by Arlette.

She searched every grime-infested nook in his apartment. Nothing but the remnants of a lonely old man.

Maybe Lili didn't have anything else in her bag . . . or the killer had known what to look for and found it. Frustrated by another dead end, she slumped against the cupboard. The circumstances of Javel's murder puzzled her.

He'd probably spent most of his time in his shop so she decided to search that next. The sharp tang of leather assaulted her as she entered. Under the display of arch supports, she found his cluttered work tray. Tightly wedged against the wall, it took her several tries before the tray came loose. Under leather scraps lay a small book, beat-up and well thumbed. Black spiders crawled over Lili's handwriting. With trembling hands Aimée lifted the journal as skeins of multicolored wool trailed to the wood floor. She brushed the spiders off and stuffed the journal under her designer jacket.

In Javel's room, she poured cat food into the bowl. As she left, she made the sign of the cross, then whispered to Javel, who gazed sightlessly at the ceiling. "You were right. I'll get him this time."

BACK AT Leah's, Aimée read from a torn page of Lili's journal:

> I know it's him. Laurent, the greedy-eyed wonder who sat by me and copied my answers on math tests. The one who sniggered at Papa working behind the counter, who called us Yid bloodsuckers to my face then dared me to do something about it. The one whose family owned a building but acted like he owned the block. WORSE than the Nazis, he made sure that everyone in school who'd ever rubbed him wrong paid. Power, pure and simple. Sarah's parents were the first, he even boasted about it. Earned one hundred francs for each denunciation. But me, I killed my parents the day I took a stand and refused to let him cheat. My big moral standing sent them to the ovens. Jewish or not, he informed on anyone. Arlette, greedy and stupid, laughed at him, her big mistake. And he's going to do it again.

Sarah's hand shook as Aimée passed her the torn fragment. "Would you recognize him after all these years?"

"If Lili could . . ." She rubbed at the tears in her eyes. "He had a birthmark on his neck, like a brown butterfly."

"Of course he could have hidden it, done something surgically," Aimée said.

"I always wondered who denounced my parents. Laurent was older, in Lili's class. I never said much, tried to avoid him. Something about him I didn't like."

"There has to be proof in black and white," Aimée said. "That's why Lili contacted Soli Hecht. But I need documentation to prove it. Can you recall where he lived, this building Lili mentioned?"

"On rue du Plâtre around the corner from school," Sarah answered right away. "His parents were slumlords; it was once the prettiest tree-lined street in the Jewish ghetto."

"Stay here, Sarah. You're not safe on the street."

Frightened, Sarah crossed her arms. "But I can't do that. I have a job. Albertine needs my help, she counts on me."

"Call her," Aimée said. "She'll find someone else for now."

"But there's an important supper party this evening—" Sarah started to say.

"It's not safe for you or anyone with you. You'll put them in danger. Stay here, off the street. Albertine will manage." Aimée could tell Sarah hesitated, still not convinced. "If Lili recognized Laurent and got killed for it"—Aimée paused and spoke slowly—"don't you realize you're next?"

AIMÉE ENTERED the schoolyard off busy rue des Blancs Manteaux to see lines of children filing up the lycée steps. Probably just as they had done fifty years ago. This time there were no yellow stars, only clumps of adolescent dark-skinned children with big eyes walking past taunts and insults.

As she approached, a teacher noticed her and quickly admonished, "*Arrête.*" The jeers subsided.

"Are you a parent?"

"I have business in the office."

"May I see your identification? We take bomb threats seriously." The puffy-faced teacher looked like she needed another night's sleep. "Ministry of Education's edict."

"Of course." Aimée showed her.

"Over there and to the right." Behind the teacher a fight had broken out and she left to break it up.

Inside the school office a rotund ebony-faced woman squinted as she checked the computer. "Records are in the basement if we've kept them and the silverfish haven't eaten them," she said.

"Thanks, can you check?"

"Last name?"

"First name is Laurent and the family lived on rue du Plâtre," Aimée said.

The secretary raised her eyebrow. "Years of attendance?"

"Between 1941 and 1945, during the war."

The secretary looked up immediately and shook her head. "After ten years, everything is sent to the ministry of education." She shrugged. "Check back in a couple of weeks."

"But I need it now!"

"Everybody needs it now. Do you know how many children attended the school at the time?" She looked at Aimée. "Frankly, I'd say don't waste your time, nothing got put on microfiche until the sixties."

"Any teacher or custodian who might have gone to school here?" Aimée said.

"Before my time," the secretary paused, "but Renata, a woman in the cafeteria, has worked here as long as I remember. That's all I can suggest."

In the yellow-tiled cafeteria, Renata, a woman with a thick gray braid wound across the nape of her neck, narrowed her eyes in suspicion.

"Who did you say you were?" she asked.

Aimée told her.

Renata just shook her head.

One of the servers, a prune-faced woman, walked over to Aimée and nudged her. "She forgets to turn on her hearing aid."

Aimée thanked her and pointed to Renata's ear. Renata only scowled.

"She's quite vain about it. Thinks none of us know," the woman, whose name tag said SYLVIE REDONNET, confided. "As if we cared. Half the time we go around yelling at her since she can't hear."

Renata stirred the ladle of a steaming pot of lentils.

Aimée turned to Sylvie, who grinned. "Maybe you can help me?"

After Aimée explained, the woman nodded her head. "Believe it or not, I'm too young to have been here in the forties," she chuckled. "Now my sister, Odile, a few years older than me, was. Go ask her—she loves to talk."

"That would help me, thank you."

"You'll be a treat for Odile, she can hear." Sylvie glanced in Renata's direction. "But she's wheelchair-bound. Around the corner, number 19 rue du Plâtre."

Aimée felt a glimmer of hope when she heard the address.

ODILE CACKLED from five floors above as Aimée huffed up the steep metal-grilled staircase. "One thing I don't have to worry about."

Aimée reached the landing at last. "Odile Redonnet?" she said. Looks certainly did not bless this family, Aimée thought, looking at the shriveled crone in the black steel wheelchair.

"Pleased to meet you, Aimée Leduc, my sister phoned about your visit. Come in." Odile Redonnet wheeled herself ahead of Aimée into the apartment. "Please shut the door behind you."

After two potfuls of strong Darjeeling tea and exquisite freshly baked madeleines, Odile Redonnet let Aimée get to her point.

"I'm looking for someone," she began.

"Aren't we all?"

"A boy named Laurent, his family owned a building on this street. He'd have been about fifteen or sixteen in 1943."

In answer, Odile wheeled over to an oak chest and slid open a creaking drawer. She pulled out a musty album. Several loose black-and-white photos danced to the floor. Aimée bent down to pick them up. In one she saw a radiant Odile standing upright with her arms around an RAF-uniformed man.

Aimée looked at her and smiled. "You're beautiful."

"And in love. That always enhances one's looks," Odile said. "This should help my memory." She laid the heavy album on her dining table and motioned to Aimée. "A ride down memory lane. Can you slip the phonograph on?"

Reluctantly, Aimée went and stood over an old record player that played 78s. She cranked it several times, then laid the needle on the scratched black vinyl. Strains of Glenn Miller and his forties big band filled the room. Odile Redonnet's eyes glazed and she smiled.

"I left the lycée in '44 to work in a glass factory," she said, turning the floppy pages.

"Are there any class photos?"

"Can't say we were so sophisticated then," Odile said, searching the tired pages. She hummed along with the scratchy clarinet solo. "This is the closest thing to a class picture," she said, pulling some gummed photos apart.

Aimée almost spilled her hot tea. It was the same photo she'd deciphered from the encrypted disk Soli Hecht had given her. "Which one is Laurent?"

Odile Redonnet's gnarled finger pointed to a tall boy standing by Lili in the Square Georges-Cain. "Laurent de Saux, if that's who you mean. Lived at number 23, two doors down."

This black-and-white photo showed the café with strolling Nazis and the park with students.

"How did you get this?"

"Madame Pagnol, our history teacher, took it to illustrate the statue of Caesar Augustus. See." She pointed out the marble statue in the background. "We were studying the Roman Empire."

Of course, Aimée realized now. What had appeared as a random street scene worked as an illustration of the magnificent Caesar Augustus statue. That's why it had been taken.

"Did she give one to each student?"

"Oh, no," Odile said. "Only to those who could afford it. After this I left school. Never finished."

She struggled to contain her excitement—*Here was the proof . . . but proof of what?*

"Laurent informed on students during the Occupation."

Odile closed her eyes.

"Or was it you?" Aimée said.

Anger flashed in Odile's eyes. "Never." She pushed the album away.

"Nostalgia isn't what it used to be." Aimée had had enough. "That good-old-days stuff doesn't work."

Odile stared out the window. "Nothing disappears, eh?"

"Bald and ugly truth doesn't."

Finally Odile spoke. "Laurent asked me to inform. Anonymous tips got one hundred francs. The Gestapo offered several hundred francs for outright denunciations. But I wouldn't. I saw the hate and fear in classmates' faces after Laurent walked by. He assumed the Nazis would win the war and protect him."

"How about you?"

"Wrong person, wrong time. I sheltered that RAF pilot during the Occupation. So they taught me a lesson." She pointed to her withered legs.

"Who?"

"The Gestapo doctors doing research on spinal nerve endings. They chose me to experiment on. Took me to Berlin, then exhibited me as a freak."

"Please forgive me." Aimée shook her head. "I'm sorry."

"I was, too." Odile smiled. "But I still try to remember the few good old times."

"What happened to Laurent?"

"Didn't see him towards the end. Disappeared with a lot of people. Who knows?"

"What about his family?" Aimée said.

"Shot." She pointed out the window. "Against that wall. His stepmother and father in 1943. Rumor had it that he informed on them."

Aimée almost choked on her tea.

"Who took over the building?" she finally managed.

"Some cousin from his mother's side. You see, he took his mother's name, she had the money. After she died and his father remarried, he kept her name."

"Which name?" Aimée said.

"Always called himself de Saux. Hated his father for marrying again."

Odile Redonnet paused, looking at Aimée for a long moment.

"It's all about him, isn't it?"

Aimée nodded.

"Evil incarnate, but I can't even say that because he was amoral. No conscience. He'd do anything to hold power over someone. But Laurent disappeared, like so many collaborators after the war. He was seventeen or eighteen at Liberation. Who'd recognize him now in his sixties?"

Aimée paused, recalling the torn page from Lili's journal. "I know it's him. Laurent." Lili's phrase that Abraham had repeated to her—"Never forget." Lili had recognized Laurent because he'd sent her family to the ovens. She'd never forgiven him.

"He's back, isn't he?"

"May I have this?" Aimée stood up. "I have to find out who he is and this should help."

She put the photo in her bag, then took her teacup to the kitchen and put it in the sink. Odile's kitchen window looked on to a series of dilapidated courtyards. Number 23 was probably one of them.

At the door, Aimée turned. "Thank you," she said. "But I disagree, Odile."

"How's that?" Odile asked from her wheelchair near the table.

"I'm beginning to believe he never left," Aimée said.

THE FIRST bell she rang was answered by a fortyish woman in a zebra leotard, with flushed cheeks and a light beading of sweat. Aimée could hear the pounding beats of heavy drums in the background.

"The owner? Don't know. Send my checks to a property management," she said, out of breath.

"How about the concierge?"

"Isn't one." Her phone started ringing. "Sorry," she said and she closed the door.

None of the other doors she rang answered. She wandered to the back of the building where the garbage cans were kept, hunting for the gas meter. At last she found it behind a rotted wood half door. She wrote down the serial number of the meter. Easy to trace if she accessed EDF—Électricité de France, otherwise a tedious search at the tax office for ownership. Of course, she still might end up going there. Now she needed computer access and pondered breaking back into the Victor Hugo Museum to hit the keys on their state-of-the-art computer.

SHE CALLED ABRAHAM STEIN from a public phone in the Metro station at Concorde since her cell-phone batteries had died. Sinta answered.

"Abraham's talking with some big-nosed *flic*."

"A chain-smoker, with suspenders?" Aimée asked.

"You got it."

"Please get Abraham, but don't tell him it's me." Aimée waited while Sinta fetched him. She heard the radio news broadcast blaring in the background, with a reporter's terse comments. "Riot police have been called to clear away demonstrators from the Elysée Palace where the European Union Summit Tariff will be signed. Sporadic confrontations between neo-Nazi groups and the Green Party are happening here and in parts of the 4th arrondissement, notably around Bastille."

The phone scraped something as Abraham picked it up. "Yes?"

"It's Aimée. Don't say anything, just listen, then answer with yes or no if you can."

He grunted, then she heard him say, "Sinta, offer the detective some tea."

"Is his name Morbier?"

"Yes."

"Has he mentioned me? Asked when you've last seen me?"

"Yes, doubly so."

"To do with Lili's murder?"

"Yes."

All of a sudden she heard Abraham clear his throat and Morbier's gravelly voice came on the line.

"Leduc! Where the hell are—?"

"Why are you setting me up, Morbier?" she said.

"Wait a big minute. You didn't meet me or return my calls and now your partner got shot up," he said.

"Cut the crap," she said. "Who's behind this? I'm clicking off before your three-minute tracer locates me. I've got some questions."

"By the way, your partner is cranky as hell," he said. "Pissed you left him. Seems he might not want to be your partner anymore."

"Why are you asking Abraham questions when you've been taken off Lili's case?" she said, checking her watch.

"Just curious if he's heard from you," he said.

"Why the hell ambush me?" she said.

"You're paranoid, what's gotten into you? Listen, Leduc, take a reality pill. No one's after you."

"The only other explanation is that my phone was tapped, they heard where we were meeting. Javel . . ."

He interrupted her. "Why are your prints all over his place anyway?"

Her fingerprints were all over the rooms of a supposed suicide. Two minutes and fifty seconds showed on her watch as she hung up the pay phone.

Aimée heard the whine of metal grinding metal and whish of air brakes as the train pulled in. She slid through the door of the train bound for Porte de Vanves, full of Parisians going home from work. She clutched the overhead rail as her head spun and she felt sick to her stomach. Who was telling the truth? Could René, her partner and friend since the Sorbonne, have turned on her? Had he really been protecting her when he told her to run? Of course he was. His protective behavior ran consistent with how he always treated her. Usually to her annoyance.

Then there was Morbier. He'd lied about investigating Lili and had certainly been acting out of character.

She got off at Châtelet. At the kiosk she bought a recharger for her dead cell phone. Commuters washed around her like a wave on the platform, parting before her at the last minute. In the black designer suit she blended in well with the professionals at rush hour. After she had inserted the charger her phone beeped immediately.

"Yes." She looked at her wristwatch.

"About time," Thierry said. "You're a hard lady to reach. Found her?"

"We need to meet," she said.

"Bring Sarah to my office in Clingancourt," Thierry said.

No way in hell would she do that.

"Meet me at Dessange in Bastille, thirty minutes."

"You mean that hair place? How can . . . ?"

"In thirty minutes. After that I'm gone." She clicked off and called Clotilde.

JUST BECAUSE she was on the run, with skinheads and the police all searching for her and unable to return to her apartment, it wasn't reason enough to have greasy hair. Clotilde lathered Aimée's hair with henna as Françoise, the proprietress, escorted Thierry to the shampoo area.

Nonplused, Thierry asked, "What's this all about?"

"Sit down. You could use a trim," said Aimée.

He snorted. "Cut the smart remarks."

"A full-service salon, nails, facials. Why not take advantage?" she said beneath the suds, smiling at Clotilde, who massaged her scalp. Thierry fiddled with his hands and looked uncomfortable. She indicated a space in the light and airy salon, bustling with colorists in lab coats, women with tin foil wrapped in strands like antennas from their heads, and huge blown-up photos of waiflike models on the walls. Hair dryers and vintage disco music kept the beat in the background along with the hot ammonia smell of permanent waves.

Thierry either had to stand and talk down to Aimée or lie back on a chair and get a shampoo. He chose to stand. "Have you found her?"

"If I have, what does that mean to you?" Aimée said as Clotilde rinsed her warm soapy hair.

"That's your job. I asked you to help me," he said. "Now that we found my father. My real father."

"Why do you want to meet her?" she said.

"It's only natural, isn't it?" he said.

As Aimée sat up and Clotilde dried her hair, she noticed his bloodshot eyes and jerky movements. He clutched and unclutched the leather belt of his storm-trooper coat. She would never engineer a reunion between Sarah and Thierry in his present condition.

"Look, I'm going back to the demonstration at the Elysée Palace," he said. "We're forcing the Greens to back down. Showing those idiots that people will take a stand. The agreement will be signed."

He sounded petulant and whiny for a fifty-year-old man. And scary.

"Do you mean the European Union Trade Agreement?"

He nodded. "Let me see her, talk with her."

"I'll ask her. Why did that scum in lederhosen have a heat-seeking rifle?"

Thierry's eyes narrowed. "What?"

"Tried to pepper me with bullets like a rabbit. In the courtyard of Hôtel de Sully." Aimée slouched under the warm wet towel as Clotilde kept tousling her hair.

Thierry reluctantly followed them to a hydraulic chair that Clotilde pumped with her foot. As she looked in the mirror, Aimée found she resembled a drowned furry creature while he looked predatory and disheveled.

"Maybe you want to tell me about it," she said.

"Sounds like you're getting paranoid," he said, shaking his head. "He's busy organizing the demonstrations."

"Not anymore," she said. "And it's too late to ask him."

Thierry twisted the chair around so fast that Clotilde's scissors and set of combs went flying. Canisters of mousse and styling gel clattered to the floor. All eyes turned to her, straitjacketed in a barber's smock, and a nearly frothing Thierry, who gripped the armrests, shoving his face into Aimée's. Several stylists automatically picked up hairbrushes and one clutched a heavy-duty hair dryer defensively.

"You took out Leif?" Thierry eyes opened wide in disbelief.

"Him or me. That's what it came down to," she said uneasily. "Leif looked too greasy to be Nordic."

"Idiot!" he said. "A recognized *Korporal* in our corps."

"He shot at me from the roof," she said. "I won't apologize for making it out alive."

All of a sudden, Thierry looked up and noticed the stylists watching him with raised beauty implements.

His voice dropped to a whisper. "Bring the Jew sow," he hissed. "Meet me at the office tonight. If not, the dwarf won't make the morning."

It was her turn to be surprised.

"Room 224 in Ste. Catherine Hospital—your partner, René Friant."

And then he was gone, leaving a whiff of stale sweat.

Françoise rushed over. "Should I call the *flics?*"

"No, please," said Aimée. "Thanks, but nothing really happened."

Françoise nodded. "Bad news, eh?"

"In more ways than one," Aimée agreed.

With dripping hair, she grabbed her cell phone and immediately called Ste. Catherine's Hospital.

"Friant, René? He was discharged five minutes ago," the floor nurse told her in a flat voice.

She called their office. No one answered but she left a message in a code they'd worked out. She warned René and told him to meet her at her cousin Sebastian's later. She left the same message at his apartment. Now she felt somewhat reassured. If she couldn't find René, she doubted Thierry could. At least not right away.

The hum and buzz of a busy salon had returned and Clotilde looked at her expectantly, comb and scissors poised.

"Let's talk about color, this brown's too mousy," Aimée said.

Clotilde just winked and pulled out some swatches. Aimée pointed at several. With a new hair color, dark glasses, and the tailored suit, no one would recognize her in a crowd. In her radical departure from jeans, leather jacket, and scuffed boots she could sing the computers electric anywhere.

While Aimée sat there, she played out all the scenarios in her head. Even though she wanted to blame Thierry for the attack on her, he had seemed genuinely surprised.

Suppose Leif worked for Laurent, whoever he was. Could Laurent, with Leif's help, have disposed of Lili, shut Soli Hecht up, tried to kill her, supposedly shut down Morbier's investigation, trailed Sarah, strangled Javel, and made it look like suicide? To do all that, they'd have needed more help.

One part she didn't get—why not put the rope in her hand, make it look like she killed Javel? The only reason she could think of was that maybe a customer had come in and the killer didn't have the time.

Or the killer wanted attention deflected from Arlette's murder in the past. Make Javel out as morose; after missing Arlette all these years, he'd decided to join her in memorial. That would make sense, Aimée thought. Ever since the TV and morbid tabloid coverage of the Luminol extravaganza, things had heated up. The killer or killers had certainly been working overtime.

And that all brought her back to Laurent. She had to ferret out his identity and protect Sarah.

Her cropped hair now streaked with pale blond highlights, Aimée stepped out into the small cobbled street. A loud appreciative whistle came from the old man behind the nearby fruit cart. She winked at him and smiled to herself.

Opposite the salon, a well-dressed Yves came out of the wrought-iron entrance doors of Brasserie Bofinger. For once she knew her hair looked fantastic and she was dressed to match it. Nervous and delighted, she wondered what to do.

He looked dapper and businesslike in a navy blue double-breasted suit. Not like a neo-Nazi. Clotilde had brushed off the lint so the black suit looked runway-ready. A few buttons, remnants of the dumpster, had rained on the floor of the salon, and Aimée had told Clotilde the story as they giggled.

She seriously contemplated raising her arm to hail Yves, when an unmarked Renault screeched to a halt beside him in the small street.

The car wedged him into a doorway. Two plainclothes types pulled him, struggling and kicking, into the backseat. The doors slammed and the Renault screeched down the street.

She leaned against a window, shaken. She assumed they'd been undercover cops. After all, he was a neo-Nazi . . . wasn't he?

Friday Afternoon

HARTMUTH AND THIERRY SAT across from the Victor Hugo Museum by the playground in Place des Vosges. Children's laughter erupted from the swings under the barren-branched plane trees. The vaulted stone arcades surrounding the gated square, filled with fountains and grassy patches, reflected the late autumn sun's last rays. Over the worn stone cobbles wafted the smell of roasted chestnuts. Hartmuth's hands shook as he folded the newspaper he'd been pretending to read.

"I only agreed to meet because you said it's important," he said. "What do you have to say to me?"

"Millions of things. You are my father," Thierry's eyes shone, almost trance-like. "Let's start by getting to know one another. Tell me about my German family?"

Hartmuth stirred guiltily. "You had a sister once," he said after a long pause as he watched the children. "Her name was Katia. I wasn't a very good father."

Thierry shrugged.

"Who raised you?" Hartmuth asked.

"Some conservatives who lied to me." Thierry kicked at a pigeon anxious for crumbs. "But I've always been like you, believed in what you fought for. Now I know why I joined the *Kameradschaft*, it's natural that I would carry Aryan beliefs like you."

Hartmuth shook his head. He stood up and walked along the gravel path. He stopped at a slow gurgling fountain near the statue of Louis XIII on his horse.

Thierry stirred at the memories of Claude Rambuteau handing him crumbs for the pigeons at this very statue. Why hadn't the Rambuteaus told him his true identity?

"I said goodbye to her," Hartmuth said. "Here."

Startled, Thierry asked, "Who do you mean?"

"Your mother, before my troop shipped out to the slaughter at the front." He paused. "She's still beautiful," he murmured wistfully.

"How can you say that?" said Thierry, aghast. This wasn't how he imagined his Nazi father would act.

"I loved her and I still do," Hartmuth said. "She thinks it's all in my mind. Let me show you where we used to meet." Hartmuth strode across the square, pulling Thierry along.

None of the scurrying passersby paid much attention to them, a piercingly blue-eyed man and slender silver-haired gentleman, who, if one looked carefully, had a definite resemblance.

Halfway down the rue du Parc Royal, Hartmuth turned and pointed up at the arms of François the First, the marble salamander sculpted into the archway.

"I first saw her here, on these cobblestones," Hartmuth said. "But over there is where you were conceived, underground."

"Underground? What are you saying?" Thierry asked uneasily. Opposite, on rue Payenne adjoining Square Georges-Cain, Hartmuth agilely climbed over the locked gate. He started rooting in the plants among the ancient statuary. Thierry could hear clumps of dirt landing in the bushes. He was afraid Hartmuth was losing his mind.

"What are you doing?" Thierry asked, after he climbed in behind him.

"Come help me," Hartmuth said. He beckoned to Thierry, his eyes shining as if possessed. "Move this pillar." Hartmuth tried to push the broken marble column. "It's got to be around here."

"You're crazy. What are you going on about?" Thierry raised his voice.

The dusk was settling and the street lamps came on one by one.

"The entrance to the catacombs!" Hartmuth said. "We'll find it, they've been here since the Romans. They haven't gone away.

This city is honeycombed with the old Christian tunnels." He took Thierry's hand and stared at him. "I used to hide in them with your mother every night."

Thierry felt embarrassed by the longing evident in Hartmuth's eyes. "Why do you call her my mother? I never knew her, she abandoned me, she was a filthy Jew!" His hysterical laugh climbed to a high pitch. "Filthy, that's perfect! Rutting in the dirt with an Aryan."

"Odd. She said the same thing." Hartmuth shook his head sadly. "You mustn't hurt her. You do understand, don't you?"

"That an Aryan could sleep with a Jew?" Thierry said accusingly. "Was it because you were far from home and lonely? Maybe she seemed exotic and seduced you?"

Tears welled in Hartmuth's eyes. "Where did you get all this old hate?"

"I know Auschwitz was a lie," Thierry said. "My responsibility has been to expose those death-camp coverups."

"I smelled the stench of too many of them," Hartmuth said wearily and leaned against the broken marble column. "Your grandparents, Sarah's parents, ended up there."

Stunned, Thierry shouted, "No, no! I don't believe you."

A few passersby on the sidewalk turned to stare, then moved on.

"Our regiment troop train was bombed somewhere in Poland," Hartmuth said. "We had to rebuild the tracks in the snow while partisans shot at us from the woods. There was a terrible smell, out in that godforsaken forest, that never went away. We didn't know what it was because we saw no villages, only tunnels of black smoke. When the train ran again we passed a spur track. An arrow pointed to a sign saying Bergen-Belsen. Rotten corpses of those who'd jumped off the train littered the side of the tracks. I'll never forget that smell." Hartmuth spoke in a faraway voice.

Thierry glared at him. "You're lying, Jew lover!"

He climbed over the fence and ran off down the street. Hartmuth sank to his knees among the ruins but he had no more tears left. From deep inside came the old lullaby that his grandmother sang to him: *Liebling, du musst mir nicht böse sein, Liebling, spiele und lach ganzen Tag.*

He sang the words as he dug earth and moved stones. Long after the streetlights shone he was still digging.

SATURDAY

SOLANGE GOUTAL LOOKED UP from her work, her eyes swollen with crying. "Soli's dead . . . the rumor is that he was killed."

"It's more than a rumor, it's the truth," Aimée said, setting her leather bag on the granite counter below the chiseled words *Never forget.*

Solange averted her eyes. "Go in, the director will see you now."

Annick Sausotte, director of the Centre de Documentation Juive Contemporaine, bustled over to greet her. Extending her hand, she pumped Aimée's, then pulled her into an office.

"Ms. Leduc, it's unfortunate we meet after Soli Hecht's tragic death." Her quick darting eyes flicked over Aimée's suit and took in her leather bag. "Please sit here. I'm all yours for five minutes. Then I must run to a memorial luncheon."

"Thank you for seeing me, Ms. Sausotte. I'll get right to the point." Aimée perched on the edge of an uncomfortable tubular metal chair. "The Temple Emanuel has retained my services in the murder of Lili Stein. I believe Soli Hecht, at Lili's request, was investigating someone whom she recognized as a collaborator from the war. There's a connection and I want to know what Soli worked on the day he supposedly got run over by the bus."

"Supposedly run over by a bus you say, Ms. Leduc?" Annick Sausotte said.

Aimée looked at her sharp dark eyes. "Someone pushed him in front of the bus," she said. "But I can't substantiate that, Ms. Sausotte. Don't you wonder why he would take a bus when his rheumatoid arthritis had been so severe he needed help down the stairs and with his coat? And after he told Solange he'd take a taxi?"

"What do you want from me, Mademoiselle Leduc?" Annick said.

"Access into computer files that Soli worked on that day," Aimée said. "I came across his name in Lili's belongings. I believe she'd recognized a former collaborator and asked Soli for help to obtain proof." Aimée paused. "That's what got her killed."

Annick Sausotte leaned forward, her chin cradled in her palms, elbows mirrored on her polished desk. "Soli was the only one who could have authorized access to his files, but now . . ." She stopped, a look of sorrow crossing her face. "Of course, that's impossible. Only the foundation can grant such permission."

"I know he was murdered in the hospital. But I can't prove that either." Aimée stood up and leaned close into Annick's face. "There's another woman in danger, a survivor whose family perished in the Holocaust."

"Are you Jewish, Mademoiselle Leduc?"

"Is that a job requirement? Because I get the feeling that might be more important to you than someone's life." Aimée paced over to Annick, who rose. "Someone's after me, too, but they don't seem to care about my religion!"

"You're taking this personally, Ms. Leduc. Please understand . . ."

Aimée interrupted. "I tend to take things personally when my life is in danger. Will you help me or not?"

Annick Sausotte escorted her to the door. "I don't even handle that end of the center's operations. Let me check with those responsible and Soli's foundation. Call me in a few days."

Aimé shook her head. "You don't seem to understand."

"That's the best I can do," Annick said as she put her arms into a too large overcoat that engulfed her small frame. "Please call me tomorrow or the day after."

As Annick Sausotte rushed out, loud buzzing erupted behind

the reception desk. Aimée paused at the desk, studying the visitors' log intently.

"Solange, there's a delivery in the receiving bay," Annick said. "I'll hit the door opener here if you can go down and take it."

Solange grabbed her key ring, as Annick's footsteps echoed in the marble foyer.

"I'll use the restroom then let myself out with the director," Aimée said.

Solange hesitated. A shrill voice came over the intercom. "Frexpress delivery, I need a signature!"

Solange nodded at her, then disappeared behind the rear door. Aimée heard the click of the front doors closing and quickly scanned the security system. Security monitors showed Annick Sausotte striding to the narrow street and Solange signing a clipboard, handing it back to a uniformed driver, and then turning towards the camera. Then Aimée couldn't see her anymore.

She pulled open drawers until she found the one with plastic identification cards. Underneath were several passkeys and Aimée grabbed all of them, sticking them into her pocket. Aimée stepped inside the partially open door of Annick Sausotte's office. She figured she could stay in the office until closing time, which would be in about ten minutes. Aimée had just kicked off her achingly high heels and crumpled into the tubular chair when she heard Solange's voice.

"Annick, did you forget something?" she said.

Aimée looked over and saw a bulging briefcase on Annick's desk. She realized there was no closet and the desk offered no hiding place. The only other piece of furniture, an antique black-lacquered armoire, stood delicate and three-legged. She opened it to find it full of fragile porcelain.

Nowhere to hide.

She heard Annick's voice as a phone rang. "It's on my desk. I'll get this call."

Aimée grabbed her heels and flattened herself behind the door.

As Solange walked to the desk, Aimée pulled slowly on the door, almost covering herself behind it.

Solange had picked up the case and turned to leave when Annick said, "Solange, look for that press packet on the deportation monument, will you? Second or third drawer of my desk."

She couldn't see Solange but prayed that she'd find it. Quickly. Her nose itched. Unfortunately, her hands gripped her heels and she couldn't pinch her nose shut without banging the door.

She heard Solange rooting through the desk, rustling papers. "I can't find it. Which drawer?"

She tried pushing her nose against the wooden door to stop her sneeze but that only pushed it open more. She was just about to explode when Annick called out, "I found it."

Solange strode out of the room, banging the door shut behind her. Aimée dropped her heels on the carpet at the same time, muffling her sneeze with two hands as best she could. From behind the closed door came low conversation then silence.

While she slipped her heels back on, she dialed Leah's number at the button factory

"Leah, how is Sarah?"

Leah's voice answered in a low, conspiratorial tone. "At last check, all's well."

"How long ago did you check, Leah?" Aimée asked. "Our guest rates among the nervous variety. Probably could use company."

"Looked in a few hours ago," Leah said. "I'm closing up so I'll check. There's a gruyère soufflé with a caper tapénade relish in the oven . . ."

Aimée realized she hadn't eaten yet today. "Sounds wonderful. I'll be tied up a while, so please reassure her. I'll call you back."

Soli Hecht's foundation on the fifth floor resided in what had been poetically called a garret in the last century. Now it consisted of whitewashed rooms with slanted eaves and rectangular windows. White particle board ringed the office with continuous counter and shelving space. Several computers sat near a state-of-the-art copy machine and white metal file cabinets took up the remaining space.

The general antiseptic impression was marred by the photo covering a whole wall. A small child's foot hung out of a crematorium oven next to piles of ashes with smiling uniformed Gestapo members poking it with their riding crops. Bold letters below said NEVER FORGET . . .

Aimée's stomach lurched, but she forced herself to stay. She sat down at the nearest flashing computer terminal. She leaned her head against the screen, but still the photo wouldn't go away. What about that little foot? The mother who'd washed it, the father who'd tickled it, the grandmother who'd knitted socks for it, the grandfather who'd hoisted it on his shoulders? Probably all gone. Generations gone. Only ghosts remained.

So Soli Hecht reminded himself of why he worked here, Aimée realized. As if he needed the motivation, being a survivor of Treblinka himself. She started punching keys, playing with possible passwords to access Soli's hard drive. She considered the possibility of the attic effect, that all data storage survives on the hard drive. A user, like Hecht, would think he'd erased information by deleting it. But nothing ever went away. All written code was routed through the computer hardware and lodged in there somewhere, something she was paid well to find in her computer forensic investigations.

She discovered the password *Shoah* and found the terminals in Soli's foundation linked with the center's system downstairs and rubbed her hands excitedly. Methodically, she began accessing the hard drive, checking both data banks for Lili's name.

Soli's last computer activity was dated Friday, the day of his accident, two days after Lili's murder. No files had been opened or new files added. As she read his email she grew disappointed. There was only a brief message from the Simon Wiesenthal Center. Where would Soli's floppy backup disks be?

The locked file cabinets yielded to a wiggling paperclip and Aimée searched, keeping her gaze averted from the photo. Hundreds of pages of testimony from survivors about Klaus Barbie, the "Butcher of Lyon" which Soli had successfully documented. Aimée kicked the nearest cabinet; nothing newer than 1987. Baffled, Aimée began a systematic search of the whitewashed rooms. She emptied the files and took the file cabinets apart, checked under the computer for anything taped to its underside, and checked the carpet seams. Three hours later she remained thwarted. Nothing. Not even one floppy disk.

Something to do with Lili had to be here, she felt it. Would Soli have taken it with him? Even if he had, he'd have a copy or backup disk. At times like this, Aimée knew it was best to walk away and come back with a fresh eye to catch something she might have overlooked. She decided to go downstairs and check the center's microfiche file for cheat sheets from the Occupation.

The third-floor library system was clear, concise, and immaculately cross-referenced. Microfiche files of Jewish newspapers and bulletins rolled before her eyes.

An hour later, she found the old grainy photo with a brief article, *"Non Plus Froid"*:

> Students at the lycée on rue du Plâtre demonstrate patriotism for our French workers in Germany. This wool drive contributes to keeping our men warm this winter.

She saw Sarah and Lili, yellow stars embroidered on their dresses, standing by piles of coats in a school yard. There, too, was the face Odile Redonnet had identified as Laurent de Saux. On his neck, peeking from his shirt collar, was a butterfly-shaped birthmark.

She copied the article, complete with photo, on a laser copier standing flush with the wood-paneled library entrance. It eliminated distortions and blurs due to yellowed unarchival newsprint so that even minor facial distinctions were clear. The quality was excellent and irrefutable. She wondered how Laurent de Saux had hidden that birthmark.

Here was proof that Laurent knew Lili and Sarah. His identity remained the question. She had to check the bloody fingerprint against the French national file. Of course, she thought. Find a Laurent de Saux and check him against the bloody print!

That was when she heard the echo of footsteps. She froze. A raspy, hacking cough came from the hallway. Security? She dove under a nearby trestle table, clutching the copy in her hand. Then she realized the copy machine's cover stood suspiciously open and the red light blinked irritatingly.

Her leather bag lay on the marble floor by the machine. She peered from under the table and saw an elderly man, probably a retired *flic*, in a security uniform. She'd have to overpower him to log back on to Soli's computer and finish her search.

He hawked and spit into the metal garbage can near her head. Finally he switched off the machine, closed the cover with a thump, and flicked off the lights. He left a scent of last night's onion meal in the library.

And then she realized where Soli could have hidden things. Somewhere disturbing and offensive. That had to be it. The only place she hadn't looked! Silently, she rolled the copies into her bag, slipped off her heels again, and padded back up to the fifth floor.

Inside Hecht's foundation she approached the wall. Up close to the Gestapos' leering faces in the photograph she felt around. Smooth all the way to the tips of the riding crops, then she felt an indentation and slight groove. Pressing it, she heard a click, then felt a part of the wall open to her right with a swinging whoosh. A drawer slid out on tracks holding several disks in envelopes. She found a floppy titled "L. Stein." Steadying her hands, she took a deep breath and attempted to open the disk. But it didn't work.

The floppy was a WordPerfect file that had been protected with a password. She tried Soli's birthdate, his birthplace, events and names from the Holocaust. No success. Then she tried the names of all the concentration camps. Nothing. She tried Hebrew prayers and simple configurations of biblical references. Nothing. She needed René's code-breaking software to pick the lock of the file on Soli's disk.

She prayed that René had made it to her cousin Sebastian's by now. She punched in Sebastian's number on Hecht's white phone.

Sebastian answered. "He's here."

René got on the line.

"Are you all right?" she said.

"Just a graze, I'll live," he said. "I've hooked up the laptop."

Thank God, René was a computer fiend like she was. "Download this and let's try to crack it," she said. "Let's talk it through step by step."

René's fingers clicked over the keys nonstop.

Aimée checked her screen.

"Okay, download complete," René said. "What are we looking for?"

"We're searching for Soli Hecht's password. I can't open the disk."

After a few minutes, René mumbled something that sounded like "Azores."

"What's what?" Aimée asked.

"Beat your neighbors out of doors," he said.

"Care to elaborate?"

"The old card game," René said. " 'Beat your neighbors out of doors'—popular during the war. Even in her eighties my grand-mother could ace me every time."

"Am I missing something here?" Aimée asked. "What are you talking about?"

"Remember the Jigny case?" he said. "I used our software to pick the password lock and got the first couple of letters."

"Go on, René," she said.

"Well, after getting the first couple of letters I guessed that the key was in a fantasy game," he said. "The guy's kid loved Dungeons and Dragons, a real aficionado, so that made it easier. I got the password and opened the file. We bought a new computer system with our fees from that one."

She blew a noisy kiss through the phone. "Haven't I said you're a genius! I don't know if Soli played many card games in Treblinka. He'd have been fourteen or sixteen then. All I know is he was intense and methodical—that's from what I've seen of the office in his foundation."

"Let me sink my teeth into this," René said. "I'll call you on the cell phone."

She thought about what René had tried. Games. Did Soli play games in Treblinka? Survival would have taken up most of his time. What games could Soli play in a death camp . . . if he'd played any? Something that could only be played on the rare occasions when the guards didn't watch. Something that prisoners could make that could be hidden easily. Something that required thought, planning, and deliberate moves. Just like the way he'd finally assembled his case against Klaus Barbie.

Of course! Chess could be played in a concentration camp. C H E C K M A T E opened the file immediately. She pulled out a fresh disk from her bag and started copying the now open file.

While she did that she called Leah.

A perky-voiced Leah answered, "Allô?"

"Did Sarah enjoy the soufflé?"

"But she's with you," Leah said, suddenly awake. "Isn't she?"

"No!" Aimée panicked.

"She said she was going to meet you, something about the salamander," Leah said.

"What?" Aimé trembled. Why would Sarah have left?

"That man picked her up," Leah said. "He said they would meet up with you."

"Who?"

Leah described someone who could only be Thierry. Aimée hit

"Eject," grabbed the floppy, and ran down the stairs. By the door, she deactivated the security system in just the way Solange had described. On her way out, she tiptoed past the guard, who didn't even snort himself awake.

By the time she stood at the traffic light on the corner of rue de Rivoli, she knew she was being followed. She ducked into the Metro, remembering how she and Martine used to hide from their cronies after school. Latched to the tiled walls were hinges that held the swing doors of the Métro, and enough empty space for two giggling teenagers. Now it was a harder squeeze for her. But she just fit. A big rush of hot air, the screech of brakes, and the whoosh of pounding feet as passengers disgorged up the steps past Aimée. She counted to thirty, then ran back up the Métro steps and found a taxi by the western entrance of the Louvre.

"WHERE IS SARAH?" AIMÉE asked into her cell phone.

"You haven't found her?" Hartmuth said.

From the second floor of her cousin Sebastian's cluttered antique poster store on rue St. Paul in the Marais, she surveyed the narrow alley wedged below her. Sarah, not realizing the danger from her son, had gone with Thierry. Or maybe he had forced her.

Aimée pushed that thought from her mind. She had to get to a computer with municipal online capability and find Sarah.

Sebastian, in black leather pants, jacket, and matching black bushy beard, was helping outfit René. She'd rescued Sebastian once, her cousin by marriage and a former junkie. As he often said, he owed her for at least one lifetime.

René emerged from the upstairs loft, his arm hanging in a sling, wearing a fisherman's vest customized with flashlights Velcroed in all the pockets. Sebastian gently lifted him up and down into thigh-high rubber fishing boots.

"What's the salamander?" Aimée said into the phone.

Hartmuth let out a ripple of breath. "The marble arms of François the First."

Loud rumbling noises from below reached her ears. Sounds of distant thunder came from the direction of Bastille.

"Skip the history lesson," she said, frustrated that she might be too late. "What does it mean?"

"The salamander is a sculpture, carved in the arch of the seventeenth century building she'd lived in, opposite the catacombs."

Below her on narrow, medieval rue St. Paul, the street slowly filled with a line of khaki light utility tanks. Sleek and streamlined

Humvees rolled over the cobblestones, straddling the stone *bouches d'égout* that led to the sewers. Aimée hadn't seen tanks in Paris since the riots of 1968 by the Sorbonne. Parked cars stymied the tanks' progress and they emitted clouds of diesel exhaust in the chill November afternoon.

"Has there been a bombing?" Aimée said.

"Radicals versus rightists," Hartmuth said. "I'm afraid I have something to do with it."

"What do you mean?"

Hartmuth's voice sounded tired. "My failure to vote. The EU was unable to ratify the trade agreement with its exclusionary policies."

"Thierry took Sarah to the catacombs," she said. "How does he know about them?"

"I showed him the old exit," Hartmuth sighed. "Hidden in the Square Georges-Cain."

"Meet me there," Aimé said. She clicked off.

"We won't get through on any surface route, Aimée," René said as he walked over to her. "Checkpoints all over, armed militia is sealing the Marais."

She kissed him on both cheeks. "I cracked Soli Hecht's locked file with 'Checkmate.' "

René smiled. "Ditto."

"Great minds think alike, eh?" she said. "That's why we're going underground."

"The catacombs don't extend this side of the rue St. Antoine," he said.

"But the sewers do, René."

He rolled his eyes. "You know I don't do well with . . ."

"Rodents, me neither, but Sebastian's got something to help us with that," she said. "Did you bring the laptop?"

"Talk about addicted to computers!" he said. "Making a wounded man just out of the hospital borrow pirated software from friends!" He growled but his eyes shone. "I love it! What is the plan?"

"Hook the laptop to the municipal system and access FRAPOL 1 incognito," she said.

"Why?" René winced as he slung the backpack over his good shoulder.

"So I can identify that bloody fingerprint and find out who owns the building in the Marais," she said. "I'll nail the killer in dot matrix or laser gray scale." She quickly changed behind a 1930s poster that proclaimed "Ski the Alpes Maritimes" with parka-clad figures cavorting stiffly among old-fashioned ski lifts.

"Unload here or outside?" Sebastian asked, his beard muffling his voice. He had arranged everything she asked for.

She nodded to the rear door, which opened on a rain-soaked alley. He bundled up the bulky materials, then crouched under the eaves of his shop, his black leather pants glistening with raindrops.

"Thanks." She sidled near him in her dark vinyl hooded jumpsuit.

She gripped the handle of a small gray box, while Sebastian lugged a large backpack. They trudged in the light rain along the cobbled alley to the Quai des Célestins, a block away. René kept up the rear.

"What about the inhabitants below?" René said. "The ones with long greasy tails?"

She pointed to the box. "Sonic disturbance. They hate it. At least that's what the advertisement promised."

"It's high tech all the way with you, Aimée," René puffed.

"You're the one who's bothered by the rats, remember? Didn't you mention the epidemic proportions of rabies among the rodent population as recently as last week?" She tried not to sound out of breath. "This is the best I can do on such short notice."

Sebastian smiled out of his beard and René just glared.

"The back door to my place is always open, Aimée; just jiggle the hinges and slip in the bolt," he said.

"Sounds obscene," René muttered.

Sebastian grinned and was gone.

Aimée slid a thin metal rod out of her sleeve and hooked it under a sewer lid. Using a quick twist and thrust, she hauled the lid up and onto the pavement with a loud scrape. As inconspicuously as possible—on a quai overlooking the Seine with a dwarf at twilight—she gestured elegantly.

"After you," she said.

She hefted the backpack, then gripped the box as she climbed down the slippery rungs. Finally, she pulled the heavy, scraping lid back on top of them and it clanged shut.

A rotten mix of vegetables, feces, and clay and the smell of the sewers wafted through the damp tunnel. Dripping concrete arches oozed shiny patterns as if a giant snail had slimed over them.

Whenever René moved, the flashlight beams bobbed and bounced off the subterranean sewer walls. Splashes came from down the passage, and when he turned, pairs of beady red eyes were locked into the flashlight beams. It was no time to be squeamish but hordes of squealing rats were hard to ignore. She opened the box and switched the sonic meter on. The arrow wavered, dipped to zero, then shot up to five hundred decibels. Flat buzzing was emitted from the box, echoing off the dripping sewer walls.

"It's a good thing this frequency is only audible to animal ears," she said.

René looked dubious. "Do they get hypnotized like deer?" he asked as the rats remained staring at them.

"I doubt it," she said and shivered. These rats were the size of rabbits.

She wedged the sonic box into a pocket in the backpack, then secured it with Velcro holding straps. She had neglected to mention that the range had been shown effective at about two meters to repel penned canines. No studies had been done in wet underground conditions with rodents.

She also pushed aside the thought that they could be rabid.

René turned slowly, his beams illuminating clumps of glistening brown fur and hairless tails, littered down the long sewer.

She consulted her sewer map. The brown stained concrete wall had a white indicator number with an arrow painted on it. "Let's go," she said.

As they trudged along in the continuous sludgy stream, Aimée pulled her ventilation mask over her mouth and adjusted René's for him. The smell wasn't so bad if they did that. Their footfalls echoed with the continuous drip from the clay pipes draining from the streets above. Behind them scurried an army of rats, their tails slapping the walls, maybe two meters behind them. They covered three blocks in five minutes, but the rats were gaining on them.

"Even with you driving, René," she said. "We couldn't get this far so fast."

Up ahead, the wet brown walls dripped with rivulets of rusty slime from a ten-foot-diameter netted pipe.

Aimée pulled out her wire cutters from inside her jumpsuit and started cutting. Loud squealing sounded nearby.

"No way am I going to crawl in there," René protested. "I go through enough shit in a day as it is."

"It's not exactly what you think it is, René," she said, cutting through the thick wire. "It's not a toilet drain."

"Well, the smell could fool me," he said. "What is it?"

"The waste-station chute and the only way into the morgue," she said, helping him slide into the gaping hole she'd cut.

"Oddest break-in I've ever done," he muttered.

"Maybe a little blood or fluids that have been hosed down from the embalming tables might find their way down here," she said. "But it's all diluted."

"Makes me glad I haven't eaten today," René said, slowly climbing up the wet steel rungs, using his good arm.

Aimée pressed a button and the waste chute's hinged metal cover swung open. She pulled René up and realized they had climbed into a large storage closet. Mops, vacuums, and industrial cleansers took up most of the space. Several blue lab coats, worn by maintenance, were hanging from hooks along with plastic hair nets and rubber gloves. She stripped to her black leotard, donned the lab attire, and put her jumpsuit in the trash. She pulled René's boots off. He slipped on sneakers.

"We'll leave out the back door after I do a fingerprint match, okay?" Aimée whispered and looked at her watch. "With your help, it should take fifteen minutes."

"Why couldn't we have come in the back?" René said.

"Police guard," she said. "I wanted to time it for a shift change but that got complicated. We're in and out and no one knows the difference."

"Why the morgue?" he said.

"After we finish, I count on finding Sarah in the catacombs right behind the morgue wall."

Inside the morgue, only one of the fluorescent strips of light flickered in the hallway, the rest had burned out. The abattoir green tiled walls echoed with their footsteps. She pulled open a stainless-steel-handled door labeled PERSONNEL ONLY.

The vaulted room reeked of formaldehyde and was frosty cold. Gray-sheeted bodies were laid on wooden plank platforms, only their toes visible, each with a numbered yellow plastic tag. The scene reminded her of some fifteenth century medical print. The only things missing were the leeches and incisions permitting evil vapors to leave the body.

Aimée pushed open another swing door. The scales used to weigh organs hung suspended from the ceiling on metal chains. A corpse lay on a stainless-steel table, angled over the floor drain: a female, young, with long brown hair and discolored needle tracks along her hands and arms. She'd been slit from chest to pubic bone and sewed back together with black thread, harshly outlined against her chalk white skin. The top flap of her skull had been sewn back on but her hairline was too close to her temples. Sad, Aimée thought, and a pretty bad job. They usually tried for the parents. Maybe there weren't any.

She made her tone businesslike. "The medical examiner's computer should be through there." She popped Nicorette gum into her mouth and pointed down the dim hallway.

"Breaking and entering used to be more fun than this," René said and stopped. The hallway plunged into darkness.

"Where's the light timer?" She groped along the rough wall for the switch. Finally she found it and flipped it on. Ahead of her on the medical examiner's door was the biggest lock she'd ever seen.

THIERRY PUSHED SARAH PAST the bushes bordering the Square Georges-Cain into the dark hole obscured by the decaying pillar. He shoved her forward, forcing her to climb down half-rotten timbers. Inside a bone-pocked cavern, smelling of mold and decay, he motioned for her to sit down.

"Remember this?" he said. He shone the flashlight beam over the crumbling catacomb walls. Cistern water dripped down into black, oily puddles.

Her body shook. "How do you know about this place?"

Thierry held the fax he'd stolen from Aimée's office with Sarah's picture: her tar swastika, her shaved skull, and him as a baby in her arms. Sarah's face fell.

"Nom de Dieu!" she said. "Where did you find that?"

He remained silent, lit a candle, and pulled out a strip of silver duct tape.

"What's going on?" she asked uneasily. She started to get up, but he pushed her down in the wet dirt. "What do you want?"

"Your undivided attention," he said, binding her ankles with the tape. "Admit it," he said, sitting cross-legged across from her on a jagged marble slab. "Wasn't I a cute baby? Did you croon nursery rhymes to me here?" In a cloying falsetto he sang, *"Frère Jacques, dormez-vous?"* He kicked at the dirt.

Sarah's black wig hung off her ear and the scar showed plainly in the candlelight. Damp air filled the cavern. "Why are you doing this?"

"You see, you should be proud of that." Thierry stood up and traced his finger over the raised swastika on her forehead.

Sarah trembled.

"You earned the Führer's seal, as few Jews could," Thierry said. "But you're still a kike. Tainted."

"Oui. Une Juive," she said. She stopped shaking. "But I don't live in fear because of it. Not anymore."

"But you have to pay," he said.

"Pay?" Her eyes widened. "I haven't paid already? My family taken by Gestapo, giving you up . . . isn't that more than enough?"

She shook her head. "As soon as I got back to Paris, I stood outside the Rambuteaus', watching you go in their door." She wiped her eyes with her dirty raincoat sleeve. "Right where I'd kissed you goodbye as a baby. You know what I did? I fell on my knees, in a puddle on the sidewalk, thanking the God I've despised for years that you were alive. Alive, walking, and breathing, a grown man." She struggled to continue. "I went to the temple, where I'd gone with my parents, and begged God's forgiveness for my hatred of him. You're healthy, you had loving parents."

Thierry snorted. "Loving parents? Nathalie Rambuteau loved the bottle."

"I'm sorry. So sorry."

"No matter how she promised," he said, "when I came home from school, she'd be drunk and passed out, stuck to the floor in her own vomit." He slammed his fist into the caked dirt wall. "That was on a good day. I thought it was because I was adopted."

"Adopted?" Sarah picked at the duct tape. "Did she tell you . . . ?"

He interrupted, stooping down to bind her wrists with strips of duct tape, "To make my bed and clean behind my ears?" He grinned. " 'Maternal' doesn't describe Nathalie."

"You survived!" she said.

He took her arm, peering at her as if she were a laboratory specimen.

"You show no pronounced Semitic features." His eyes narrowed.

"Must be some ancestor raped by Aryan invaders back in the steppes and you carried the recessive genes."

"Killing me won't make you less Jewish." She raked her taped hand like a claw in the dirt. "Or change that I'm your mother."

"Proven inferiority." He pulled out a Gestapo dagger, which gleamed dully in the candlelight. "We've talked enough."

Saturday Evening

AFTER TEN MINUTES, AIMÉE still hadn't picked the Zeitz lock on the medical examiner's office door. Her hand ached.

"This is taking too long," she said.

René crouched near her on the scuffed linoleum and pulled out a Glock automatic.

"Not a finesse approach," he said. "But it will save time."

She hesitated, but kept winching the tumbler. A minute later, the huge metal lock clicked, then dropped open with a metallic sigh. Aimée rubbed her wrist as René reached on tiptoes to remove the lock and open the door.

"After you," he said.

Settling into an alcove office desk, he quickly plugged his code breaker into a surge protector under the reception desk, then hooked it to his laptop.

Aimée knew she hadn't wasted her money as she pulled the yellow stop-smoking gum out of her mouth. Even though she'd kill for a cigarette. She stuck two wads on opposite sides of the inner door jamb, then affixed the cheap alarm sensor Sebastian had purchased at the hobby store. The medical examiner's office area, painted institutional green like the rest of the morgue, lay quiet except for the sound of René's fingers clicking on a keyboard.

"Spooky," René said, accessing Soli Hecht's disk. "I know the clientele won't bother us but I'd feel better with the door closed."

"Air needs to circulate." She nodded towards the broken air vent in the wall. "Otherwise the formaldehyde reeks. Besides, if anyone trips my alarm sensor, we'll hear."

Aimée tried to hide the doubt in her voice. She plopped into the ME's chair.

"Bingo!" René said.

"That's his access word?"

"Take a guess what the ME's code is." René rolled his eyes.

Aimée looked at the framed photo on the desk: a paunchy, middle-aged man, tufts of gray hair poking out from a beret, cocked a hunting rifle under one arm and held a limp-necked goose in the other.

"1Stud," René said.

"He's a legend-in-his-own-eyes type." Aimée shook her head. "After opening bodies all day, how could he want to kill any living thing?"

Working in a morgue would make her want to celebrate life—not hunt it down and shoot it. France's obsession with *la chasse* had always offended her. But was she doing that? Doubt nagged briefly. No, hunting down a killer and bringing a murderer to justice wasn't sport, like bagging an innocent creature.

She refocused and typed in 1Stud, which immediately accessed the system. Once inside, she tapped into EDF, Electricité de France, which connected to Greater Paris municipal branches. She navigated online to the 4th arrondissement.

Once inside the utility system, she pulled up the listing for the meters of number 23 rue du Plâtre, Laurent's old address. Extra energy points had been awarded to the building due to moderate use and conservation of energy. Nothing more. Another dead end. Disappointed, she logged into FRAPOL 1 and requested the bloody fingerprint found with the Luminol at rue des Rosiers.

As the fingerprint came up, she typed in "de Saux," then ran the standard search program.

"René, this high-speed modem is like power steering after driving a tractor!" she purred.

"Don't get ideas, Aimée," he said. "They're too expensive and you're spoiled as it is."

Ten seconds later, a single phrase popped on to the screen: *Unknown, no records found.*

Of course, she thought. He's too smart to have left any trace. That's why he killed Lili. She'd recognized him and he thinks Sarah will, too. Is it just because Lili identified him or is something happening now, she wondered. He must have more at stake.

All collaborators had good enough reason to hide. Especially from the families of victims whom they'd informed on and sent to the ovens. How could she trace him? Little if any information from the forties had been entered into the government database.

"I've got it! *La Double Morte,*" Aimée said to René. "Someone had to pay tax on that building, either inheritance or capital gains. It always comes down to that, eh? Death and taxes, the only two sure things in life."

The screen blipped while Aimée accessed the tax records of number 23 rue du Plâtre. Records stated that the property stood free and clear of lien, was zoned for three units, and that ownership resided with The Crédit Agricole real estate division. Okay, she thought to herself, let's scroll back in time. The Crédit Agricole had paid all taxes since 1983, when they'd purchased it in lieu of payment in a bankruptcy proceeding of a Jean Rigoulot of Dijon. This Rigoulot of Dijon had faithfully paid taxes on the property since 1971. A 1945 probate tax had been billed and never paid. She skipped back to 1940 when the property tax had been paid by a Lisette de Saux. Must be Laurent's mother, she reasoned. However, the next owner, a Paul LeClerc, had paid the lien and probate tax in 1946 as part of the purchase agreement. She scrolled back into 1940 again and discovered an addendum. Lisette de Saux had changed the title into her husband's name. That's when she saw Laurent's new name and Soli Hecht's dying syllables made sense. "Lo . . ."

Lo . . . ! Laurent Cazaux. She almost fell off her chair. If she didn't hurry up, the collaborator, Lili's murderer, was about to become the next prime minister.

THE FLUORESCENT lights fizzled and the warning light on the surge protector blinked. René frowned. "Not enough juice.

Let me fiddle with the fuses, this ancient wiring can be amped up with a little work."

"We don't have time, René," Aimée said, joining him in the alcove.

"If the power goes, the computers crash. We lose everything," he said.

She knew it was true. He waddled past the sensor that obligingly beeped an alarm. She punched the hallway light switch for him, since he barely reached it.

"I do this all the time," he said and grinned. "Everyone loves me in my building."

She reset the alarm and phoned Martine at home. After ten rings, a sleepy voice croaked, *"Allô?"*

"Martine, I'm going to send you a file at your office," Aimée said. "Download it and make copies right away."

"Aimée, I just got to sleep after being up two days with the riots," Martine said.

"What time do you go to press for the Sunday edition?"

"Er, in a few hours, but I'm off," Martine said. "Give it to CNN."

"So you've been leading me on for years?" Aimée said. "I thought you wanted to be the boss! This info has your new job description on it as first female editor of *Le Figaro*."

Martine sounded awake now. "I need two sources to confirm. Impeccable ones."

"You'll have the third within twenty minutes," Aimée said, glad that Martine couldn't see her cross her fingers.

"This better be good," she said. "Gilles's shift is over in half an hour. I'll meet you down there."

"Does *mademoiselle l'éditeur* have a nice sound to it?" Aimée said. "Hold on to your chair when you read this or you might fall off like I almost did."

Aimée pulled up the bloody fingerprint from rue des Rosiers, then requested a match search on FRAPOL 1 with Cazaux's name. At the corner of the screen, the progress box blinked "Searching records." She drummed her chipped red fingernails on the ME's wood desk.

The alarm bleeped and she sat up, gripping the Beretta inside her leather backpack. Her fingers found the safety and flicked it off. She'd taken the handgun from the man in the police uniform outside Soli Hecht's hospital room. The office lights blacked out; only the red light on the surge protector wavered. Stay calm, she told herself, hugging the bag close to her.

From the hallway, a shadow moved, then a flashlight shone on the walls. The citrus scent gave him away before she heard him speak.

"Maybe you'd like to tell me what you're doing," he said.

A smoldering Rothmans orange cigarette butt landed on her keyboard, briefly illuminating it.

"I've got a gun," she said. "If I get upset I'll use it."

"Don't play with me, you don't have a permit," he chuckled. "This is France."

The fluorescent lights buzzed then flickered on. She looked straight into the green-gold eyes of Herve Vitold. Behind him in the hallway, René hung by his suspenders to a large circuit-breaker panel, plastic gloves stuffed in his mouth.

"Ms. Leduc, we meet again," Vitold said. He slid next to her in one fluid movement, his eyes never leaving hers.

"I knew you were too good-looking to be internal security," she said.

He moved so close she could see each hair on his upper lip. Almost intimate. His chest heaved rhythmically, which was the only way she could tell he was laughing. The Luger in his hand didn't move, though; it rested coldly against her temple.

"I've been waiting for you to break into FRAPOL 1 again," he said as he scanned the screen intently. "Your technique is good, I'll use it myself next time."

"You're the tidy-up man, eh?" she said. She knew that as soon as she got a match, he'd erase it, eradicate all traces.

He looked bored. "Tell me something new."

"You want to crash the whole system," she said. "Destroy all law enforcement files and the internal network of fingerprint and DNA identification, Interpol interfaces," she said. "Just to erase his fingerprints. But it won't work."

"Pity," he said. "You've got talent. Wasted talent."

"Each system has its own safeguard network. You'll never get past them." She wanted to keep him talking. "Any break-in attempt trips the system alarms. Freezes all access," she said. "You can't do it."

"But I can," Herve Vitold said. He smiled. "I designed the alarm alert for FRAPOL 1 and the defense ministry." Expertly, he snapped the cartridge in and out of the Luger with one hand. "Disarming them will be easy."

"Cazaux is finished," she said.

"Quit playing games," he said.

"Untie my partner," she said, glancing at René. "I'm getting upset."

Vitold ignored her. René flipped uselessly like a caught fish, his feet dangling above the scuffed floor, trying to bang the metal circuit breaker with his shoulders. Vitold backed up and pointed his gun at René's head. René's eyes blinked nonstop in panic.

"Be still, little man," Vitold said. With his other hand he opened a cell phone and pressed memory. "Sir, I've begun," he said.

"Didn't you hear me?" Aimée said.

Vitold sneered as he cocked the trigger by René's ear.

"Now I'm upset," Aimée shot through her leather bag, drilling him three times in his crotch. Disbelief painted Vitold's face before he doubled over, thrashing wildly. He yelped, dropped his cell phone, and collapsed in a bloody sprawl on the linoleum.

"See what happens when I get upset?" she said. She straddled Herve Vitold, his still surprised eyes focused upward. But his frozen stare told her he'd checked out.

She pulled the gloves out of René's mouth, then gently lifted him down.

René spit talcum powder out of his mouth and flexed his fingers. "And I thought Vitold liked you for your looks," he said.

"They never do," she said and pointed to the screen.

"Match Verified" had come up. She typed in Martine's email address at *Le Figaro* and hit "Send." She picked up Vitold's Luger and his cell phone and brushed off her shirt. Before she could copy everything on a backup disk, the amplified clanging buzzer alarm sounded. Startled, René dropped his laptop. From the hallway, red lights flashed on and off. She picked up the laptop, slipped it inside her backpack, and slung that over her shoulder.

"Hurry!" she said, and canceled the command. She grabbed her backpack. "Go, René."

Now the only documentation with Cazaux's photo and fingerprint identification awaited downloading on Martine's computer at *Le Figaro*. But would that be enough?

Right now it would have to be. She'd copy and make a backup disk at Martine's office, but would be nervous until she could download the evidence on Cazaux. Their faces alternately blood red and splashed in blackness, Aimée and René jumped over Vitold's lifeless figure and sprinted down the hall.

In the vestibule, she grabbed two paramedics' vests and helmets with red crosses on them that hung from hooks. She threw one to René.

"This will get us through the crowd and past police lines," she said.

"From sewer rat to paramedic all in one day," he said. "Who said life wasn't an adventure? Now if I could just get some stilts, we wouldn't stick out so much."

A wheelchair was parked in the vestibule. "Get in," Aimée said.

"You've got it the wrong way round," he said. "Paramedics don't ride in these, patients do."

She pushed him down. "You're wounded in the line of duty, I'll do the talking."

THIERRY'S DAGGER GLINTED IN the sputtering candle-light. Cold air seeped from the ruined catacomb walls.

"You're handsome," Sarah said shyly. "I used to kiss your little feet and blow on your toes. You'd laugh and laugh, such dulcet tones."

"How touching!" he said. "A madonna and child fresco! We're back in the dirt, too."

Sarah looked down at worms wiggling blindly in the earth next to them. "Those who flee the past are doomed to repeat it. Is that what you think?"

Thierry's eyes were far away. "You abandoned me," he said in a little-boy voice.

She reached tentatively for his hand. "I didn't abandon you," she said. "I let you live."

"She used to tell me I was a casualty of war, some freak accident. Then she'd smile, torturing me, refusing to say any more."

Sarah shook her head. "My milk dried up and there was no food," she said. "At sixteen years old, I'd been branded as a collaborator. You had no chance with me! Nathalie had lost a child. She had milk and she wanted you. They were of the bourgeoise class, politically conservative. I was a Jew who consorted with a Nazi!"

"So it's really true," he said. He stuck his dagger in the packed earth and sank down beside her, looking dazed.

With her bound hands, she stroked his shoulders, afraid everything would end as suddenly as it had begun. Seeing her old lover and being trapped by her lost son stirred yearnings inside her. Impossible ones. That old deep hurt had opened again.

Her few loose fingers stroked his back. "We lived around the corner from here. One day I came home from my violin lesson, the courtyard was deserted. So was the building. Our Mezuzah, ripped from the front door, lay on the apartment floor. Papa had just had it blessed by the rabbi. That's how I knew. My parents warned me and fooled the Germans. They never came back. I never forgave them for leaving, I missed them so much. So I understand how you feel; a child whose mother leaves him will always think himself abandoned. If only . . ." She sighed deeply. "If only I had escaped . . ." Her voice trailed off.

"I can't believe I'm a Jew," he said.

"Nathalie promised me that she would tell you the truth. Not torture you with it," she said, her voice anguished. "What good comes of it? Give me the knife."

Thierry shot bolt upright, as if remembering his mission.

"Defilement of the Aryan race merits summary execution," he said hotly. "You know that."

He pulled the dagger from the packed earth, slicing his wrist lightly. Sarah's hands shook. Thin beaded blood trailed over the tattooed lightning bolts on his hand.

"Please don't kill me," she begged. "Please, we need to—" A loud crack came as Hartmuth batted Thierry's hand. The dagger clattered, hitting the half-buried limestone arch beside them.

"Oh my God," Sarah screamed.

Hartmuth reached for her and stumbled over the mound of bones.

"I couldn't hurt her," Thierry faltered.

Hartmuth gripped a rotten wood post. Shocked, he stared at Sarah. Thierry cut the duct tape from Sarah's ankle and helped her up.

"I wanted to," he wailed. "I wanted to, but I couldn't, oh God."

"So pathetic," Hartmuth said in disgust, "there are no words. How can you threaten your own mother?"

"He's confused," Sarah pleaded. "Everything has turned upside down for him. He doesn't know who he is."

Hartmuth reached in his pocket. He pulled out a small pistol and leveled it at Thierry.

"No, please," she begged.

"If she's Jew scum," Thierry said, bewilderment shining in his haggard face, "so am I."

"Sit down, Thierry," Aimée said, interrupting the strange scene. Holding Vitold's black Luger, she climbed down the bits of wood jutting out from the caked dirt in the cavern walls. René followed behind her.

"It's under control," Hartmuth growled. "Put your gun away."

"You first," she said.

Hartmuth hesitated. Sarah put her hand tentatively on his arm. "You don't need this," she said. Slowly, he lowered the gun.

Aimée reached the catacomb floor, where her heels sank promptly into the dirt. The last ladder rung splintered. She turned and caught René before he landed on a pile of rubble and bones.

"Come here, Thierry," she said.

Thierry perched on a rotten timber, his eyes twitching. "Let's play possible scenarios," he said, his voice rising in a high pitch.

"Thierry, calm down," Aimée said. "You need time to work things out."

He ignored her. "Son tries to knife long-lost mother because she's a Jew pig," he said. He stood up, his face contorted in the flicker of light. "Father shoots son because he's a two-bit Nazi wannabe. Father puts bullet in his own brain because long ago he disobeyed the Führer." He laughed manically. "I like it. Let me do the honors." He reached out to Sarah.

Aimée moved towards him but Hartmuth had leveled his gun.

"Leave her alone!" Hartmuth yelled.

Thierry stumbled.

Too late. Hartmuth shot, but not before Sarah had flung herself in front of Thierry. The shot reverberated, almost deafening

Aimée as Sarah's body slammed into the earth wall. Blood spurted from her chest as she thudded to the ground, clutching at her heart.

Aimée grabbed Hartmuth's arms, while René quickly took the gun from him. Rumbling rose from deep in the cavern as bones and pebbles slid down the walls. The wood posts trembled above them. Dirt showered over Aimée's face.

She ran to a moaning Sarah, wanting to cover her ears and shut out this woman's agony. Instead, she knelt, attempting to staunch the blood pooling in a dirt puddle.

Hartmuth fell to his knees. "What have I done?"

"Maman," Thierry said. "You saved me." He knelt and stroked her clammy forehead.

Sarah's breathing came in shallow gasps as Aimée propped her head up.

"My baby," Sarah crooned, pulling him close. "My baby."

Aimée applied direct pressure to the hole in Sarah's chest.

"Hold on, Sarah."

"The ambulance is on its way," René said, putting the cell phone in his pocket. "It won't be too soon either." He looked nervously above him.

"Sarah, you can make it," Aimée said. "Just a little bit longer."

Sarah nodded. "Thierry, your Jewish name is Jacob, the healer of men." She smiled weakly. "After your grandfather."

Hartmuth remained in a heap near the bone mound, curiously immobile. Aimée realized he was in shock. His eyes focused somewhere distantly in the catacombs.

"Thierry?" Sarah wailed as her eyes clouded, gripping him tightly. "My son!"

"Bring your father, Thierry," Aimée said. She gestured towards Hartmuth. "Reunite them." She didn't need to add "before it's too late."

Hartmuth meekly knelt with Thierry. Aimée gently put Sarah's head in his lap. Wordlessly, he caressed her face as Thierry gripped his shoulders and looked away.

"I need your help, René." Aimée whispered instructions while she pulled him aside.

As she climbed up the ladder, her last glimpse was of a weak, smiling Sarah being held by Hartmuth and Thierry illuminated by a flashlight beam.

THE MEDICAL crew couldn't get Sarah to let go of Thierry until Morbier arrived. Finally she let go. He nodded to the attendants, who slipped her onto a stretcher they'd unfolded.

Panic sparkled in Sarah's eyes. "I gave them all the food!" she screamed, now struggling to get away from Hartmuth. "We're hungry. *S'il vous plaît*, my baby is hungry!"

"Take any statements?" Morbier swiveled his head, addressing the young uniformed sergeant at the scene.

The sergeant shook his head.

Morbier leaned closely over Hartmuth's outstretched palm. He sniffed. "Notice the residue oil from the bullet chamber?" He pointed at the glove. "Your theory, sergeant?"

The uniform shook his head again and cleared his throat unsteadily.

"Strong smell of gunpowder on his right hand." Morbier cocked his eye down at the sergeant, now taking notes on a pad hastily produced from his pocket.

"Sir, I . . ." he began.

"Gather the evidence," Morbier snarled.

"Let's get up." Morbier gently took Thierry's arm. "You can ride to the hospital."

Empty and spent, Thierry climbed out of the catacombs. "Why couldn't I believe her?"

Morbier grimaced, handcuffing Hartmuth's wrists behind him. He muttered under his breath. "This is for your own protection, Monsieur." Hartmuth remained mute, staring vacantly.

"Does he mean why couldn't he believe Aimée?" Morbier looked at René.

René nodded.

"Take him to the station," Morbier directed.

The sergeant saluted, hustling Hartmuth forward and up a makeshift ladder.

"Why don't you tell me about Aimée's plan?"

René smiled grimly. "I thought you'd never ask."

"Where is she?"

"Partying," René said.

Surprised, Morbier dropped his cigarette.

"We're invited," René said.

AIMÉE KNEW if a person had been listed as dead and wasn't, he or she needed an identity. Thousands of refugees during and after the war had lost identity papers since buildings with records were bombed, their countries gobbled up or renamed. These people were stateless. A piece of documentation had been created, called the Nansen passport, to legitimize their existence. If she found this proof, she'd have him.

She headed for the elegant Musée Carnavalet, which was located around the corner from the catacombs and housed in the former *hôtel particulier* of Madame de Sévigné. The museum courtyard was open. Inside the deserted marble-ceilinged restroom she switched on her laptop but realized the battery had died. She found a socket, plugged it in, and breathed a sigh of relief when she logged on.

She hacked into the Palais de Nationalité files and found him. Laurent Cazaux had been approved for a Nansen passport in 1945. But her triumph felt hollow. She had to stop him. Quickly, she downloaded the application and approval forms.

She pressed the redial button on Herve Vitold's cell phone.

"Meet me alone, Cazaux. L'Académie d'Architecture bureau, at midnight," Aimée said into the phone. "If you want to make a deal."

SEARCHLIGHTS SCANNED in pewter strokes across the sky. The sliver of a moon drooped low over the Seine, hardly a ripple on the surface. Aimée rubbed her arms in the frosty chill.

Before her, the windows of l'Académie d'Architecture in Place des Vosges glowed with the light of hundreds of hand-lit tapers. A stream of dark limousines deposited guests at the entrance of the former seventeenth-century Hôtel de Chaulnes. Tonight's commemorative gala was in honor of Madame de Pompadour, the true arbiter of style at the French court, who still influenced what passed for elegant today.

She, along with the rest of Paris, knew Minister Cazaux was scheduled to begin the celebration by attending the fashion show. Her rough plan, formulated in the Musée Carnavalet's restroom, several blocks away, held major obstacles. First of all, she had to surprise him at the gala before their midnight appointment and force him to reveal his guilt in public. But that seemed minor, since she had no invitation to this heavily guarded soirée. However, before that she needed to meet Martine at *Le Figaro* and copy the disk with her proof.

As she rounded the corner, her heart stopped. The bomb-squad truck straddled the sidewalk. Workers swept up glass blown out from the wrought-iron entrance doors of *Le Figaro*'s brown brick facade. She wondered if Martine had been hurt.

"Any injuries?" she asked.

A stocky jumpsuited man shook his head.

"Much damage?" she said.

He shrugged. "Go figure. The next prime minister's around the corner and someone throws a bomb into our newspaper. But the upstairs offices weren't touched," he said.

She hesitated, then walked inside. The smells of cordite and burnt plastic mingled with the familiar scent of *le vin rouge* from the uniformed guard. He stopped her by the reception desk.

"I have an appointment with Martine Sitbon," she said, showing a fake press card.

He read it carefully. "Empty your bag."

She put her laptop on the counter and dumped the contents of her pack: wigs, tape recorder, cell phones, sunglasses, tubes of ultrablack mascara, and a battered makeup case. The Luger thumped out and shone dully in the chandelier light. "I have a permit." She smiled.

"Ah! *Comme* Dirty 'arry!" He fingered the piece. His tasseled loafers squeaked as he moved. "I'll hold the gun since our metal detector got damaged." He smiled back. "You'll get it on your way back. Fourth floor."

She wouldn't bother to debate, he'd pocket the Luger anyway. The blast had also ripped up part of the concrete steps, damaged the wooden atrium, and shaken off some sections of the lobby's ceiling. Dust covered the lobby furniture but the lift worked.

She had to work quickly: copy the proof she'd emailed and convince Martine to publish it, then confront Cazaux. He'd withdraw from the ministry and politics if he knew *Le Figaro* was going to expose his true identity. He couldn't deny living in Paris during the Occupation because she had Lili's class snapshot and the microfiche photo from the Jewish library showing him, Lili, and Sarah. Most of all, she had his bloody fingerprint at a fifty-year-old homicide.

Inside the lift she pressed 4, then pulled a blond hairpiece from her wig bag, clipped it on near her roots, then worked the hair into hers to look natural. She pinched her cheeks and swiped red lipstick across her mouth. As soon as she'd copied the download and briefed Martine, she'd figure some way into the gala next door and confront Cazaux.

The fourth floor held editorial offices; below, the copy room and printing press occupied the first three. As features editor, Martine occupied an office nestled in an unlocked suite of front offices.

Martine's leather jacket hung from the back of her chair. Red lipstick traces were on the cigarette burning in the ashtray next to her computer screen, which displayed the message "Download time remaining approximately three minutes."

All she had to do was find Martine and copy the disk. The computer on Martine's cluttered desk clicked faster.

"Martine."

No answer. Aimée's spine tingled. She heard a noise and turned. The lobby guard stood at the door with the Luger aimed at her.

A deep voice came over the intercom. "Target One has been secured at the perimeter."

"The dwarf carrying computer printouts?" the guard asked.

"Affirmative," the voice said.

"What's Target Two's status, Colonel?"

"Inspector Morbier's unit is en route to demonstrations at the Fontainebleau periphery," the voice replied.

Plans of Cazaux's ambush died. Now she was on her own. They'd nabbed René and sent Morbier to the outskirts of Paris.

The computer whirred. "Download accomplished" flashed on the screen. The guard's shoes squeaked as he stepped to the terminal. The second lesson at René's dojo had been to react defensively and naturally. When he looked at the screen, she kneed him in the groin. As he bent over in pain, she jerked the mouse wire, then wrapped it tightly round and round his wrists. She glanced at the screen, hit "Copy," then tied his wrists to the armrest of Martine's chair and stuffed his mouth with pink Post-Its.

Garbled noises came from his mouth.

She eased out the Beretta from where it was taped to the small of her back and pointed it between his eyes.

"Shut up. Subtlety isn't my strong point." She straddled his leg, pulling open drawers in Martine's desk. She found postal tape in the drawer, then taped his ankles to the swivel-base chair.

"Copy completed" came up on the screen. She leaned over and hit "Eject."

The disk popped out. She yanked the mouse wire and looped it several more times around his wrists.

He struggled, his eyes bulging, and tried to spit out the Post-Its. His patent-leather shoes beat a rhythm against the desk.

"He's very proud of those shoes, Mademoiselle Leduc," a familiar voice said from the open office on the left.

Cazaux winked at her. He stood flanked by a pistol-toting bodyguard. The guard snatched the disk from her, handed it to Cazaux, and body-searched her.

The guard shimmied his hands over her body, then shook his head. "Nothing," he said after he had set her gun on Martine's desk.

"Have you grown more hair, Mademoiselle Leduc?" Cazaux said. "I remember it shorter."

Fear jolted up her spine.

The guard felt her hair, then ripped her hairpiece off. The small microphone clattered onto the floor. Cazaux nodded to the guard, who threw her laptop at the wall. He stomped it with his boots until little fiber-optic cables spurted out, like so much techno blood.

"You won't win, Cazaux," she said.

"Why not?" He held up the disk.

"René sent copies to every newspaper in Paris," she said.

"Go downstairs," he told the bodyguard.

He gestured towards the other office. "Let's discuss this privately."

Once inside, he locked the door and sat down, indicating for her to do so. "You're bluffing." He smiled. "But I would, too, if I was in your situation."

"Laurent de Saux is your real name," Aimée said.

"Well, young lady," he said. He smiled indulgently, as if humoring a child. "How could you prove that assumption?"

She glanced at her watch. "You better read the Sunday edition of *Le Figaro* to find out, which starts printing in thirty minutes."

"That's impossible." He chuckled. "Gilles is in my pocket. And your girlfriend Martine is sleeping off a tranquilizer." He leaned forward, resting his elbows in his lap, and stared at her. "Please sit down."

She kept standing.

"You've been a good sparring partner," he said. "This game

doesn't exactly match my wits, but so far it's been mentally stimulating." Cazaux smiled expansively.

"This is only a game to you, isn't it?" she said. "Not real live people. Just objects you manipulate or remove to advance your position. Soli Hecht understood your thinking pattern. It's like a giant series of moves in megalomania chess."

"And you think you've engineered a checkmate . . . but how well I know," he sighed wearily. "How the corridors of power are lined with minor annoyances."

"You informed on your parents after you killed Arlette Mazenc," she said. "You probably watched them executed below your window on rue du Plâtre."

"What do you want?" he said. His eyebrows lifted in curiosity. "I've been watching you. I'm impressed. You're good, you know. How about a nice, fat EU contract designing software frameworks for participating countries? I'll make it happen. Or would you like to head the French government's online security division?"

He dangled impressive carrots.

"You should step down," she said, hesitating a fraction of a second.

He sensed weakness like a shark going in for the kill. "I know how you feel. You think I did wrong." His tone became soothing. "Sometimes we have to do things for the greater good." He shrugged. His eyes burned as he went on. "But now I'm almost at the peak. I'll scale it. The culmination of my life."

"Fifty years of lying and killing and you get to be prime minister?" she said.

His eyes narrowed. The moment had gone and he knew he'd lost any chance of recruiting her.

Loud reverberations came through the floor, the rhythmic pounding of the press. Aimée realized the Sunday edition had gone to print without Cazaux's identity. She had to make him confess, then somehow get out, get help.

"What about Arlette Mazenc, the concierge?" she said.

"You keep bringing up that harelipped harpy. What an ugly mug she had!" His tone had changed. He whined like a petulant schoolboy. "That crippled cobbler liked it, though. He would. The bitch almost conned me out of some tinned salmon. My stepmother found it, tried to make me return it. And my stupid papa, bewitched by that slut who thought she could replace my mother, backed her up. Can you imagine? I had to teach them a lesson." He looked at Aimée with a wide smile. "Seems ridiculous now, doesn't it?"

He talked as if he'd spanked a naughty child, not brutally bludgeoned a fellow collaborator and informed on his parents, causing them to be shot below his apartment window. Truly evil incarnate, just as Odile Redonnet had said.

"And Lili Stein saw you, she'd hidden in the courtyard. She escaped, only to recognize you fifty years later, so soon before the election," she said. "You carved the swastika in her forehead."

"She was a self-righteous busybody who took Nazi food," he said. "Like the rest of us. When you're that hungry you don't care. But I was smart. I made money out of them. Every one of them except Lili."

"One hundred francs for anonymous denunciations. You figured the swastika would point to skinheads," she said. "But skinheads make them differently. You drew it slanted, like Hitler and everyone else of your era did. A signature of that time."

"Signature?" he said.

"The 1943 Nazi flag flying over the *Kommandantur* on rue des Francs Bourgeois had exactly the same one. You passed that every day on your way to school from rue du Plâtre."

He smiled and his eyes were evil. "Lili was the smartest in class but she stopped helping me."

"Helping you?" she said. "You mean, because she didn't let you cheat on math homework, you informed on her parents."

"We all deserve what we get."

"Arlette Mazenc cheated you on black-market tinned salmon. Furious, you bludgeoned her down in the light well, where she kept her cache. But Lili was hiding in the courtyard, afraid of the Nazi officer who'd been asking Arlette questions. She saw everything. You chased her up the stairs but she ran and escaped over the rooftop. You figured she had died. The last link to your identity erased, especially since you knew of the punishment inflicted upon Sarah, the blue-eyed Jew, Odile's deportation to Berlin and your classmates shipped to the countryside. But fifty years later Lili recognizes you in a Hebrew newspaper and tells Soli Hecht. Hecht tells her to do nothing until he has more proof, then makes overtures to the Simon Wiesenthal Center. But Lili couldn't wait, she knew how you silenced opposition. She tracked you herself—that was her mistake. You found out via your government connections that Hecht obtained a piece of an encrypted photograph with you in it. Hecht hired me to figure out the encryption. He tried to tell me your name. I don't know how you found Lili . . ."

He interrupted Aimée with a wave of his hand. "But Lili was the only one who could put it all together. Of course, she was where I'd expect her to be." He gave a little smile. "*Alors*, still on rue de Rosiers."

"You saw Lili talking with Sarah and killed her before she could spread her allegations. Killed her like you killed Arlette Mazenc."

"She deserved it," he said.

Yellow slanted light came from the half-opened door into the next room. Aimée edged towards it.

"The deal is you withdraw tonight," she said.

"But that's not in my plan," he explained calmly. "I have to take care of all the people who've helped me over the years. Many, many friends. Connections I've nourished that need to be repaid."

Aimée interrupted. "Like you repaid Sarah's parents, Lili's, and all your other classmates who didn't do what you wanted."

He shrugged. "You know I won't let you get away with this." He stood up slowly. "I learned an important lesson a long time ago." Old stone glistened wetly outside the window.

"The backup disk is in the vault." But there was no vault and she felt sick inside.

Anger blazed briefly in his eyes. "Have you done something silly requiring major damage control?" he said. He continued almost wearily. "I've learned if you want something done right, you have to do it yourself."

As he turned to face her, steel glinted in his hand, illuminated by the yellow light. His arm shot out, holding a Gestapo dagger. "Nothing can be proved. You are joining history, Mademoiselle." he grinned.

"You've got it wrong," she said. "I've got the proof—the copy of your Nansen passport and the photos showing you in Paris. Soli Hecht gave me encrypted files. You're history, Cazaux. No one nominates a collaborator and murderer."

He shrugged. "You'd be amazed at the backgrounds of some of our deputies."

She peered out the window, wishing the courtyard was lined with Morbier's men, not shiny black crows cawing loudly. But they were at the outskirts of Paris. It struck her that she was hopelessly on her own.

She darted towards the slightly open door, kicked it, and barreled into the next room. Skidding inside on her heels, she ducked under a conference table in time to avoid crashing into it. The room lay deserted except for framed sepia photographs of bearded men, their lapels dotted with medals. Piled newspapers blocked her way. Aimée backed out of this room into a stark unfurnished salon. Just beyond were the tall entry doors of more office suites.

She turned to see Cazaux, with a perverse smile, pointing her own gun at her. He snapped his fingers and motioned her towards an enclosed stairway.

"Let's get some air," Cazaux said.

He swatted her head with the butt of the pistol as he marched her up the dark curved staircase. His ropy, tensile hands pinned her arms behind her. Warm blood dripped behind her ear onto her shoulder, its cloying metallic scent making her light-headed. Or maybe it was the butt of the pistol, she couldn't tell. By the next floor she was panting and he wasn't even winded. For an old man he stayed in good shape. He noticed and smiled.

"Wonder how I do it?" he said as he forced her to kneel on the top step and kicked the side of her head.

Searing pain with hot white stars shot through her brain. He held her arms so she couldn't reel to the ground.

He slapped her face sharply. "I asked you a question—don't you wonder how I do it?"

She wanted to answer, "By drinking the blood of your victims." Instead, she concentrated on keeping her balance. She felt limitless fear at the cruelty of one human to another.

"Lamb embryo injections," he said. "Keeps me young. I can keep it up for hours, too." He smiled suggestively.

She cringed in disgust. "You're sick."

Up on the slate roof of the newspaper, the peaked roofs of the Marais spread below them. Lighted windows from l'Académie d'Architecture in the building below shone and music drifted up. He shoved her onto a flat-tiled space, once a balcony. Wind whipped over her and drizzle pelted her face.

"I've warned you," he said in a long-suffering voice. "Repeatedly. Offered to give you what you want, tried to negotiate, but I'm afraid, Mademoiselle Leduc, you haven't been receptive."

He dragged her over to a parapetlike ledge. She dug her heels into the pipes crisscrossing the roof and tried twisting away.

"You're going to take the fall," he said. "For everything. I'll see to it." Cazaux had one last parting shot. "Your precious Lili sent them to the ovens, I didn't." He chuckled. "It was all her fault."

Lili's fault! And then she wasn't afraid anymore of how he would kill her. How he lied and what he did to Lili was all that mattered. She saw the jagged swastika carved in Lili's forehead as she charged into him.

"No more LIES!" she screamed.

His Gestapo dagger slashed her leg, ripping her skin, but she kept going. They fell, tumbling, into the corner gutter over snarling gargoyles, frozen in stone. He was amazingly strong and wiry. His bony fingers gripped her neck, squeezing tightly. Choking and gasping, she pushed him away. But he banged her head against the ugly gargoyle spouts. Again and again. She was sputtering for air and blinded by her own blood. Half of her body hung over the ledge. Her fingers clawed a gargoyle's wing as she tried to hang on. Below them was the skylighted roof of l'Académie d'Architecture.

"You're going with me," she gasped.

As her grip loosened, she used her last bit of strength to pull him on top of her. She heard him shriek before his fingers let go of her neck. But it was too late.

They sailed into the cold dark air. Together, they landed on the skylight, which shattered beneath them. Shards of glass, splintered and twinkling like diamonds, pierced her skin. Her splayed legs caught on the metal skylight handle, jerked, then held as she swung upside down before managing to grip the skylight frame.

She twisted her good leg around the support bars but her other bloody leg dangled uselessly. Cazaux's long body hung suspended from the ceiling, entangled in cord and wire from electrical lines. Powdery blue dust shimmered in the moonlight while his legs twitched.

"Help me!" he choked.

He was slowly being strangled. The wire had rubbed the makeup off his neck, exposing the mottled brown birthmark. Far below them, a well-dressed gala crowd gathered open-mouthed on the glass shards.

"I wondered how you hid the birthmark," she sputtered, gasping for breath. "The more you move, the tighter it gets. Here." She reached her bloodied hand towards him.

Vainly, he tried to lift his arms but they were wrapped and twisted by cord. His face was turning blue. "Air . . . help!" he rasped.

He was beyond rescue, she couldn't even reach his fingertips. "There's one thing I need to do, Laurent de Saux," she said, wiping her hand in the soot.

He was gurgling and choking but hope shone in his eyes as she reached down. She was about to draw a swastika across his forehead, brand him as he had branded Lili.

She stopped. If she did that, she'd be down at his level.

"The circle is complete, Laurent, as Lili told her daughter-in-law," she said. "Due to Lili Stein, you won't be prime minister!"

She watched as he wiggled himself to death to the accompaniment of screams from below.

She was dizzy, her leg was slipping, and hundreds of needles stung her body. She'd finished what Lili had started; after fifty years Cazaux wouldn't do any more damage. Never forget, Lili had said. Her bloody fingers couldn't grip the skylight handle any more. Below her, shimmering glass carpeted the ground and she prayed to God it would be quick. She managed to yell, "Get out of the way," before her leg slipped and she couldn't hold on any longer.

An arm grabbed her from a swaying rope ladder. Her sticky hand was grasped firmly by a pair of dry ones. All of a sudden, wind whipped around her and she was suspended in the air. Blades thupped above her. She was flying. The gray slate rooftops of the Marais were far below her. Then everything went black.

Epilogue

THE LOUVRE'S SILHOUETTE BLOCKED all but a tiny rectangle of the silver-gray Seine. Weak November sun struggled through dirty windows into the Leduc Detective office.

"Cazaux almost made it," Martine said. She crossed her long legs, tugged the short skirt of her red power suit, and fluffed her blond hair. She seriously inhaled her cigarette. "Too bad, I was out of commission. That's one conversation I'll always regret not hearing."

Aimée, her eye bandaged, shrugged. Miles Davis nestled in her lap, asleep. She sipped her espresso with her semi-good hand. "The EU is under reorganization, the treaty shelved. Especially after Hartmuth's withdrawal."

Morbier stood up, stretched, and offered Aimée a cigar.

"Cigars don't count," he said. "You don't need to inhale."

"Living dangerously suits me." Aimée accepted. She clutched the cigar in her other fist as he lit it. "That helicopter ride inspired me. I'm going to take up rock climbing. Seems to be my forte after all the heights I've been to. Care to join me, René?"

René turned his head as far as his neck brace allowed. "Ask me next year," he said. "Maybe my body will be healed."

"Seems amazing, after fifty years—" Morbier began but Aimée didn't let him finish.

"Fifty years doesn't mean injustice goes away. Sooner or later it reappears. But when this generation dies, who knows?" She shrugged. She puffed on her cigar, sending clouds of smoke into the air.

"Where's Hartmuth?" René said.

Aimée winced. "The total body count isn't over. Is it?"

Morbier inhaled deeply on his cigar. "Thierry chained himself to Sarah's hospital bed. She's out of intensive care. Hartmuth's feeding her."

"I think you know one of our undercover investigative reporters," Martine said slowly.

"Yves?" Aimée shuddered.

He'd been a good guy after all. Maybe she'd call him after her plastic surgery healed.

"They found him," Martine said. "Battered. But he'll live."

"When do you move into your new office?" she said.

"When Gilles packs his stuff into crates," Martine said. "I'll have to get my own flat now. Grow up."

"Editors do that." Aimée grinned. She turned to René. "Partner, we need to apply for another tax extension!"

"Aimée," René asked slowly, "will you tell Abraham?"

"If he asks. Otherwise, I'll let the ghosts alone. All of them," she said.

Acknowledgments

My thanks go to all who inspired and supported this endeavor: from the beginning Nina, Jean and the Saturday group, James N. Frey without whom, the Bs, Alice, Isabelle, resources of the Holocaust Center of Northern California, the work of Serge Klarsfeld, Ange who said 'why not,' the wonderful Noe Valley librarians, L, Le Centre de Documentation Juive Contemporaine in Paris for all their help, Gabrielle, Madeleine Dieudonné et Julia Curtet, agents de recherche privée in Paris for their generosity, Denise Schwarzbach who opened her heart and shared. My heartfelt thanks go to Melanie Fleishman, who kept an eye on the small details and saw the big picture; my son, Shuchan, who let me; and Jun, who said it would happen.

Continue reading for a preview from the next
Aimée Leduc mystery

Murder in Belleville

PARIS

APRIL 1994

Monday Afternoon

AIMÉE LEDUC'S CELL PHONE rang, startling her, as she drove under the leafy poplars tenting the road to Paris. For a moment she'd felt as if she were flying—flying into spring, away from the winter, when her broken body needed to heal.

Aimée groped around in her backpack until she found her phone wedged next to her ultrablack mascara. Freeing it from her extra sweater, snarled on a software encryption manual, she finally flicked it open.

"Aimée!" shouted a woman's voice. "It's Anaïs."

"Ça va?" Aimée said, surprised to hear the voice of her friend Martine's sister. In the background, Aimée heard loud voices. "Anaïs, let me call—"

"You have to help me," Anaïs interrupted.

Several years had passed since Aimée had seen her. "What's the matter, Anaïs?"

"I'm in trouble."

Aimée pushed her black sunglasses down on her nose and ruffled her short, spiky hair. How typical of Anaïs—everything revolved around her. A dull pewter sky blanketed the suburb of Aubervilliers. Within minutes the sky opened, and rain blanketed the road.

"Right now I've got to drop some work off, Anaïs," she said with growing impatience.

"Martine talked to you, didn't she?" Anaïs asked.

Impatience turned to guilt. Despite her promise to do so, she'd never called Anaïs after Martine spoke with her. Anaïs suspected her husband, a government minister, of having an

affair. Computer security, Aimée had protested, was her field—
not spousal surveillance.

The phone reception wavered and flared.

"Right now it's difficult," she said. "I'm working, Anaïs."

She didn't want to interrupt her work. Thanks to a client refer-
ral, she was dropping off a network systems security proposal at
the Électricité de France. Aimée prayed that this would get
Leduc Detective back on its feet after a lean winter.

"Please, we have to meet," Anaïs said, urgency in her voice.
"Rue des Cascades . . . near Parc de Belleville." Anaïs's voice
came and went like a piece of laundry whipping in the wind. "I
need you."

"Of course, as soon as I finish. I'm on the outskirts of Paris,"
Aimée said. "Twenty kilometers away."

"I'm scared, Aimée." Anaïs was sobbing now.

Aimée felt torn. She heard a muffled noise as if Anaïs had covered the receiver with her hand.

Birds scattered from hedgerows. Along the gully, budding daf-
fodils bowed, skirting a mossy barge canal. Aimée pressed the Citroën's pedal harder, her cheek reddening in the whipping wind.

"But Anaïs, I might take some time."

"Café Tlemcen, an old zinc bar, I'm in the back." Anaïs's voice
broke. ". . . get caught . . ." Aimée heard the unmistakable
shrieking of brakes, of shouting.

"Anaïs, wait!" she said.

But her phone went dead.

MORE THAN AN HOUR later, Aimée found the café with
dingy lace curtains. She eased out of her partner's Citroën, which
was fitted to accommodate his four-foot stature, and smoothed
her black leather pants.

Strains of Arab hip-hop remixes drifted in from the street. The
narrow café overlooked rue des Cascades; no entrance to a back-
room was in evidence at first glance. Pinball machines from the

sixties, their silvered patina rubbed off in places, stood blinking in the corner.

Aimée wondered if she'd made a mistake. This didn't seem the kind of place Anaïs would frequent. But she remembered the panic in Anaïs's voice.

Apart from a man with his back to her, the café's round wooden tables were empty. He appeared to be speaking with someone who stood behind the counter. Old boxing posters curled away from the brown nicotine-stained wall. She inhaled the odor of espresso and Turkish tobacco.

"*Pardon, Monsieur*," she said, combing her fingers through her hair. "I'm supposed to meet someone in your dining room."

As he swiveled around to look at her, she realized that there was no one else behind the counter. He put down a microphone, clicked a button on a small tape recorder, and cocked a thick eyebrow at her.

"Who would that be?" he said, amusement in his heavy-lidded eyes. His thinning gray hair, combed across his skull, didn't quite cover the bald top of his head.

A long blue shirtsleeve pinned to his shoulder by a military medal concealed what she imagined were the remains of his arm. Behind the counter, sepia photos of military men in desert jeeps were stuck in the tarnished, beveled mirror.

"Anaïs de . . ." She stumbled, trying to remember Anaïs's married name. She'd been to their wedding several years ago. "Anaïs de Froissart—that's it. She said she'd be in the back room."

"The only back room here is the toilet," he said. "Buy a drink, and you can meet whom you like there."

A frisson of apprehension shook her. What was going on?

"Perhaps there's another Café Tlemcen?"

"*Bien sûr*, but it's three thousand kilometers from here, near Oran," he said. "Outside Sidi Bel Abbès, where I lost my arm." He nodded to his tape machine. "I'm recording the truth about the Algerian war, anticolonial struggles from 1954 to 61, and how our battalion survived OAS friendly-fire bombardment."

Why had Anaïs suggested this place? Had she made a mistake?

Aimée stepped closer to the counter. "I might have misunderstood my friend. Did a woman use your telephone recently?"

"Who are you, Mademoiselle, if I may ask?"

"Aimée Leduc." She pulled a damp business card from her bag and laid it on the sticky zinc counter. "My friend sounded agitated on the phone."

He studied her, his hand wiping a falling strand of hair back over the bald dome of his head. "I've been busy with deliveries."

"This isn't like my friend Anaïs," she said. "She was very upset. I heard car brakes, loud voices." She searched his face, trying to ascertain if he was telling the truth.

He hobbled out from behind the large chrome espresso machine to where she stood.

"A blonde, wearing designer clothes and gold chains, came in," he said. "She looked like she'd made a wrong turn coming out of the Crillon."

That must have been Anaïs. Aimée maintained her composure—this man was proving to be a helpful observer.

Torn between searching for Anaïs and hoping she'd return, Aimée decided to wait. She drummed her chipped red nails on the counter and remembered Martine complaining about her sister: It was always hurry up and wait.

"Did you see her leave, Monsieur?"

He shook his head.

She was dying for a cigarette. Too bad she'd quit five days, six hours, and twenty minutes ago.

"She told me to meet her here. She'll be back."

"Doubt it," he said, studying her as if coming to a decision.

"Why?"

"She gave me a hundred francs," he said. "Said for you to meet her at 20 *bis* rue Jean Moinon."

Aimée stiffened. "Why didn't you say so?"

"Had to be sure you're the impatient one with big eyes," he said. "She said to make sure it was you."

He nodded his head toward the street. "She knew she was being followed."

Aimée felt the first hint of fear.

The man gave a half bow. "Retired Lieutenant Gaston Valat SCE, formerly with the intelligence branch of the Franco-Algerian police," he said. He stood to attention as much as a one-armed man with a limp could. He noticed her gaze. "À *votre service*. Not half bad, eh?"

Not all that surprised by his change of attitude, she figured an old vet like him would welcome action on his doorstep.

"When did Anaïs leave, Gaston?"

"Close to an hour ago," he said.

She shouldered her bag.

"And like I told her," Gaston said, studying her, "*adieu*."

AIMÉE HURRIED INTO THE sheets of rain. Her edgy feeling had been growing all week. Paris was bracing itself for terrorist attacks, the radio warned, due to enforcement of the anti-immigration policy. The *flics* were nervous and, as Aimée knew, when nervous they tended to overreact. Shopping on the quai, she'd noticed the darting *flics*' eyes. She'd seen the dark-blue-suited CRS riot police in her Métro station with machine guns questioning random riders. Even *boulangerie* patrons in line ahead of her had jumped, startled by the sudden banging of trash cans. It seemed like everyone vibrated with fear.

By the time she reached the boulevard, the downpour had ceased. Twilight covered Belleville. Parents tugged children from shop to shop under umbrellas or placated them with baguettes at the crowded bus shelters.

The aroma of cumin from the corner Lebanese restaurant perfumed the rain-freshened air. Aimée had forgotten the bustle and energy in Belleville. African dialects reached her ears. She walked by abandoned, graffiti-covered, turn-of-the-century shop fronts. Taxi *klaxons* honked, and old men bargained in Arabic at fruit stands. Senegalese women clad in bright-patterned clothing and headdresses shared the Métro stairs with black-on-black Parisian sophisticates.

A neighborhood of *caractère*, she thought, but its working-class origins had suffered the onslaught of the trendy. Chunks of the grime-blackened eighteenth-century buildings in Édith Piaf's former neighborhood had either been torn down or renovated.

The saucer-like April moon had risen by the time she'd reached the narrow street. In contrast to the busy boulevard, rue Jean Moinon lay quiet. Aimée paused. The smell of wet dog mingled with rose water from a nearby passage. She wondered why Anaïs would come here.

The streetlamp's yellow cone of light revealed broken pavement. Parked cars filled one side of the narrow street. Number 20 *bis*, or 20 and a half—as Aimée remembered her mother's explanation of the term—consisted of two floors with many bricked-up windows. That was one of the few things she recalled her American mother joking about. Number 7 *bis*, their old apartment, had been referred to by her mother as "half here and half not, like me." Not long after that, when Aimée was eight, her mother had tacked a note on the apartment door telling her to stay with the neighbor until her father came home. Her mother had never returned.

Aimée stood back and looked up at the nineteenth-century building. Dark and silent. Only one floor had open windows, their shutters weathered and broken. No concierge or *gardien*. Just a massive wooden door defaced by silver graffiti.

Gaston could have given her the wrong address.

"Anaïs?"

Had Anaïs never come—or had she already left?

Aimée didn't know the code for entry so she rang the service bell. She waited, watching the streetlight's reflection dance in the oily puddles between cobblestones. Opposite, several buildings advertised apartments to rent.

No answer. She shifted in her boots, looking around. The street was deserted. Apprehensive, she felt like leaving.

Aimée walked up the uneven pavement to the end of the street, regretting her impulsiveness to follow Anaïs's trail. This wild goose chase had led nowhere. She wanted to kick herself— why had she agreed to help? She needed to hustle for the EDF contract!

Spousal surveillance really wasn't her field. Next time she'd think twice before she ran into the rain. She turned to retrace her steps. On her way back to the car she'd try one more time.

In the distance she saw two women emerge from the door of 20 bis. Aimée recognized one as Anaïs, her blonde hair illuminated by the streetlight. The other, a dark-haired woman, wore a shiny black raincoat that swung as she moved. The woman opened the driver's door of a car parked up front, reached in, and then shoved something across the car's roof to Anaïs, who waited on the curb.

As Aimée walked closer, she saw that the car was a powder-blue Mercedes. Anaïs stuck the object in her shoulder bag, put on her sunglasses, and rushed off without saying good-bye. Odd, Aimée thought, since it was dark and rainy.

"Anaïs!" Aimée called out, hurrying to catch up with her.

Anaïs turned, noticed Aimée, and waved in recognition.

Strains of Arabic music suddenly blared from nearby, loud and piercing. "Shut that crap off!" someone shouted from a window.

The dark-haired woman slammed her car door and started her engine, and with a blinding flash the Mercedes exploded. With a deafening roar, the car burst into a white-yellow ball of flame. Aimée faltered, and everything seemed to move in slow motion, but it could have only been microseconds. Terror flooded her. Tires and doors blew off like missiles into the stone buildings.

She saw Anaïs rise in the air, as if she were flying, then disappear. The ground reverberated.

The pressure wave knocked Aimée off balance in mid-dive. She aimed for the nearest car as the backdraft sucked at the air around her, tighter than she could stand. Steel fragments and bloody viscera rained over the street.

Aimée landed on wet cobblestones, praying that nothing else would explode. Her heart hammered. She tried to cover her head with her hands. Memories of the Place Vendôme terrorist explosion that killed her father came back—his burned body ejecting from the surveillance van, her hand holding the molten door handle, and the fireball that engulfed the van as it smashed into the Place Vendôme column.

And then she realized the danger—gas tank vapors from the parked cars could ignite from the flames. She pulled herself up and made her legs move. Made them go past the metal Mercedes skeleton, burning furiously and bulging like an accordion. The intense heat singed her eyebrows. She had to find Anaïs and get out of there.

Her ears rang, and she choked on the billowing smoke. She tripped on the cobblestones, greasy with oil and antifreeze. Her hands were bloody and shaking, just like five years ago when her father was blown up in front of her eyes—the same horrible nightmare.